Baggattaway

ACKNOWLEDGMENTS
• Jud Hartmann for telling me the story of the ruse
• Rich Rhodes for expert counsel in Ojibway language usage and translations

BIBLIOGRAPHY
• Vennum, Jr., Thomas. *American Indian Lacrosse: Little Brother of War* Smithsonian Institution, 1994
• Gringhuis, Dirk. *Lore of the Great Turtle* Mackinac State Historic Parks, 1970

Bronze sculptùre *A Cherokee Ball Game* by Jud Hartmann used with permission (judhartmanngallery.com)
Front Cover / Back cover design by Russ Gossett
Photo by Andy Philion

Wordclay
1663 Liberty Drive, Suite 200
Bloomington, IN 47403
www.wordclay.com

First published by Wordclay on 3/30/2009.

ISBN: 978-1-6048-1509-2 (sc)

Printed in the United States of America.

This book is printed on acid-free paper.

PART ONE

B I R C H W A L K E R

Upright Fossils

The three of us were running in place. It had to look like penance—a middle aged guy with a paunch heaving inside a sleeveless white jersey pacing two younger sleek-bellies half dressed for lacrosse. The cage masks of their big helmets cut their faces into squares, but they weren't wearing the high gloves that protect the forearm from vicious slashes during a game. No shoulder pads either, no elbow pads, no rib pads. No socks, they never wear socks anyway. For training runs, a stick and any old gym clothes would do. First light had barely scratched the surface, and it was already so warm and humid we wanted to go home. We were stretching at a tree-shrouded trailhead in the Hiawatha National Forest on the Upper Peninsula of Michigan. You've probably heard of Sault Ste. Marie just twenty miles east. Obie Crick and Jerome French were the two stallions eyeing me through their cages as we pumped our knees up extra high to touch our outheld lacrosse sticks, the sweat starting to run, the fog of our breaths colliding. Baggattaway, as lacrosse is known to us, is a sport of lean, fast athletes. I used to be one myself. I coach now, a Chippewa warrior carrying a few extra pounds, to be sure, but with a more than decent lacrosse resume of his own to point to. Birch Charlevoix is my name, and somehow, I am to coax what would most certainly be a miracle from a bunch of underdog Indian kids—a single, pale, solitary win next June. The Indigene Nation lacrosse team has not even made it out of the round robin since 1978, so expectations are suitably low for us in the 2010 World Championships. But as to winning that one measly little game, well, we better win more than that.

I barked at them, "Do you have anything to lose?"

"No!" they yelled back at me.

"Well, do you? Anything at all?"

"No!" they replied again, even surer this time, though, I knew, they'd have said anything to get me off their backs.

We dumped our helmets and broke up hill onto a pine needle trail, slipped into the trees. Right away we were enveloped in the smells of wet bark wafting from the pines and birches and maple and ash. There were thousands of trees and they were surely alive. They towered over us. They laid down their floor of leaves and needles for us as we threaded our way through their bulges and knots, under their low-hanging branches, banging shoulders with us as if they wanted to get in on this training too. Slowly the dawn entered the glades as we quickened the pace, and roots erupted from the forest floor, keeping us on our toes. I looked forward to Obie, who with his darting quickness had sprinted ahead of lagging Jerome. We were dwarfs next to those trees. The boys were cradling their sticks non stop—that reflex swiveling of the wrists that holds the ball in the pocket of the stick—and were scooping up pine cones, imagining lacrosse balls, passing them back and forth. Behind them a hundred fifty yards or so, I could hear the thud of their steps, feel the rumble. They fired on squirrels and at imaginary goals through saplings thirty feet away. They fired over their shoulders on each other, laughing, and they picked up speed. Jerome's big heavy soles crushed twigs and there was a running echo in the green canopy above us.

Years ago I taught Obie and Jerome in the middle school on our reservation, the Pope County Indian Reservation, not even a stone's throw from this forest. I am responsible for their love of this game, I suppose, and for at least a measure of the success they have earned in it. They have come about as far as you can in the sport. They have both been offered contracts to play in the MLL, the pro lacrosse league. Not that it will bring them fame and fortune, but, unlike when I played in the early seventies, there's a professional circuit to aspire to now, a fan base, a dozen venues around the country. Obie and Jerome have finished their college careers at Great Lakes University, one of the division-three powerhouses in the sport. Obie is a longstick defenseman, and Jerome is my goalie.

I wondered why I was running so well. I seemed to have caught a second wind, the huffing and puffing converted into crisp, efficient breathing strokes through pursed lips. I was feeling the timing, the hand-eye coordination, caught a glimpse of the well-oiled baggattaway machine I was thirty years ago. I cradled an imaginary ball in the webbing of my stick, rocking my wrists, picked up a signal from the ground, an instinct that rolled through me, telling me to cut, spin, scoop, dodge, duck, jump, fire, all of which I do like a man possessed. Suddenly I found myself raring back, cocking the head of my stick so far behind me that it almost touched the ground, coiling my ample midsection into the lever for the greatest shot ever taken in the history of baggattaway. I made my run as if I was a javelin thrower approaching the line and I hurled my imaginary ball. Like a god, I flung it straight up into the green canopy. It broke right through that overhang into a patch of blue morning sky, became a round white speck and disappeared into the vaults of heaven.

Ahead of me, I searched out Obie and Jerome. Sweat was pouring down into my eyes. Lactic acid flooded my legs. They were burning and beginning to cramp up on me. I did not expect to see the rest of my team, the other fifteen stallions who make up the Indigene Nation lacrosse team, but there they were. They floated before me. Next to Jerome were Elias Lane, my Abenaki defenseman, and the fastest middie on the team, and Orin Beauchesne, who's an Onondaga. The three attackmen were lined up in front, smaller than the others, so that now it was starting to resemble a team photo. The twins, Robbie and Trevor Fenton, are Huron. They flanked Danny Brown, the only Sauk. Grubby Spratt and Normand LeFramboise, whose last name means raspberry in French, are both Cayuga and played at Finger Lakes University in upstate New York. Looming self-consciously in the back, tall, tall Russell Phaneuf plays defense with Elias and Obie. His mother is Choctaw, his father Creek. Delbert DesMarais, Philip Davidson, Jesse Olsen, Aaron Bell, Herschel Seavey, Evan Crosse and Ronnie Philibotte clustered together in a cross-armed, tough-guy, stone-cold stare at the camera of my eye. Was I supposed to blink? Was I supposed to snap this picture that drifted more and more out of focus with each passing second? Now my team was lost in a swirling mass of people, all Native Americans from the hundreds of tribes that existed once, and I was hearing war whoops in the distance. It is a thing that never was—Indian Nation, the United States of India, whatever you like, a confederation of Indigenes. Why did we not unite against the Europeans? How did the other fifteen get to the forest? I was shaken. If only I could have sat down and rested for a second. But I couldn't look away. There were millions in the picture now, and somehow I was made aware of all our nations spinning before me, circles spinning within circles, like a roulette wheel: Sioux and Cherokee, Delaware and Passamaquoddy, Ogunquit and Illinois, Mandan and Seminole, Ottawa, Navajo, Crow, Pueblo and Yakima, Mohawk, Miami and Erie. There were Missouri, Oneida and Seneca. Kiowa, Pawnee, Omaha, Comanche, Cheyenne, Arapaho. The forest was teeming with Indigenes. And the lusty whoops were beginning to merge into something intelligible. I could make out a rhythm, a chant, and, though I saw my people's lips moving, I swear the sound was coming from the trees around me.

"Birch," they groaned in the sultry air, "we cannot beat the English. We are outmanned and outgunned. Don't you see?"

This chant was repeated like a litany until it nested inside me like the fog at the trailhead. Then they scattered. Before the photograph could be taken, all those Natives tore off into the woods in every direction of the compass. There was a great commotion. They are endangered.

"No! Stay!" I called out after them. But it was useless. They were scattered and there was no fight left to retake what is ours, Anishinaabewaki—our land, Baggattaway—our game. I felt a sharp pain in my ankle and fell to the pine needle path thinking that Obie and Jerome said they had nothing to lose. I was sweating like a stuck pig, hopefully melting some midriff, and I insisted into the silence that nothing to lose means everything to gain, means you play with whatever you've got because this is life.

Suddenly I was moved to the water's edge. I was standing at the shore of great water and the moment had the look and feel of colonial times. My brothers fished and hunted beaver in birch bark canoes on the straits. I smelled cedar on the air. The waters were unusually still. Around me, the trees were changed into ramparts now, cut, sliced and planed into stockades and banquettes of a fort from which the redcoats began to open fire through loopholes upon my people. The smoke from the rifles clouded the air, the sky went dark and the moon sailed into place—presto!—over the water as if God Himself just didn't have the time to wait for it. And in the hanging smell of gunpowder and the repeating echoes of hundreds of rifle volleys, I heard a sound coming from the moon. It was my chieftain who called.

> *Hi yi yi ya ya! He yi yi ya yao!*
> *Hi yi yi ya yo! Hi ah ho ay yo!*
> *Heya, heya, ha i ya ho ay oh!*

I craned my neck to the moon.

"Birch!" I heard vaguely. My ankle hurt. "You're dreaming, Birch. Wake up. You were chanting. It's Bwon-diac, isn't it? He was calling you."

Marla had scared the hell out of me. She moved in to put her arms around me from behind. She knows I do this. I have weird dreams about reality.

"Goddamn English. The moon was right on the water. Waxing, a waxing moon."

"You need to lose weight, my dear," she warned, releasing my mid-section. "You're waxing a bit yourself. Besides, I want to know. Are you or are you not the coach of Team Indigene Nation?"

"That was in my dream, too," I offered, "Obie and Jerome and I were running in the Hiawatha."

It is a dream I do not seem to outgrow. Somewhere atop an outcropping in the forest a gray wolf arches his back and bays out at a half moon, his snout raised in plaintive howl. I admire him because he can only do what he's doing. Why does the gray wolf cry? It helps if you know what I know—that there is, in fact, a man up there, tied to the moon. And I know the man. He is my chieftain. He has circled the Earth for two hundred and forty years now, fast approaching the three-thousandth revolution. Even as its dark side again turns to face us, he continues to scold from the light side of the moon. Only I and the gray wolf and the eagle can hear what our chieftain whoops out into the Milky Way from behind the moon.

> Have you heard with startled ears the
> Deathless war-cry of Bwon-diac,
> Fearsome ripple through the Planets,
> For the Vengeance of his People?

Here's what I think: he is trying to wake us, his people, the Chippewa, the Odawa, the Potawatomi. The Council of Three Fires. He is trying to avenge an awesome defeat. And if I know him at all, he will taunt his captors into all eternity.

This is no dream.

$2009 - 240 = 1769$, the year of my war chief's death at the hands of an assassin in Cahokia, Illinois. His name was Bwon-diac, better known to you as Pontiac, and any motor car company or city in Michigan of the same name is taking his in vain. I love Bwon-diac. He was the last Ottawa standing when the lights went out. He was the light. And he went down swinging. I weep at his beautiful instinct, his reckless abandon, his love for his people, his murder. I weep at how the odds were stacked against him, of how winning, in any conventional sense of the word, was impossible. I weep for us all at the thought of his fate in the Afterlife, lashed forever to the searchlight in the sky.

"Birch, how'd you say you're going to lose all that weight?" Marla is like a white dog with a Chippewa bone, me.

The cycles of the moon, repeated on an eternal scale, give rhythm to life. We count off our seconds and days and months and years by its turns. Our calendars are paced to its recurring themes. Our oceans heave and ebb at its behest. Our women, too. Though its light is borrowed, in awe we think to put our finger on it. Yes, change does happen, I suppose. The moon starts new and black and takes the profile of the waxing crescent and then discloses a quarter of itself, all in seven days. Then, it is a pregnant lady with its telling bulge in the middle and then a flashlight in another seven days. Waning, the masquerade is reversed until, three weeks after its beginning, it slims to its last quarter. Has it lost weight? Has it given birth? Its fate is to fade, and fade it does into crescent and fades some more until the dark new moon arrives and a moon has passed. I agree—change does happen, yet if we look to the moon, it's always the same old changes.

It makes me wonder about the stages of womanhood. My Marla, for instance. We've been together for thirty years now. She's forty-nine and beset with the tell-tale signs of menopause. Hot flashes and sweating and mood swings to beat the band. Our women are whirled around by a force of nature beyond us all. It should be called menostop, don't you think? It's no pause, is it? Their cycle, their moon, has stopped. This is a headline! The woman who has bled like a clock for thirty-seven years to the pull of the moon suddenly has no more moon. What this must mean to womankind I can only imagine. I do not know if this image is correct or not, but it seems true enough to me: the onset of menostop is all fire and spit as the full moon tugs at her insides to make an egg pop out and then all the harder because it can't make a blood flow either and all that pulling makes her a lunatic. The river bed is dry. The moon, frustrated, throws its hands up. The woman is immune. She feels no pain; she is numb, vacated, released, soulless, like the Indigene.

Marla read my mind like a book. "You're thinking about that long, sad list of yours, aren't you? The tribes that are no more?"

Yes, my own moon-stopped damsel in distress, but also about you. And Neil.

You will meet my best friend in this life or any other. His name is Neil Longbow LaSalle. *Aanimendam.* That's Chippewa for *He's more than just a little off his rocker.* Neil says that the Holocaust was nothing. Don't get him wrong; he means no disrespect. In fact, this seems to be a compliment coming from Neil; a brother is speaking. Six million people go up in smoke for no other reason than they offended the haywire political order of the day. Well, that just sounds too much like what happened to us for Neil. No one knows how many Indigenes there were when Columbus "discovered" the Americas, maybe thirty million, maybe many more. Fewer than two million are left. And each tribe of the hundreds that thrived once, it seems to me, had to have a last man standing, a proud sachem over whose dead body the English colonial juggernaut rolled, or an outwitted war chief conned by American administrations into selling tribal lands he didn't even conceive of as his own for pennies an acre. Are we the invisible new moon, awaiting a rebirth out of the black void? Are we the last quarter moon in a desperate fading dance, or, in some way that I do not see, the shining full moon that rises on a line with the setting sun, revealed in our roost in the sky as a people resurrected? Is the Indigene forever washed in its luscious lemon light?

"Did you see Bwon-diac in your dream, Birch?"

How am I lucky enough to have this woman? What moon-madness made her open the sports page of the *Soo News* thirty years ago and see my picture there—the college lacrosse hero, arms raised victoriously and teeth gleaming in the spring sun and the long, straight black hair of my youth tousled by the wind? What lunacy bade her gather her newborn love child and come to the doorstep of my father on the reservation? What moon-struck feeling enveloped me at the sorry sight of them and led to a union that continues to this day, the love-child daughter now grown and gone? Why does Marla Langevin of Sault Ste. Marie, Michigan live with me in this wretched lot? What exactly did she fall in love with in that grainy picture? What great force holds us in one another's orbit?

And through the fog of menostop she asks a simple question like, "Did you see Bwon-diac in your dream, Birch?" It's well past humoring me. She's really asking. She knows that Bwon-diac is lashed to the moon. She knows that I imagine his war whoops raining down on me from the night sky. She knows that he seeks revenge from his foul perch in the Afterlife, that the twenty-eight million Indigenes died in one way or another at the instant Bwon-diac pushed out his last breath and that all of his offspring were forever rendered into fossils. She knows that the white man's texts label Bwon-diac an Ottawa, true enough, we believe it as well, but as a mother herself she allows me to claim him as my chieftain because his mother was Chippewa. This is better than marriage vows, a declaration of love as pure as the bridal veil.

But, there's my side of the bargain too. She's right. I am waxing. I should lose the weight. She tells me to jog with her. I am the chieftain of my team, I guess you could say, and a chieftain leads by example. If I am to lead this humble Indigene Nation to even a single victory in the 2010 lacrosse World Cup, I will have to whip this old body into shape one more time. Like my dreams, it will start in the nearby Hiawatha National Forest.

"I wish you could hear him," I answered.

How do I know of Bwon-diac's fate, you ask. How can I be so sure that he exists up there, pining in the Afterlife? Why, just as you would say of any of your own legends, of those who leave a great name. Yet they live on in our hearts. They spawn generations, like roots of a family tree, a symbol inseparable from its people's yearning. Neil Armstrong. General Custer. Jesus. The people's yearning is what keeps the story alive. The moon still mystifies, the frontier still teems with invaders, Paradise still beckons.

Bwon-diac? Jesus? What wicked lenses we all have to look into the heavens!

At the tender age of seven in school here on the Pope County Indian Reservation, all of Bwon-diac's children were required to learn a poem about him by heart. Our parents helped us—it is thirty-six stanzas long—with long evening hours of patient listening and nodding. And not just the words. We studied the structure of it, trochaic tetrameter as we were told, its weave like ivy around our minds, its tempo etched so that we have no choice but to sing our tribal songs in this form: four strong-weak pairs per line. That's how it works, like the sound of slow but urgent tom-toms. The poem, called *The Cry of Bwon-diac*, is anonymous, though it is clearly written by a French Jesuit who was an acquaintance of Bwon-diac, perhaps even a friend. Neil and I as kids would act it out to make it stick in our heads, Neil claiming the priest's verses because there are only eleven of them and loading the full weight of Bwon-diac's twenty-five verses on me. Because it is a poem of the imagination and it deals in the post-mortem vagaries, I take the good priest at his word. Love wrote this poem. Maybe I was impressionable at seven, but, as Marla knows, Chippewa are people who trust in dreams as divine communiqués, and it sounds to me as if the Father had a dream. Just listen to the first lines spoken by the war chief to the hated English. I can see his scowling face and head shaved but for the crest where a thick pelt of it runs from his forehead to his spine. His scalp is stained with vermilion. His voice rings deep and savage, his face and upper body contorting against his fate:

> "O! You splendid, splendid bastards.
> To the moon you've lashed Bwon-diac!
> Roped a chieftain to his anguish,
> Deposed him to Purgatory."

> "To this orb I have been fastened
> Tracing circles in the heavens
> Rising east and setting westly
> Round the river of my defeat."

Do you see what I mean? At our tender ages, this is what we learned from the poem: under the gaze of six successive moons,

Bwon-diac stormed the English fort at Detroit, believing his
Anishinaabewaki territory and way of life to be in grave peril;
ultimately he stormed in vain. He hated the English and he hated
Henry Gladwin. Listen to how bad he wanted the scalp of the English
commander:

> "In the Flower Moon I started
> Sieging Detroit from the river.
> Fort commander Henry Gladwin
> Wore the scalp I yearned to raise up."

Please understand this too: it was not just Fort Detroit. Bwon-
diac was a great war sachem who had the power of speech-making
and this gave him far-reaching influence over many other tribes. He
used this influence in 1763 to carry out a lofty-minded rebellion
against the new English overlords who had assumed control of the
Great Lakes forts from the vanquished French and listen: they did not
treat the Indians well. So, Bwon-diac, sniffing demise on the easterly
winds that ride the Great Lakes, devised the plan for a simultaneous,
coordinated attack on thirteen forts. Listen how he went down
swinging:

> "But the circumstances worsened.
> The French king his forts surrendered
> To the haughty, mighty English,
> On their way of life a cursing."

"Let us count them, let us count them.
Fort Miami and St. Joseph's,
The Sandusky and Ouatanon,
Sault-Ste. Marie and Presqu'Isle."

"On our lakes and rivers see them,
Fort Detroit, Edward Augustus,
And site of lacrosse deception,
Fort Michilimackinac stands."

"Other forts the English gave back.
Eight forts total were retaken.
But for six moons Major Gladwin
Stolen Fort Detroit defended."

"In the Falling Leaf Moon season
With the long cold winter waiting
Did I peer into my spirit—
It is over, it is over."

"At the Council of Three Fires
Was a bittersweet required.
The French king had abdicated.
Just Bwon-diac could be counted."

"On this night-sun rage and seethe I,
My head throbbing from my fate still:

> Your paid Illinois assassin
> Whose blunt tamahaac did fell me."

It strikes me: did Bwon-diac know, was he ever told, of the lacrosse deception at Fort Michilimackinac? In his endless revolutions, does he know that his story and the story of that attack at Michilimackinac have in turn lashed *me* to their orbit? Does he know I am his son, heir of his fate, like him hunting after just desserts? That I will lead the Indigene Nation lacrosse team onto the battlefield against England in a year's time? And listen how the French Jesuit imagines Bwon-diac in the Afterlife, carrying all that hate with him past the portal of life, groping for the tomahawk in his buckskin, the irony of his means of transport seemingly lost on him:

> In meandering this meantime,
> Struggles he to loose his hand up
> English skull of Henry Gladwin
> With casse-tete to rip asunder.

> Unto such a fate Bwon-diac,
> The great war chief of th'Odawa
> Grunts and groans across the heavens
> Henry Gladwin's skull his vessel!

Can you imagine? Sailing through the heavens on the very skull you wanted to plunder in life? I'm glad he doesn't know. It was written of him that he stood in the white man's path for a moment and thrust him back, revealing the tragedy of his people and the cost of human progress. Human progress. A great nation rose up, a behemoth. Yet in the forging of that nation came the petrification of its indigenous peoples, whose region known as the Great Lakes is my region, known to us as Anishinaabewaki. I say petrification because of the final line of the poem. Listen:

> His revolving eyes do well up,
> At his Nation's humors draining,
> Mighty forest of the Great Lakes,
> Anishinaabek, upright fossils.

Upright fossils? When you say *Anishinaabek* you are addressing the Potawatomi, the Chippewa, the Odawa—the Council of Three Fires, our ancestral tribal family, the Great Lakes Indians. And when you say *Anishinaabewaki* you are talking about our sacred lands themselves. We are the people of the Great Lakes, positioned on this peninsula as if aboard a ship whose prow juts out into an eternal lake, two vital bridges our gangplanks over the waters. Above us to the north is the International Bridge to Ontario, Canada. It links the Twin Soos—the Michigan Sault Ste. Marie and the Ontario Sault Ste. Marie—over the St. Mary's River. Fifty miles south of us is Big Mac, another bridge that spans the Straits of Mackinac to lower Michigan. And in the middle of these two gangplanks is my world, the Upper Peninsula of Michigan—the Soo, the Hiawatha National Forest, the sacred pike-fishing grounds of the Chippewa, and the Pope County Indian Reservation just outside of Periwinkle, Michigan. It's barely a spit of land, this U.P., more Wisconsin than Michigan on a map, its wooded shores washed by those three northern Great Lakes.

"But, Birch, you are fossils," said Marla, silently following me down a well trodden path in my mind. "One look around the rez tells you all you need to know. You were put here to be out of the way. You're a virus that's been contained. You were swept under the rug, closed in a time capsule. Can you imagine if I had raised Sheila here?"

For the last fifteen years she has been the truant officer for the Periwinkle public school district, prowling the alleys of the town and the rez like a dog catcher hauling stray mutts back to school. Everyone around here knows her and loves her. I have often wished I could be one of those Periwinkle mutts. On purpose, I would skip school every day without fail, be the worst truant case in history, ache for her to find me and willingly jump into her rescuing arms. And that line about Sheila gets me every time, she knows. Thank God for Marla's mother Sandrine who raised Sheila in the Soo during the week, enabling a rez-on-weekends-only youth for her granddaughter that had the fortunate effect of turning the rez into something akin to a recurring school field trip instead of a life sentence. Of course not. Not a white girl. Not on these streets. Are fossils alive?

I will trim my gut. I will awaken my skills in baggattaway, the *real* name for our game, in the stands and groves and lakeside pine needle paths of the Hiawatha Forest, thinking all the while of those thousands of birch and beech and pine and fir and cedar and maple trees through which I run, all that beautiful sap turned to stone, all those trees, alive but suspended in amber, struck dumb by removal and annexation and assimilation, stunned museum pieces on the mighty Anishinaabewaki landscape. It is to them I will dedicate myself.

"I do not want to be a fossil."

Ever since I put the poem into my seven year-old heart, I have wished that I could see what Bwon-diac sees. Though not his fate, I do envy him his eye-in-the-sky view of Earth and the galaxy and the cosmos. Do you know the Earth can change faces too, that it quarters and halves and can be crescent and gibbous? It seems to be a property of celestial beings. I learned that when the moon revolves around the Earth, so must my war chief, his lungs impotent against the vacuum of space. I know this does not deter him because soon enough I and the gray wolf and the eagle again pick up his scent. Homeland and defeat converge anew in his line of sight:

"Without end I face my torment,
Relive ever my last battle,
The Rebellion as you called it,
Seventeen and Three-and-Sixty."

A few hours later, he hovers above England, his nemesis. He spits at them:

"I spy on your island-country
From my lunar perch above it.
Had I only known then of it,
Grandiosity of England."

"Self-important little isle
With cupidity afflicted;
Were you given some divine right?
Why stand redcoats on my shoreline?"

"And your rivalry spilled over
'Cross the seas into your New World.
French and English competition
In Anishinaabewaki."

But his moon buggy will turn him once again toward home, and, even more than at the glimpses of constellations and distant planets and auroras borealis and the rings of Saturn, I imagine his heart warming at the sight. For it is a beautiful place. How prominently the great waters would show from afar, an intriguing mix of shapes and sizes, a constellation in its own right. I wonder if he thinks about the nature of the moon and its power over the life of man, the tides and the poems it excites. See how it has remade him:

"I am now the Wolf Moon, Snow Moon,
Am the Maple, the Strawberry;

Am the Harvest and the Hunter's,

Am the Corn Moon and the Blood Moon."

He is the changing face of the moon.

I wonder if he can see me.

I wonder if he knows that he can destroy the Earth.

I have studied maps, the view of Anishinaabewaki from space, and, without a doubt, it is the three northern Great Lakes that would catch my chieftain's eye. Not the shimmering hectares of the North Atlantic, nor the broad St. Lawrence River churning past Montreal, not Lake Ontario or Erie nor even the threadlike Ottawa River that feeds them but the Huron, Michigan and Superior, these three-of-a-kind that make up the eye looking back at Bwon-diac:

"You must know this, all my People,

In the Earth an Eye is hiding.

I can see from here its ire

Looking out upon all of us."

I am here, Bwon-diac!

Forgive me if I jump around. My story has many faces, many yearnings.

Before I slept again my moonless woman pulled me to her and put her hands to my temples, lifting the flap of her wigwam to me, laying her Indian beside the fire that holds the monster of sleep at bay.

Pontiac-Looking-Down Day

Neil said people are like raindrops. That we were distillations, condensing out of a great ether on high and that to ether we would one day return. That we raindrops were gathered up and released over and over. He said that's why people called each other drips.

It was just dawn, and I steered the model year 1969 milk truck old Matti Virkanen gave me through a warm spring mist the few blocks to Neil's trailer. The milk truck likes the dark morning time, a vestige of its working life when it carried the fresh smells of the dairy out into the homes. I keep the driver's door slid open just like Matti Virkanen did to make deliveries. I like the adjustable bar stool driver's seat, which allows you to stand and drive if you want, and all that floor-to-ceiling storage space behind me where long columns of red crates, pegged with dewy bottles and aluminum tops, used to sway and clink. With the single exception of driving it to the fort on our June Twos, though, it has never ventured off the U.P, and even then the fort is just barely the other side of Big Mac. So this old milker gets me around our endless habitat of water, forest and sky. And it can be hard to tell where the one picks up and the other leaves off. Human beings do seem an afterthought at times, like Neil says, a fleeting, occasional apparition between heaven and earth. I told you Neil was crazy, *aanimendam*, afflicted in both body and mind, but I can assure you he is not yet out of the game. He has mostly decided to ignore it, the game, and he made that decision long ago. He dropped out of

Periwinkle Middle School during eighth grade because he had no use for slanted stories and the white kids taunted him mercilessly for not even *trying* to fit in and his grandfather had had enough of it, too. He was meant to be outside, a nature boy, busy with his hands, not cooped up in some classroom learning colonial American history. He learned infinitely more from his grandfather anyway. His grandfather would take him and his dog St. Anne on long hushed walks in the Hiawatha, stopping in the dappled sunlight of the forest to bend an oak bough or a maple branch to himself and trace the veins of leaves before Neil's young face. Stepping slowly on the crunchy pine needle trail, he would suddenly hold out his hand to stop Neil and without looking point to the top of a tree where white-crested woodpeckers were hammering the side of a black walnut three stories above, Neil opening to the world of the canopy. He would lay the palms of both hands on the thin bark of the birch and caress it with eyes closed as if he were reading a pulse through the skin of the tree and instructed Neil that this forest that housed such a vast wildlife with its owls' nests and beaver dams was also a sanctuary for man, a place where he played his part, his own cradle and his own grave. As if to reinforce the point, Neil's grandfather taught him how to set controlled small brush fires to clear undergrowth. They would walk the forest's wetlands, its granite outcroppings, its densities of spruce and cedar, birch and maple, ash and hickory, until from three hundred yards the roar of plummeting waters announced Tahquamenon Falls. Once in its full presence, the roar made St. Anne chase her tail until they laughed and drowned out the human voice. But over the din the grandfather, perched on a big angled rock, would lift his voice, holding forth for hours at a time on the kind of knowledge Neil did crave: disappearing Sault Chippewa traditions like sugar camping as the winter waned and the maple trees swelled with sap, and pike fishing from birch bark canoes in the bustling rapids of the St. Mary's River, and communal chants and legends sung in Ojibwemowin about baggattaway and the winter bear and beaver hunts, and the art of mixing bear fat and dyes or charcoal for war paint, and the throwing of dogs over the sides of their canoes as a sacrifice for safe passage or in thanks for a good catch, and the enduring role of the French language which retained its honor as a trading tongue from the earliest contact with the white man and in whose words the Jesuit priest had originally scribed the *The Cry of Bwon-diac* whose lines they would sing over and over in both French and English under that cascading water, and then the art of mimicking the baying wolf the screech owl the crying dog. There came a test, to be sure, at the end of all this instruction, the construction of an eleven-foot long birch bark canoe. Under the watchful eye of his grandfather, Neil set to the task outside this very doublewide trailer he now inhabits. He knew where his grandfather kept the crooked knives and draw knives and awls and hand drills for a long time already, in the long deep narrow drawer of the old dining room hutch, and gathered them along with axe and mallets and wedges and saws. Watched by his grandfather, he felled the straightest white birch he could find and removed the bark in long lengths, rolled them up inside out and set them aside. He felled a white cedar and split it for the gunwales and ribs. He dug up spruce roots for lashing and peeled the bark from them and cut them into man-sized lengths, and from those same spruce trees he gathered sap from points where grubs had burrowed through the bark. Using a putty knife and his bare hands, he would seal the seams and joints of the vessel using no more than this gum and just the right amount of fat. He built a form according to his grandfather's instructions in the side yard of his lot and when he put the bows in the gunwales, when he planed and soaked and steamed and curved the cedar planks to make the ribs, his grandfather bestowed upon him the name *Longbow*. Neil's grandfather died a happy man, I think. On the morning they were to launch the canoe, a test of early manhood, Neil and I found his grandfather dead in his bed. He looked to be still sleeping. St. Anne was standing at his face. Her tongue was out all the way. It appeared that she was speaking to him, maybe trying to coax him back to life, but to no avail. I was shocked and looked at Neil, but he was unmoved and simply said that we must go to the river anyway. There was no adult to tell us what to do.

"You take the canoe and paddle. I'll take my grandfather."

With that he lifted his grandfather's vacated body and folded him over his shoulder. Neil moved outside less self-consciously than I did. It felt like we were doing something wrong. Glad to hide myself, I hoisted Neil's canoe and paddle up over my head. Neil grabbed a spade with his free hand and, with St. Anne bravely leading the way, we trundled deep into the Hiawatha to the precise spot where Neil had felled the birch and white cedar trees. A long enough section of the birch trunk remained from that operation, bark intact. Neil had me gather a kind of ceremonial mound of pine needles and we laid his grandfather down. I dug the grave while Neil stripped the birch bark for his grandfather's burial suit. We placed the corpse into the bark and closed it over his body except for the sunlit centerline where the bark had been cut. Neil stared down at his grandfather's face for a long time. We cut some longer spruce roots and slung them under either end of the bark casket and lowered the body into the heart of the Hiawatha Forest. "No one will know," he said matter-of-factly, "you don't have to worry. My grandfather has walked on. We will walk on."

He motioned us onward into the forest toward Tahquamenon Falls. St. Anne figured it out before I did. We were going from the interment to the canoe launch. Neil walked in front of me and I spotted his back every now and then as the boat was jostled above my eyes. He seemed bigger to me now, older. We laid the canoe gingerly on the surface of the water, deeper where it pools and eddies at the base of the falls, and St. Anne jumped in at the prow. Neil paddled the three of us down river. We could not bring ourselves to inspect for leaks or to jump for joy that there were none. No one said a word. St. Anne sat on her haunches with the same look on her face as when we found her that morning by the side of the bed, her tongue practically scrolled out of her mouth. I believe that was the moment in my young life I learned the meaning of the word irony. It was an abstraction to me before that, something older and wiser people said, but if it meant what I was feeling right then, I had become, along with Neil and possibly with St. Anne, older and wiser. What irony meant to me? The taste of sad and happy in the same eternal instant, right and wrong holding hands, and the mind left to deal with the opposition. Neil steered the canoe to the bank. We stepped out after St. Anne, and Neil said to me, "The dog is grandfather to the man, Birchwalker." And so, as his grandfather had loved him with a name, my best friend loved me, too. Longbow and Birchwalker.

With no legal guardian, Neil and St. Anne came to live with us until he turned sixteen.

You do not forget it when your grandfather, your teacher, your elder, walks on. Nor do you speak of it. In a little less than a year, Neil and St. Anne had reinhabited the double-wide and lived out his adolescence as his grandfather would have wished. And in the thirty-seven years that followed, little had changed. He tapped rock maples and hung birch bark sap buckets every March. He collected the sap by hand and poured it into a big wrought-iron kettle and boiled it down outside his trailer, chanting loudly in Ojibwemowin as he mocked progress. He gave maple syrup away for free on the reservation. He made maple taffy and sold it once a month for traveling money, as he called it, to our friend Mickey Blake in the Soo. His hips bothered him. But, listen, something *had* changed: Neil Longbow LaSalle began to make lacrosse sticks with his bare hands.

There it was. I wondered what his grandfather would say. His trailer, like my milk truck, was a thing stuck in the past, a quaintly hip look about it. Planted on the far side of his oblong plot, the familiar double-wide was bedecked in rainbows and peace signs and insurgency of all stripe and hue. Sap buckets were scattered in a heap in the big side yard. Over there was his precious birch bark canoe, still kicking after all those years. That day, as on every other June Two, we would wedge it in the back of the milk truck and drive down to the fort. We would hide it near the head of the Mackinac Trail at the southern tip of the U.P., tucking it in lovingly among some high red fescue and painted trillium above a small pond, and there it would summer. From there, he could easily haul it down to the straits and paddle to his heart's content, slaloming through the giant concrete piers of Big Mac and the bobbing blue buoys. First, though, he had to get himself down to the pond, usually with me in the milk truck but sometimes in a dirty taxi cab.

Though you might not imagine the words *birch bark canoe* and *baggattaway stick* in the same breath, it has always made sense to me. I know this because I was without a doubt the catalyst for this extension of his basic craft. You see, though Neil never did, I got off the rez after high school. I went to college, and I played lacrosse, and I played it well.

There was smoke coming from his outdoor fireplace on that morning, which meant he was steaming ash or hickory to bend into baggattaway sticks. Off to one side of the yard you could see his metal die, a plate screwed shoulder-high to a big ash tree. It had two protrusions on it, a pair of vertical knobs that serve as levers for bending. He made Iroquois-style sticks, one by one, and sold them to the chief of the Onondaga Nation where they still play the Creator's Game, by Indian rules, baggattaway. The chief of Onondaga Nation is a man named Parry Four Bears Beauchesne, and if ever a man was a purist, it is the chief. You could say he *is* the market for Native sticks. The craft of stickmaking, of course, is a disappearing art selling into a dying market, yet he insists in the face of superior new materials like graphite and titanium that his young Iroquois players use the traditional wooden crosses, a reminder of whence they come when they go to play on the white man's fields. And that is how an Iroquois and a Chippewa came to be in business together. Listen: that is a rare thing, because for centuries the two tribes have been at odds over a battle that took place out here on the U.P. two hundred years and some ago. There are plenty of people, Iroquois and Chippewa both, who won't let go of the grudge. But Neil and Parry and I were as silent on that point as Neil and I were on his grandfather.

Neil and my father were two of a kind, a relationship cemented that year he lived with us, a relationship that continued when I went down south for college on a lacrosse scholarship. It seemed to me in those years when I made my visits home that Neil and my father were somehow declining together, that insistence on the old ways taking its toll on them as the world outside the reservation kept moving forward. So, I had a choice to make, and it was an easy one. The two of them are the reason I decided to return for good to the Pope County Indian Reservation after college. Some of the symptoms were troubling. Neil would lapse more frequently into French or suddenly go on a fast or a drunk that lasted sometimes for days, and he was angrier. Maybe it was living alone for so long. Maybe it was a lot of things. He grew inclined to pick fights he didn't have a prayer of winning; he developed an occasional taste for fast food and started to hang out with no apparent purpose at a barbershop in the Soo to defend the honor of the owner. You can see why I came back to just be near him. If I lost either or both of these guys, these Chippewa brothers, I would be lost myself.

Still though, all those years later, paced by the acquisitions and eventual losses of St. Annes One, Two and Three, the fourth embodiment of St. Anne graced Neil's prow with her perfect posture and spittle flying in streams from either side of a mouth with a flopping tongue, her barking harangues borne off on the wind. Even ice on the Straits, even the whipping winter weather did not stop him. He followed no modern nautical line of thinking, obeying instead an ancient Chippewa gene. It was the seam of air and water where the condensation happened, the fickle surface, that was sacred to Neil and all Anishinaabek. Renamed the Straits by the white man, the five-mile wide beating heart of Anishinaabewaki connected Lake Michigan and Lake Huron and, despite barges and tankers and haulers, remained an altar. Big Mac, with its two platinum towers, lorded north-south over the waters. And my friend glided along like the small unwitting detail that holds an entire landscape painting together, the detail you might miss at first because he does not pretend, the detail you will never miss again. He paddled south from the pond, doing figure eights under Big Mac, lured like a fish by Fort Michilimackinac on the opposite shore. He and St. Anne had attained a quiet local celebrity for their escapades in the straits. Ferry boat captains never missed the chance to point out Neil to their passengers, over the din of the fort's crackling muskets and peals from the carillon, urging him on the public address to please go ahead and throw St. Anne out of the canoe, egging him on with a pull at the foghorn for good measure. It was the ultimate tourist distraction, I suppose, seeing a painted-up Indian in a birch bark canoe tossing his beagle into the water and watching him swim back to the canoe. The fort staff, too, looked forward to Neil's approaches, especially Jan Zwiebel, a well-meaning tour guide who waved to him unrequitedly from the cannon.

Through the bedlam, however, he stayed in his moment. Here he played with an eddy, doing doughnuts like you do in your car in snowy parking lots, there he would build up speed and break into showy Indian pirouettes upon the Straits, the curved blade of his paddle the rudder on which the turning depends. All with skill and aloofness. And do not be alarmed should he throw St. Anne overboard, it was only to teach her how to swim back to him. Above, Bwon-diac himself presided, receiving Neil's prayer from arms stretched skyward in pure supplication, from a son of the Great Lakes, from a birch bark acolyte.

Can you relate? Layer by layer our identity has been remade, our Chippewa blood diluted to the meager twelve percent that remains in my friend and me. I think this is the labyrinth where Neil was somehow bidden to live, and where I have learned to merely visit. Remember: our Chippewa forefathers drank the sweet blood of their enemies, and ate their hearts! And the bear of this Native spirit still prowls during our long winter. Only now he has taken refuge in a deep cave, though he does not sleep. You cannot find him. His tracks were covered by the snow in which you came.

Neil said we Indigenes, condensed from the ether into the white man's world, are worse than orphans. We are…occupied. The most remote of all his fancies was at once the saddest and most beautiful. In the labor of love which was the act of the making of each baggattaway stick, Neil believed he had created a life. He saw it. Attached to the long handle of every stick he fashioned was a Chippewa warrior. He called them his sons. He claimed to have fathered a thousand of them. He said he had been granted the powers of a conjurer and that his simple task was to rejuvenate the decimated and shamed ranks of the Anishinaabek. Single-handedly if need be. He believed that his conjurer's powers matched those of the sky and the water in Anishinaabewaki. Around his plot these sons ran and caroused, causing poor Neil no end of exhaustion and woe but also infecting him with the hope of rising once again. He said the lacrosse stick was a paintbrush the Great Spirit handed down from the clouds with an Anishinaabe attached who sprang to life the second his moccasins touched the ground, the army by which we would reclaim our sacred lands and cast off the slumber of the white man.

Like I've said, it was June Two, 2009, and just like June Two of every year it was a kind of boys day out. This custom was the personal invention of Longbow and Birchwalker, and even my Marla could not resist or control it. It was after I returned to the reservation in 1978 that we bestowed upon the formerly unadorned June Two the name *Pontiac-Looking-Down Day*. I guess we needed something to do. We tried to gather up the harmonies from our long-broken song.

We sang first and foremost of the virtue of righteous resistance in the almost famous and almost successful rebellion of our war chief. We bowed to his fate in the Afterlife tethered to the moon and noted at the same time that there was no better vantage point than a horizon moon from which to watch our humble little commemoration. We resurrected baggattaway, the Creator's Game, passed from heaven to the Anishinaabek and co-opted by the white man after our bear entered the cave, the game once played to the exclusion of all else here in the Great Lakes and now no more, and let us not overlook our great fortune in being able to reenact such a sacrifice on the very altar it was first celebrated—Fort Michilimackinac.

I had fasted for a mere twelve hours in honor of the occasion. Neil for at least four days.

"Neil!" I yelled out five paces from his rickety front stoop. "Neil Longbow LaSalle!" St. Anne Four barked and barked at me.

"Chippewa brother," I heard faintly from inside. "Bienvenu, mi wigwam es su wigwam."

Even before I entered his Chippewa peace van, I could smell the smoke. Neil was as high as the great ether. His place was, on a good day, rustic. His one concession to modernity was a lousy old TV as old as the Sports Entertainment Network Enterprise that spewed live sports into his brain. The network was better known as *SENE,* and that would have dated his set at about vintage. He had a rotary phone in the sitting area to speak with me or Marla or Parry Four Bears. A veil of propane odor had seeped into the walls, the same walls that cried out for spackle and paint. His grandfather's hutch stood right where he left it, the knives and lacing awls and all the rest of his whittler's cutlery still a mess in its long top drawer, only Neil had draped an old Indian runner over it, ten feet long. It was every bit as ugly as some prize find at a flea market, but it spoke to him like a myth. Tassels and small bells hung from either end. Black horses with wide eyes galloped on its pale yellow field, beadwork swirls of thunderbirds and fine flowers flared up around them.

He stood in front of a mirror which swung precariously on the wall by his front door. He greeted me with bloodshot eyes. As if I needed a reminder of the gulf that can occasionally separated us, I checked my blue jeans and hooded gray sweatshirt against his chosen garb. I watched my Chippewa brother apply vermilion to his forehead and his feet and calves and in zigzags to his forearms and across his face. He was naked except for the breechclout, a kind of deerskin loin cloth which only accentuated his bowleggedness. On the table a few feet away in the kitchen lay two brightly colored kingfisher feathers which, over howls of protest from St. Anne, I helped him tie into his hair at the crown. He shushed St. Anne, who ran suddenly for the door, banging hard into my leg on her way, on purpose. Then he made thick gray braids out of the rest of his hair, winced sharply while sliding a feather through his nose. He painted his wrists and hands yellow and drew parallel lines of the same yellow on his thighs. He outlined the colors with bear fat and charcoal, giving it the gravity of war paint, but smudging it in the deep lines of his face. Neil put on the Big Indian for all our June Twos.

Finished, he turned to me, a vision. "Ready, Birchwalker?"

Adorning his walls like fence pickets was a full squadron of three- and six-foot white ash baggattaway sticks, fashioned by his own hand. I can help you with this: the intention of the arrangement on the walls would come clear after some reflection, high-low pairings of the traditional length stick and the longer defenseman stick used in the white man's version of baggattaway. They were made in the Iroquois style and sometimes in my periphery they seemed like mismatched snowshoes on the wall of my friend. I wondered if he saw the pairs as a series of portraits, himself pictured with each of his thousand sons. Breaking the wave of pickets on the side walls were two framed pictures, each depicting an aspect of Anishinaabek antiquity that had long since claimed Neil's heart. Relics. One was Indian, telling of Chippewa encampments on the St. Mary's River swollen with the autumn pike run. In the foreground dozens of lacrosse sticks were stacked pyrelike for a blessing at the edge of a bonfire, the players standing behind them and the river in a tight circle. The twilight fire glowed in their faces. The second picture was a simple black and white sketch of Big Mac, distorted a bit to make its center span bulge out like a fish eye. It was done in fine lines to commemorate the day the bridge opened to traffic in 1957, the same year Neil and I were born.

Neil took down a high-low pair of sticks and ambled over to a wooden crate in his den. He bent over awkwardly and removed two vermilion balls and threw them to me. I prayed that the perforations did not hold unseen pints of St. Anne's drool. Stretching tradition to the breaking point, Neil favored the original Indian lacrosse ball, constructed not from rubber but from the knot of a white willow, charred and scraped into a circle, tinted the color of life, red, and perforated to make it whistle when thrown by your head. You would not want to be struck by one of these. He emitted a little war whoop, a blessing on the equipment.

"Birchwalker," he said, "they should use these in the World Cup."

To the white noise of St. Anne barking outside, he plopped down next to me on his blanket-strewn sofa. We both knew what had to come next. He was floating in his red eyes yet alert to the presence of something besides me. In this enlightened state he would regale me with a legend from the vast bank of baggattaway stories. All indigenous peoples have legends about the role of lacrosse. The Iroquois say that the game was played before human beings were even created, a battle between Good and Evil settled by a game of ball. The Chippewa have several of their own. The fables about baggattaway and life and death do not follow the white man's form. They are as weird as Bible lessons. And be warned: our parables have teeth. Neil did not offer me the pipe shaped like a tomahawk. When he finally put it down, his gesturing became wild and he rose and fell on the sofa, he cried. I knew better than to interrupt this legend, his duty.

"The young man had three sisters. His name was Madjikiwis. He said, 'I'm going to go see my new brother-in-law.' He took up his war club. It had a big ball at the end of it; when he picked it up, sparks flew all over the room. That's how powerful he was. There was thunder and lightning. When he got to Wakayabide, he said, 'My friend, I want you to be my brother-in-law. When you go into the wigwam, go to the smallest woman. That's the sister I want you to marry. All right, get up and follow me.'

"He kept on until he came to a tiny woman. When Madjikiwis hung up his club, Wakayabide saw sparks fly out." Neil's red eyes opened wide, his palms followed in kind. "Madjikiwis's sister started to teach him: 'We have all kinds of games here. I want you to be careful. The people here are dangerous. They kill each other. You won't live very long if you play in their games.'

"Everybody heard that Madjikiwis had a new brother-in-law, so they all wanted to see him and invite him to play in their games. The first man he met was a grizzly bear. The next one was a polar bear. Wakayabide found out that these people changed into animals."

St. Anne pawed at the door. I let her in and she ran to Neil. Absently, Neil rubbed her fur, and I realized that she knew the story as well as I did. He came slowly to his feet, held an imaginary bullhorn to his mouth.

"The next day, early in the morning, there was an announcer going around the village, saying, 'Today we have a lacrosse game. Madjikiwis's brother-in-law must play too.' Wakayabide's wife said, 'Be careful! I don't want you to go. They'll kill you.' He laughed. 'They can't kill me. I'll go and watch, anyway.' Madjikiwis was losing the game and had already lost all of his clothing."

"He wanted Wakayabide to play for him. Wakayabide stood with his bow and arrow, watching. One of the players, the grizzly bear, came over to him. 'Here, Brother.' He gave him a lacrosse stick. He took it, but Wakayabide had left his belt in the wigwam, so the wolf wasn't there. You see, out in the woods, a wolf had told him never to leave the belt but always take it along."

Neil was choking back tears.

"The ball was coming. His partner said, 'Grab the ball and run!' He grabbed the ball with his stick and ran for the goal. The other man followed. Instead of taking the ball away, the bear jumped on his bare back and tore the skin to the bone. Wakayabide dropped dead right there. They cut him up into pieces and shared the meat.

"His woman was worrying about him. She asked people where he was, but they didn't tell her. That night all the families feasted on the meat. The wolf knew that something was wrong with his master. He started to howl inside the belt. The woman heard that noise. She kept quiet and listened. It sounded like a wolf howling."

And now my friend's mouth was a circle. He came to his feet.

"At first it was like a wolf way off in the woods. Then she saw that it was coming from the belt. She found a little pocket. She opened it and found a tiny dog. She set it on the ground. She knew right away that it belonged to her man. The dog shook and began to grow. Then he dashed outside and ran all over town. He got all the bones and put them together in the shape of a man. Then he hollered. The bones jumped together. He hollered again. Flesh came on the bones. He hollered again. Then his eyes opened up. When the wolf hollered the fourth time, Wakayabide's breath began to come. The wolf said, 'You didn't listen to me, my grandchild, so I came to save you. That's what happens when you don't listen. Get up now. We'll go home.' His wife was glad to see him again. She said, 'I found that little dog in your belt. He's saved your life. Always take him along now.'

"The next day was another lacrosse game. Wakayabide's wife scolded him, 'Don't go. They'll kill you again.' He said, 'No, I want to go.' He wanted to get his revenge on the one who had killed him. He put on his belt and went out. He was looking for that bear.

"At Ball Up the bear said, 'I'll show you how to play!' He took the ball. Wakayabide followed him with two arrows in his hands. Wakayabide jumped on the bear with his two arrows and buried them in his skin. He tore the bear to pieces with the arrows and killed him. Then he walked away. The other people cut up the bear and cooked him. They passed the meat around to all the families. He had some of it too. It tasted good, nice and fat. The bear came alive again the next day too. He was a powerful man."

Neil looked off into space, as if returning the story to the vaults of heaven.

"It's the wife who saves Wakayabide, right, Neil?" I asked him, like always.

"The dog."

"The dog? Dogs were god-bait," I reminded him. "It's the wife who saves."

"No, Birchwalker, the woman beguiles man. It is the dog who saves him. The dog is grandfather to the man. Birchwalker. Le chien est le grandpère de l'homme."

"C'mon," I said. "Let's do it. Let's go. Let's go down to the
fort and walk that field of clover and oxtail in honor of the last great
Chippewa defiance before we all turned to fossils. For crissake, let's
go get your head aired out."

We portaged the canoe to the milk truck and wedged it into the
back. Neil had packed it with a change of clothes, a pair of mismatch
crosses, a dozen or so tins of his Bigwig maple syrup, a few dozen
sticks of Bigwig maple taffy and the tomahawk pipe in a deerskin
quiver. He jumped into shotgun position, careful not to mess the
kingfisher feathers, and we chugged away southward. St. Anne, on
Neil's lap, fired an eager yelp.

"Birchwalker, maybe someday we should get ourselves a
Pontiac," he said with a self-satisfied grin out the windshield. "Step
on it, Indian."

His knees were red despite the spring warmth. They were
telling me we were probably already too old for this, yet we had to
continue this pilgrimage. It would be as unthinkable as you not
trimming your folks' gravesites on Memorial Day. In no time flat we
were idling at the Big Mac toll plaza, and finally we were dropped
like silt at the mouth of the river of remembrance that is Fort
Michilimackinac.

On our lakes and rivers see them.
Fort Detroit, Edward Augustus,
And site of lacrosse deception,
Fort Michilimackinac stands.

Once upon a time, we were maize growers and ice fishers and beaver hunters and *zinzibaakwad*—maple sugar campers. We were stewards of the Straits and all the adjacent lands; we allowed the French to put up a Jesuit mission on the cedarlined shore; they called their church St. Anne de Michilimackinac. Even Bwon-diac, still alive then, could not help but be moved by the tough-love message of Christianity preached into the spiritual void of Anishinaabewaki by those genial Jesuits:

> "Stockade sentries of our father
> For his black-robed priests intended.
> Christian Crucifix they taught us,
> Though they honored our Great Spirit."

> "As I think back and remember
> On the first time I did listen,
> I believed not in Salvation
> Rather in the Crucifixion."

Back then, we had to paddle for four days to reach the Soo. Now, it's an hour in a milk truck. I felt the story of the mighty lacrosse deception welling up in me. Neil would listen to my story of the massacre on the young king's birthday two hundred forty-six years ago.

"Longbow, you be Bad Sky this year," I suggested.

"Mais non! Tabernac, Birchwalker! Enfin, je m'en fous!"

Makoons and Bad Sky

"How could you throw that cute little dog off your canoe? And not just the one time, but time and again?"

Jan met us right out of the museum shop, her voice sweet but pinched. "Would it hurt you to wave every now and then?" she scolded, looking right at Neil. She folded her arms across her chest, awaiting an explanation. Neil looked at me, a plea in his eyes. I drew a breath to speak, but Jan was on a roll. "Poor little thing," she said, stooping down to pet St. Anne. "He throws you overboard, doesn't he? Is he teaching you how to swim? Poor thing." And then, back to us, "Did you think I'd forget? Huh uh. I remember you two from last year, and how we stood in the rectory while it hailed bloody murder and you told me all about bag…bag…"

"Baggattaway," I helped her.

"Right," she said with a wave of her hand. "Do you remember? But I never knew about the dogs…"

I looked down at my sneaker, watching it shuffle the gravel on the pedestrian path that leads to the fort entrance. "Our people, the Chippewa, used dogs to, they, uh, needed to appease the, uh…"

"Oh, glory be, just come out and say it. They sacrificed the poor helpless things, didn't they?"

"They bound their legs up so they couldn't swim," I admitted.

Neil stared her down, challenging her to say she had seen him bind St. Anne's legs.

"You better wave next time," she warned Neil with a stare of her own. She stepped off to the side, opening the path to us and then walking alongside. "We had a good turnout Memorial Day for the reenactment, lots of tourists, lots of curiosity about that 1763 lacrosse game. But as you can see there's nobody around now." Suddenly she grew animated and turned to block our way, holding her hands up to her head. "Wait, this is Pontiac-Looking-Down Day, right? The guy tied to the moon? I remember now! Who's gonna be Bad Sky and Makoons this year? Isn't that it? Did I get it? Did you find a Weniway and a…oh, who is it…"

She is short and circular and was beaming now ear to ear, proud of her memory and rightly so. She had retained those hard-to-hold Chippewa names for a whole year.

"Minavavana, Jan," I told her. "He was the chief of the Mackinac Island tribe. Good job to remember Makoons and Bad Sky, though."

"How could I ever forget the name Bad Sky, since that was the whole reason I learned about him in the first place. Say again. Minne…But, wait…it's your real names I can't remember."

Neil drew his shoulders up, squinted and pursed his lips at Jan.

"Yeah, I remember all right. It was my first year working here and I had to encounter the likes of you. I remember our little talk."

Neil harrumphed.

Jan was right. As we'd walked up the path to the fort gate last June Two all hell broke loose in the heavens. Lacrosse ball-size hailstones blew down from tall clouds. There was sudden lightning and white caps appeared on the lake. Geese and barge calls on the wind. We shuffled into the restored colonial rectory, attached to the church where the heathen were punished with Enlightenment in the middle of the Eighteenth Century. We rode out the storm on the bench pews, talking war paint and breechclouts. It was my lecture. Jan was a lively audience, listening intently even as she kept an eye on Neil. To the steady tom-tom beat of big hail on the wooden shingles of the tiny hut, I had spilled the beans to Jan about our little commemoration.

"Why do you boys do your own reenactment? We got the one here every Memorial Day!" she'd exclaimed. "People come from everywhere to see it!"

I'd just smiled at her. I'd explained to her that ours was private. Neil was never a fan of initiating the uninitiated, even a trained staffer like Jan. As I explained the catapult shot, he'd amused himself by repeatedly sticking his crosse out a window casement, catching hailstones in the net, eating them. We were kind of stranded there, so I told her everything, not only of the infamous shot but also about the event's carnage so minutely recalled every Memorial Day. Baggattaway games were never pretty, and the one in 1763 was particularly gruesome—even by Chippewa standards. I don't know what had gotten into me. Unlike Neil, I just wanted her to *know*. Her forefathers and mine had been bitter enemies. And it was not lost on her that the victors' great-granddaughters trade the anguish of Indian extinction for a tourist's slack jaw.

"The Chippewa drank their blood," I'd told her shocked face. "They cupped their hands inside the opened gut and drank the enemy's blood. They scalped the English soldiers while they were still alive," I insisted. "Plundered the fort's supply houses and went off into the row houses like rabid dogs in search of those whimpering cowards whose skin oozed a fear you could smell."

"I guess you don't want me to labor under any romantic illusions about this, do you, Makoons?" she'd said.

"It was ugly, Jan. The Chippewa and the Saulk used whatever weapon they could get their hands on, the lighter and more lethal the better. Their women and children tossed them the weapons on the run, you see. Like the pipe tomahawk. Neil has one. They're long, slender cylinders of wood, usually ash or hickory like a lacrosse stick, and nearly as long. At one end is a pipe bowl for sharing tobacco at peacetime and on the other end you'll find a tomahawk blade for those…hard-to-settle disputes. What they'd do, the Chippewa and the Saulk, they'd catch an Englishman from behind and plant the tomahawk in the neck just below the right ear." I slashed with an imaginary blade behind my ear for effect. "Don't worry, though. Neil uses his exclusively for peaceful reasons."

Neil had flashed Jan a toothy smile.

"How did that catapult shot work again exactly?" she wondered again this year.

"Jan, even if you'd seen it, you might not have believed it. That shot gave us a miracle victory, even if it was short-lived, a little like…Palm Sunday maybe," I said, hoping she'd see the point.

"Then I'll be your Doubting Thomas, won't I? You'll have to show me. You boys show me the catapult shot, and I'll refund your entrance fee. I want to hear the whole story, including the gory parts. Tell me your real names again?" She looked right at Neil. St. Anne barked once and scrolled her tongue out at Jan.

I could see the light in Jan's eye and it dawned on me that she was dying to learn, learn from someone authentic, someone related to the original cast, every detail of this staged game. Maybe she was an encyclopedic gatherer of Indian trivia. Maybe she wanted to get a promotion. Maybe she had a little thing for Neil. Whatever the motive, she was a determined seeker of this knowledge, and I, for one, was happy to oblige.

"I'm Birch Charlevoix. The cute one playing Bad Sky is Neil Longbow LaSalle."

The best part about June Two, 2009 was that it fell on a weekday and the tourists were back at work. So Jan walked with us into the fort, marching us past its historically significant structures, making a beeline for the landgate on the other side. Though the original land gate and most of the trees were long gone, my mind easily reconstructed the scene. Through the mist of history I saw the thirty houses of the garrison, the inside banquettes and the firing loopholes for defense, the Jesuit priest saying Mass for the few heathen intrigued by the dying man nailed to the cross, the raucous traders peddling their guns and rum for marten and beaver and otter skins. I was filled with a retroactive shudder over my people's fate. I wished I could have warned them that their victorious experiment in sport and warfare would not hold. They do not hear me when I warn them in my dream.

The ground outside the fort was wet and very green, dotted with oxtail and strife. Jan leaned against the land gate, an opening in the cedar stockades of seven or eight feet in width. St. Anne sprinted out into the wildflowers and barked bravely at the Straits. Neil and I walked out the land gate, the wind off the lake tossing my hair. Neil drew a deep breath, suddenly at home. The sun was breaking through and warming the air quickly. He knew what I had to do. My job was to reminisce, to recall my story. The Saulk and the Chippewa had already taken the field.

"The waves are lapping and pockets of cedar drift on the wind. I pause for them to speak a word, to let their memory fill mine, to receive their blessing. There is Bwon-diac on the moon above, looking down. On the twenty-fifth birthday of the young King George III, the two teams gather at the centerfield, forty Chippewa and forty Saulk, their women and children huddled in blankets along the south picket wall. Some of the women carry babes on their backs. Others make friendly conversation with the soldiers and invite them to place bets on one of the teams. The English soldiers have all come out of the fort after the midday meal in their unbuttoned redcoats, relaxed and ready for entertainment at the invitation of the tribes."

"C'est vrai, Birchwalker. Très bien commencé," Neil agreed in French.

"The game is announced: the winner would be the first to score four goals; play should take around an hour; the goal is the space between two stripped cedar posts, each guarded by two goalkeepers; the Chippewa defend the southwest goal; the boundaries of play are the stables and gardens to the southeast and the mounds to the southwest, making a short field for the eighty players of about two-thirds of a mile."

Neil leaned on the long stick, his eyes closed. St. Anne had become a brown, black and white speck running down the shore. Jan inched closer.

"Underneath the surface of the contest between the two tribes roils the brewing war between these same tribes and their new rulers, the English. The English have greatly irritated the Indigenes. Without notice, they have halved the prices for skins formerly paid by the French. The colonial scent is of plunder and occupation and seizure of lands and life and limb. The present fort is deemed vital in the trade lane from Montreal to the lands west of the Mississippi and in all areas of the Great Lakes, so that whoever holds the fort also controls a pivotal regional depot and gains significant trade and military advantage. No less a thing than life is at stake in the eyes of the Indigenes as they make their preparations for battle disguised as sport.

"The Chippewa ballplayer called Makoons arrives by canoe with his woman and child after a journey of two weeks. He has traveled with baggattaway sticks partially carved, with beaver and marten pelts for trading, with stores of maple sugar and utensils, some tokens for his Odawa host family. A deception is designed by the Saulk and the Chippewa that will gain them access to the inside of the fort. The aim is to seize it and to kill the entire English garrison and to plunder the stores. An invitation is made to the English commander by Chief Minavavana of the Saulk island tribe. A game of baggattaway is to be held for the pleasure of the English soldiers who will enjoy a holiday on their king's birthday. A good game is promised as the Saulk seek to avenge last year's loss to the Chippewa."

Neil began a bowlegged lope around the field, cradling one of the perforated vermilion balls in the webbing of the long stick above his head, his lips moving in some kind of chant. St. Anne stood on the shore barking at him though her bark could not be heard over the wind.

"The ruse depends on a catapult shot by Makoons. He has arrived early to practice the difficult shot with a partner named Bad Sky. They practice and practice in a field far from the fort until they have mastered the catapult. It is not intended to result in a goal. It is only a way to launch a ball farther downfield than would be normally possible with the Great Lakes style sticks. Bad Sky, with Makoons approaching at full run, will slide his right hand up the long stick to a point just below the webbing. His left hand remains at the butt end of the stick so that his stick is held horizontally and braced for the contact to come; he plants his legs apart and holds the stick high."

I watched St. Anne chasing Neil. Then he pivoted as quickly as his arthritic hip would allow and faced the other way, sliding his right hand up the shaft like Bad Sky.

"Oh," muttered Jan, staring straight into my face.

"Makoons approaches, scooping the ball on a long bounce from Weniway, the tall one painted all in black except for the big white circles around his eyes. Makoons is as fast as the wind and very intent. At the point of impact he will slide his right hand down on the short stick to get as much whip as possible before slamming his into Bad Sky's. The ball is to be thrown into the open land gate of the fort where the players will pursue it in their droves, exchanging their baggattaway sticks for the weapons hidden under their women's blankets—war clubs bulging with hard knots of maple, scalping knives, tomahawks. They will attack and kill the garrison with all due dispatch. There is to be much stabbing, clubbing, scalping, smearing and drinking of blood, eating of enemy hearts, and the fort will be won."

"Dear God." Jan covered her mouth.

"The evening before the match, preparations are intense. The eighty players have begun their fast and will have no sex with their women. They will sit two-by-two in a sweat box for an hour at a time. Medicine men are rubbing the sticks and balls in vermilion, as well as the weapons of war, and blessing them with water from the great lake to the purpose. Makoons is bending a few new sticks just in case, steaming them in a big copper kettle. His woman, Boodoonh, is preparing to do the lacing, burning holes into the wood with a hot awl.

When the time comes next morning, she will wrap her man's braids and paint his face and torso. She will tie kingfisher feathers to the webbing of his sticks, an Indian prayer that the ball fly true and swift. Boodoonh will station herself near the land gate with weapons under her blanket. The women are in this game too.

"The tactic is to remove the spectating soldiers as far from the open land gate as possible, and this is tricky. They must find a way to put the English at ease, which they began to accomplish in a trading visit the day before. They talked up the game and made a census of those to be killed and took stock of the bounty they would seize after the battle. Some took their young sons to display the skills of baggattaway. The boys drew a friendly crowd of Englishmen, piquing their curiosity. The Chippewa and the Saulk know that the English have never witnessed the ball played by the Indians, that they are lured by the promise of brutal encounters, broken bones, war whoops. All of that is planned for. But there must also be the expectation of wild shots so that the one Makoons finally launches into the fort will be seen as part of the contest. Three wild shots are devised. Two will be flung against the picket wall on either side of the land gate, and more importantly the third will be "accidentally" flung into the water of the great lake by a stumbling Saulk player who is trying to get the ball downfield toward the Chippewa goal near the shore. Much commotion will ensue, as tens of players enter the water after the ball, slashing and dunking one another amid continuous whoops of intimidation. Englishmen will be lured to this scene far from the gate, and within minutes of the retrieval of the ball from the water, it will be forwarded to Weniway who will spot Makoons who will nod to Bad Sky who will brace himself for the catapult, and all will be wagered on the success of that moment."

Neil had migrated to the shore and was standing with his stick and St. Anne looking out over the water toward Canada, his back to me.

"The day arrives. June 2, 1763, the birthday of King George III of England. The weather is sultry and warm, but there is no rain. The soldiers have eaten their midday meal and stride leisurely out of the fort. They see that women and children have lined the fields of play. They see the small boys stationed behind the goals to catch and return errant balls. Some have brought rum with them. They note the wagering going on the far side and are invited to participate. They are engaged by the Indigene women in a friendly way. They are at ease. The referee who is a medicine man of the Saulk calls the players to the centerfield, a huge huddle of eighty baggattaway players with never so much to gain as in this game. Fair play is encouraged; Minavavana curses the English and sets fire in his players' hearts with his own wild eyes. The sides break, and two players from each team go off to the goals. Ten from each side take defensive positions, which leaves twenty-eight a side at centerfield, Weniway towering over all of them in his black and white paint. *Ball Up!* is called. The referee tosses the ball overhead and runs out of harm's way. Thirty or forty sticks clash amid great whoops and the lurching and jostling of masses trying to gain possession of the ball. As the game progresses, it draws the soldiers out away from the gate according to plan, the two picket shots working to enchant the English with the notion that a baggattaway ball can end up just about any old place. At 3-3 a pause is called to let the players get a drink, for final wagers to be placed on the game's outcome and as the signal that now is the time for the water shot."

St. Anne had begun to turn circles on the beach now, chasing her tail, and her owner was loping around the perimeter of the field, still cradling the ball in his webbing. His mouth was shaped like a baying wolf, but still I couldn't hear him.

"In no time after the break a red ball is bobbing upon the great water, and two dozen players are in hot pursuit, pushing and dunking each other in the water, hitting one another with their sticks, yelping war cries. After sufficient commotion to lure the soldiers, the ball is cleared back to Weniway who wheels and fires to Makoons. He never lets him out of his sight. Makoons bends down very low to scoop the ball with his stick and comes up running at full speed toward Bad Sky. The English soldiers seem to understand that a play of great moment is unfolding and are rapt with attention. To them it must look like Makoons will bowl Bad Sky over. At twenty paces, they both slide their hands in opposite directions on their shafts, like mirror images. Makoons lets loose with wild whoops and begins to cock his throwing arm. The motion stands him up and with a mighty heave he cracks his stick into the horizontally held stick of Bad Sky. The ball is catapulted on a very high trajectory, arcs down toward the land gate where it strikes the open right gate and bounds into the fort, finally coming to rest under a trader's table." I paused, seeing it as clearly as if I had been there, every sense tingling.

"Don't stop now, Birch," yelled Jan Zwiebel. "You've gotten to the best part. Aren't they going to rush into the fort and scalp everyone in sight and loot and pillage? Aren't they going to take over the fort with war whoops and dancing? Aren't they going to smear a lot of blood and eat those English hearts?"

I couldn't think of anything to say to her.

After a long, uncomfortable silence, Jan put her hand up to her chin. "You know what? I'm just sitting here wondering if you boys do school assemblies. I really am."

"Birchwalker," said Neil, breathy from the run back up the hill to the land gate, "let's go Lockside. You can buy me a pizza. We'll get a haircut, come on."

Soo Locks

When Neil says Lockside, he means the decrepit old downtown where the fog lies heaviest on the streets of Sault Ste. Marie. If there's a part of town that has been locked away in a time capsule, it is Lockside, a twelve-block square whose northern edge is washed by the St. Mary's River. If you find yourself on Easterday Avenue, you've gone too far south. Ashmun Street meanders along its eastern flank. Boundless Lake Superior itself hovers westerly. These few acres of commerce and city parks overlook the intricate system of canals and water locks built on the river in the 1850s. The locks dominate here. You will hear them hoisting and heaving; you can learn about them in the museum; you can take a dinner cruise and be hoisted yourself. They act like water elevators, leveling the twenty-three foot gradient between Lake Superior and Lake Huron. But you must know there's a vintage movie house Lockside, a barbershop, a pizza place that sells snowmobiles on the side, an Amoco station, a tobacconist and a sports bar, too, that mark our movements in the Soo, a circuit that Neil has always called the trail of tears because most Lockside visits include an encounter with a guy named Roy LeRoi.

Thirty years ago, all I knew is what I was hearing as a kid at Periwinkle High School. This new kid from the Soo starts showing up in the parking lot before school, during school, after school, hanging out, making friends. He liked to be called The King. He was just there all of a sudden, and the kids flocked to him. He promised them booze.

He revved his bright red muscle car and flashed his broad smile and, sometimes, a shiv. At first the shiv came out to titillate, later it would come out to intimidate, and later still to cut. He was nothing, a strutting peacock, a rabble-rouser. But he had a bad compulsion. He was an Indian hater. You could tell so easily, the way he stared me down as I walked past the throng into school, the way he looked at all the Indian kids, picking us out like salmon in a pike run. His hate lay openly in the eye. And on the tongue. He slurred us in ways shocking to people even back then. But some of the kids ate it up. He told them he went to Soo High but that he didn't really bother with school all that often, bragged about how he already had all the education he needed. He told them he lived with his father's cousin in a shack near Sugar Island, that originally he was from Big Soo across the International Bridge in Ontario. He claimed he served time in a juvie hall twice in his young life, once for digging up Indian graves in a cemetery on Sugar Island and then a year later for assault with intent on some Sault-Chippewa kids. There's a lot of Chippewa across the bridge. There's also a lot on Sugar Island and in our Michigan Soo, and then there's us out at Pope County. That's a hell of a lot of red meat for a Bone Digger, as I came to call him. We do make juicy carrion for those vultures— and they're still out there—who live to redden their curved beaks in the entrails of the near dead. And it was surely an easy enough thing to rally other white kids against Indians. Who are these holdout compulsives like Bone Digger, driven to eliminate every last vestige of our existence even after we have long since ceased to exist? Roy LeRoi was our reminder that the ladder of life would eventually run out of rungs. He was the guy that stood above us on the ladder and stomped on our slipping fingers with his boot heel to break our grip on the bottom rung, meaning to send us into eternal freefall.

He was supposedly already twenty and boasted that he'd already bagged himself many a precocious schoolgirl and had even fathered a child across in Big Soo. He flirted openly and lewdly with our PHS girls, grabbing his crotch and howling as they passed. The girls, some of them, smiled at the attention or at his boorishness; others he scared or just plain disgusted. The boys too. How they admired his derring-do, his loud wit, this man of the world, this driver of muscle, this truant father who so blithely threw down a challenge to the accepted virtue that Native Americans had to be tolerated, integrated, adopted.

Like I told you, Neil had dropped out of school in eighth grade. When I told him about this new kid named Roy who was castigating the Native population, he said, "King, le roi." I'll never forget it. Roy in French. "Is his name Roy LeRoi?" he asked. He went to school with me the next morning. Neil walked right up to him, asked him the same question he'd asked me, only he didn't wait for an answer. Neil clocked him, sucker punched him in the gut so he folded forward; then he tagged him with a quick right to his chin that sent him flailing off wildly to his right and finally down on the macadam. Roy scrambled quickly to his feet and began to dance wide circles around Neil, yanking at his chin and laughing like a crazy man. The kids formed a large circle and chanted for action. No one was pulling for Neil. Roy landed one on Neil's chin that turned him right around. He tripped him to the ground and got on top of him. When he pulled out his shiv, I jumped on his back and dragged him off Neil. Feigning surrender, Roy gave Neil something to remember him by as they stood up, making a sudden lunge and a wild swipe with the shiv that cut Neil just above his hipbone and left a bad scar. A burly bus driver broke the fight up and reported the incident to the office, but it was only the first of many fights to come. Roy was belligerent, caustic, touchy, and he was just getting warmed up. The whole senior year went on like this, our friends and his ducking open places and broad daylight to tangle, his French kids against us Indians.

But the unpaved roads of '74 did not stop Roy LeRoi from venturing out to the Pope County Indian Reservation and cruising our alleys at dusk. His fat predator tires crunched over the gravel and dirt. His incursion, along with three or four other cars filled with his new followers from school, focused the mind, bringing Chippewa fathers and mothers, Neil and me and plenty of no-bullshit Indian kids to their stoops to face them down. Engines were cut. A row of car doors slammed shut. Twelve or thirteen boys emerged acting so cool, looking every way but right at us, then they squared off across the alley, when Roy began his taunts, backed by the chorus of yes men. You could smell the beer on their breath. Eyes would signal. Heads would nod. Though unarmed, we were not afraid. We were proud, and we were ready to fight, but not in our parents' alleys. We were also as fast as the wind, and on that night we tore into the dark Hiawatha which we knew like the back of our own hands. Fools, they chased us.

We knew the trails. We knew the trees, we knew the falls at Tahquamenon, we knew that if the fight was taken to the Hiawatha the outcome could hardly be in doubt. To Neil's owl hoots, we jumped them from above, we surprised them from hollowed-out trees, ran them ragged across streams into the darkest places in the forest, countering their advantage of numbers and the shiv. They got lost. They finally turned back, shouting epithets of a scurrilous nature as you might believe and promising a return match.

The idiots would only make the Hiawatha Forest mistake one other time. But the harassment continued. My father reported them to the Periwinkle Police. They blew him off. By then we were at each other necks, a blood feud that promised danger and vengeance, lust. I remember the exhilaration I found in being hunted. There's no time you feel more alive.

The second time we lured the fools into the Hiawatha, Jimmy Blackbird pushed one of Roy's posse fifty feet off the viewing platform at Tahquamenon Falls, putting him in the intensive care unit in the Soo. With this more egregious offense, the police issued Roy and his friends a restraining order and imposed a curfew on the reservation.

Then I went away to school. Roy's yes-men got jobs in the Soo flipping pancakes or pumping gas or wherever else they could. A few went to college. I had no idea what had become of Roy, The King, Bone Digger. He must have known that Neil remained on the reservation, but Neil never said a word to me about it. The teenage lust was spent. We all went our separate ways into the forest of life.

Four years later I finished college and was named to the Indigene Nation lacrosse World Cup team. My picture ran in the papers, the *Soo News* and even in the Sault *Star* over the bridge in Ontario. It must have been that picture that fetched Roy onto our alley ways once again, only now he was driving a bright red ton-and-a-half, four-by-four pickup truck. His license plate read K-I-N-G. In the open bed, five or six different kinds of fertilizer bags lay in stacks and some were stood up open, some empty, and crumpled-up bags lay crushed under a concrete block and a dozen gas cans; he had mowers and spreaders. In broad daylight this time, he drove right by my father's house where I was standing out front and our eyes met briefly. He just drove on, but he was letting me know that he was still around, that the blood feud was still running hot. We were just older now. It seemed to me he wasn't sitting quite as high in his seat as before. As I watched his face in the big sideview mirror, it occurred to me that a bastard is what he was. We were young men in 1978, in our early twenties, and there was a very adult feel to that look we exchanged. The next time I saw him was at McKeon's Sports Bar in the Soo.

Back then, Tommy McKeon told me Roy was a maintenance man at the locks, mowing lawns and fixing snow blowers and tending the acres of city parks that run along the canals. "He's in here all the time, a goddamn menace. You'd think we were a goddamn saloon in the wild west when he's in here, Birch," Tommy told me. Tommy's concerns were mercantile. Thus, his establishment tolerated The King and his always simmering compulsion even after everybody else had gotten over the ancient blood feud. While he was a harmless loudmouth to most, a special kind of loathing had condensed in him for us Indians, a steady viscous drip of blood, urine and pus into the root cellar of his gut, growing a twisted thing that ruled him. Bone Digger spat at our modest social gains, if you could even call them that, since gaming had put us on a corner of the map, regarding them no doubt as the darkest hour before the dawn of our annihilation. I did not underestimate him. A fiery leader, he could still recruit enough bodies, though they were mostly the Frenchies who had signed up with him back in the parking lot of Periwinkle High, and that was why Tommy had trouble just throwing Roy out. They'd take their dollars and make some other watering hole their home. If Roy could be said to have any virtue at all, it was surely persistence, his dogged determination to shut us out of his world, which included the possibility that the local bad boy will one day carry it all too far, just to finally satisfy that awful thing that was growing in the root cellar. He'd already put two scars on Neil. He was in his fifties now, all that pent-up bile looking for an out.

I watched Neil carry a pair of jeans and a T-shirt into the rest room at DePaul's Amoco station, and I didn't imagine he'd get all the war paint and grease off his face. St. Anne Four barked at me from the driver's bar stool while I filled up the milk truck. Neil returned looking ever more modern and skinny, no hint of the smudged charcoal or the war-paint cosmetics, the effect of his bowlegs muted in the long pants. The kingfisher and nose feathers were gone. He'd done his homage to Bwon-diac. The buildup to Pontiac-Looking-

Down Day took an emotional toll on my friend. History, after all, can be heavy. First, he fasts for nearly a week and makes himself up and tells that baggattaway legend about Wakayabide and runs that windy field with his arthritic hips feeling the heat of our chieftain's stare from lunar orbit and is forced to deal with the unwashed like Jan, and finally he, we, must simply slump to the ground exhausted in the bitter memory of the English retaking the fort. Naturally, he comes up from all of that self-denial and reminiscence as hungry as a bear and ready for some action. He was looking for fast food and mayhem, and Lockside was just the place.

The first stop on the trail of tears is always Tony's Pizza and Snowmobiles. St. Anne was happy to be out of the milk truck and pranced ahead of us. Neil slung the quiver over his shoulder, stuffed with taffies and maple syrup tins. We passed Blake's Cigar Shoppe where Neil had been displayed for two summers as a living cigar store Indian. (Of all people, Neil is the one who proposed it to Mickey— posing out front in kingfisher feathers, war paint, buckskins and all, while holding an open box of White Owls to lure customers inside. He had just moved back into the double-wide after his grandfather walked on and really needed the paltry paycheck. He has never described to me the self-loathing he had to feel.) These days, Mickey Blake has a life-size Indian statue out front. I went in to buy a Montecristo for Tommy McKeon, and when I came back out, there was Neil squared off with his replacement, standing on his tiptoes to go eyeball-to-eyeball with the wooden Indian, calling him out.

We were Tony's first customers of the day. His grills and ovens were ready to go, the smell of heat and tomato sauce in ascent. He kept track of the days with a girly calendar. We noted that he'd scribbled in *Bwon-diac-Looking-Down* for June Two.

"Aaniin, inini," Tony said without looking up from the counter he was wiping down for us. His white apron was spotless. He possessed superb salt-and-pepper hair and a matching mustache, was slim and polite, and never stopped probing the hungry consumer inside you. He'd sell you anything, like a bazaar vendor—watches, pizza, snowmobiles, even Neil's maple syrup, which Neil set down near the cash register to a knowing nod from Tony. In one smooth motion he set out Soo Chamber of Commerce paper place mats, some stained silverware, two filmy Coke glasses, greasy salt and pepper shakers, hot red peppers. He's the only one on the trail of tears who has bothered to learn even a word of Ojibwemowin. "Gentlemen, I trust you had another uplifting Bwon-diac-Looking-Down Day. Can I interest you gentlemen in a snowmobile perhaps? Got some great off-season deals. Used, too. Were it only winter, I could offer you a test-drive at the snowmobile oval, inini."

"Maybe just a pepperoni pie and a couple vanilla Cokes, Tony."

"I can help you with the financing, inini. I'll carry you interest-free for a period of six months. I'll even advance you the down payment in maple syrup futures, Neil."

"You know we don't buy on credit, Tony. What would our chieftain say?" Neil pointed at the calendar, the word Bwon-diac.

At the invocation of that sacred name Tony straightened and held up his hands in surrender, a sensible retreat. St. Anne Four and I watched Neil dig into the pizza after his spring fast. He devoured it, eating six slices to my two and then proceeded to down the twelve ounces of vanilla Coke in a single gulp, his theory being that the acid in the soda would burn a path through the wad of pizza and begin an accelerated digestion which would clear out enough room for beer at McKeon's. Pleading whimpers from his beagle produced no scraps from the master. He pocketed two fifties from Tony for the syrup but left me to pay the tab while he worked up a magnitude-six belch delivered with a parting smile for Tony.

"You're welcome anytime, I'm sure, Neil."

Next we walked to Neil's top spot along the trail of tears, and that is McKeon's Sports Bar, down the street from Tony's and over a block and a half on Ashmun Street. At noon the Sports Bar too had the off-hours feel of those wee-hours establishments, the odor of stale beer and deep-fry from last night tamped down by room deodorizer. Still, after the pie we were ready for a beer or two. There were a dozen or so guys already here, third-shifters. They seemed calm and unhurried, like they had located themselves presciently at Tommy's, in advance of the beer-lust that would soon overtake them. But for now their hair was still wet from the morning combing, the T-shirts still fresh, the eyes still glazed over from sleep. Tommy McKeon had all sixteen televisions going, no sound; only a few of the third-shifters watched.

The atmosphere of McKeon's riled St. Anne Four just as it had done to her three predecessors, driving the poor thing into a tail-chasing frenzy. If Jan Zwiebel could only have seen it! It's the same thing that happened on the shore, her dervish dance with whitecaps. As soon as the signal of the TV screens descended on her, she chased and nipped at her own rump with such abandon and such fierce need that I can only compare it to the agony of a groin fungus. The patrons got a snicker out of this performance, then looked at us, then back at the TVs or their *Soo News*. In St. Anne's defense, as we watched her tight circles, I had to concede that the power of sixteen televisions over your head is overwhelming, regardless of what might be playing.

Tommy has one of those NFL TV packages, called Sunday Ticket, so he can present every single early, late, and late-late Sunday football game in its entirety during the football season. So on NFL Sundays, of course, it's all the different games live. Passes, runs, sacks, injuries, replays and challenges, touchdowns, field goals and extra points, stats and announcers, timeouts and commercial breaks—a constant stream of sporting images carried to the reptilian brain that will resolve during sleep into Monday's narrative at work. It's a flickering pandemonium for the eye of a sports fan, the ultimate fix for the everyday football aficionado and the very staff of life for the more addicted Fantasy Football League player. Overexcited announcers and former players blare opinions from each set. Halftime shows create an intermezzo to freshen up the drinks and splatter the gutters in Tommy's rest room. A passer-by on a winter Sunday would look through one of Tommy's frosty front windows and see the potentially disturbing sight of sixty or seventy male heads, in every possible stage of balding and combination of team colors. He would see them pivoting on the swivel at the top of their cervical spines at the array of sets overhead, unable to fix on the Lions-Packers game or the Buffalo-Pittsburgh clash, the Cadillac commercial or the Celebrex ad for more than it takes to play a series of downs before looking around at each of the other sets for additional stimulation. This goes on for hours upon hours. They cannot detach their eyeballs from the screen. I've even heard Tommy say he might put a set in the john.

The Saturday throng at McKeon's is different, looser, more affable. This is the NCAA crowd, lighter spirits, amateurs. They're the kind who revel in the rich variety of sport—the Summer and Winter Olympics, golf, tennis and even NCAA baseball and lacrosse. In fact, Tommy is one of these selfsame amateurs and, ever since *SENE2* began broadcasting the year-end college tournament a few years ago, a budding lacrosse aficionado to boot. Televised over Memorial Day weekend, the college lacrosse championship is quick-hitting and fun to watch. This year Tommy put it on all sixteen sets, the quarters, the semis and the lopsided 11-2 final match between Finger Lakes University and Mid-Atlantic Military.

I think often of the Eastern sports franchises that people cheer every weekend, where they are, and I see the map of Bwon-diac's Rebellion in 1763, his plan of attack. Listen: the Buffalo Bills, that was Fort Niagara; the Pittsburgh Steelers, that was Fort Duquesne; our beloved Detroit Lions, that was Fort Detroit, the one that Bwon-diac himself laid siege to for six long months; the Green Bay Packers, that was Fort Edward Augustus, as the English called it, at the end of the bay; and then you've got the colleges and universities like Pittsburgh and Wisconsin-Green Bay and it is plain to me that the Indigene fields of baggattaway are buried so deeply under the white man's macadam and artificial turf.

On this late morning of Pontiac-Looking-Down Day, though, Tommy had the doors open and *SENE* on all sixteen screens. A major league baseball highlight show was airing, raining down sixteen identical talking heads and plays of the week on poor St. Anne from every conceivable angle. After two minutes of tail-chasing, St. Anne, dizzy and exhausted, came to, staggered over to Neil and leaned into his leg, looking as though she's had one too many herself already.

"D'you see that lacrosse final, Birch? Not much of a game, huh?" Tommy asked from beneath the stratosphere of television. He slid Neil and me a beer. "Your buddy's here. Be good."

"I was here for the final, Tommy. Remember? Is his last name really LeRoi?" I asked, nodding toward Roy.

"I don't do last names, Birch," he said. "All I know is Roy. The King, like he keeps on telling everybody."

After Neil and I had seated ourselves at a window booth, Roy swaggered over to us with one of his salesman smiles. He was missing an eye tooth, I noticed, since I'd last laid eyes on him. He'd moved up a weight class, too. Roy, especially drunk, was not a fan of people bringing dogs into public eateries like McKeon's, and we were not even people.

"Seen you brought your mangy beagle into the bar again, Indian. Seems you people don't learn too good. You slow or somethin', Kimosabe? You're high, ain't you? Look at you. You still smoking the evil weed from that fucking tomahawk pipe of yours?" Roy was rolling up his sleeves, hitching up his blue jeans, the cocky smile now a sneer. A big ruby ring looked ingrown on his right hand.

Neil chafed, peered into his face.

"It's just fine with Tommy, Roy," I said. St. Anne was barking at him breathlessly now and attracting the attention of the whole bar. "Careful," I told him tongue-in-cheek, "or I'll run you into the forest and scalp you." We eyed one another like we had on the rez thirty years ago, remembering the kid Jimmy Blackbird pushed over the falls, an action that had yet to trigger its equal and opposite reaction. "Look, we're just having a beer and watching tube along with everyone else."

But he and Neil were locked onto each other.

St. Anne crouched backward, seemingly loading her body for a catapult shot, and emitted a long low growl.

"I don't see no fuckin' forest," said Roy, nonchalantly knocking Neil's beer off the table, the ruby ring clinking on the glass. I saw Tommy's head snap around to us. "Dogs in places where people eat, that ain't kosher. They drool and bark; they got fleas; they stink a place up, just like all you damn 'Native Americans.'" Roy broke into a broad grin and put the palm of his hand to his open mouth, mocking us with his best impression of war whoops, and Neil charged him as fast and hard as his bowlegs and bad hips would allow, putting his head right into Roy's stomach and folding him in half as they fell to the floor in a flurry of arms and legs. I dove in on top.

"Roy!" Tommy yelled out. "How many times I told you, goddammit! Pick fights with me if you want. My customers, you leave 'em be. Now, back off!" Nobody in their right mind would pick a fight with Tommy, a big-boned lumberjack, shaved bald with bushy red eyebrows, a square-jawed brawler himself backed by his own Irish army. Plus, he poured the beer you'd be denied if you pissed him off.

As we dusted ourselves off, Roy pulled the shiv and waved it through the air at us. "Just cleaning up this little corner over here for you is all, Tommy," he said into Neil's eyes, sniffling emphatically. "It smells. Somebody took a shit and it come to life, I guess."

"That's it! Drag your ass! I will have that goddamn knife, too, Roy. You come in here with that thing again, it'll be mine," Tommy bellowed at him.

Neil shushed St. Anne, sat down and ordered us another beer. Though he did not discuss the encounter with Roy, something told me Neil knew Bone Digger far better than I, that the two of them had more history. With St. Anne suddenly fighting sleep at his feet, Neil reminded me about the haircut. Paying this tab too with my friend sitting on those twin fifties, I noticed that Roy had huddled with a bunch of his cronies, including a number of young Frenchies I'd never seen before. A skinny young guy I took for a Chippewa had his eye on me.

"See y'around, Birch," said Tommy McKeon in his rumbling bass voice. "Wait. Birch. You said you're going down to Ottawa for that lacrosse meeting, right? For the World Cup? Where's it being played? Hey, bring me back some promo stuff I can hang up around here, will you? I'll do what I can to spread the word for you. We will get the whole damn Soo behind your team."

I kept forgetting that Tommy was a born again baggataway fan. He looked and sounded so much like a prison guard. "Supposed to be next June in London, Ontario, Tommy." I slid him the Montecristo down the length of the counter.

"Hey, London ain't that far away. Don't forget my poster now, Birch," he reminded, pointing with a thumb over his shoulder to an open spot on the wall by the cash register.

"The sponsors will have one out soon. I'll bring you a couple."

"You ever watch the Summer Olympics, Birch?" he asked, wiping down the tap pulls and countertop. He was eyeing the cigar.

"Yeah, sure," I said, turning around to face him, "if I happen to be standing under a bank of TVs."

"I love the gymnasts. You ever see those guys, doing their giant circles around the horizontal bar or ripping a pommel horse routine? One-handed handstands on the parallel bars? Like the freakin' Wallendas. We couldn't do a tenth of their shit."

"Even on a good day, Tommy. I'll have to watch them closer next time they're on."

"You should. You know what my favorite routine is? The floor exercise."

Finally, Tommy had lifted the cigar and was sliding it back and forth under his nose.

"Believe that? The goddamn floor exercise, and the best move in the history of the Olympics, maybe in all of sport," he insisted with jabs from the still-wrapped Montecristo, "is that little move called the y-scale. You know the one I mean? In a standing position they cup an ankle in their hand and just lift it up straight up? Even with their head? Try it once, Birch—I guarantee you'll fall on your ass and pull muscles you didn't even know you had! Anyway, good luck at your meeting." Moved by his own description, Tommy was still purring to himself, shaking his head in appreciation of the unlit Montecristo now unwrapped and dangling from his mouth, when Neil, St. Anne and I took our leave.

Who knew, I thought with the *Soo Locks* coming into view, that something as harmless as a barber pole could have generated such passion? The next stop on the trail of tears was the barbershop of Thaddeus Sokolowski, his pole's swirling red, white and blue stripes endlessly peaceful. Peaceful, yes, but not if you're Lockside where there's only one such pole and not if it was somebody else's pole to begin with. As the three of us approached, the familiar smells of the *Soo Locks* came wafting over us, a masculine potpourri of barbering effusions that calls to mind the musk of a boxer's cornerman and his cutting and gauze, his stanching elixirs, herbal and aromatic, sweet and caustic and stinging. Already I could make them out on the air: there was Vitalis, witch hazel; there was rubbing alcohol and Barbasol shaving cream, after shaves and colognes to suit any taste, talcum powder drifting over all of it. Sounds also wafted through the open door, barbering sounds, like the snip-snip-snip of the scissors around

the ears; the clipped patterns of male banter; the radio that Thad keeps
at a modest volume, always tuned in to the broadcast home of the
Detroit Tigers; his vintage cash register that records a sale like a
phone ringing; the slap of his straight razors on the leather straps that
hang from the antique chairs, the crank of the pedal he uses to raise
and lower the chair; the whisk of the hydraulic lifts. Then, there are a
few sounds you'll never hear—the screech of electric hair blowers,
the buzz of electric clippers or the female voice. Thad was as
unchanging as Lockside itself.

  Standing in his open doorway to say our hellos, we observed
basketball-tall and slender Thad standing in his aqua-blue tunic over
the crown of a young boy, snipping away at a stubborn cowlick,
administering what looked to be a layer cut. The sight of us made his
eyebrows arch and he smiled and waved at us with the hand holding
the scissors, motioning us in. The boy's father slouched in a waiting
chair under a shelf filled with tall bottles and short cans—liniments
and balms and salves and cranial seasonings that only collect
dust—reading the *Soo News*. You could eat off the floor, if you were
so moved, swept on Pontiac-Looking-Down Day by a slow-moving
teenage boy sporting an iPod and a soft-bristled broom which he
guided intently in and out and around the three chairs. It's homey
inside, old country, with the faded map of Poland hung prominently
on the back wall; big unframed mirrors looking back on each of the
three chairs; his linoleum tiles curled and cracking in the corners; drab
olive paint on walls adorned with posters of hairdos you wouldn't be
caught dead in and a grainy black-and-white series of Thad's turn-of-

the-century relatives at Ellis Island; a price list that includes pompadours and D.A.s and crew cuts. The *Soo Locks* is a gentlemanly throwback, its sole proprietor just trying to eke out an existence like everybody else in present-day Anishinaabewaki. And you could come in for a cut anytime, because Thad Sokolowski lived in the back rooms.

Listen: it just doesn't help at all that Neil and I were known to Roy's Frenchies as the Indians who installed Thad's barber pole.

You see, this artifact of Soo history hearkened back to the time thirty-plus years ago when a passing of the guard occurred between the two Lockside barbers, the retiring Frenchy, Gerard Bonenfant, and the young Thaddeus Sokolowski. Though Gerard Bonenfant's barber pole had always announced *Le Coupe*, the very symbol of French savoir-faire in the tonsorial arts, he nevertheless decided to bequeath the pole to the young Pole, Thaddeus. Gerard did not speak good English, and when he retired at the age of seventy, he negotiated by hand gestures with Mickey Blake to hire Neil and me to pull up the barber pole and hoist it the three blocks to Thad's place of business across from the movie house. This transfer of a cherished icon did not sit well with the Frenchies, who saw in the deal outright blasphemy. The rotating red, white and blue stripes of the barber pole were viewed as nothing less than the French flag itself set aspin, and Gerard's professional *beau geste* would be forever held against its recipient. I still remember the day. Thad, blissfully ignorant of any and all ethnic considerations, looked on proudly as Neil and I troweled in the cement around the base of the pole. The Frenchies will never forgive him the egregious sin of accepting Gerard's gift, nor will they forgive us our role in cementing the deal. As a minimum recompense, they wanted Thad to change the name of his shop—*The Barber Pole* would no longer do. They insisted on it, meeting and rallying at Gerard's former pole to demand the change. They doused it in beer, launched stink bombs at it, tried to set it on fire, pissed on it, spat on it, you name it, but they could not quite bring themselves to topple it because it was Gerard's. The crisis escalated. They spray-painted profanities on it—*Fuck you, Pole!* and *Eat shit and die, Thad!* Years later he remained a marked man. The embers of this fire were fanned and kept aglow by Bone Digger and his Frenchy henchmen to the point that, even when Thad finally did accede to their demand and changed the name of his establishment to the *Soo Locks*, they were not appeased. Still, he had to know he would have the last word in this imbroglio, for now he was barber to them all.

Once, Thad actually tried to explain the history of the barber pole to the Frenchies, to imbue it with a history that might inform their attitudes toward it. He taught them through chants of *Thhaaad, oh, Thhaad* that in medieval times the barber was a bloodletter, a kind of sidewalk surgeon who could fix what was ailing you, that the swirls of red and blue indicated blood and bandage and, in the end, the grace of a healed state. Of course, that only made matters worse. The tribe came in ever greater numbers to deface the bloodletter's pole. Exasperated and growing frightened, Thad called the cops to disperse them, only to find that the Soo's Finest had dispatched Officer Dennis Charpentier, a former recruit of Bone Digger's from Periwinkle High who had meandered into local law enforcement after atoning for previous misdeeds through brief arrests and hours of community service. Charpentier took a hands-off attitude toward the matter, preferring to treat the alleged abuse of private property as harmless fun that warranted no further surveillance on his part and positioning himself a couple blocks away at the doughy counter of St. Mary's Lockside Bakery.

You must know that this was a situation custom-designed for Neil Longbow LaSalle. With no natural ethnic ally and a look-the-other-way stance from the Soo police department, Thad remained a sitting duck to the rabid Frenchies, and Neil's every instinct rallied him to the correction of this injustice. He had always played a kind of self-appointed sheriff to the Bone Digger's vigilante. It had become the closing ritual of our Pontiac-Looking-Down Days, the benediction that closed the circle of the trail of tears. He would show up just often enough to send a signal to the Frenchies that Thad had friends and police the barber pole *he* had planted into the sidewalk in the stretch between the two streetlights on Ashmun Street kitty-corner from The Soo Theater. A simple man was Thad Sokolowski, who desired neither riches nor fame, not undue personal advancement nor even unmitigated happiness, though certainly the freedom to pursue it. And Neil meant to provide just that.

Over the years, some serious fisticuffs had erupted between Neil and Roy at the barber pole. In his earlier years, Neil was pretty intimidating, not physically, but spiritually somehow, as if he could

conjure minor gods to his side for any brawl with mere mortals. Roy
was never cowed. Ever since the day at Periwinkle High when Neil
walked up to him and clocked him, Roy had taken a special delight in
persecuting him, and the barber pole became their home plate, a thing
to defend and a thing to retake. I'm sure Neil embodied for him the
essence of Native America itself, its detestable harmony with the
wild, its weird primitive character, its ignorance of the written word,
in short, the very traits about it that annexation and removal and re-
education were supposed to have driven out. But Neil retained them in
abundance, threatening and defying Roy by merely existing. The face-
offs had started harmlessly enough with Roy spear-heading a posse,
St. Anne One or Two guarding the back side of the pole and Neil
standing at its front like a cigar store Indian, staring straight ahead,
unmoved by Roy's invective, watching the circles grow ever tighter,
until finally they could look right into the whites of the other's eyes.
And listen: they took their feud to the limit. On a Pontiac-Looking-
Down Day fifteen years ago, I watched this crazy dance they do. It
had built up like a boil that needed lancing. Taunting Bone Digger,
Neil had unsheathed the tomahawk pipe from his deerskin quiver and
held it out sideways at him as if Bad Sky himself were defending the
Soo Locks pole. Roy grinned that unnerving grin of his and waved his
posse back. "Well, red man, I see you do still have your weed pipe.
Gonna use it on me?" He looked over his shoulder back to his people,
crazy-eyed.

 "Frenchman," Neil answered, "sometimes it is a tomahawk
pipe and other times it is a pipe tomahawk. Right now, I would say

you are looking at a pipe tomahawk. And I'm bound to use it on you."
Two crisp barks from St. Anne Two reinforced his message.

   "You're already wearing one of the King's scars," he whined,
"Want another one, do you, Injun?" He released the blade from the
shiv with a loud metal snap and lunged at Neil. Neil parried it with the
tomahawk shaft and let loose with an eerie combination of war
whoop, dog growl and owl hoot. He straightened his back against the
barber pole and circled around it, ducking and bobbing to avoid Roy's
thrusts. Sensing that it could only end in a standoff, Roy raised his left
forearm over his head for protection against the blow that he knew
Neil would rain down on him, and with the timing of a prize fighter
dropped his head and shoulders underneath his upheld arm and
followed the opening this gave him tight in to Neil's midsection.
"Ahhh," I heard him say. His shiv had only a T-shirt to penetrate, and
I saw him try to lift Neil up on it after it had entered Neil's stomach.
St. Anne Two jumped completely off the ground and took a piece of
Bone Digger's neck, shaking her head back and forth like she had a
sock. In the meantime, Neil had swung the tomahawk with his right
hand from the outside, planting the edge of his blade in the muscle on
the back of Roy's arm just below the shoulder. They both went down
spurting blood. Thad Sokolowski came running out with the broom
and the hose after the two of them were taken to the emergency room
at St. Mary's Hospital. Roy took fifteen stitches in his neck and
another fifteen in his shoulder. Neil did earn his second scar from
Roy's shiv, but, lucky for him, the strap of his buckskin quiver had
deflected the full force of the blow. Still, he took twenty stitches of his

own. The Soo Police detained them both for a work week in the city lockup for mutual assault with intent to inflict bodily harm on another.

On the most recent, 2009, edition of Pontiac-Looking-Down Day, Neil had strapped on the buckskin quiver and stood facing the street and showing only the pipe end of his weapon. Thad Sokolowski waved hello from the doorway and renewed his standing offer of a free haircut anytime we liked. St. Anne Four took the back of the pole and I looked at them and wondered how long they'd wait and what I was supposed to do in the meantime. Within minutes, we heard Roy's big mouth from around the corner and other voices too. I wanted to do one of Tommy's y-scales, some incredibly martial yet Buddhist move that would end this thing before it began. But there they were.

"You guys take Charlevoix. I won't need no help with Neil here," he snarled.

With that, Roy jumped Neil and wrested the pipe tomahawk from him, as the other Frenchies obeyed orders and jumped me. They were not strong but they were quick and I took a couple of punches to the ribs and face. It was the younger guys I'd seen at Tommy's, wearing their woolen tuques on such a warm day. I was able to push a couple of them back, giving myself more elbow room to launch big swings at them. St. Anne Four had latched onto the arm of one of them, growling deep in her throat and shaking her head viciously from side to side. The Frenchy was screaming for her to stop. This gave me some backbone and I started swinging wildly, randomly, in every direction, landing good punches on occasion and air on others, but generally speaking giving better than I was getting. There was one on my back and I could see Marla's face suddenly because at times like that you know for sure if you're carrying too much weight for the fights of life. Roy brandished the tomahawk blade. Neil, defenseless now, beckoned him forward, urging him to bring it on. Out of nowhere, the police cruiser of Officer Dennis Charpentier, with Tommy McKeon riding shotgun, squealed onto the scene to break things up. St. Anne had gone to the side of her breathless master, whose braids had fallen out; Roy dropped the pipe with a clang on the street. Thad Sokolowski leaned on his broom, shaking his head back and forth. I had a bloody mouth and a couple of sore ribs, but so did two or three of the Frenchies who were fighting me.

"You two again. Don't move a muscle! Every one of you is under arrest!" said Dennis Charpentier. "Every one of you!" he emphasized to Bone Digger. "I got you for loitering, public trespass, drunkenness, assault and anything else I might think of later."

"Come on, guys, you heard the man," said Tommy, shoving people toward the squad car. "This shit has got to stop."

I wanted to tell Officer Charpentier what he missed as he lowered my head, what we were doing, since its innate beauty had only then occurred to me.

What we were doing?

Well, you had only to look below the surface of events: Lockside was the field of play. The *Soo Locks* was the goal. The barber pole was the post. Neil was the goalie, and the pipe tomahawk was his stick. I was the defenseman. The Bone Digger and his goons were the attackmen from the other team. Officer Charpentier, you were the referee. Thad Sokolowski the spectator. And St. Annes One through Four? We could call them the Indigene cheerleaders despite the fact that we'd most likely throw them in the lake one of these days.

Gosh, Officer Charpentier, we were just having a friendly little game of baggattaway, you know? The French against the Indians.

Naanganikwe

1978 was when I first saw my mother's head bob and ran out of fingers and toes to count my father's hourly lapses of memory. 1978 was still of that era before casinos and gaming profits when we took on actual human dimension, got our alley ways paved and plowed in the winter. 1978 was worse than 1850 in many respects, bloodlines were thinning rapidly, blurring our identities, our people had hardened into upright fossils and were lined up to perish forgotten on the rez. I'd been four years in a white man's school, playing his/my sport, pampered on the luxury coaches that carted us around the Midwest, pampered in the good hotels and restaurants, pampered in the warm dorm rooms and movie theaters. It was hard to come back to Pope County. Fresh off the '78 World lacrosse championships, you see, I had respect. I had won a fleeting glimpse of that rare bird and become somebody. I hated myself for even thinking it, but when I came back everybody on the rez was nobody. I considered my older sister, Minerva, the only entity standing between my parents and demise, who herself would evaporate into thin air when they walked on. I considered my old best friend Neil down the road, how important he'd been, wondered if he could still recite his part of the *Cry of Bwon-diac,* wondered why he toiled day-in and day-out at the insane tasks he set himself just to spite the white man and keep alive the old ways that only could lead to fossilhood. We hadn't stayed in touch. I supposed he still lived in his grandfather's double wide and kept beagles named St. Anne and paddled his homemade birch bark canoe on the Straits of Mackinac and steamed bends into ash and hickory and sewed them up with leather webs. I wondered.

Wondered, as I considered the job offer of a milk truck route from Matti Virkanen, if I could live, if anyone could be truly said to live, on the Pope County Indian Reservation. But a bobbing head, a tongue in knots, an old best friend and an overburdened sister woke me from the lie that I even had a choice. My flirtation with the white man's world was probably over for good, a transient luxury afforded me solely by my athletic abilities, the rez was my home. I would take the job from Matti Virkanen, get up at 3 A.M. every day and love it. I would help Minerva tend our elders. My prowess on the white man's lacrosse fields would be duly remembered from time to time, mostly at McKeon's sports bar, where too many of my kind already pickled themselves with drink in order to forget the future.

Welcome home, Birch Charlevoix, said an echo that led me backwards.

And then through the window screen I heard her ask, "Is this where Birch Charlevoix lives?" I stood up and saw her, an apparition on our front stoop. This was no long lost relative come to call. The air around me went all electric, and as my polite but bemused sister let her in and showed her to a chair, you could have heard a pin drop. There should have been a halo around her head. I guessed her to be nineteen or twenty, and she offered so many distractions all at once that I flitted around like a butterfly trying to touch them all. There was a khaki knapsack flashing peace signs of all colors and sizes strapped over her shoulders, and a baby girl thrashed within it, winding her chubby fingers through her mother's brown ponytail and pulling at it like the mane of a horse. My mother asked her just who the hell she was.

"Marla Langevin," she said.

Marla wore pink Converse sneakers, a tank top that issued a whiff of sweat and frilly, cut-off jeans revealingly short. Leaning forward in that chair with the fidgety papoose still attached to her back, she had won our undivided attention. We were quickly taking her measure, both the urgent tangibles on display and also the intangibles of personality for she had charisma, Marla Langevin. A thin upper lip and a pouty lower one, a strong nose and chin, brightly confident hazel eyes, all of these alluring singularities populated her face and in collaboration even unleashed a multiplication of themselves, but the spinning lure that hooked my jaw was a two inch scar in the shape of a smile high up on her left cheek, and it glistened. She kept lifting her hand to it yet always stopped just short of touching it. Fair, fair skin that seemed a hopeless thing in this climate, powerless against the bite of the cold snow moon. She lengthened her neck and turned her head to release the baby's fingers from her ponytail. Her actual appearance was secondary, though, to a higher sense or need. In a single chaotic minute I knew she'd been made for me. It was surely that mythical moment that arrives, that grand suspension of time during which a man recognizes his mate and falls in love.

My father and I could not take our eyes off her.

My sister Minerva, examining her mind for reference points, finally marveled, "Wow, this is like an invasion."

Marla would quickly size up the dynamic of my family, that my mother, the she-bear, was the one she had to sell.

"For the love of…" my mother chuckled incredulously. "You show up out of nowhere at my door in your pink shoes and your baby on your back, like some kinda hussy, all sexy in her tiny shorts and her low-slung top. What do you want, missy?" Looking her up and down, she lit a cigarette, inhaled crisply.

The baby began to cry. Marla hoisted her—did I say it was a girl—from the knapsack, swung her out in front, raised her tank top up over her left breast and released the cup of her bra. The child latched onto the nipple like a shark.

My father and I followed her every draft. My mother, unfazed, shushed us.

"Well, Jesus, I never…What's the matter with you two?" she scolded my father and me. "Ogling the poor girl like that. Ain't you never seen a mother's breast before?" Again, she turned to Marla. "What is it that you do want?"

"Just some water with ice, please," replied Marla, to which my mother responded by getting right up in her face. "No, *what do you want*? You got some nerve just showing up here and baring your bloated boob in my living room like we're all just dying for you to flop it out and here we are never laid eyes on you before, so, what is it you want, missy?"

After an awkward silence gently paced by the infant's lapping and swallowing, Marla drew a breath and held it, raising not only those swollen mother's breasts but also the attached suckling's face. My father leaned in. I too gulped in anticipation of her offer.

But my mother beat her to the punch. "How'd you get out here anyway?" she squinted at Marla, draping each word in ironic drawl. "You from the Soo, ain't you?"

Marla let the breath out. "I walked. Yeah, I'm from the Soo, Lockside. Just took baby Sheila here and hoofed it out to 6 Mile Road. It was a good day for a walk. Never got a ride, so I kept on going. When I got to the end of the paved road, I just asked for the Charlevoix residence. Everybody knows where you live."

"Well, aren't you the clever one. Why you here?"

She dug a crumpled piece of newspaper out of her pocket with her free hand. "Actually, I was reading the sports section of the *Soo News* last week, which I never do, at least not often. I mean, what's to know? It's sports. You dribble or run or shoot or pass and put a ball in a goal. The other guys defend you. That day, though, there was a picture of Birch on the front page, up at the top, with a caption that read, *Local pride: One of Soo's Own Maryland-bound for '78 World Lacrosse Championship*. Something like that. You were standing in front of the goal, and, well, I did some research." She held up the picture, of me, pressed it into my hands.

"Oh, yeah?" my father rang in.

"I can't believe you just walked," Minerva worshipped. "What's your baby's name?"

"Thanks for asking," she said to Minerva, "Sheila. But if you don't mind, I'll come right to the point. Mr. and Mrs. Charlevoix, I need help from a good man. From a man I can trust. We're about the same age. Okay, Birch might be a year or two older, but he has the look I want in a man. You know the picture? A look of confidence but not too much of it, a look of knowing who you are, a look of sympathy for people, a look of sorrow that there has to be pain in the world and a look of hope that works to fix it."

My parents looked at one another, then my mother waved her off. "Jesus, missy, that's a whole lot of looks. You seen a whole lot more in that stupid little picture than I did. I think you're just looking for a daddy for your baby, right, missy?"

"Dingo bingo!" my father cried out. "The dingo dam at the rez! She'll hide her pup in a knothole and stand guard and hope the snakes don't get it from the inside while she's blocking shots on the outside."

I couldn't tell if she was able to penetrate the scrambled references to Native fable and sport, but Marla handled his excited utterance with a smile and a pass at her scar. I explained to her that the wild dingo bitch protects her litter by tucking them into a knothole and standing vigil. The only trouble is, like outbursts from my father, serpent attacks from within the tree can never be ruled out.

"You hit the nail right on the head, Mr. Charlevoix!"

He was knocked back in his chair.

"Mr. and Mrs. Charlevoix," she said holding them in her gaze, "I don't even know how I know it, but Birch is already walking a path

I'm just starting out on. I need a friend, a lover, a partner, a survivor, and that is your son, as I say, if he's not already taken."

"Are you asking for my son's hand in marriage?" puzzled my father.

"How do you know he don't drool or have some damn venereal disease?" shrieked my mother. "How do you know he can support you and your little baby? For the love of God, missy, you don't even know him!"

Presumptuous? You might say. She presumed with abandon, yet we could all see that she was as rational as she was direct, as vulnerable as she was insistent. She had a plan of attack— disarming honesty at all costs. But it was no put-on. She set up a stark mismatch between her fragile circumstance and her bald presumption which completely buffaloed my parents, my sister and me, too. From as flimsy a set of props as a newspaper photo in the sports section of the *Soo News* and a nursing daughter, she spun a dream, tried to snare four Chippewa.

My mother looked around and gave an exasperated little chuckle. But she was far from defeated.

"Where'd you get that scar, honey?" she asked, bobbing, as she set an iced tea in front of Marla. "It's a whopper. You some kind a pass-around or somethin'?"

Again Marla made that move, instinctively reaching for the scar and stopping just short of touching it. "Let's just say I've seen enough of the Soo and its men and leave it at that."

"So, let me get this straight. You're telling me that you picked my son to be your husband based on a stupid picture and a story about his lacrosse playing? You walk for miles out to the rez with your little baby hanging off your nipples and claim him like a shirt off the rack at the dime store? You expect him to jump into your arms at first sight? And just what's so hot about a bunch of sweaty Indians playing ball? Jesus, missy. Talk to me."

As Marla answered, I stared at the picture. I liked it too. It isn't every day that an Indian kid from Pope County gets his picture in the *Soo News,* held up as a hometown hero to the white community. The college lacrosse star, gleaming in the sun, arms raised in victory, tapped for the all-tribes Indigene Nation team. I was trying to see the picture from Marla's point of view. But surely some greater force had propelled her to my father's front stoop, baby in tow, to lay claim to me.

Then, training the beautiful force of her character straight on me for the first time, she asked, "How do you make money now, Birch Charlevoix?"

She had a look, too. Implicit in this one was the proposition that any answer was already beside the point. Take a shot at playing professional lacrosse or coaching, *Whatever you want*, the look said, *Immaterial, as long as you put bread on the table and a roof over our heads and joy in my heart.* Inside I was crumbling like a cookie. I could have this woman simply for the taking? How sad life was on the rez she could not have known. I hemmed and hawed, finally blurting out that I had just hired on for a milk route.

Then, out of thin air: "Did you ever think about teaching, Birch Charlevoix?" The Chippewa word for teacher fell into my mind: *gikinooamaagwaaniin*, one initiated, which is what it felt like she was doing to me. "You'd make a great teacher."

This caused my mother, who'd been ever so slowly and reluctantly warming toward her guest, to guffaw. She corkscrewed right up out of her chair. She hissed and chuckled and groaned under her breath, bared her palms like the she-bear pawing back an aggressor. "Just wait a minute now, missy. Where do you get off telling my son what he ought to be doing?"

Marla just fixed her face on her baby and took a tone like women do at a quilting bee.

"Look, Mrs. Charlevoix, I don't know anything about anything, but it's plain to see that the rez is Birch's home and that his second love is lacrosse and if he were to bide his time for a while on the milk truck and get his teacher's certificate, then he'd be ready to jump if, say, a phys. ed position ever came open at the…"

"Periwinkle School District?"

"There you go, Periwinkle. Love the name. Is that where the Indian kids go to school too? Then Birch'll get them all fired up about middies and goalies and defensemen and attackmen, how the season starts in the freezing cold and ends in the blazing heat, the buzz of scoring a goal, the talk, you know, their lingo—face-off, crease, pipes, cradle, long stick, scoop, lax. All of it. How can you possibly beat that?" she said, eyeing little Sheila. "It's life in a game."

"Research?" my father jumped in from somewhere. "Did you read that lacrosse is an *Indian…?*" Marla had him so flustered. "…baggattaway," he recovered, with raised eyebrows and a lilt in his voice.

She rolled the strange word around in her mouth. "Baggattaway. Well, if it is, I will have to learn all about that, and I promise I will. And don't you think that if Birch could combine his love of lacro…bag-gat-taway with a calling like teaching, wouldn't that make a life worth living?"

My bobbing mother was silenced, outflanked by the dingo dam, her plan, her optimism, her truths. And slowly the weight in the room collected on me. Marla's intention was clear. How should I answer, now that every answer was a wall closing in on me?

I know.

I know!

I could have erupted in anger; I could have thrown her out for her arrogance. I could have told her I was already taken. I could have charged her with aggravated assault with intent, that bared breast. *How dare you step into our miserable menagerie of zoo animals who hunt no more? Can't you see we've been defanged? How dare you bare your perfect white woman's breast and suckle your new life? Can't you see? We are dying here! Have you no respect for the dead?* My mental calculations must have numbered in the millions per second as I watched her, a donnybrook in my head over what my response should be, and it had to be now, in front of my parents and my sister. Should I just give in, grab this Pocahontas-in-reverse and kiss her? What in God's name was she doing here? And just what was this irresistible power I had over her? I had no wealth, no prospects for creating any. I had, in no particular order, an amnesiac father, a bobbing head mother, a decent lacrosse story and a milk truck route—a hell of a dowry, all of that, yes, but otherwise no secret weapons or intimidations with which to surprise her. How, after this invasion, would I ever be able to surprise Marla? I was a cute little Native American dog in the window of the Humane Society. And what did she know of us? She was a pure outsider, ignorant of my ancestors' penchant for oddities like tossing beagles from their canoes as a sacrifice to the manidos for safe passage. How dare she enter the Pope County Indian Reservation? And shame on me. How dare I simply be here for such a brazen annexation?

So, I said, "There's somebody I want you to meet."

She detached the baby, buttoned up her blouse, wiped Sheila's mouth, wedged her back into the carrier and came quickly to her feet, ready for anything. There was no script for this. Though I hadn't seen him much, it seemed only natural to walk down the road to Neil's. Still, I had the vague feeling that he was expecting us, and his greeting still gives me goose bumps thirty years on. He stood there in the alley, held out both hands in welcome.

"Naanganikwe," he said to her from three paces. Daughter-in-law.

He made her blush, and I tell you it was beautiful. She doesn't blush deep red in the face, but blotches irregularly in her Lockside paleness. She looks away and swallows. She hopes you don't notice. She reaches for her scar.

On the night of Marla's invasion, St. Anne Two was just a puppy, a peppy one at that, nipping at our heels as we entered Neil's dingy trailer. Neil was definitely high, lots of nervous energy. He unburdened Marla Langevin of her carrier and cooed at Sheila as he propped her up on the floor and left her to the playful attention of St. Anne Two. We did not acknowledge the long hiatus in our friendship. He was gnawing on a stick of maple taffy and chasing it with Jack Daniels. Marla and I both started drinking with him. But within the space of a few minutes, Neil would completely transform the tone of our gathering. Suddenly a high priest, he fitted a Sioux headdress onto his crown and motioned for us to follow him. He sat down at a mirror and began to apply stripes and lightning bolts of red, yellow and black to his face, arms, calves, everywhere. He saw that Marla was curious. He stood to offer her his seat. Then, as she followed his every move in the mirror, Neil crouched and slithered around her like a shaman, chanting in Ojibwemowin, and sculpted her air with the palms of his hands. Sheila, too, was watching Neil like a hawk.

"Are you fluffing my aura, Neil?" she laughed. She sat straight and still for him, somehow giving herself over to this probe as you would to an MRI. She closed her eyes and did not open them as he took her long brown hair in his hands and braided it for her ceremonially, chanting all the while. He laid the heavy braid of my apparition over her shoulder, stood her up and placed a buckskin coat over her shoulders, pinned her hair with three kingfisher feathers, dabbed her face with his paints and laid an extra thick covering of black over her red scar. Then he put an index finger to his lips, gently hoisted the now sleeping Sheila onto his own back and tiptoed outside into the long shadows of the two ash trees on his plot. He set the carrier down by the fireplace with more than appropriate delicacy, and there we stood, unquestioningly, in his thrall. Between the ash trees in the distance, like a distant baggattaway ball arcing between goal posts, a bright half moon lit up Marla Langevin's painted face. It seemed even Bwon-diac approved.

"Are we getting married, Birch?" she asked, happily confused. "Am I being confirmed or something? How the hell does he know, anyway?" she whispered around the rim of her whisky glass. She grabbed my arm in momentary panic as Neil and St. Anne then proceeded to fill the night air with barks and whistles and bird calls and the baying of wolves, a Chippewa call to order. He began, with no further ado, to recount a legend, a kind of first reading for Marla from the Native old testament.

"In the birch bark wigwams my people made their dwellings. Two girls slept outside the wigwam. One asked the other, 'Which star do you choose, the white one or the red one?' The other answered, 'The red one.' 'Then I will take the white one,' said the first girl. 'He's the younger, the red is the older.'

"When the girls awoke, they were in another world, the star world. The girls saw that the two stars had become men, and that the white star was the older and the red was the younger. The girls remained in the star world, the first one sad that she had chosen the old white star.

"There was an old woman up in this world who sat over a hole in the sky, and she moved to show the girls the hole. 'That's where you came from,' she told them. They looked down through the hole and saw their people and grew homesick. One morning the old woman told the girls, 'If you want to go down where you came from, we will let you, but first gather roots and twist them into a rope.' The girls worked for days. They made plenty of rope and tied it to a big basket. They got into the basket and the people of the star world lowered them down. They landed on an eagle's nest, but the people above thought the girls were on the ground and stopped lowering them….."

Neil paused for a moment, pursed his lips and decided to go no further with the tale. "There is more to that one," he said to Marla, "but you get the message."

He withdrew, fussed over Sheila a bit, planted his skinny haunches on a stump and began to puff away on his tomahawk pipe. Marla did not seem bothered that his pot smoke lingered and swirled around the baby but looked at me with that happy puzzlement in her features, and we continued to pour freely from Neil's jug of sour mash whisky. We sipped in the baggattaway-ball moonlight for long minutes before St. Anne Two barked at him, roused him, it seemed, and Neil came to his feet again, bade us to do the same and cleared his throat to speak to Marla the second lesson, a Native legend of salvation.

"As our young witness seems to have no objections, we may continue," he began. "A great prophet among our people had a hunting dog, a black wolf. The sea god was jealous and swore to take its life. So he appeared before it as a deer, and as the dog rushed to seize him, he drowned it in the sea.

"The prophet vowed revenge. He waited for him in tall rushes until he came ashore. He drew his giant bow and shot a poison arrow that pierced his heart. In anger, all the creatures hurled mountains of water at the prophet which he tried to outrun but which swept away the forests like grass. He called out to the God of Heaven, and a great canoe appeared with pairs of beasts and birds aboard, being rowed by a most beautiful maiden who let down a rope to him and drew him into the boat."

At this point, Sheila awoke with a vengeance, flailing every limb she owned, her face turning red and then some, and she wailed right through the rest of Neil's second reading, just like in a real church. Did she know something we didn't? Again, Marla Langevin was unbothered by the outburst, urging Neil to continue if he could.

He obliged by dropping his voice and projecting out into the night over the Sheila screams, but then St. Anne Two began to howl along with the baby and they nearly drowned him out altogether. "The flood raged on, but the prophet was safe. He then said to Waw-jashk, the Muskrat, 'Go down to the bottom and bring me up some earth, out of which I will create a new world.' Down he plunged, but he came back lifeless. The prophet blew into his mouth and he came back to life. Then he saw in Muskrat's paw a clump of earth, which he rolled into a small ball and tied to the neck of Raven saying, 'Go, and fly back and forth across the surface of the deep that dry land may appear.' The waters rolled away. The prophet and the maiden were united and repeopled the world."

The high priest folded his hands and lowered his eyes. The baying and wailing stopped.

She moved over to pick up Sheila and said with genuine gratitude, "Neil, I love that! Am I a most beautiful maiden? Have I saved Birch from drowning? Will we repeople the earth?" She was flattered, let in on secrets, radiant.

Neil lifted an amulet of some kind from around his own neck and held it up to Marla's face. When it came to rest on its chain, we saw that it was a vermilion turtle.

"Naanganikwe," he said, thumbing yet another layer of black paint into her scar, "four hundred years ago, the sachem Minavavana set this very necklace around the neck of the French priest Father Castin, a sign of welcoming." Under the brow-furrowed scrutiny of baby Sheila now safely wrapped in her mother's arms, Neil placed a hand on our outside shoulders, pushed us gently into one another and raised his hands to the night.

"Mingled fires crackle now. Tom-toms drum your wish across the sky. Above you moons are born and die, the eternal hourglass. Already, great waters lap at the sands of your shore. My brother, my sister, you have saved one another." Playfully, he smudged black paint onto the baby's nose and took her from Marla Langevin. "Please," he said to me, "kiss the bride."

I had no diamond to place on her ring finger, but I did kiss her. And then I kissed her again and again in that moonlight. She stayed in full Native character, slipping out of all but the buckskin coat, the war paint and the vermilion turtle around her neck. An event divinely inspired and devoutly attended, the consummation of Marla's invasion was a wildfire that did not burn itself out until almost dawn, when only charred trees and smoking stubble remained of us sleeping lovers. Neil had given shelter to a dingo dam, made a knothole for her baby out of the Pope County Indian Reservation.

And the bull's eye he pierced with his seeing-eye arrow, the single idea that raises red at her nape even to this day?

That we, Marla Langevin and Birch Charlevoix, had saved one another.

The Beet Garden

There have been reported in legend and in fact any number of encounters between the white man and the Indigene woman. Pocahontas, for example. Seduced by a power unimagined, they fled with their secrets to the enemy camp and dared to love that power. Bwon-diac's first assault on Fort Detroit is said to have been waylaid in this exact manner, betrayed by a young Indigene smitten by the grandiose notion that she could trade up in life. Sacajawea married Toussaint Charbonneau and gave aid and comfort to the white men named Lewis and Clark. Less frequent, I'm sure, are reports of traffic in the opposite direction, white women, like Marla Langevin, high-stepping the river to the Indigene encampments.

It is resolved, then, that among other reasons Naanganikwe was dispatched by the fates to cheer my father in his waning decades.

"When has a white woman, a winner in the game of history, pulled back the flap of the wigwam?" he used to ask us rhetorically after her invasion. "What makes the living walk the grounds of the dead, the cemetery of Anishinaabewaki? No matter what evil she may do, what promise she may break, what injustice she may work, what law she may transgress, what feelings she may stomp, she can never, ever, be diminished in my eyes," he swore on numerous lucid occasions. At age ninety-one, he was not so great, lost in mental cloverleafs of place and tense, a confusion of offense and defense.

He'd be wearing his green and white flannel shirt with the long sleeves and button-down collar topped by a gray cardigan sweater even on this sultry July morning. He took chills. He was a stick. He wouldn't wear his glasses.

Before this…retirement? He did not have a so-called career, one where you park your ass behind a desk and make phone calls and jet here and there for the company. That's a white man's idea. A crazy one, at that—work, work, work for fifty years so you can make enough money to insulate yourself against leaving it, saying in so many words that you hated every second of it, failing to realize that work is life. Don't leave the net open, or you are defenseless against the balls that will continue to whistle at your face, even in retirement. Stay in the crease, play through infirmity, suck in your final breath with gusto and let it out with a laugh. Go down with a great lunge, swatting your stick at the shot that flies by you into the net. Stay hungry. Arrive in the heavens still breathing hard from the exertion. Then, you have lived.

My father taught me that and I hoped he would remember it for himself. For a man who had lived his entire life in poverty, he managed to cobble together enough jobs, positions, stationings, postings and half-careers over the years that, if a normal career can be likened to a plaid stable blanket, then his was a rose-embroidered Derby quilt. By the time Naanganikwe knocked at his door, Louis Charlevoix was sixty-one and, at least through the eyes of his son, had certainly made the world a better place. A tough, scrawny kid, he'd been taught to fish pike and play baggattaway. I count these as forward indicators in his career. They tell of inbred Chippewa instincts. Be it a wily pike holding his breath so he can wedge free through your gill net or a baggattaway ball singing past your ear, there is net play common to both pastimes. At fifteen he would paddle out onto the rapids with fishing teams and drop the hand-sewn nets, pull up the less clever or fatter fish and salt and stow that precious haul, an entire village fed for the small price of scarred hands and aching shoulders. And on land he would spend every spare minute playing the Creator's Game. Though baggattaway had not been played on the U.P. for decades by the time Louis was a kid at Pope County, it was certainly played across the river in the Ontario Soo. They played box lacrosse there, a funnelized version of baggattaway contested on small, vacant ice rinks where a kid's hand-eye coordination was honed and put to the test. He and a couple dozen friends from Pope County would ride the early steamer over to Ontario and forget to eat because the game had consumed them all day and into the night, when they would have to sprint to the river yelling to the captain to wait for them, the last boat of the day chugging right over their pike schools. Louis played goalie, and for his friends to put him in net, well, that made him first among equals. Swatting away shots on his goal from vicious angles, down low, up in the weak corner, his hands slid for position on that shaft, like Makoons and Bad Sky, constantly recalibrating every joint and limb he owned in an effort to fend off the short hop or the close-in over-the-shoulder shot.

When the Great Depression fell over America and the rest of the rich world, it gave them a taste of the everyday of the Indian on the reservation. But listen: That drawn-out misery was still a parsec better than any second on the rez, and that is a pi worth of light years. My father did not sit it out. He shelved his nets and started working for himself. For pennies in 1934, he swept the Hiawatha in the Indian CCC, then he quit high school to hire on in the copper mines out in the Keneewa Peninsula, right on Lake Superior. He loved it a lot more than Periwinkle High. Counting the ride to and fro, his days were often sixteen hours long. He didn't care. He ran a noisy steam hoist until the mining company scaled back operations due to price controls passed by the government during World War II. When he turned twenty-four, he embarked on his first half-career, driving a milk truck route in Sault Ste. Marie for Matti Virkanen's dairy farm. Almost ten years. He loved that too, proclaiming the joy of delivering the pasture's bounty to the stoops of his customers enough to deliver a man. It was a far sight better, he said, than standing on a clanky assembly line in Detroit, and, besides, Matti had set no limit on the consumption of chocolate milk. The villain in this piece was, once again, the federal government. As he was single and able-bodied, the U.S. Army burst this pastoral little bubble and buttonholed him right out of Virkanen's running milk truck, cropped his hair, made him do a million pushups and sent him to the first U.N. war, on the Korean Peninsula. Thirty-three years, and he had never even so much as set foot off his own Peninsula.

He was drafted in the summer of 1950 when the Chinese had invaded the south. He joked about it to his friends and to his parents. "It's no big deal. It's the U.N. against the communist bastards who took what wasn't theirs," he said, "it'll be like an all-tribes baggattaway game. Besides I'm just hopping from one damn peninsula to another." He survived the landing at Inchon, General MacArthur and the Chinese counter-offensive, the gulag winter of North Korea. By sugaring season of the next year, the U.N. forces had reoccupied Seoul, cinched a belt around the country at the 38th parallel and Louis was home for Christmas. Wearing his blue milking tuque, Matti Virkanen came over personally and offered him the gift of his old milk route.

He ran the milk route again for a year but simply couldn't find himself in it as he had before. The stint in Korea had enveloped him in a strange new relation to his home. Things were different all of a sudden, and not just because of the war. You had to get with the new program—cars, cars and the roads and bridges that enabled them. Yes, even the U.P. was being dragged into that speeding present. The seduction of a nation was at hand. He thanked Matti, apologized for leaving and took on as a laborer in the engineering adventure down in Mackinaw City, the creation of the five-mile suspension bridge that would link the U.P. to the rest of Michigan. He definitely wanted in on that. He wanted in on the idea of his Anishinaabewaki joining the mainstream. The game was progress, and the country was awash in it. The bridge would be about connection. The U.P. must belong to the world. The bridges and interstates would be the tracks. The steel company paired him with another Chippewa, a guy named Johnson Plaice. They built caissons on the Straits, lots of them, deep enclosed capsules that they sank into the water and pumped out so the concrete piers could be poured. Peering down into the caissons was dizzying, like canyons two hundred feet or more deep and crisscrossed all the way down by steel I-beams descending like a staircase into a dark distance. Johnson Plaice dared him to jump down and walk each of the steel beams. My father asked him what prize he was ready to put up for such a dare. Johnson said, "Come on, Louis, it's just catwalks. I'll get you a date with my sister Edina. She's a looker, too, I swear. Look, you get down there in one piece you take the elevator back up. Any Indian could do it, and I promise you it'll be worth your trouble. Her name is Edina."

My parents, Louis Charlevoix and Edina Plaice, never told us whether my sister Minerva is a love child, and it really didn't matter, but we were pretty sure that my father walked the tightrope of each of those beams and that the first date with Edina went real well, because, whichever came first, in 1955 Louis became a husband and father. My mother, who always claimed that she had been the victim of an arranged marriage, was indeed a looker. I've seen their wedding picture.

In the five years between the Big Mac and International Bridge projects, Louis laid over as a sugar farmer in the sap season weekends and a year-round mason tender. He didn't care. He hauled maple sap on an oaken yoke bowed by a sixteen quart tin drum at either end, chugging back up the hill from the sugarbush to the boiling house. Year after year in those wicked first-thaw temperatures of late winter and early spring, he took a permanent chill that took up permanent residence in his bones and angled in on his net, arms raised for the shot. He could no longer flick his quick wrists like he once did in the box games, only dress himself in green, gray and white in defense against this chill, and hope he could hang on. *Dad,* I wanted to say, *do you remember when you fed this Chippewa toddler maple candy so pure and sweet it twisted me inside out,* but that ember no longer glowed in him.

When blueprints finally came to life in 1962, he jumped at the chance to work on the International Bridge. Another cog in the wheel of his connection-dream, it was the second bridge built in a five year span, meant to lift the U.P. up to the world, this time to the north. The ribbon was cut within a year, and that timing was fortuitous for my father because it happened to coincide with the rumble of the U.S. government's paving trucks dropping their steaming hot piles of macadam through Michigan and up in the U.P. itself. The federal interstate highway program was on the march. It fit his view. He was a simple grader. He didn't care. It was the final piece of the puzzle, he said, striping the fifty north-south miles between St. Ignace and the Soo with an asphalt hide a modern-day Chippewa could be proud of. This was the completion of his uncertain vision after Korea, his Anishinaabewaki, smothered though it may be by white culture, linked to its means of survival.

Might as well go down swinging.

Might as well be in the world.

Dream realized, he could have retired happy right then. But he was only forty-five, and now that Anishinaabewaki was easy-on and easy-off, it should have been Easy Street for Louis.

Minerva and I were just old enough to remember his second half-career. He had got his card as a stone mason. The work wasn't always steady, but when it was he'd be out of the house before dawn, back at dusk covered in dirt and sweat and carrying a six-pack in the door. He troweled mud and pointed seams for a construction company from the Soo called Sandusky Builders who were the only local builder to weigh the Chippewa gifts of quick able hands and work ethic against an inclination for alcohol and still hire them. Predictably, after twenty years of this reaching and bending and grabbing and hoisting and setting of blocks and bricks which arranged themselves into schools and factories and hospital additions, Louis's forearms got big and knotty. He grew some legendary bumps, big rangy amphibians, like cysts or ganglions, contortions of the nervous system. They had locomotion. They nested inside our father. They scared us. He told us they were frogs, bad spirits, manidos, who had jumped through his skin into his forearms, warts and all, a plague he must suffer because of his bad, bad children. He loved tormenting us with them, balling his hand into a fist and rocking his wrist so the tendons and muscles of his forearm would set the frogs in motion. He would screw up his face and pretend to writhe in pain. He would hold them up to his ear as if listening to them. "Yes, manido," he would say. He could make them slow to a disgusting crawl, slithering wickedly up and down his arm under the skin until we groaned. Or, he could make the frogs practically leap out of his skin, make them dart to and fro like polliwogs in a pond. He could gather them together in a huddle and send them out to play, anything to upset our children's stomachs. He told us we must never touch them. By the time I was twenty-six and back on the rez, this frog-play had disappeared. The frogs had begun to bite. They hurt him. The knots got as big and tight as Adam's apples. He tendered his papers to Sandusky. We saw unaccustomed tears wash from sixty-six year-old Chippewa eyes that night. We watched as he covered the frogs with the green and white flannel sleeves, and the frogs were spoken of no more. I wanted to ask him. *Dad, still got those frogs in your arms?* At age fifty-two, I would have preferred to explode sad family taboos, but he no longer remembered why his sleeves stayed buttoned snugly at the wrist.

Still he was not through.

In the mid-eighties on the boundary of the Pope County Indian Reservation, they opened the first high-stakes bingo casino on any reservation in the country. People called it the Three Fires Club, a big old cinder block cube my father had helped build in his days as a stone mason. It stood there for better than two years vacant and unmarked, not even defaced or spray-painted with graffiti. We wondered if some wise man among us foresaw the advent of Indian gaming and the millions to be made from it, because, aside from the secret nocturnal bingo games to which you were admitted only with a password, the little structure had no obvious intended use at all. And then with the passage of the 1988 Indian Gaming law, class III gambling was permitted and immediately the whole operation sprang to life. It was painted Miami Beach green; a Three Fires Casino sign showing three kindling sticks and a single flame was commissioned and mounted over the front door; some surrounding land was leveled for a lighted parking lot. *Come on out and lay down a bet!* smiled a cartoon sachem in headdress in the *Soo News*, the first advertisement taken out for the club. If you were a tribal member of the Chippewa, the Ottowa or the Potawatomi, you were automatic for the menial positions in the casino—valet parker, housekeeper, dishwasher, chambermaid, bouncer. Entrepreneurship had erupted on the reservation, shielded as it was from any tax—federal, state or local. Imagine: Blackjack and baccarat and chemin de fer on the sacred grounds of Anishinaabewaki, the white man chased onto our reservations to take his pleasure in an activity deemed illegal in the United States of America, whose border lay a mere fifty feet from the front entrance of the Three Fires Club.

In part because of the frogs that had jumped into my father's arms during its construction, he was among those Chippewa favored, winning a job dealing blackjack. The white shirts had long sleeves, and besides, he said, now the people of the Three Fires would have work on their own land, profits to plow back into the reservation. He was back. He girded our loins with his spit and fire. His optimism was infectious, and we felt ourselves dealt right back into the game again. Born with a face that betrayed every feeling, he brimmed with misplaced social energy at first, his ready quips and shit-eating grins and raised eyebrows lighting him up like the flashing rows of one-armed bandits behind him as he dealt. But he was determined to be a success at this, even at the expense of his inborn gregariousness. He came home with stories of unimaginable sums of money wagered and won, wagered and lost, of a glamorous aura that enveloped the club, of local celebrities and contented customers laying down bets on harmless games of chance, of the sums risked in a good cause and that was, in my father's mind, the Pope County Indian Reservation. He hoped and prayed that everybody might soon come to this enlightenment, that maybe Uncle Sam was saying after all this time, *Sorry about any inconvenience we might have caused.*

But, as my father should have never forgotten, this was the not that dreamy America but the Soo. It was the same place where Thaddeus Sokolowski's barber pole drew hateful taunts. It was peopled with the same lowlifes that came out to the rez to fire dice and hoodwink dealers and generally tempt fate while getting drunk on watered-down hard liquor. There were Indian haters among them as well, like Roy LeRoi, who couldn't handle the hooch and picked fights with drunken Indians out under the halogen lights in the parking lot when they ran out of money. Such escapades were to be expected in any startup operation, and they only added to the frontier allure of the Three Fires Casino, in turn encouraging even more riffraff from the Soo. Tommy McKeon, in a display of mercantile counter-punching, hung sixteen televisions from his ceiling.

By the mid-nineties, the place was going so strong that a huge new project was undertaken. Ground was quickly broken on a full-scale casino after the image of Las Vegas. Golf courses, four-star restaurants, world-class hotels, a galaxy of tourist attractions would be offered, including ferry boat rides and visits to colonial forts and jogging paths through Chippewa forests—no stone would be left unturned in the attempt to draw the white man to the gaming tables of the once and former Anishinaabewaki. In anticipation of ever greater numbers of customers from the rich south of Michigan and the Greater American Midwest, Louis Charlevoix and older Native Americans were openly demoted, pushed out of their earned positions of consequence, redeployed as the waiters, bussers, dishwashers and barkeeps they'd been at the start. Especially the elders were deemed expendable in the drive to professionalize the staff of Three Fires. Billions of dollars were set to change hands in reservation casinos, the newest rabbit hole for Indigene culture. It's a good thing Louis could schmooze. They made him a bartender.

The Three Fires spawned so much money that disputes over tax bills erupted between the Chippewa Nation and the state of Michigan. Court battles were fought. In the legal haze it became a white man's resort. The older Chippewa were fired. That included my father, finally finished with his Derby quilt at the age of eighty-seven. I did not hold it against my friend Jimmy Blackbird that he let my father go. It broke Jimmy's heart. He'd known Louis from way back. Jimmy was a smart guy, an MBA in Finance who had to deal with lawyers and state revenuers and eavesdropping technology and the shady probabilities of human nature and preferably not with a disgruntled eighty-seven year-old Chippewa bartender. *Dad,* I wanted to say, *remember when you worked in the casino*, but even that fresh ember no longer glowed.

I can sum it up for you: Louis Charlevoix gave his life to the dream of launching a better world for mankind, a dream in which the white man would sit alongside the Indigene, cross his legs and smoke the pipe. And when it turned out that only fingers were crossed, he lost heart, and he broke.

"That Birch?" he called out feebly from inside.

"Did he plant his garden? Did he cry?" I asked Minerva's open brown face.

Looking a little annoyed with me, she insisted under her breath, "He's in trouble, Birch. He's planted his beets, yes. He plants them every year on Pontiac-Looking-Down Day. You know this. It's how he reaches out to you. His beets are the baggattaway balls for Neil's sticks now. While you and Neil are at the fort, he is on all fours hunched over the garden bed. And, yes, of course he cried."

As Minerva spoke I saw that my father's beet garden was like a Chippewa reservation. A little plot whose edges demarked a set-aside existence. A patch within a patch, residents bunched according to genus. Where once a few Jesuit outposts stood at the heads of streams and lakes in proud Anishinaabewaki, now a few beet gardens were permitted in the upper Great Lakes of the United States of America.

"He's missed you," she whispered as I entered.

Of course my father cried over the beets. He cried over the beets because he found even this set-aside life a beautiful thing. He cried over the beets because they had become vermilion baggattaway balls. Blood-stained lacrosse balls growing in the earth. June Two, 1763 has taught me many things about life, and none truer than this: If your opponent whistles one by you into the net, you are already dead.

And here was Louis Charlevoix standing in the net, and he couldn't tell a Red Ace beet from a baggattaway ball from a damn bullet coming at him. I wished I could see the shots coming and punch them away from him.

"Marla?" asked my father. His dog Tipi never looked people in the eye. He just sat tall by my father's bentwood rocker, aloof as a bodyguard. My God, he should have had sunglasses.

"She's at home, Dad."

"This is her home. This is where she came to get you."

"I know, Dad."

"I love her spunk."

"I know, Dad." I walked over to his bentwood rocker and hugged the familiar green, white and gray threads that held his bones together. "You got your garden planted. It looks good. I can see the tops of the greens pushing through."

"Sheila? She want a bath?"

"She's in the Soo, Dad. She's thirty-one now."

"I love her spunk, too. I'm her grandpa. The beets are in."

He was chatty, yet my mother would not talk to him and Minerva lost patience. He needed someone to talk to, and of all people Marla filled that void. How lucky Louis was that the fates had sent Naanganikwe. Often, she did well just to keep my parents apart. The she-bear was not well herself, a spate of mostly minor ailments. She stayed out of sight, in her bedroom usually, avoiding contact with my father, and in the confines of this tiny house where he slept only a few hours a night and reclaimed the bentwood rocker for himself before dawn, she was left sitting for long hours by herself on the bed. She planted her hip on the side of the bed and adjusted her mind to the past, staring blankly out the window. She firmly believed that she could be infected by my father, that he could and would contaminate her mind in the same way his was. She said she'd read this in the paper and that she could die from contact with his pots and pans, his expelled breath, his clothing, his bad jokes. So, naturally, my father made a game out of it, rolling licked whorls of skin onto every article they own, fingerprinting his sickness around the house in a trail for his bride Edina.

My mother heard my voice and came out of the bedroom, groping along the wall for fear of infection by my father.

"Hi, Birch," she cooed to me with a big smile. "Going somewhere?"

Her head bobbed. How did she always know when I was leaving?

"Your mother eats her soup in the bedroom to avoid me," my father said. "I'm trying to poison her, I guess."

My mother smiled at me. "Birch, how do you break bread with a man who sees red beets floating on broth as vermilion baggattaway balls floating on the waters of Lake Huron? Answer me that one. Huh?"

"Get the ball back in to Weniway!" my father cried out.

"Tell them where you're off to, Birch," prodded Minerva.

"I knew he was going somewheres," my mother said, her head shaking no.

"Just down to Hull, down to Ontario. I'll be back in a few days. Take care of those beets now, Dad, and look after Minerva and Marla, will you? Mom, don't forget Neil, either. You know how he loves company. It's a good thing you two are around to keep us all in one piece, cuz we'd all be a mess without you. I've got a meeting of the World Lacrosse Council. Should be interesting. You know? I'm gonna try and turn the clock back for you."

Walking to Matti Virkanen's old milk truck, a dazzling picture jumped into my head, a firing diamond just peeking out from the topsoil of my father's beet garden.

Vision

Did I ever hear get an earful about the French and Indian melee at the *Soo Locks*.

Six weeks after the sectarian brawl school was out for the summer, and I was still nursing a swollen eye, a split lip and three bruised ribs. The bunch of us spent two days in the city jail, which meant that, including Pontiac-Looking-Down Day, I missed three days of work in early June, forcing a substitute teacher to survive that End of Days of the school year. Fortunately, my beat-up face was only of passing interest to the students, but there were parents who wanted my hide. The principal was obliged to reprimand me. Marla repeatedly rang up the family name my father had spent a lifetime constructing, and which in a single stroke I seemed prepared to destroy.

"Barber-pole sitting? That's what it is, right? My God, Birch, you're a teacher! I don't care if Thaddeus vouches for you. I don't care if this guy The King egged you on or not. I don't care if he pulled a knife. And I don't much care if they destroy poor Thaddeus's pole, either!" She was disappointed. "Maybe I'll go pull the damn thing up myself. Just to be rid of it. My God, I've never heard of anything so stupid, even in the Soo! You're a teacher! What were you thinking? Haven't lessons been learned from fifteen years ago when he and Neil nearly killed each other? Are you even thinking about Hull? God,

Birch, you have to be careful. You're under the microscope now. Forget about this Roy whatever-his-name-is idiot."

"I am going for a long run in the Hiawatha," I said.

"I am going to make you some food to send with you," she replied, perturbed.

I grabbed my stick and took off. In the summer after my junior year in high school, my father goaded me into running the entire length of the Hiawatha Shore Trail—one hundred twenty miles of root-strewn bridle path alternating with flat, boring macadam along the southern shore of Gitchee Gumee from Big Bay to Grand Marais—over four and a half marathons long. In a single day. I'd heard that Indian boys were supposed to be locked down in a sweat box and have a vision.

My father made sure to tell me his. When he was thirteen, my grandfather told him to pick a tree in the Hiawatha, climb to the highest branch that would support him, then go up one more. He was to sit in the crotch of this tree until a vision presented itself. With nothing but a rope, he scoured the forest overlooking Tahquamenon Falls until he found the perfect tree, a ninety foot black walnut. He climbed up seventy-five feet and tied himself facing west onto a precarious branch where he proceeded to sit for four days. He had no food or water, a quiet witness to near skies and far ones, sunsets and moonsets, bark mites and mosquitoes, birdsong and cascading waters. In the middle of the third night the sun came up all around him and he received the dream of the two gods playing that primal game of baggattaway—the one that decides the fate of man—right before his eyes. They bumped hips and tried to break each other. They were killed and came back to life. They took the forms of predatory animals and birds. He thought he was unconscious or out of his mind, his eyes glued to the two of them and their speeding vermilion ball that left a red vapor trail through the clouds. At moonset of the fourth day he felt a hand on his shoulder, and it was his father. He hadn't even heard his approach. And my father told him he knew that there is life in the next world and that our game is how we arrive in it.

He told me he knew I couldn't run the entire one hundred twenty miles in one twenty-four hour period. This advice he gave me: "Listen for the tom-toms, boy." I would experience pain and I would drive myself through the pain and learn to ignore it and then no longer feel it. I would find a spirit guide. Placing one foot in front of the other for mile after mile, picking my way through the upright fossils and plodding along the shore, my mind slowly cleaving from my body, I too would arrive on a plane of existence where visions are the normal state of affairs. Pain was the key, and the breaking through it.

Yet the pain that wracked me was that he was right.

I never heard the tom-toms, not even in the distance. The first miles were the worst. The spirit and body were at war, clashing over every single step, making each a victory of ragged will. In time, the breathing steadied to the footfall, and you settled in; you were whole, a perfect machine living out its intended purpose. You could go on in this euphoric state for hours. And then, finite being, you became aware again, and you registered the wear in your bones and in your skin and your breathing came a cropper and you slowed. At that point

I had nothing to show but feet pocked with blisters, a mangled skeleton and a broken spirit.

When do the tom-toms kick in, I asked urgently.

I would, though, manage two of the four marathons and run well into the third, reaching Marquette thirty miles down the road by one in the afternoon. I was a hollow log. But when I saw my father's pickup tracking me, the thought of quitting flew from my mind. I vowed to reach Munising another forty miles along the shoreline. At nine-thirty that evening, cramped and defeated, I limped into the little port and gave up the ghost at the rusty Rotary Club sign at the outskirts of town where my father scooped me up and drove to the emergency room of Munising Community Hospital where even a Chippewa boy would be refurbished.

"So," he said. I could scarcely even hear him. "Seventy miles. No one ever said you had to do it without resting once in a while. You only used fourteen and a half hours."

"Maybe I wasn't done," I huffed.

He laughed right in my face.

Sitting in a tree, if that's what my father had done, would not be for me. I started to run after those elusive visions, after the sound of those tom-toms. I stalked them, figuring that either I would eventually bag one or that I would run right out of myself, and that would be that. I called them Hiawatha marathons, the long tracks I invented that wound elliptically over thousands of acres; mile after mile I would run, ever faster ever farther over the pine needle trails, bush-whacking through virgin forest and sprinting in open stretches, leaning and straining for those tom-toms. I sweated out all the sodium and electrolytes I owned and puked my guts more than once too. I cramped in my calves and thighs, my arms and hands went numb, and I fell in a heap and slept loglike, dreaming that I was still running. I would scale maples, like a wintering bear, and have no memory of how I got there.

Yet I was unworthy of the vision. Why do we need to show up our fathers? That Louis possessed what I vainly sought tormented me. I had tried too hard, I had forced it. In that period, the Hiawatha became for me what Fort Detroit had been to Bwon-Diac, a dread place that defied puny human will, and for a long time I avoided it like the plague. Maturity whispered that I had to let the dream come to me, but I was fragments without it, denied my due.

With my stick, I turned west and within half a mile I entered the forest I had once shunned. My ankle was weak, given to twisting as I ramped up to speed. Tommy McKeon's big prison-guard face popped into my head, his comment about the Olympic gymnasts doing their y-scale, and I stopped to try it. It is a ridiculous move. Unable to balance or to get my foot up that high, I finally wrapped my left arm part way around a big ash tree, cupped the inside of the right ankle and lifted my leg up in an ugly pike about waist-high. I discovered: You cannot have midriff and do the y-scale. It felt good, though, almost vision quest good, quiet, strong, total. Four and a half miles I ran after that, reasonably renewed and suddenly intent on staying alive until June Two of 2010, when, somehow, against all odds, I would coach my Indigene nation team to a win over Team England on Pontiac-Looking-Down Day. Coach's intuition.

The milk truck was purring in the street. Hull awaited some five-hundred miles from here. Marla had crafted three varieties of high protein, high fiber sandwich (peanut butter, turkey, egg salad), a freezer bag full of sesame sticks and a big thermos of ice tea.

"You better get a move on if you're going to beat that storm," she said, kissing me good-bye and wishing me luck.

It was a tropical late July evening, and the western sky behind me was a layered dark with tall white thunderheads raging out from it. Standing at the wheel so my skin didn't stick to the seat, I traversed the bridge my father built forty-one years ago. I could easily picture my forebears on the river below, canoeing through snow squalls after sturgeon and trout, hunting red stag at the water's edge. There were no bridges, no locks, no canals in the river then. I saw them track the beaver in his poplar dams, stalking the washes through silent snows, I saw them snowshoe across frozen lakes with shouldered bows after the sleeping bear, I saw the women and children boiling sap on Sugar Island.

And just that fast, Ontario, and up onto Canada's longest highway, Route 17. The world that can be known thinned out and vanished as I drove. Every gas station I pass advertised itself as the last chance for fuel, and it felt like I was surrendering control of my vehicle to the moon rising up in the clear eastern sky. The few fast food franchises that attached to the roadway are empty. The electrical storm, advancing from behind, gobbled them up. I didn't care. I didn't even have to move the steering wheel. The miles just happened. I was hypnotized. Pitchblende darkness flapped a ragged blanket over the huge farms where combines had been left for the night among strewn haycocks. I had outrun the storm, or it just fizzled out like they sometimes do, I couldn't tell. The peanut butter and the egg salad were gone, as was an unknown portion of sesame sticks and a good slug of the ice tea. The sky, purple and yellow one minute, had finished black. I was reminded as I reached down to turn on the high beams: This vision I would propose to the Council was Neil's. I was merely the spokesman for a genius. He'd come to me and said, "Opportunity, Birchwalker, is knocking. Drive me out to meet the war chief?"

"Birchwalker," he'd proclaimed, "the 2010 World Lacrosse Council championships would be the perfect stage for a reenactment of Minavivana's lacrosse deception at Fort Michilimackinac. If we get it by Parry Four Bears, you can sell it to the Council."

In no time, we had fleshed the idea out and arranged a meeting with the chief. I drove us out to New York State to meet Parry Four Bears. We hemmed and hawed, probably didn't make a lot of sense at first. Like any politician, Parry had to see that the result promised enough to justify the personal risks, and he was a busy man so he was looking for the full clarity of our bottom line. It was a lot to ask. Powerful people in the modern game of lacrosse would object to tradition being bucked, vested interests being threatened. Parry would have to approve, or the vision was kaputt, stillborn.

Then Neil had stood and gestured leaderlike with his hands, "Let us not consider whether the downside is a battle worth fighting. Let us rather consider if the upside packs a wallop for our people and our sport, lest both be forgotten forever. For example, Chief, can you see a tournament where the players from every country use the traditional Iroquois stick? Where they run barefoot over a two- or three-mile field? Where the vermilion balls of the old days are thrown between stripped spruce saplings for goals…..?"

Not only did Parry Four Bears' face warm to the concept, he immediately came to his feet and added three quick, grand twists of his own. Also these, I believe, had been anticipated by my friend well in advance.

The chief had then said, inspired yet with calculation, "What if a hundred thousand, from every Indigene tribe that still exists, were present at such a game? What if the tournament, played under Indian rules of baggattaway, were televised?" Then, turning to face me, his mind obviously racing, "Birch, you will coach the team. I need you to get to the semis. I'd need you to beat the English."

Neil and Parry together like that? It was the Big Bang, like watching teammate gods in an act of creation. It was better than the thunderstorm I had just left behind me. We had sold him. Neil's vision had inspired equal ones in Parry until an idea had been birthed that was broader than sport or history or humanity alone, the sum and the product and the square of all three. Forever. Amen.

The sparse road signage told me that Mattawa, Ontario, was the next exit, a little border town right on the Ottawa River. And across the river loomed the western edge of Quebec Province. My head had started to pound in waves, circling my skull like the thunder. I pulled off Route 17 at Mattawa, following a sign that indicates a campsite somewhere along the dark riverbank, and turned onto a dirt road that suddenly spilled the front end of the milk truck down into a run of birches and poplars that shrouded the water. I shut off the motor and got out for a walk. My ankle and ribs had stiffened up, too, during the long drive. With no obvious cause, I felt alone here, penned in, spooked at the border of Anishinaabewaki. My mind was panicked, looking for a fence to jump over, a way to break out. The place names out there, Chippewa names, speak the very truth of our annexation: Nipissing, Petwawa, Nosbonsing, Kaotisinmigo, Wahwashkesh, Ottawa itself, Memesagamesing, Amateewakea, Nepewassi, Manitowing, Wikwemikong, Wakomata—towns and lakes and islands I know of. Place names are our only epitaphs, names on placemats in greasy spoons that no one can even pronounce. In the deafening silence of place names, up into that chill of time and space our Chippewa spirits have been blotted, our entire civilization reduced to points on a map.

The pain in my head was now a steady hurt, and I plopped down on the riverbank to the unbroken sound of rushing water. Downstream I saw a white disk glowing in the night as if an alien saucer had landed among the trees, a power plant, and that thought did not fit at all because now the sight of the intricate Chippewa beaver hunt had entered my mind. I could have been hallucinating in my anger at being nothing but a place name, because suddenly I was in a birch bark canoe with other Anishinaabek brothers and it was cold and we were tracking beaver. A gray wolf bayed out of sight and an eagle soared overhead. It was dusk and we let the canoe glide. We threw a bound-up dog overboard to curry favor with the manidos. We spotted the domed top of the beaver house and stationed the canoe at the edge of the ice, knowing that they would soon come out to gather food. We decided not to wait. We broke up the house with trenching tools and waited for the family to flee into the washes, revealed where the ice returns a hollow sound when struck. We found their faces in the bubbles through the ice, saw their breathing. We fetched them out one-by-one with our hands, suffering sharp bites in the process. We skinned and cooked the beaver and ate its meat.

Waves of nausea and intense pain behind my eyes almost overtook me. St. Anne was suddenly standing at my side, barking in Ojibwemowin. I had no idea which of the four sisters it is. What next? I stepped out onto the rapid waters of the Ottawa River, led by St. Anne, and we were whisked into the seam of water and sky and sucked upward through a hole, evaporated with a hiss into the sky above the sky.

Shhh. Bizaan. Shhh. Hear how I finally had my vision.

It is calm here. My anger is stilled. We are in a dream. I believe that this is the moon. My feet are touching its surface. The pounding in my head has moved outside my head and has become the dark drumming sound of tom-toms out in the void. I am looking at

Bwon-diac. It is shocking. It is not how I imagined him, but I feel certain it is my chieftain riding the heavens on Henry Gladwin's skull. It is the picture of ultimate suffering. Maybe he knows that I am here with him, but he seems aware only of himself. My chieftain is bound in his limbs like Gulliver, in an unrelenting state of distress as he tries to free himself from the predicament. His eyes swing to the right corner of his eyeballs and back again, and I think he is looking for his tomahawk. It is there in his buckskin, but out of the reach of his stretching, trembling fingers. I am afraid to intervene, to take it out and give it to him. I look out into the nothingness and see gibbous Earth. I cannot discern Anishinaabewaki, but there is a vault of stars around Earth and behind it in an endless tunnel, a cornucopia spinning slowly counter-clockwise. Far below and to the right of me, the white sun spews light frantically from its rim. It lights a portion of Earth and, I suppose, a portion of the moon.

My chieftain is covered in vermilion, looking as if he has been stripped of his skin, and now I hear him bellowing out into the cosmos. The sound he emits is difficult to understand at first, and Bwon-Diac is squirming like a fish in a net. Now his sounds have shape. St. Anne barks away. They come out of his mouth in strips that knife out into the darkness, paper strips, and the words are dots on the paper that appear to me to be a code. Now my chieftain settles. He goes limp and his face relaxes but the paper keeps coming from his mouth. Button candy. This is the picture of a tortured man spitting out button candy into space to the beat of tom-toms. The paper streams out like a ticker tape and the little dots of button candy attached to it are his words. I am forced to think of a player piano, and I see that my chieftain has been programmed, that he is destined for all eternity to spit out the same words he must have died with. Is this the Afterlife? Now again he tenses and there is a huge bellowing sound that pushes the button candy outward. Can you hear it? Do you know French? Mon pére, mon pére, pourquoi vous m'avez abandonnè? *He is talking to the king of France, the father who forsook him and left him in the hands of the English. Over and over again he sees it, says it.*

I experience the suffering of Bwon-diac with my own senses. I taste in my mouth the bitter gall he swallowed at the news of his father's defeat and his decision to cede also Canada and the Indian territories to the English. I have the sense of blood rushing to my head as he recalls his coalition tribes giving up the siege at Fort Detroit. I feel the sting of salt in the wound—the news that the hated English retook the forts within days of his victory as he escaped to the Illinois. He does not want to die. He wants to live. The pain of loss twists and slithers in him, working him in this sepulcher inside and out like a worm.

Though I do not register the actual audio command that emanates from my chieftain on his lunar deathbed, I apprehend it as clearly as the sound of the rushing waters of the Ottawa some-where below me: Take them back! Take them back, *he tells me.*

Then I awoke on the near bank of the Ottawa River, yanked back well before I was ready to return. It was pitch black except for a hazy chokecherry moon. I had the image in my head of sixteen red balls bounding into sixteen open gates at Fort Michilimackinac, all on Tommy McKeon's TVs. Though my head was still pounding, now it was with excitement. There was an eerie quiet in the air. My senses were lit up, I heard with St. Anne. I had met my chieftain. I felt like I could walk across time and I wanted to wake my father and tell him that I had had my vision, that I had heard the tom-toms. He would joke that I had finally reached puberty. I wanted to hear him tell his vision again. I whooped out into the darkness to Bwon-diac, and St. Anne was no longer there.

Polishing off Marla's turkey sandwich, I eased the milk truck into a parking spot in the underground garage of the swankest hotel in Hull. Three commands wound around my brain like ivy shoots on a trellis. On the way to the hotel's front entrance I passed a few storefronts, one of which was a jeweler. I beheld sparkling diamonds set into necklaces and rings and earrings and realized I had scrimped and saved long enough. It had the feel of inspiration. It was clear. I would present, at long last, my French-Chippewa bride of thirty-one years with a proper engagement ring. Over the clatter of the check-in process, the three ivies weaved into a single, bell-clear voice:

"Opportunity, Birchwalker, is knocking."

"Birch, you will coach the team."

"Take them back!"

The World Lacrosse Council

I knew the Q&A with Marla after Hull would be a marathon, like a private press conference just for her. In confessional fullness, my short-term memory would be relieved of every detail of the meeting, all its personalities and encounters, its sinners and saints, its naked ambitions and lost opportunities, its winners and losers, so I prepared its top and bottom narratives as dispassionately and as completely as I could on the ten-hour drive back home from Hull. She'd busy herself doing dishes or cooking as she listened with the ears of a priest. I would confess to her thusly:

I made some friends in Hull, not from around here. I made some enemies, too, mostly from around here. Here's how Archie Mellon opened the two-day meeting. He's an Aussie, the new executive V.P. of the World Lacrosse Council. First, he let loose with a piercing whistle to get all those jocks' attention. He was a hotshot international executive in the pacemaker business, I guess, with a reputation for banging heads and compromise. He's retired now with plenty of money. He stays alert, as he says, in this new venture as an international lacrosse executive. Keeps him in the game. I liked him right away. He's coming to the U.P.

Really? Sounds like your father's kind of guy. Louis and Archie should meet. Did he ever play? When's he coming? Do I get to meet him?

Let's see. I suppose he is a little like Louis. Archie has never picked up a stick in his life. But listen. "Men," he began, looking us all square in the eye from his spot at twelve noon on the huge mahogany table, "here's the thumbnail. We have a lot going for us, but we suffer from public apathy. We have great venues and the world's best players. We have the new blood of European and Asian countries who have joined us in the last five or ten years. We have a beautiful crystal trophy. We have the world at our fingertips, but nobody seems to give a damn. We have never come close to filling a stadium for our championships, and that's going all the way back to 1974 when I was still a young buck with a thirty-two inch waist. Plainly put, we are not organic until we can do this, and if we are not organic, we are not growing. So, how do we move forward fast? Simplify, maximize, grow." Then he banged the heel of his oxblood loafer-clad foot on the table and kept talking, showing us that he might be new but he was well informed. "Unless you watch *SENE2* in the American wee hours, you've never even heard of these world championships. Hell, the NCAA final round in May drew almost fifty thousand a game! The college kids put us to shame, for Pete's sake. It makes the name of our tournament sound wishful—the *World Lacrosse Championships*. So, since the world isn't exactly beating a path to our door, I want ideas, right here, right now. I want to hear what you think will put us on the map," he said. "Don't be afraid. Who's up first?" He rubbed his palms together and motioned to the Japanese contingent.

He gets right down to business, huh?

You'll see. The colonials…

Colonials? Oh, you mean England?

Throw in the U.S., Canada and Australia for good measure, guilt by association.

Okay, the baggattaway colonials.

You know the type. In their forties, fit, tanned, brash, brusque, not a wallflower among them—ex-jocks staying busy in the sport they can't leave. Razor-creased chinos, loud argyle socks wrapped in penny loafers, Ivy League haircuts, sherbet Izods, beefier now, but still with strong chins and lean-muscled forearms twirling pencils like they were cradling sticks.

Didn't you kind of fit in with that look, honey?

Maybe, but I don't have their sheen. Parry Four Bears sure as hell didn't.

What'd he wear? Buckskins and moccasins?

Parry? No. Beautiful tan two-piece suit and floor-length Onondaga headdress.

Wow. They laugh at him?

You'll see. The guys I liked the best were the ones who weren't native English speakers.

Sounds right to me.

I looked around the table and knew that absent divine intervention I did not have a prayer of converting these hardened lacrosse souls to baggattaway.

Birch, can you start with the ending? I need to know how you did!

Just relax, you'll see. This was my first encounter with World Lacrosse since I was the face-off middie for Team Indigene Nation in the second WLC championships in '78.

I know, I know. I seem to remember a picture…

Me too, but what I was thinking is that we were skunked 17-0 by Team USA in our first game. I doubt you remember the name Drey Foss? I faced off against him eighteen times in that game, and it looks like now we'll be facing off again as coaches.

No, is he an annoying colonial?

Hell yes. I also knew Harald MacManus of Scotland and Andrew Sophie of Canada, but the rest of the delegates were complete strangers to me. Listen to this: We've got delegations from China, Hong Kong, Japan and Korea now.

It's really going global then.

The poor Japanese coach was barely intelligible. He spat out a few words about how the growth prospects for lacrosse in East Asia were limitless. He touted the vast sports television market of the Orient and then he spat out an introduction of the Chinese delegates, the coach Li Rui and his boss Mr. Yuan, welcoming China to the club.

Are you going there, you're going there, aren't you? They want you to travel.

Maybe. And I'd do it in a heartbeat. Next up was the German party. Their coach, Karl-Uwe Feldenheld, has a red face and his cheeks puff up when he talks. He said these were both common afflictions in Bavarian people. He wants to get the European public into lacrosse by staging the championships in Florida, where they all just love to spend their holidays. He said that if we combined Florida, lacrosse and, he said this with raised bushy eyebrows, *the American Indian*, then Germans would come in the thousands. Then he walked over to Parry Four Bears, begged his pardon, took off his headdress and tried it on his own huge Bavarian head.

I don't know about Florida. Maybe the Choctaw…

He was just talking, Marla. These were opening statements.

Germans would come?

We want them all! The next guy who spoke, Russell Pape, the faintly mustachioed coach of the English squadron, as he calls his team, I didn't care for him. And I don't guess he exactly warmed to me either. Another smug colonial, whiny, makes loud, bad inside jokes that no one but the English-speaking crew gets and then has the arrogance to subject us all to this howling laugh of his whenever he thinks he's been funny. *In the main*, as he said, *it's all about the bloody telly. Get a sponsor, sell it to the big networks. Don't forget the rights to Asia,* he said gratuitously as he made a deep bow to the Japanese coach. *Promote the hell out of it, keep the tourney in North America where it belongs and don't expect the football and cricket-loving English to care one way or the other.*

He sounds obnoxious.

You haven't heard anything yet.

"Next," Archie yelled, looking at his own people, the Aussies. The coach Graeme Fletcher rose to speak. He speaks outback, you know, and it was a while before I could even follow the guy.

Another colonial type?

No, he's a good guy. Uncomfortable public speaker, though, and didn't have a whole lot to add. He jokingly proposed that we stage the tournament in the outback because the world loves Australia, *Invite them all to the bleedin' outback*, he smiled.

That's good, a Commonwealther who's not a colonial.

But listen to Foss. He blew up, trying to be a comedian. *Prisoners! You're nothing but a bunch of rejects! Crazy-ass prisoners who just managed to be a little bit smarter than the aborigines whose lands you stole. Who the hell is going to fly fifteen fucking hours to the god-forsaken outback?*

Now that's a high-strung colonial boy.

He's a loose damn cannon. "Next!" Archie barked at the Danes. The Danish coach is Lars Asferg. I like this guy a lot. He's bright, articulate and rational.

Just like you, honey.

He's smarter than I am, but I've got him by a mile in body mass. He's a tiny guy, small framed, you know? In his perfect English, he said that Graeme Fletcher might be on to something. The Danes, he said, are relative newcomers to lacrosse, but, as Europeans, they know that war and sport are two sides of the same coin. He actually cited the Berlin Olympics in '36, just before Hitler started his war. Basically, his idea was that playing fields and battlegrounds are equivalent places. He said we could move our games out of closed-in stadiums to open fields, like on a Civil War battlefields. Lars said *This would be very imaginative.*

Oh, my gosh. Lars is warm.

Then Archie pointed at the Czech delegates. The Czech coach stubbed out a cigarette as he stood up. *Kovak*, he said mysteriously. I had to check his nameplate, the first name was Karel. He looked at the ashtray. *A bad habit I picked up after my playing days. Jesse Owens, after those same Olympics, took up the habit too.*

There's a novelty, a smoking lacrosse man.

You'll see. Novelty does not do this man justice. Right away, Kovac wanted to be provocative, combative, and his manner all but ensured it. The American coach bit first.

Foss?

Right. *Don't flatter yourself*, he said. *Smoking killed him. Maybe so*, Karel Kovak answered with an odd sense of calm, *maybe so. But the stress that killed him was a lethal combination of international celebrity and his role as, how do you say, a sacrificial lamb in the American civil rights movement. Hardly the cigarettes alone, I think. As to promotion, we need a man not unlike Jesse Owens, an authentic hero to the people to give our little track meets some...juice. Like Herr Feldenheld, I think our Indian friends offer interesting possibilities. Are there famous ones?* he asked, looking smugly around the table.

He's creepy. Feldenheld is a great name.

So that brought the Scot to his feet. Harald MacManus commands attention, though for all the wrong reasons. First, he has patches of orange freckles and green eyes and a pasty face, and he's got a halo of puffy orange hair. And the brogue, it should be corked in an oak cask and shelved forever. He was a troll, gruff but smart. He called us *bahstards*. He said we have to go global. *Look around the table. Do you want to go missionary?* he asked us. *Then get South America. They've got great footballers and tennis players, they're thin and fast and wiry like us lax players used to be.*

He's wild, Birch. He's right, too, right?

He was certainly right that not a single Spanish speaker graced the mahogany table. Archie took notes on that. Harald called Scotland the *provairbial engine of European lacrosse*, saying we would grow a spectator base if we globalize, music to Archie's multinational ears. I can almost imitate him, *Dealing people in, that's sport; dealing them out is war, and that's a fine line. We need an athlete, a team, to emairge in our game. D'you know, lads? An underdog, like me and Scotland, to steal the show away for the common man. Not bloody likely!* Russell Pape yelled out before he could even finish. *You'd have to ply the competition and the bloody spectators with barrels of your single malt before that would ever happen, MacManus!*

That Pape, he's the English coach?

Yes. But Harald got the last word. *Now there's a sensible idea, Pape*, he said. *If you'd like to bullshit with me a bit further on this topic, I can be found belly to the bar in about three hours. Join me, you bahstards, and we'll throw back a single malt or even a fooking dooble if you like, talk some Scotch lax!*

MacManus is crazy, huh?

He's a Scot. But Pape wasn't through yet, either. *So*, he said, *just to recap, MacManus. You're an advocate of the missionary position*? Asshole is always trying to get a laugh, and he usually doesn't. Andrew Sophie was next.

I know that name.

Yeah. Canada. He was great, at first. Pleasant. Introduced himself as the host for this Council meeting, his country as the birthplace of modern lacrosse and ice hockey…

Of course. But what do you mean, at first?

… as well as the host of the 2010 championships again. And Marla, for some reason, I was driven to my feet right then.

She would look at me, direct and unblinking.

Parry Four Bears was stoical. I saw Archie's eyebrows lift up and his lips go round. I was choking on unformed words and ideas. Andrew Sophie yielded the floor grudgingly, throwing me a look. Marla. Around the table were Finns, Americans, Indians, English, Scots, Japanese, Italians, Chinese, Koreans, Aussies, Czechs, Danes, Dutch, Canadians, Germans, Irish, Kiwis, Swedes and Welsh, each one staring at me in anticipation. Splashes of colors from this array of flags stole my attention for several seconds. Reds, whites and blues were the most common; yellows and blacks, greens and orange and the purple and white of the Iroquois. Listen, Marla: The Council is a mini-U.N. run by a bunch of ex-jocks! And just like the U.N., some members are more important than others. The Security Council is the U.S., England, Canada and Australia.

The baggattaway colonials.

Yeah, the 1974 charter members, rule makers, enforcers and, usually, winner of the tournament. Of all people it was Drey Foss who snapped me out of my reverie. *Waddya you got, Birch?"* he said. *"How's that Cub Scout troop you call the Indigene Nation look this year?*

He must have played, right, college and MLL?

A standout in college and as a player and coach in the MLL, and as Connecticut-Yankee as a jock can be. He can back up his arrogance, though: American teams have won seven of the nine WLC championships.

So what? Keep going, Birch, tell me what you said!

Somehow I found a voice and I went for it. *You want turnout,* I boasted. *I can give you turnout. I can give you a hundred thousand if you understand Section 2.5 of the WLC constitution the same way I do...* I had to raise my voice over the catcalls from Drey and Russell. *...which states that lacrosse shall include all versions of the game. And all versions means all versions.* Foss objected right away. *What'd you do, stay up late reading the WLC constitution last night? What the hell is Section 2.5, Birch? I did,* I said. *Let me see if I can paraphrase it for you in its entirety. Lacrosse shall include all versions of the game. Were you able to follow that alright?* He ignored that and began to taunt the Indian in me. *Well, maybe we should consider your brainstorm over a peace pipe. Got one, do you, Birch?*

She'd stop and narrow her eyes. What was Archie doing during this little exchange?

Just watching, hanging back. *Where'd you get that shiner, Birch?* Foss then asked me.

I told you so!

I said I ran into a barber pole.

What was Parry doing all this time?

You should have witnessed the save. He came to his feet urgently but calmly, shut them all up real fast. Finally, he said, *We are brothers at this table. Save the competition for the field.*

I love Parry Four Bears. And Archie…what's his last name?

Archie Mellon. He banged his oxblood heel on the table again and ordered me to keep going. He wanted to hear more about Section 2.5. *Archie*, I said, *section 2.5 of our own constitution couldn't be plainer: Lacrosse shall include all versions of the game, and we intend to base a proposal on it. This game is the lifeblood of my people. A prayer to the Creator. The way it's played today is fine, but it is confined and linear—field shortened, goals narrowed, loaded up with body pads and technologies we never dreamed of. Let's open up the game just once more, set it free. Let's take advantage of television, the hungry eye of the public. People want to see beginnings, comebacks, a story with roots, they want to learn. Baggattaway gives them all of that.*

She would applaud me. That's strong, Birch. I like that. What'd they all say?

Stunned silence. Drey Foss then spoke up, naturally. I can even imitate him: *Oh, Jesus, you can't seriously…You realize what's he saying, don't you? The venue's been set for four years now. He want to undo all that, does he? Change all the rules to make it some throwback, a goddamn nostalgia tour?*

Were the foreign coaches following all this?

They had no idea what was going on. It was too fast for them. But Andrew Sophie put two and two together, asking, *You mean we're actually not going to play in London, after all the work we've…all the commitments we've…all the…?* Archie jumped back in and said for everybody to just cool off. "Here's what I want," he said, shuffling a short stack of papers. "Simplify, maximize, grow! We don't have to do keep doing the same-old same-old if it doesn't work." With that guidepost, he issued committee assignments, taking a personal interest in Constitution and Rules, and urging all the delegates to seek me out on the interpretation of Rule 2.5. He had swung his weight behind us a little bit, even branded the idea *entrepreneurial*. He chaired the Marketing Committee himself, which handles all the corporate sponsorships. He charged the Promotion Committee, comprised of Canada, U.S., Indigene Nation and Denmark, to generate ideas to 'create gate,' as he called it, to maximize the damn spectators.

Committees are dull, Birch.

Not mine. You'll see. I was determined, Marla. There was no losing this fight.

Spoken like the coach of Indigene Nation!

So the Promotion Committee's little breakout room was what you'd expect, a small table, a water pitcher and some glasses, some padded chairs, a tripod and a flip chart. Drey Foss tried to open the window but couldn't. *Shit*, he said, *we can't open the window. I need some fresh air.* He just stared me down as if Parry, Andrew Sophie, Lars Asferg and their co-delegates were not there. *What exactly do you want, Birch*? He was antsy, irritated. I told him to relax, that we were on the same team here, asked if he could imagine a large gathering of human beings about to engage in a game of ball, a battle, two encampments, opposing tribes, stripped saplings planted three miles apart, scores of players swarming in patterns of offense and defense, swinging this way and that, defending their goal to the last and attacking the opponent's goal like their lives depended on it.

Did he buy it? Wait, let me guess, no.

No. This is what he said: *Hold on a minute, Birch. The game is called lacrosse. I want you to imagine all the pace you're stripping out of the game.*

Did you tell him the rest?

Yeah. I said it gets worse. Only natural materials can be used, so, no graphite sticks, no plastic or titanium or metal. No pads or helmets. Some players fast and abstain from sex. Before the match, we light a bonfire. The men lean their sticks with the heads facing the fire in a circle and stand behind them. Thanks is offered to nature for providing the wood, to the animals for providing the gut and leather. A medicine man says a prayer and you have Ball Up. *Ball up*? he said, *What the fuck is that? And you're saying this is what we should do for our championships? Turn them into Indian pomp and use their shitty equipment*? I said yes, if you want to rouse the sleeping giant. *And just who would the sleeping giant be, Birch*? The Indigene, I told him. *Hordes, right*? he spat. A hundred thousand or so. He laughed at me. *A hundred thousand or so when we can't even give away five thousand tickets now, that sound realistic to you? You'll have to bus*

*in goddamn homeless people and retards to get that many spectators.
You're nuts!* He was fuming. *Look, you had your time. It's over. It
may have been your game once, but it has passed you by. A hundred
thousand? Help me with that, Birch. Yeah, go ahead and get specific.
Break that down for me, will you?*

You had him right there, didn't you?

I did. Okay, I said. Add these numbers in your head:
Chippewa—106,000; Choctaw— 88,000; Iroquois—49,000;
Potawatomi—16,000; Delaware—9,000. Lars went to the tripod,
writing the numbers I was reeling off. Drey half watched, his own ox
was being gored and he was powerless to save it.

Did Lars add them all up for Drey?

Drey did, actually. *That's almost three hundred thousand,* he
said, rubbing his forehead. Right, I said, and there's plenty more
where that came from. I didn't count Creek, Seminole, Cherokee,
Sioux. And don't forget the white folks… All of a sudden, Archie
Mellon was standing in the doorway. Told me he wanted to hear it
right now. I should go ahead and lay it out. I should spill my guts.
Parry nodded at me. I took a breath and let fly. *We'd want to schedule
the final for June 2, 2010. That's a big day for us. That's what will
bring our people out. We'd want that particular game to be played at
Fort Michilimackinac, Archie. That's in Michigan, way at the top of
the lower peninsula. All the better if it were to pit the Indigene Nation
against the English, but that's another discussion. We would play the
semis at the fort too. The twelve round robin games would be played
at Fort Edward Augustus, that's Green Bay…*

What'd he say, Birch? Did he get it? Did he like it?

He just said, "I'm listening." So I told him we want a bye into the round robin for the host North American teams—the U.S., Canada, Indigene Nation; that we'd want the field lengthened from a hundred ten yards to three-quarters of a mile, that the goals should be saplings planted eighteen feet apart instead of six and guarded in the Indian way, with two goalies. He kept listening, so I kept talking. We would allow only ash or hickory sticks, I said, nothing else. I have a stickmaker on the reservation, a friend…

Neil?

Archie Mellon interrupted me there, wanted to know if Neil— I didn't mention his name—would be able to make sticks for every player from every team. Weighing the risk-reward of the idea. "How many sticks would he have to make?" he wondered. Then he asked, "What about that, Drey?" But I jumped in before Drey could draw a breath. In for a dime, in for a dollar, Archie, I said. That'd be around four hundred sticks or so, which we would offer at no charge, though I'll have to run that by my friend before I commit.

Birch, I can't believe you said that! What's Neil gonna do if Archie says yes?

I don't know yet. I told him we'd use the ball-up our ancestors used instead of the face-off, and we'd play with wooden balls which a team could paint any color they like. We would lose the referees and relax the penalties, probably not call any unless someone was injured by a flagrant foul in which case you don't need the ref anyway. And since it is kind of self-policing in that way, I said, each side would play up to forty players, on the field, at all times.

Neil won't know whether to jump for joy or jump out a window! Four hundred sticks? My God, Birch!

Archie was bowled over, too, awe-struck. So I invited him up. *Come see for yourself*, I told him. *Come to the U.P. and see the fort, see the crosses being made*, said Parry Four Bears. He said he would.

He's definitely going to jump out the window. Birch, no charge?

Hey, I was on a roll, and it just came out, but that will have to play itself out. Drey argued from his knees. Lars Asferg overruled him to say that the European teams would support the Indigene Nation proposal and that the Indian presence is the heart and soul of the plan. *Archie*, Foss begged him, *please tell me you're not letting this go forward. They're conning you. Don't you see? It will ruin World Lacrosse and the game itself. Can you imagine the chaos with forty people on a team playing at some fort on some trail of tears or whatever? And I, for one, would never give up my titanium stick. I mean, come on, ash or hickory made to order by Birch's buddy for free. You can't make these guys play with toy sticks like that. And, oh, by the way, three quarters of a fucking mile*! Archie, though, was all full of tough love. "Drey," he said, "aren't you learning anything here? We've already taken their big game and squeezed it between our sidelines. Simplify the presentation by depicting the origins of the game. Maximize spectator participation by bringing in the tribes. Grow the sport itself with the new fan base. Get it? This could be a bonanza, forty-five, fifty million if we do it smart and get the right corporate sponsors. Do you see a downside there, Drey?"

Four hundred sticks for free.

Did you hear that, Marla? Millions!

There should be some left over to pay Neil then. You know who's going to help him, don't you? What about all the time it will take, and materials and fingers rubbed raw?

I told you that will have to get sorted out later. So anyway Parry raised his right index finger and said, *We would like to send our share of the proceeds to the poorest reservations. Also, some of our people may need help with their travel expenses.*

Birch, stop. Four hundred sticks for nothing? Everybody gets a piece of the action but the guy who will work the hardest. He'll have to have them ready by...

Okay, I wish I hadn't said anything! I screwed up, okay, you're right. He'd need a damn assembly line...

Yeah, named Marla and Neil.

I know! Marla, what can I tell you...

Tell me you'll be an Indian giver.

Listen, though. Archie said, "I want *SENE2* to come to *us*," and then, "What places would they be traveling from?"

Birch, this is a huge learning curve for an Aussie from the pacemaker world—Native lacrosse, a hundred tribes from all over the U.S., managing a championship like this his first time out and you throw baggattaway into the mix. He might need one of his pacemakers before this is over.

He might. But Parry explained to him: South Dakota, Oklahoma, Michigan and Ontario. Then I volunteered that *SENE2* might consider doing a piece on Neil, it'd be quite a story.

It sure will be. Do I get in on this fifteen minutes of fame, too?

Absolutely, honey. So, by now Drey was slumped in his chair, defeated, disgusted, nowhere to go.

Good!

"Where is your reservation exactly?" Archie asked me. You can ride back with me, I told him. A mere ten hour drive. But he's decided to fly out after he briefs the president of the WLC, I guess. In a few days he'll be here. Oh, then he asked about June Two, why that's so important since we'd be playing the tournament a month earlier than normal. *Which means*, I offered, *we could ride the coattails of the college tournament on Memorial day weekend.* He liked that. I told him about Bwon-diac, about the beginning of the end of the American Indian story, and that that is the reason our people will come out. "I'd come out, too," he said. "Does everybody here know that story? The one with lacrosse at the fort?" he wanted to know. The next morning garment bags and suitcases were piled up in the lobby for check out. Archie was hung-over. They had tipped a dozen bottles of single malt whisky in the hotel bar with Harald MacManus.

Talk about a captive audience.

Here's how it went. Nothing against Germany, of course, I started, but since Lars and Kovac opened the subject yesterday, imagine for a minute that it's 1943 and the Germans have conquered

Canada. They have their eyes set on the U.S. and come down the St. Lawrence Seaway, winning battle after battle with their superior weapons technology. They occupy all of the military bases in the Great Lakes area because of its strategic importance. They intend to control shipping lanes and supply points from Montreal to the Mississippi River and the American West and then to brainwash a suspicious native population in their racist ideology. There is no purchase, though, with the disgruntled natives and the issue develops to the point where General Eisenhower devises a plan to retake the bases. It will be a ruse of sport, coordinated attacks in nine Great Lakes cities. He invites the German commanders, who know nothing of baseball, to attend a grand spectacle of the American pastime on an open field near one of the bases. It is a game to be played between two of the region's best teams, and the contest is scheduled for April 20, Hitler's birthday. This will relax the minds of the German occupiers and give them something interesting about native culture to write home about to their hausfraus. Suppose they all come out in shirtsleeves on a glorious spring day, coolly confident in giving their occupation force a well-earned day off. They see players warming up, hitting balls, taking some infield practice, signing autographs for the thousands of fans who have begun to arrive. The smells of food and drink waft on the air, along with the public address announcer's voice which gives the starting lineups for, let's say, the Chicago White Sox and the Detroit Tigers. Adoring fans bring the conquerors copious quantities of their favorite drink, beer. Beautiful women encourage them to place a friendly bet on the outcome of the match. Assured by

Eisenhower of a close game, the occupation force feels the gritty tension of a sports rivalry, a grudge match that goes back decades. They hardly notice that it is Bat Day and that each spectator has been given a bat just to celebrate the offensive-minded character of baseball. The game is exhilarating and the score is tied 3-3 at the seventh inning stretch. This is Eisenhower's signal moment for attack. The occupation force is called to the infield to be honored by the natives and then it happens. To the soaring strains of God Bless America, those same spectators, who have now completely encircled the Germans, descend on them with their legions of baseball bats, mashing their skulls with white ash clubs and retaking the military base. Their jubilation is unmatched, but also short-lived as the Germans send reinforcements and retake the base in a matter of days. Eisenhower flees into the forest but in a fury Hitler himself hires a member of the St. Louis Cardinals to track and kill him, which feat is accomplished some years later. After putting down this final revolt, the Germans go on to a relatively uncontested annexation of the continent, relocating ethnic groups into isolated clusters around the country. They want the melting pot to cool back into its original ingredients. Plots of land are established for each group to maintain a trace of its identity but they are subject to the laws of Germany now. Imagine that German culture grows up and matures in this New World, enveloping what was once American culture and smothering it completely. Imagine that the country is now called New Germany and that its reign has continued for two hundred forty-six years.

Oh, my God, Birch.

The message was received loud and clear. Gruesome thought, isn't it? I summed up. Yet, this is our life. I have taken liberties with history to illustrate for you what happened to our civilization in 1763. Two Great Lakes tribes called the Saulk and the Chippewa staged a last-gasp game of baggattaway to reclaim their sinking world. With a sense of purpose only quarry knows, they entertained their captors with a false ball match that appeared perfectly normal to the English force until a warrior named Makoons launched a catapult shot off the outheld stick of a teammate named Bad Sky who had received a long, downfield pass form a six-foot-ten inch Indian named Weniway, who was painted in the smudged black of charcoal and bear fat from head to toe except for the white circles around his two eyes. The vermilion ball caromed off the right door of the fort's landgate and into the trading area. As the Indian players ran after the loose ball, their women swapped weapons for lacrosse sticks and they were turned into warriors …

Birch, that's really pretty good. Did it sell?

Drey Foss didn't think so. He jumped to his feet and screamed, *So, finally we have it! Vengeance. It's about vengeance, your idea, not some innocent and pious reenactment, but blood lust for the loss of your lands. That's it, isn't it, Birch? As much as you say you're over it, you want to cut our hearts out, don't you?*

I hate him. What did you say?

That we are so far beyond the need for vengeance that we are in danger of forgetting who we are. We must remember! Will you deny us that last wish? *So*, he appealed to the rest of the Council, *we*

dub 2010 the Year of Baggattaway and we get all teary-eyed over
what happened in colonial times and walk hand-in-hand down
Memory Lane with a bunch of dour, forlorn Indians and we screw it
up for the rest of us and have to wait another four years to set things
right again?

What does this guy have up his ass, Birch?

Then suddenly—"Meeting adjourned!" Archie yelled,
surprised the hell out of everybody.

The poor clueless foreign coaches.

"I'm adjourning the meeting," he repeated. "This is going
nowhere. Maybe a little dose of good old-fashioned fascism will be
just what the doctor ordered for us, too. I want to hear from you guys.
Write me, call me, email me, but talk to me somehow. I'll be in
touch." And that was that. Talk about a sour ending to a meeting.
Drey Foss and Russell Pape both gave me the finger as they stormed
out of the room. We all left Hull knowing two things: a whole bunch
of lobbying was going to take place behind the scenes for the next few
weeks, and Archie Mellon was coming to Anishinaabewaki.

Wow, so we wait.

We wait. Oh, last thing. Andrew Sophie asked me if I was
happy now, dripping with sarcasm as he shoved one of the promo
posters he had printed up for the championships in my face. *Take as*
many as you want, Birch, old pal, he said. *Take hundreds if you want,*
because we won't be needing them anymore, will we? Look, he said,
pointing, *London, Ontario, July 7-16, 2010.* I tossed the bunch of

them in the milk truck, but I only need the one for Tommy and his meat-eating patrons.

And if he hangs that pearl before those swine at his bar, will it make a difference? She'd give me a hug and decide that I'd had a long four days, that she could sweat me about Neil and the four hundred later.

I would have to be careful to shroud this fact from her, though, my final act before leaving Hull: I walked to the jeweler's and put her diamond ring on layaway, hopped in the milk truck and drove back on Route 17.

Walk On, Louis Charlevoix

You pick out a diamond ring. You point your vintage
Virkanen milk truck at the western horizon and you drive in the
luxury of timelessness, spurred in the recollection of what just
happened around the mahogany clock table and what was promised
from it, passing the spot on the river where you were shot to the
moon, vacantly a sesame stick now and then and a swallow of iced
tea, marshaling the cascade of events and statements and declarations
and bravado and lies and hope into a pleasing narrative for your wife
with the ears of a priest, and, oh, yes, calculating the omission of your
own missteps. But she's not always just sitting there waiting for you
to arrive and recount your glories. She is sometimes overtaken by
even bigger events much closer to home, occurrences outside your
own bitty, quantum world. Marla had wanted to be there for me, I
knew, but she'd had her hands full in the small front room of my
parents' house where a family had suffered in my four-day absence,
where an aanimendam father wearing a green and white flannel shirt
and a gray cardigan sweater had fallen face down into his beet garden,
apparently as if something had tugged him into the bed, while digging
up his ripening baggattaway balls. Louis Charlevoix was dead before
his only son could turn back the clock like he promised he would.

"Marla?" I called. She'd left me a note. *Birch, You better come
right away.* She'd signed it with an 'M' inside a heart. I ran for my
father's front door. I watched her burst into tears in the doorway, and I

knew. The blood drained out of my head. I stumbled around to the skinny side yard my mother stares at and to the back where his beet garden was brimming with life. "No," I said when Marla threw her arms around my shoulders.

"Minerva found him, Birch. He was out here working in the garden. She saw him from the kitchen window; he fell flat on his face into the dirt and beets. She said the earth took him back."

She could not answer my angry and pointless questions, only reach for her scar. "Marla, you didn't call me?"

"Oh, Birch, it was all so sudden, and I didn't want to come between you and your dream. I thought about it every minute. It just happened yesterday morning, and we've been running around, and I thought the last thing you'd want to know on a ten-hour drive through the middle of nowhere was that your father had just died."

No harm, no foul my moonless woman. "Was it…?"

"We're guessing. Your mother says this or that, and Minerva says nothing. The way he just fell forward, I thought it might have been a stroke. The saddest thing is that it's ninety-five degrees in the shade and he was out here in his damn gray cardigan and flannel shirt on, happy as a clam, weeding his beets. Maybe he just got too hot, Birch."

I got a strong hug from teary Minerva who could not look me in the eye, a weak one from my bobbing mother. She barely put her arms around me, she was confused but under control.

"Where is he?" I asked.

Marla was the only one who could answer. "Birch, Jimmy Blackbird..." She had to compose herself. "Jimmy called a funeral director friend of his in the Soo. I forget his name. He's in a vault there, Louis, not Jimmy or the funeral guy, but this is the part...Jimmy is collecting money for the funeral..."

There was no stash under the mattress for this, no prepaid funeral expenses held in interest-bearing CD's or term life insurance policy, just one of those things that gets organized in the moment. But, I realized, there was a stash. The ring. I could repay Jimmy with my savings.

"Minerva and I had to write the obituary. She's really hurting, Birch. Hasn't said a word in almost two days, since she found him and dragged him inside."

"Minerva dragged him inside? My father's in a vault? What's Jimmy doing?"

"He's spent the last twelve hours contacting your father's old friends, employers, lacrosse buddies from eons ago. He's taking donations from the Sandusky brothers, the sugar farmers, anyone that Louis worked with."

"Jimmy."

"He says he hopes to get enough for a cremation and a simple urn for the ashes. He said he'll make up the difference between whatever he collects and the actual cost. Says it's the least the Three Fires Casino can do for one of the family like Louis Charlevoix."

"Jimmy."

"Oh, and I put the word out to the team through Obie and Jerome. They're all pitching in, too. They want you to know how sorry they are, and if they can do anything, just…oh, Birch, I'm so sorry." Her tear-stained face folded up again. Naanganikwe in mourning. "They'll all be at the funeral."

"How was your trip, Birch?" asked my mother. "Lost a little weight, ain't you? Anybody hungry or thirsty?" She shuffled into the kitchen mumbling about the heat.

I sat down in his bentwood rocker and thought about the seam between the water and the sky, the hissing sound that evaporates you up and out of this world in which a man is but an occasional apparition condensed from Neil's great ether. And about the hole of the mitèwin that sucks you up into the Chippewa land of stars that spins in a spiral tunnel around the Earth. No, but I know what you saw, Louis Charlevoix, my very aanimendam father. I know what you saw with your terrible eyesight as you weeded that last beet. As your face met the soil, you saw an irresistible ninety foot black walnut, and you climbed to the highest branch that would support you and then you went up one more and you roped yourself facing west to its highest branch where you settled in for all eternity to watch the gods fight over you, those fertile beet garden rows your own Pearly Gates.

Marla crouched down in front of me and asked about Hull, her brown eyes two wet smiles, not yet realizing I had already told her everything in the milk truck on the way home.

Jimmy Blackbird suddenly hopped the stoop, shaded his face and peeked in the front door screen. "Hey, Birch. Marla."

"Jimmy!" I cried out and bear-hugged him. "Thanks. Marla told me."

"Birch, you know it's nothing. We all loved the guy. We're sorry to lose him. Listen…"

My mother came in from the kitchen with a plateful of fry bread and a dish of boiled greens with beets sliced over the top. "Oh, hi, Jimmy," she said. "Hungry or thirsty? Birch?"

Jimmy had rounded up a few thousand dollars, enough to pay for a cremation, and he kindly offered the casino for the wake. Who were we to look such a gift horse in the face?

Minerva broke her silence. "Can you get him cremated right away so we can have the ashes? Can you let people know that fast? Can you do that for us, Jimmy Blackbird?"

"Jesus, missy," my mother said. "Aren't you rushing it a little? Show some respect for the dead. Let's do the four days first, maybe, then have the party."

We would pick and choose in the moment as we endured this trial, which of the old ways and which of the new ways to favor in commemoration of my father. But the timing of things was strictly up to Edina, and if she wanted four days for the sake of the old ways, then she would have them. After that, the mourners would party.

"Just saying, the wake and the party are the same thing," my sister insisted.

Jimmy turned to my mother. "If it's okay with you, Louise. I could display the urn in the ballroom upstairs where people can pay their respects, and then, if the weather cooperates, we'll have some refreshments down in the parking lot. You think Louis would approve? Minerva," he said with a flourish, "consider it done."

Baa Maa Pii, we hugged Jimmy good-bye.

"Jimmy," my mother yelled after him, "as long as it's gonna be a two-fer, could you maybe spike some of them refreshments out there in the parking lot?"

"Has anybody told Neil yet?" If anyone answered I don't remember it. My system was shot, and I was minutes away from what Archie Mellon might call organic sleep. And the next minute Archie himself called from the road to tell me he was already halfway from Detroit airport to Anishinaabewaki. He had decided to meet Neil and see the fort before briefing his boss about Hull.

At the edge of awareness, I told Marla.

"Let's get you home," she said.

I was in a steep descent when she undressed me. If she thereafter took her bawdy pleasure with me, I was not aware of it nor do I now have any recollection of it. I do recall that I dreamed thick as a jungle, wet as a monsoon, stark and real. I dreamed that I was a teenager, and so were Marla and Neil, that the three of us teenagers had somehow killed my father and that we determined his Path of Souls would run through the tomb of the Hiawatha. We took St. Anne and went into the forest and got high, drinking and smoking, built a fire, cooked some marshmallows, dipped them in my father's open thorax and swapped ideas on how best to dispose of the body. *We could do an old-time air burial*, said Neil, *and lay him out on an outcropping, shake some tobacco all around and let the birds have at him.* I said *no we should do a ground burial in the darkest glade of the Hiawatha where the manidos would never find him. Louis would wear the flannel shirt and sweater, and the frogs in his forearms would finally have their way with the rest of him, beating the worms to the punch, and, nourished, bounce to another man's skin.* Marla said *no, no, no, the Hiawatha is not a tomb but a womb, we should stand him up straight in a hollowed out tree trunk, bear him on our shoulders to Tahquamenon Falls and ship him over the edge, just to give him a shot at rebirth in the next hell.*

St. Anne then spoke human, in Indigene meter.

Louis Charlevoix is not dead.

He is merely in transition.

Tipi knows the way to guide him

On the Path of Souls, don't worry.

Neil turned into a bear and clawed Naanganikwe until she bled blood that spurted from her in the shape of billowy yellow crescents. We left her and St. Anne, licking her wounds, and proceeded to do pretty much what she had suggested anyway. We carried Louis's corpse to the spot where we had buried Neil's grandfather so long ago. Neil pointed at a birch tree and it fell, stripped the bark, pulled up a spruce root that had no end to it, lashed things together at such a speed I couldn't follow it and poured holy water on it, presto, instant birch bark canoe. Smiling like a magician, he produced a lacrosse stick from his hip that changed shapes when he cradled it—from the bent ash stick into a Chippewa warrior, like a hologram, back and forth, one side glistened the other side hissed, over and over until not only did I lose control of my eyes, spinning around helter-skelter in my head, but I drooled like an animal. *This will be Louis's paddle,* said Neil. We went to the falls and threw the canoe over, Louis, his dog Tipi, wearing sunglasses, and the lacrosse stick warrior paddle, frolicking at the cusp, balancing against gravity for the longest moment, then falling prow first into the river. I heard Marla moan. I went back to the spot and tied a spruce root love knot around her left ring finger. She came to life like a goddess reborn, threw me down and straddled me, shook her hips over me and extracted whatever it was she needed. She growled at Neil and said, *get the body back, bring it to me.* He retrieved it from the river and returned. *Almost,* Naanganikwe shouted, *there must be turnips and there must be fire!* So we performed the same rite all over again except this time before we shoved the canoe over Tahquamenon Falls we dumped a burlap bag of fresh turnips in, set fire to it and my father went off in a blaze of glory onto the Path of Souls to wander for the allotted four days.

I must have been calling out in my dream. When she woke me I was sweating. It felt like the middle of the night. She smoothed my hair back. Then she got up, walked to our dresser where we keep a bottle of Jack Daniels and two cut-crystal glasses on a lace doily. We sipped while I tried to make sense of the dream to her. She laughed, furrowed her brow, got disgusted, laughed again. We clinked our glasses and knocked back the last of the drink. She turned out the light and I thought she had left the room, put off by my dream. Then, like a shot, she was on top of me, naked and silky. It stood me up right away. It was as if my crazy dream had become real. Her knees were splayed out a yard apart over me, wide open, trying to choke herself on me. I did not have to do anything. I was not supposed to do anything. In the dark I saw two slashes of red, dangling and smiling. One was Minavivana's vermilion turtle that she has never taken off her neck since the night of the invasion, the other was her shiny red smiling scar of whose genesis I am still ignorant. It was blood-stained, vermilion love she pushed on me, into me, a new love that spat at every wisdom, that hurt it was so finished. The Great Turtle carrying my heavy goddamn world on its back, that's who she is. The womb of my moonless woman was speaking to me, that was the point, showing me that emptiness has a heart in it, a big, beating heart.

The next thing I knew it was morning and she was standing fresh and showered above me.

"So what happened in Hull," she smiled.

Jimmy had some serious ground to cover. He assembled a small crew at the casino who pumped out dozens of rainbow-colored telephone pole signs: *Wake for Louis Charlevoix to be held at the Three Fires Casino on August 1, 2009 at 12:00 p.m. If you knew Louis or would like to share your condolences with the family, you are welcome. Smart casual dress preferred.* He and a small army posted the signs around the reservation and along the trail of tears Lockside.

Jimmy met Marla and me at the door of the briskly air-conditioned ballroom and pointed to the mantle of the fireplace as the best spot for the urn. I set my father's ashes and adjusted the handles that made him look a little like a trophy. In the cordoned-off parking lot, Jimmy had people setting up hors d'oeuvres and a bar. My mother would kiss him for it. He walked me over to the window. "Might be a pop-up thunderstorm today," he said.

"Look, Jimmy, I've got some cash…"

Jimmy turned and scooted off toward the double doors that were under a sudden attack from the outside. "Birch, I'll run you a tab," he said, waving off the offer.

I considered the trophy of my father's ashes as a wad of people was pushing through the French doors. My mother's bobbing head, Minerva in a blue dress with the two dogs, St. Anne Four and Tipi, they drifted en masse toward the mantle. Tipi strutted like she was on a fashion runway, sat back on her haunches on the hearth, stared Sphinxlike into the distance. St. Anne broke loose and tore around the room, bumping table legs and human ones, threatening the delicacy of the moment and the knees of all the guests. Jimmy finally corralled her and carried her over to stand guard with Tipi. She saw she had no choice but to accept this temporary muting of her personality, and it made for a bizarre little crypt scene, canine gargoyles guarding the remains.

"I hope Neil appreciates I gave both the dogs a bath and trimmed their claws and brushed them, and I hope he did the same for himself," said Minerva confidentially to Marla and me. This was a lot of words for my sister. It was our father's wake, though, and she was resolutely present. She floated over to talk to Jimmy who had posted himself at the double doors in a vain attempt to try to sluice the flows of traffic. A slew of neighbors from the rez appeared. Good friends like Russell and Penny, with their two grown children and spouses and six grandchildren in tow, offered their sympathies as their young ones broke for the dogs; neighborhood friends, Rich and Vern and Kenny and lots more, guys who had stood by Neil and me so many times in our high school skirmishes against The King, they stood by us in this hour too. My old high school girlfriend, Laurel, came in with her husband and three teenage children, blowing a kiss and a sad face. The only kids here, it struck me, would be Chippewa kids. There had to be fifteen or twenty of them already, from babes-in-arms to toddlers to teenagers. There were families from Sugar Island who knew Louis, and some Ontario Anishinaabek who had made the trip over his International Bridge.

With a grand flourish, Neil arrived, brushed Jimmy imperiously, had Minerva remove his headdress and made a genteel bow to the crowd from the waist. To applause and laughter, he pirouetted like an Indian dandy. He had outdone himself for Louis's wake. The pipe tomahawk swung on the wide belt and tracked like a loose dagger down the outside of his legging; a leather pouch of tobacco and ten or so tubed Montecristos hung around his throat like metal sharks' teeth, so that he could shake his head and click like crickets. His body painting was not quite solemn, vivid reds, blacks and yellows arranged in semicircles and straight and jagged lines like the peace van itself. He had splashed Aqua Velva over the bear fat and charcoal and created a dizzying rainbow of odors about himself. He had put on the Big Indian for the family, and he also played drum major for my father's wake because yet another parade of people followed him through the doors, and Jimmy was once again submerged in it. Obie and Jerome and the entire Indigene Nation lacrosse team filed in (but who could be sure in such a mob scene?), a Methodist minister whose name I couldn't remember. What a crowd Jimmy's pastel posters had fetched out to the Three Fires Casino! Everyone dressed to the nines for it, too. My stallions, hair brushed, shirts tucked in for the most part, decent shoes and they were even wearing socks. The throng pressed steadily into the hearth, drawn by Louis's ashes. The children were chasing St. Anne, cornering her, petting her, making her bark, and the noise was deafening. St. Anne tried to hold her ground, got that look about her that said overload might be near. Tipi was still a Sphinx.

"Are there drinks? Can we get a stiff one in honor of Louis?" The community salve was about to flow. Next person past Jimmy was Jan Zwiebel—my jaw must have dropped a foot, and I walked over to shake her hand. "It was hot pink, Birch. Someone put up a hot pink poster at the fort announcing the wake, and I was more than glad to come because I have some news." Tall tall Russell Phaneuf tapped me on the shoulder, smiled and handed me an Irish whisky. I glimpsed Marla for a second, surrounded, talking a mile a minute. She blew me a kiss, too. The room was threatening to burst its sides when a new round of people streamed in past Jimmy. "Mr. Lavoie! Mr. Lavoie!" The brothers who own the maple sugar farm where my father worked so many sap runs came right over, shook my hand, told me he'd be missed. "Are you Birch," asked a coarse voice behind me. It was Mr. Sandusky from the construction firm that had gambled on the work ethic of the Chippewa. "Your father was a great guy. I swear to God, to this day I don't know how he got those damn frogs in his forearms. Wished I didn't have to let him go. He was a fine man. A sense of humor and a sense of hard work. A brother." I turned around and bumped directly into the one boss my father and I had in common, old Matti Virkanen. He took my right hand and folded it into both of his and looked me in the eye, and there was so much between Louis and him that he couldn't bring himself to say even a single word. As he pivoted into the people behind him, though, he found his tongue and said he wished Louis hadn't had to go to that other peninsula back in 1950. "Bad for business," he grimaced. I was corralled by Chippewa friends who had worked with him in the early days of the Three Fires; they took both my hands and shook their heads from side to side. "Jesus," I said out loud as Tommy McKeon, Mickey Blake and Thaddeus Sokolowski walked in from the trail of tears. Jimmy had started to close the doors behind what he supposed must be the final mourners, Marla's daughter Sheila, who was nervously adjusting her black dress, and a very anxious Sandrine, Marla's mother, but then suddenly he threw them open again for a guy he was questioning but whose face I couldn't see. Jimmy reached out his right hand to whoever it was and offered his broadest customer service smile and in walked Archie Mellon in a tie and dark suit, looking every bit the part of the sharp, retired international pacemaker executive doing his golden-years philanthropy in the mission of an orphaned Native game. Elias Lane took my empty glass and replaced it with a Jack Daniels. I wanted to get to Neil but the space between us was so thick with people. He was crouched at the fireplace delivering a lecture to St. Anne about something as he primped and fussed over her. I mean, there was plenty to talk about with him. He didn't know I'd put a ring on layaway in Hull; nor that he would be steaming some serious ash and hickory for the four hundred plus sticks—he would want the Reader's Digest version of the meeting in Hull; he didn't know he was about to meet Archie Mellon; there was my vision quest on the Ottawa River, the y-scale…It wasn't until Roy LeRoi slipped in the unguarded doors that Neil made his way over to me. "Riffraff stage left, Indian. The fox is in the henhouse. Gonna watch him like a hawk."

"How does this bastard have the nerve to show up at my father's wake?"

"Slag from the trail of tears. Dry rot. But like it or not, he's a part of us, Birchwalker."

"The Bone Digger? Nuh-uh, Neil. Not me."

"So, we must be strong today. I've lost my partner, Birchwalker. Who will make the vermilion balls now? I would like to take over the planting of the beets in his honor, and I believe I would like to say a few words to the guests about my friend Louis."

"Neil, I'll be right back," I said. I maneuvered over to Archie, glad-handing all the way. After all, he had come to my father's wake.

"Archie. You made it. Gimme a whistle?"

He jutted his jaw out, stuck his index finger and pinky in his mouth and fired out a shrill, two-syllable, arcing note that stopped countless conversations in mid-sentence.

"Hey, everyone, listen up!" shouted Minerva.

The assembly turned to Archie who indicated me with an upturned palm and a graceful step to the side. But it was Jimmy who took the floor.

"Boozhoo, everyone. Welcome. Why don't you folks who would like refreshments file out to the parking lot. I know it's hot and muggy out there, but I'm sure you understand. If you like, you are welcome to get a drink and return to the ballroom for a private communion with Louis. The Charlevoix family thanks you for coming and looks forward to greeting each one of you. Go ahead now, and thanks again."

The room gradually decompressed as the huge throng threaded out the French double doors for booze. Weather was coming. Thunderheads were forming, and even inside there was a sour smell on the air. Jan Zwiebel approached with a napkinful of cheese and crackers and a dewy tumbler of brown alcohol and ice cubes. "The dogs are perfect! That beagle's the one you boys throw into the water, isn't it? The one that chases Neil around the meadow and barks at the Straits? She's precious. And the other one! Ohh! So princely. And the way they guard the urn is just fantastic! What are their names?"

"The prince is Tipi, my father's dog; Neil's beagle is St. Anne." I envisioned Tipi stoically going over Tahquamenon Falls in my dream.

"I am so sorry about your father. I didn't know him, of course, but...did you say St. Anne?"

"That's right. You'd know that. The church at the fort, St. Anne de Michilimackinac. Jan, thanks for coming today. What was it you wanted to tell me?"

"I guess you've been away a few days, right? Anyway, something's come up and I've spoken with Neil about it. Remember I told you on…Pontiac-Looking-Down Day…are you impressed I remembered, Birch?...I told you I wanted you two to do a school assembly?"

Oh, no.

"Well, it's all set. You and Neil are booked to give the assembly on the first Friday of the school year. That's Friday, September 8. I hope you can get the morning off. My daughter goes to Soo Elementary, you see, so I had a little talk about the two of you with the principal and she said, what do they do? So I told her you do this reenactment every June 2 and explained everything… everything, Birch," she said to reassure me that the more graphic bits had in no way been skirted. "And the principal pulls out her appointment calendar and says, 'Do you think they could do June 2 on September 8?' It was the lacrosse thing and the Indian thing that she really liked. I guess her son plays for Soo High or something, and she's into kids getting exercise, you know?"

I began to look around for Neil.

"I had no idea how to contact you two," she continued excitedly. "Then I saw Neil's picture in the *Soo News*. I'd recognize those legs anywhere."

I must have looked surprised.

"Oh, yeah, it was front page for your famous friend and St. Anne. She was in the picture, too. So I got his number and called him and invited him to come in to school for an interview with the principal."

"Here he is now," I said to Neil as he entered the conversation. "Seems you've been a busy Indian while I was gone."

Neil just blinked at me, and he didn't even acknowledge Jan.

"Were you going to tell me about September 8? And your new-found fame?"

"When the time was right, Birchwalker."

"Hey, Neil," said Jan like a smitten schoolgirl. "I'll leave you two to talk. Stay in touch now. Bye. And I'm sorry, Birch, for your loss."

After she left, Neil looked right at me and said, "What's the big deal? We teach little kids about the lacrosse deception, sing a few songs, tell a legend or two, have a lacrosse play-around and schmooze with Jan and her principal friend for a thousand dollars."

"Apiece?"

"Split two ways, Birchwalker, two ways. Listen, let's go have a drink," he said, ignoring the Jack Daniels in my hand and grabbing my father's ashes from the mantelpiece. He motioned to the two gargoyles that they should follow. A blast of thick hot air hit us as we filed out of the building. Jimmy had organized a flute and tom-tom, and it didn't match up with the circus tent mood of noise and conversation. The dogs and kids ran at one another. Neil set Louis's ashes on a serving table, the podium, no doubt, for his talk later. You could just hear distant rumbles of thunder over all the hoopla. Tommy McKeon found me. He looked like the bouncer Jimmy should have hired for this wake-slash-walking on. I saw Marla chatting with Archie Mellon. Tommy slid a new drink into my hand.

"Birch? What the hell is that evil Neil's wearing around his neck? *Pure* evil! Not exactly GQ cover material, that's for damn sure. Montecristo cigar tubes, for crissake, which reminds me. Meant to thank you for that Montecristo, Birch. And how was the trip? I am truly sorry about your dad. Did he, um, die while you were gone?"

"Yeah, Tommy, it's been tough on the family. But Jimmy's been unbelievable."

"Jesus, I loved the dogs and the urn upstairs." A momentary bolt of sunshine escaped the thunderhead, and it began to spit rain. "We're gonna get hit big time, Birch."

We craned our necks to the black and white towers. Lightning crackles and thunder growls inside the cloudbanks. "The trip was great. I heard you met Archie."

"Yeah, I did, but first things first. Did you get me a poster?"

"Well, sort of, Tommy. I got you a ton of them, but they're unusable."

"What do you mean?"

"Well, the WLC might be changing the venue and the dates."

He slapped me on the back. "Yeah, Archie made reference to some kind of change in the rules, like Indian-style? Tell me you talked them into Indian rules."

"Okay, then, Tommy, I did. I made my case for Indian rules and I'm hopeful."

"But the fat lady ain't sung yet, right?"

"I won't tell Archie you said that."

"This is really turning out great, Birch. I'll still use those old posters, you know, till you get me new ones. At least it's something. Hey, Birch, do you need to be full-blooded to play on your team?"

I aimed my face at him. "Well, you know, blood isn't the only test for…why? You got a ringer for me?"

"Hey, you know, what can I say, I'm always looking out for you, Birch. There's this guy who hangs out at the bar lately, older kid, and I guess he is one hell of a lacrosse player. They say he's got an incredible stick from both sides and is supposed to have some kind of hot-shit air-walk shot where he makes a run from behind the net—flying over the defense and twisting his torso through it in mid-air—then fires over-the-shoulder into the weakside high corner. One slippery bastard, they say. Pascal, Pascal Lefebvre. He's a CC, I guess. He's fast, too, Canada Chippewa and fast. You might want to keep him in mind for your roster if somebody gets hurt. Plus they say he can do a y-scale," Tommy added flexing his eyebrows.

"Who's the *they* you keep referring to, Tommy? Who told you about him?"

Tommy became a little agitated, looking around. "Roy, I guess. Your fucking good friend Roy. He wanted me to pass it on to you. 'No sweat,' I tell him, Birch, 'if he's that good Birch has to know about him.' For the team, you know?"

"Right, Tommy. You're looking around like he might be here."

"Who, Roy?"

"No, I know he's here. Pascal."

"You talking about my boy Pascal?" said The King himself, bumping me from behind like St. Anne would do and slurring his words badly.

"Yeah. I want to see him do the y-scale."

Roy pushed Tommy out of the way to square up to me. "So, you want to give him an audition, huh, Indian? You want to check out my boy? Pascal!" he yelled out, never taking his eyes off me. His loud mouth and swagger had already drawn a good portion of the crowd. Under the awning people were counting the seconds between flashes of lightning and cracks of thunder.

Pascal Lefebvre sidestepped his way through the crowd with ease, a wiry twenty-eight year old physique, at least six-feet two inches tall, a hundred ninety pounds, a black braid down the middle of his back like an Indian, nimble and quick, silky and aloof. He was wearing a jogging suit and sneakers at my father's wake. I knew with a glance he was stronger than he looked. He had the undisposed energy of a guy just waiting for a fight to break out, and that's how I knew I'd seen him—he was one of The King's new Frenchy recruits wearing their tuques at the barberpole. It was easy to picture him on the lacrosse field, cradling a ball on the full run down the sideline. With the exception of Obie or Elias, I didn't have one like him. He was, like Tommy says, Canada Chippewa, and I wondered if I was being set up through an unwitting Tommy McKeon for a poaching violation involving a player who rightly belonged to Andrew Sophie.

"Go ahead," Roy urged him. "Do a y-scale for the nice coach here."

With a bitter smile, Pascal lifted his right knee, cupped the ankle and effortlessly elevated it over his shoulder, held it for a second, then pushed it up over his head until it was almost perpendicular to the floor. The standing split. His face had reddened, but he was still smiling. He held his body perfectly still as he maintained the position for ten, twelve seconds.

"Wow!" yelled Tommy and he broke into sustained, enthusiastic and solitary applause.

Roy strutted around in a small circle like a rooster at dawn. "What do you think, coach? Got room on your Indigene Nation team for a talent like that?" He stuttered like a drunk. Fat raindrops had chased all but Pascal and Vern and a few of my other buddies to the cover of the awning. Minerva rescued my father's urn and led Tipi inside, but St. Anne stayed with Neil and me and our friends from Pope County, and, lo and behold, we had a rematch. The same old battle lines were drawn by the same old contestants as thirty years ago when we'd suckered Roy and his yes men into the dark Hiawatha. Locked in a prefight staredown, we all took pains not to look affected by the gusts that now pushed the rain sideways and made us sway on the very feet through which we were even able to record the rumbling thunder. The air smelled like fire.

"Now, why would I take a kid from Canada for my Indigene Nation team?" I asked. "As I see it, the kid's already got two strikes against him. One, that tricky little thing called citizenship, and two, he's *your* boy, Roy." I leaned into him.

"Hey," he said right back at me, "Canadian or no, he's an Injun, ain't he? Or do you say In-di-*gene*? Besides, ain't it up to him where he wants to play?"

"Are you still recruiting on the rez, Roy? What are you doing at my father's funeral?" I had begun to back him up on the macadam. The rain was digging pockets of gasoline out of the asphalt. In no condition to fight, Roy could only laugh my taunt away and retreat. Neil and our friends were all walking him back with me, showing him to the far end of the parking lot. He finally saw Neil.

"Well, lookie here, if it ain't my good friend, Neil. All dressed up in cigar tubes and sport-ing the pipe tomahawk, I see. Are you good and high, Injun? High on the evil weed?"

Neil rattled the cigar tubes at him, puts a hex on Roy LeRoi.

"You still haven't answered my question, Bone Digger. Where do you get off coming to my father's ceremony?" With that, I lost what little composure I had and hauled off and cold-cocked The King, put him on the asphalt with a shot to his left eye that hurt my hand probably as much as it had his face. We were all standing over him, we gave him a silent eight-count in the eye of the storm. He slipped several times coming to his feet, and no hand was offered. But Roy was jawboning all the way up, in grunts, laughing too. "You still have not answered my question. Who the fuck do you think you are coming to my father's wake and insulting my people? Tell me!" I screamed.

Roy rubbed his cheekbone, he was still laughing. "You wanna know why I hate you goddamn Injuns?"

"How do you hate for so long?"

"Oh, you intrigue me so! First off, my tax dollars support your ass. But overall I hate you cuz you're dead men walking. You stink. You stink like death. Yet you try to schmooze your way in, come and go where you like, hang with your betters, but you have to go back to your fucking prefab coffins, embalm yourselves with fucking weed and make like you ain't already face-up dead. I just wanna put the final nail in the coffin, put you out of your misery. And now you want to play lacrosse by dead man's rules. Look, I want you rotten apples out of the barrel. Pontiac, my ass! Michilimackinac, my ass! Indigene Nation, my ass! There shouldn't even be no separate team. There's already Team USA. Let's see *your* boys make *that* team."

My mother pushed her way through the crowd. Her brow was creased. Her face was red. "I told you so!" she yelled at me. "Do what you got to do."

The storm blew over, and the guests dared to file out into the parking lot again, stepping tentatively to ringside, where waterlogged fighters were still taking their measure of one another.
I felt my jaw clench so that the words were meted out syllable by syllable. "If you don't think we even deserve our own team, why are you giving me Pascal?"

"Ooooh, nosy tonight, ain't ya?"

His left eye was swelling up. He pushed back on my chest. "Then put this one in your buddy's pipe and smoke it: he's my son, asshole. Let's just say he has a kind heart; he wants to play for the underdog, see, wants to make your sorry team into a winner."

"Get him the hell outta here," I said to one of Jimmy's security guards who had already come to do just that. I could not take him literally. It was a bad and cruel joke beyond all possibility that Roy LeRoi, Indian hater supreme, could ever have slept with a Chippewa woman. Ever. As he was being ejected from the proceedings, I saw him catch Pascal's attention, aim his jaw at Neil, signal with his eyes at something.

The crowd converged on us. Sheila came over to check on Neil. "You okay, Uncle Longbow?" At thirty-one years of age she was still his adopted niece. She and Neil had history. They were confidants and, going all the way back to those weekends she spent on the rez during her junior high school years, fellow pullers at the tomahawk pipe. She was still tugging at her hips, looking like she'd been poured into a dress a size or two too small. The two of them stood there hugging. Sheila was a far cry from the cute little tyke who wound her fingers in her mother's hair during the invasion. By now she was divorced, childless and, into her own adulthood, beset by her unknown paternity—a lifelong detective game that had turned her into an early cynic about love. We all ached for her to find her father, to get a grasp at last on who she was, but we also feared she would just plain kill him for having the gall to conceive her in the first place. She worked as a school secretary and took online courses at Lake Superior

State. She had always fought weight, unlike her mother, and held this, along with other perceived injustices, against Marla. She resented her mother as much as she loved her, and it was this confusion that chased her to the peace van on her weekend visits, into Uncle Longbow's blameless great ether and also to Louis's beet garden, the only two men, the only two places, she knew how to love.

"Birch," she said tugging away, "I have to read a poem I wrote for Grandpa Louis. Not that I particularly crave the attention or anything. Don't make me explain, huh? I really want to get it over with, too. Do you mind if I go now? It's short and sweet, I promise you."

"It's a beautiful poem," Sandrine assured the white people.

"Go, Sheila," I said, climbing up on a chair. "Hey, listen! Louis's only grandchild has a word to say, a poem in his honor. She's Marla's daughter, Sheila. Bizaan, please." But the buzz continued until Archie cut loose with another piercing whistle that focused the crowd on her.

"Let's give the young lady a lead-in," said Jimmy and nodded to the flute and tom-tom players.

She corrected me, the picture of discomfort. "I'm his *adopted* grand*daughter*, and it's not in *honor* of Louis Charlevoix, it is *to* him." With a final tug at the dress, she began. The faces of the people were circles, pried open by our rumble in the thunderstorm, ready to finally bear witness to my father. "This is short, Grandpa, short but real," she started. She spoke from a wary heart. It was not the tender voice of the fifteen year-old grand-daughter I heard, but she knew to deliver her lament in trochaic tetrameter, the beat of Indigene song. Jimmy hushed the flute and tom-tom, and she read out into their hanging echoes.

"Aanimendam Grandpa Louis,
Tipi sits beside you coolly.
I will plant and pull your beets up,
Carve them into round vermilion.

Blissful parting, mournful hour
Body burned up, spirit walking
Linger with us, linger with us
Or, I beg you, take me with you."

Tears were cascading down her cheek by the end of the first line. At the finish, Neil raised his glass in praise, and Sheila blushed up the same way Marla does. Showered with warm applause, she managed only a brittle smile. She had physically and mentally overruled herself to perform his eulogy, that's how much it meant to her. I met her with a big hug, but she was already changing the subject, deflecting the unwanted attention with waves of her hand.

"So, you're famous," she said to Neil, dabbing her eyes. "Your picture on the front page of the *Soo News*." She knew exactly how much this would dig at him. I could only assist her in the effort.

"Yeah, so, what happened anyway? I'm out of town for four days and my friend has me doing a school assembly and he launches a show biz career."

Neil swayed from side to side.

With Sandrine at her side, Sheila lovingly rubbed salt in the wound. "Oh, let me tell you, Birch. It was a typical slow news day on the U.P. Some tourist lady saw him from the fort and snapped a couple pictures and sold them and her story to the damn rag we call the *Soo News*."

A small appendage of the crowd was drawn back to her.

"Yeah, this woman from Florida has a pet dachshund on a leash and she's visiting Colonial Michilimackinac, the fort? And she's looking out over the Straits, when she spots Uncle Longbow and St. Anne in his canoe, paddling around under Big Mac. She zooms in on them with her digital camera and shoots him planting his oar into the waves and spinning his canoe around, doing his Indian pirouette, right? But what really freaks her out is the sight of this Indian fellow in war paint who then threw his cute little beagle dog overboard. And then this other woman from the fort explained that that was once the Chippewa custom. Anyway the lady said *Over my dead body*, and she reported it to the police in Mackinaw City, surrendering her pictures as Exhibit One in the case of the tourist v. Uncle Longbow, and the local rag picked up the story on a slow news day as I say and ran it on the front page."

"Aren't they all slow? And look what it got you, Neil, back in the game with Jan Zwiebel," I winked at him.

"Hey," said Sheila, "That's her name! The one who was talking to the tourist lady. You got a girlfriend, Uncle Longbow?"

Neil was beyond anger, beyond embarrassment. He chose that moment to draw his tomahawk pipe from its belt and hold it up above the crowd, without a word, and it amazed me how quickly that gesture quieted them down. The Indigene Nation lacrosse team moved in as one around Neil, who continued to hold up the pipe and stare the crowd down with a scowl. Archie and Marla, standing on tiptoes to see, closed the five-deep circle around my aanimendam best friend. Jimmy and his bar guy distributed a final drink to everyone; whatever they'd been drowning their sorrows in all afternoon, they get one more courtesy of the Three Fires Casino.

It was Neil's audience now, and he knew just how to play to it. First, an extended silence while he detached the tubes and pouch from his neck, filled the bowl of the long tomahawk pipe with tobacco, tamped it down with a great sense of moment and lit it. This sent great billows of white-gray smoke out over his headdress into the departing thunderheads.

"Louise, we love you."

He had my mother already, red in the face and ponds in the eyes.

"A great tree has been felled in the Native American Fossil Forest. A mighty Marten bids farewell to his family, his clan, his people, and a Fish has come to bid him Baa Maa Pii. There has never been another like Louis Charlevoix to appear on the land between the sky and the great waters. From the loins of this beautiful man came

my best friend Birchwalker in 1957 and as perfect a creature as
Minerva Charlevoix. He is served in death as in life by Tipi, the proud
sentry you see now guarding his ashes. From his simple garden year
after year he pulled the finest beets which became red lacrosse balls in
his mind. At the end, Louis was said to be aanimendam, brain sick,
but whatever, okay? He loved a game so much that he thought of his
beets as its game balls. Did he love life any less? More! He always
had a dream, and he is living it now, without boundaries or
limitations. Isn't that what life is, hemming in, defining, limiting,
denying the soul its range, its running room? Louis and I had a joint
dream, you may know. The vermilion beets that were Louis
Charlevoix's baggataway balls are played by my sons, my
baggattaway sticks. I have a thousand of them already. They play
unceasingly with Louis's beets, running the edge of the earth from
dawn to dawn cradling for the pleasure of the gods."

He reached up to the clearing sky in supplication.

"Louis, tell us there is baggattaway in the Afterlife. Do we
play once more on the green meadows of Anishinaabewaki?"

He greeted the crowd again, eyeball to eyeball. "Of course,
we cannot hear Louis's answer. We can only look to our Chippewa
stories, that among them we may uncover a picture of the unspoiled
Indigene. Like, for instance, these lines, sung of Bwon-diac but
apropos today for Louis and the rest of us as well."

Neil hunched down, crouched forward, like he was telling a
story to children, letting them in on a secret. His voice was a hoarse
whisper, singsong, bound to trochees.

"Must they hunt him? Must they kill him,

Noble savage who defied them?

Must they vanquish every vestige

Of the unencumbered spirit?"

Righting himself, he raised his arms out in conclusion. "The unencumbered spirit. Please flatter me too with that epithet when I die. Such an unencumbered spirit was Louis Charlevoix; such noble savages are we all. Now I invite you to let his spirit fill you as you share the pipe of peace in his memory."

Neil drew once more on the pipe and passed it to Louise and Minerva and myself, Marla, the Indigene Nation players and on, in silence, to Jimmy who smiled at me first, to the Methodist minister and the Sugar Islanders and all of the celebrants of this requiem for my father, and finally into the hands of Jan Zwiebel and Archie Mellon.

Neil put his hand on my shoulder, "Birchwalker, get your Aussie and meet me at the peace van. I heard he wants to see how the sticks are made. So, let's make him one, dammit."

Baggattaway Barbecue

Listen: close your eyes, press the caves of your ear against the chambers of your white man's heart and you will be rewarded with a vision. Your breathing will cease and you lips will round. You have glimpsed them, the absorbed ones, below your awareness. Untold millions of them, upright fossils leaning from the waist, perched over the edge of a wan sunlight, just waiting for your words, ready to fly. Give them passage. From the cage of your heart to the expanse of your mind, I pray you, give them passage. The Great Nation That Never Was awaits the whispered affirmation of a lone Aussie, "Oh, I see," hopes beyond hope that the tandem of Birchwalker and Longbow can bend a retired pacemaker man with a keen eye for creative conflict to their vision, lead him to see and believe. That the fossils may breathe again, that their buried Game may be exhumed, that their hands may once again cradle and their feet may once again carry them downfield. This is the prayer I prayed.

After a quick shower and a change of clothes which took barely thirty minutes, Neil and Archie and I were nursing two fingers of Jack Daniels out of Neil's souvenir tumblers from the 2005 Sault Tribe Powwow. "This ain't the Conrad Hilton, you know," he told us as we ogled the dancing Indian figures etched into the glass. From the kitchen, we watched what was left of an orange sun sinking into the tops of the trees in his big side yard. Two blank sticks simmered in the steam hole of the outside fireplace. As Neil was showing no signs of relenting on the sloppy pours of whisky, we seemed committed to inebriation. Archie had shed his sports coat and tie, loosened his collar and seemed generally quite taken with us and the Upper Peninsula. Our Aussie guest was matching us drink for drink, busying himself at the moment with an inspection of Neil's sons hanging in their high-low pairs on the walls of the next room.

"These are beautifully made, Neil," he said in Australian. "Are these all Iroquois style sticks then? You know, they look like snowshoes, all lined up on the wall like that."

Neil didn't answer him. He just nodded to me and picked up the bottle as he walked outside. He's got three ragtag lawn chairs at the fireplace where he steams the wood for his sticks, comfy as a baggattaway barbecue. He'd just poured us another round when Archie too found his way down the rickety steps.

The setting sun had tinged the sky with salmons and pinks, a motion picture scored by the relentless drone of tree frogs and cicadas.

"Smells like honeysuckle," said Archie loudly.

"Let us show you how the art of Native stickmaking comes from way beyond the sunrise," said Neil moving toward the steam hole to tend his sons-to-be.

Then the unencumbered spirit in him suddenly lifted his throat to the twilight sky and sent out a series of animal kingdom sounds. He yowled, hooted, yelped like a bitch in spring rut and danced for the gray wolf. It infected St. Anne Four and set her spinning like a top again, chasing her tail in tight circles, collapsing lacrosse blanks like toothpicks and knocking a pyramid of stray sap buckets to the ground. Archie was duly nonchalant.

"Welcome to Neil's house," I told him over the chaos.

"I'm glad he wasn't with you in Hull."

And then this statement issued from Neil: "A man has only so many moons to give, Birchwalker. I will have to raise up a son to replace myself." Neil volunteered this intimacy as if Archie wasn't even there, yet, seemingly for his benefit. He could get maudlin, and I usually ignored him. But this time, even pickled in the vapors of grain alcohol, my hackles were raised to what he hadn't said.

"How many moons do you have to give?" I asked to call his bluff and make him stop talking crazy.

"Five," he answered, fully expecting the question. "Five full ones, Birchwalker."

"What are you talking about?" I said. Every so often, he just loved to cough up a mouthful of his life's venom for us to wallow in. It was no use probing him. He would only say that dying was the spirit wresting itself free from the bear trap of being alive. Like his eulogy of Louis. Then he toasted me through tree frogs and cicadas, "And another thing, Birchwalker, I'd much rather have a friend than a name."

"So, I take it there are different models of the Native stick, besides the Iroquois?"

Neil pulled three red scarves out of the sleeve of his buckskin and handed one to Archie and me. We followed his lead and tied them around our hair like dew rags, making like old time stickmakers. He turned the blank stick in the steam hole. "I will make you a stick to take to your president, one of Iroquois design. So, please notice that once the blank is done you already have the suggestion of a finished stick. But a suggestion is no son. It must cure for ten months before it can be carved and sanded and laced. Only then does it take on life. Only then are you in possession of a full creation, a living being."

"Like a good whisky, I suppose. Just how long have your people been doing this?" asked Archie.

"From beyond the sunrise," said Neil.

"No, but I mean, is it a hundred years, a thousand?"

Neil produced two sticks and held them out in front of Archie's eyes, banging them together like the jaws of an alligator. "Since there was fire. Since Wakayabide and Madjikiwis. Since Makoons and Bad Sky." Neil was drunk, venting, confusing Archie. I told Archie it might be four or five hundred years, nobody knows.

"All blanks are steamed in the fireplace to make the wood soft and supple. First, the Southeastern stick, the design of the Choctaw. The Choctaw still play the Creator's Game in their native lands in Mississippi and Alabama. They chose the shape of a teardrop for their racket head and a simple rawhide lacework, and each player holds two of these sticks during play, one in each hand. Long ago they brought their own refinement to the skill of the cradling run downfield—the bottom stick where the ball nests and the top one as a lid."

"So if baggattaway had been a religion, it would have had three branches, right? Iroquois, Choctaw and Great Lakes? That right?"

Neil laid the Choctaw sticks against the smoking fireplace and hoisted a Great Lakes stick high in the air so that its outline was cast in moonlight. His breath was heavy from ten feet away. "Well spoken, Archie Mellon. The Great Lakes stick is a thing of beauty in its own right. But, alas, the game is no longer played in Anishinaabewaki. Did you know this? No longer played! Our sons go east to the Finger Lakes to learn the game, to the Iroquois, but still the Anishinaabek are counted among Birchwalker's best players—Obie Crick and the goalie Jerome French; the twin attackmen Robbie and Trevor Fenton, Danny Brown."

"The Great Lakes branch has died off."

"But still capable of rebirth," Neil fired back. "And that's where you come in. If you allow the games to be played once more on our sacred lands we can bring baggattaway back to life here." Neil cleared his throat, shoved the stick under Archie's nose. "The Great Lakes design requires a level of skill in cradling and scooping and passing and catching that not every player reaches. Maybe that's why the branch lies broken. Yet, it is the stick played by the warrior-athletes of those Chippewa and Saulk tribes that retook Fort Michilimackinac. The very stick with which Makoons and Bad Sky performed their catapult shot."

"That's right. I remember now. Your story at the meeting, Birch. You're going to show me the fort, right?"

"You have to see the fort. It's the venue for the final round."

Neil dropped the Great Lakes stick in Archie's lap and then threw him a Southeastern stick as well, watching as Archie examined them in the dark, taking their weight and balance and lacing into his eye. "You might want to compare them to this one," he added, tossing him a white man's lax stick. "Lightweight metal and plastic, lots of whip, sexy, as they say. Of course, Indigene stickmakers have made concessions to the technology of the white man. We use their electric drills and sandpaper, their synthetic leathers instead of deerskin. But the traditional stick does not go away," he smiled, an index finger jabbing at his temple.

"Like boomerangs, I suppose. That sound crazy? I don't really know shit about it, just that the Aborigines bend and carve wood for sport. I think they use birch," he said, looking at me.

"All men are Aborigines," said Neil, meeting Archie's eyes in the dark. "It's just that some remember better than others."

"Show him how you bend the blanks before it gets too dark," I said.

Neil led us into the deep shadow of his white ash where he levered his wood into sons.

"We want you to approve the Iroquois stick for the tournament. We will unify the tribes around it."

"The aborigines have to stick together?" joked Archie.

"Damn straight they do. You are catching on, Archie Mellon. Look. Hickory is the wood of choice for the Iroquois stickmakers. The trees must be harvested after the sap run and after all the leaves are down. It must be dry and free of knots, and when you can tie a splinter of it into a knot, you know it is supple enough."

Neil walked right up to Archie, cradling a blank length of hickory like a middie on the run. The tree frogs and cicadas went still. Neil's eyes caught light from somewhere. "Nature provides us with what we need. You speak of the boomerang in your homeland. I can see this. I can see how your Aborigine, just like us American wood benders, puts his own blood in the art, breathes his own mind into it, places his own heart in it. This is why the boomerang can return to its maker, its thrower. It is bound to return. The human spirit of Native return is embedded in it, and this is the beauty of stickmaking, drunk or sober, I can assure you."

Archie breathed in a gulp of air and sat on it a moment, finally pushed it out. "Hey, what if I say I'm sold?" he asked with a big shrug of his shoulders. "Any fool can see that this is a labor of love and of spirit, a tradition from before the sunrise, that says it all to me. I'm just not so sure your WLC colleagues are of the same mind, Birch."

Neil ambled over to the fireplace and yelled back to Archie as he pulled a hickory shaft from the steam hole in the chimney. He was fully engaged in the tapered end of the shaft as he returned to the bending plate. "You see, Mr. Archie Mellon, like a mustang lassoed for the first time, the first bend is wildly resisted by even the supplest of wood and must be held in place by a metal wire."

Neil inserted the tapered end of the blank into the space between the lower knob and the flange, traveled gracefully down the handle and pulled it down into himself over the top knob with a sharp grunt. "This forms the crook. See how the bark is left in place around the outside of the crook?" He slipped a wire around the freshly-bent shaft. "The second and third bends are a piece of cake." He guided the crook into the stack, then pushed the handle up to convert the crook into a triangle. Then he reinserted the crook between the knobs up to a point about fifteen inches from the top of the triangle head and pushed the handle straight up, imparting the final bend at the throat of the stick.

Archie nodded. "So, I just bend the rest of them to my will, Neil, that what you're saying? Exert the full force of my office upon their small-thinking heads?"

"There you have it, Archie," he said proudly. "A son of baggattaway, a son of Anishina-abewaki. All that remains is to give him a heart, a mind, a soul. Let's go back inside where there's light and the bugs don't bite." He stooped over stiffly to pick up the whisky bottle.

But exhaustion had overtaken me, and the new ache of missing my father. Even Neil's ratty couch looked downright inviting, and I plopped down just to take a load off for a few minutes. Neil turned on the kitchen light. He and Archie were hunched over the bent hickory that he would now give a heart and mind and soul to, like a couple of lubed-up GYNs. I heard the clinking of glass and bottle and ice cubes and smelled whisky on the cooler night air that seeped into the double-wide. They were talking—or rather Neil was holding forth—in a kind of low, monotone, his teaching voice, instructing his Aussie student in the black arts of drawknife carving, sanding and lacing. I could no longer make out the tree frogs and cicadas over the whirr of an electric drill Neil was aiming at the throat of the racket. I did not know how I was still awake. There were strands of rawhide, catgut and clockcord draped over the edge of his table, on the floor. Fading into an overdue slumber, my last thought, Archie was fine, in good hands.

"STAND AND BREATHE, MY SON, ARISE NOW!"

Like a shot, I was off the couch! Lord! I was drooling, my eyes wouldn't focus, my clothes were a mess and St. Anne was barking so damn loud. The din of the previous night's tree life had moved inside my head. Cool morning light poured in through the filthy windows of the peace van. I could not get my bearings until I smelled the whisky and Bigwig maple taffy. The voices. I heard Neil and Archie laughing. At me, I thought.

"Not you, Birchwalker," chuckled Neil. "You can go back to sleep."

Through the fog of a mighty hangover I could see now that the two of them were standing a few feet away in Neil's stick gallery, both holding an end of a new son of Anishinaabewaki. I realized Neil was presenting it to Archie; a solemn ceremony was underway. A delivery had occurred in this night. I had slept through the labor-intensive intricacies of carving and lacing. And now I was witness to a kind of consecration—a baptism, maybe—of his newest warrior son. He drummed a piece of hickory on the table, began to chant in that

familiar meter of our childhood poem of Bwon-diac. I did not know
the baptism of his new sons of Great Waters had evolved into this; he
squeezed his eyes closed in a private send-off to his son.

"Stand and breathe, my son, arise now!
In your clockcord crook we're cradled.
Through that handle flows your lifeblood,
Scoop the ball and run it moonward.

"For from there you have descended
Like the chieftain long lashed to it.
Bring you word from our Bwon-diac?
Has he signaled for attacking?
"Sure of mind and quick of stick be,
Safeguard always our dominion,
From whome'er would snatch it from us;
Most of all beware the English.

"Let them smite you not, my proud son,
Neither chase you from Great Waters.
Stand your ground and paint your face up,
Trade your game stick for a war stick.

"Lead them to the Straits of Big Mac
On an eve of Full Moon Rising,
Then that metal scaffold climb up

And upon the Moon do clamber.

"Disappear inside the hissing,
Up the hole of mitèwin fly
And await with all your Brothers
Time of Indigene returning.

"There you'll sparkle midst the Planets
Nobler than your Persecutors—
Though they're ignorant about it,
After life we are their North Star.

"And if in that time you languish
Then take up again your game stick
Toss the comets round the Heavens
With a whoop announce your Vengeance."

Neil placed the stick fully in Archie's grasp. "You have not
made the long journey to Anishinaabewaki as a tourist. You are
seeking to understand the Native game in your official capacity for the
WLC. You are at the threshold now, Mr. Archie Mellon, you have
only to walk over it onto the long meadows of play bordered by the
streams where the players dip their sticks and into the villages whose
entire populations cheer from the hills. You have only to think of
origins, of restoring an original work of art that has been painted over

by a forger. And I see in your eyes and in your mind that you are a man who can do this."

Neil tied a splinter of perfectly supple hickory around the butt end of Archie's new stick. "His swaddling clothes. He will be called *ningwis*, my son. Give Birchwalker what he needs, Mr. Mellon. Allow him this celebration. Allow him to lead a great parade that touts the heritage of this game that is our lifeblood and that we have shared with our white brothers. Level this playing field just once. Give us our game back."

Archie's voice was a morning octave lower. "You know what happens when you mix sports and social justice in the same bowl, don't you," he responded, as if we both did. We looked at him blankly.

"Politics," is what he said, his red eyes narrowing. "As in—you better be careful what you wish for, gentlemen, because you might get it one day. Birch had a taste of this at the meetings in Hull. Resistance from powerful interests who want to keep the status quo. Look, I have loved this idea from the beginning and love it even more now that I've seen the reservation and learned a bit about Native stickmaking. Boomerangs, I tell you. What goes around comes around. If the decision were up to me I'd order four hundred twenty of these sticks right now and tell the teams they better get practicing."

Neil looked at me with a rare broad smile, questioning, then at Archie, and he seemed to grasp the potential for a stick order that would keep him pinned to his knobs and smoke hole forever, bending hickory shafts right into the Afterlife.

"I accept your kindness, Neil, of the baggattaway stick, and I will present it to the president of the WLC along with a recommendation that we seriously consider the Indigene Nation proposal. May God help us all! I do not know what he'll say, but if he approves it, beware, Birch: You will have celebrity. And while it theoretically solves our gate problem, the actual road to that solution will be paved over a gravelbed of self-righteous denunciation from all corners—nut cases out there are going to come at you from all angles. It will be a media war, I'm afraid, and your own people will be dragged in, too. Are you awake enough to lead me down to the fort? I'll be able to get to Detroit from there."

Archie and Neil shook hands and looked into one another's eyes for a long time, and Archie made his way down the stoop toward his rental. Neil walked toward the little kitchen where straps of catgut and rawhide still littered the floor and countertop. He was looking for something. He walked to the bedroom muttering to himself.

"What are you looking for?" I asked.

"Where's my bloody tomahawk pipe?" he asked back darkly.

"Oh, that?" said Archie, framing his face to see through the screen door. "I was the last one to smoke it at the wake. I just laid it down on the hors d'oeuvres table. I must have left it, I suppose."

Was all of this the answer to my prayer?

Assembly

Two months later the prayer remained unanswered, we still waited.

"Let's make a thunderstorm!" said Neil into the din of three hundred grade school kids who hadn't nearly settled in. Again he was decked out in the Big Indian, in full regalia for the September 8 assembly we had promised to Jan Zwiebel. In his kingfisher headdress, war paint and buckskins, my friend would teach the children and revel in the severing of even the white man's toddlers from any budding vanities. He frightened some to tears, their distress echoing off the hard surfaces of the hall. The late bell rang. Mothers moved up into the bleachers to console their babies, Jan one of them. Late arrivals from a delayed bus blew through the doors and raced noisily up to their classmates. The principal of Sault Elementary had laid aside a rule about animals and allowed St. Anne Four into the building, and she shadowed Neil's every move with her tongue unscrolled. The kids stood up and pointed at her, oohing and ahing over the cute little beagle. A group of the older boys let loose with hand-to-mouth war whoops, sounding a lot like kid versions of Bone Digger at the sports bar, and Neil seemed temporarily clueless. In apparent denial of the chaos, teachers and staff nodded and smiled near the double doors that led out past the lockers and the cafeteria and back to the classrooms. I had invited Obie and Jerome and Pascal to come along. We set up a lacrosse goal at one end of the gym, and bunches of Neil's sticks lay mounded in the pipes. A janitor threw a wayward ball back to them. A video camera swept the scene. A shrill voice crackled out over the PA. There was a mild smell of something burning, and the cafeteria ladies hurried in to a smattering of applause.

Neil suddenly brandished a baggattaway stick over his head like a war club in too subtle a gesture for calm. He did not still the crowd. Disgusted, Jan trundled down the bleacher steps and took the mic out of his hand. A secretary from the school office entered and handed Neil three stacks of paper.

"Okay, listen, children. I am the reason you are sitting in this assembly this morning and not in your classrooms. We are honored to have these gentlemen as our guests today, and if you disrespect them, you disrespect me. If you want to go that route, we'll just have to dismiss you back to class, and I will personally call your moms and dads. These two men are my friends. They have come to share some fun things with you this morning. They have an interesting tool," she ad- libbed, glancing at Neil, "it's called a pipe tomahawk. That's right, two for the price of one, a pipe and a tomahawk on the same shaft. You can smoke it or you can use it to keep ungrateful students in line. So, children, this is Mr. LaSalle."

You could have heard a pin drop.

"Like I was saying, let's make it rain." He began to snap his fingers, alternating hands, and to explain how young humans can imitate nature. "Not just rain," he urged the youngest ones, "but a sweeping, rolling flood blown across the land by strong winds. Join in

the snapping when I point to you, and do it as loud as you know how."
It was hardly the rousing start he had hoped for, as only about half of
the kids could actually snap their fingers. Jan's friend the principal
and another teacher came running over on tiptoes to help the young
ones, snapping emphatically and with raised eyebrows and terribly
urging smiles. In a few seconds they managed to coax out, if not an
outright downpour, then at least a respectable pitter-patter.

"Middle!" Neil yelled into the mic with his stick held over his
head. The drizzle emanating from the K-2 group stopped suddenly,
the kids thinking their work was done. "No, no, keep going!" Neil
laughed from the center, "keep snapping!" The principal was winded,
finding even this much exercise an aerobic trial. The center section of
the bleachers was occupied by the larger remnant of the third grade,
fourth graders and a sliver of fifth grade. To a man, they stood
hunched forward, intent on the mechanics of their finger snapping,
eager to show Neil that he would not regret asking them, the middle
grades of Sault Elementary School, to help him make rain. "That's
good," he said to them, "don't stop."

He sidestepped on his arthritic hips to a point in front of the
seniors of this assembly, a large fifth grade that would not be refused,
revving itself like the pole car under a green flag. Their faces said
they needed no instruction, that Neil had only to raise an eyebrow or
drop his hand and they'd be off. He raised the stick, held it aloft a few
tantalizing seconds and, finally, let it drop. The fifth graders did not
disappoint. They reached out at Neil in a heated competition for
attention with each snap of their grimy little fingers, throwing the

sound at him, and then, there it was. "Do you hear it?" asked Neil. "Keep going! Listen to your driving rainstorm." The kids liked it and Neil let it go on for another minute before raising his stick again to make the rain stop. "Give yourselves a big hand," he said.

I heard him introduce the players and me, tell the kids that the Indigene Nation lacrosse team would compete in the 2010 world championships, now only nine months away. His voice began to recede in my head as he recounted the legend of Wakayabide and Madjikiwis. I saw him hold up the stick again and walk it into the seats. He fondled the hickory shaft and traced with his hand the bends in the wood. Somebody yelled out from the top row, *What's your dog's name?* and the whole place cracked up when she barked four times and Neil said, *St. Anne Four*.

Suddenly the children before me were Anishinaabek, tryouts for the Indigene Nation team. From among them, I was to select my stars. All those faces out there in the night sky! They knew what I wanted on that field—hard bellies and noses that smell the ball and minds that see on the run. They knew I wanted them to play with abandon, nothing to lose. *A little crazy*, I would tell them, that's what unnerved a competitor. Each game of ball had to be a vision. Every pass, every shot, every check, dodge and scoop. If you happened to die in the playing you would be reborn, like Wakayabide and Madjikiwis. Obie Crick and Jerome French came down from the sky. Then, Robbie and Trev Fenton descended, my Huron twins of attack and divine handlers of the stick down low in the close quarters of the crease, and their friend, Danny Brown, took their place in the lineup. Then came tall, tall Russell Phaneuf, my jumper, my Ball Up man. And Grubby Spratt and Orin Beauchesne and Norman LeFramboise, the starlike cluster of midfielders, great churning workers of the ball downfield, and Elias Lane, spinner and dodger and cradler and juker, and Pascal Lefebvre, the brightest star, and Delbert DesMarais and Philip Davidson, Jesse Olsen and Aaron Bell, Herschel Seavey, Evan Crosse and Ronnie Philibotte, my defenders, formed a circle around them all. The constellation of Team Indigene Nation spun before me.

BAH-GAH-TAH-WAY! the assembly roared, and I awoke.

Neil had moved to the goal. In a grave miscalculation, he motioned that the kids should all come down from the stands and have a go at this homemade lacrosse camp, or, as he made them say in blaring unison before leaving their seats '*Bah-gah-tah-way*!' The teachers had to elevate quickly to frantic, doing crowd control, posting themselves in the middle of the torrents that descended onto the gym floor, their presence cleaving the kids into columns that merged again behind them into a semi-circle around the pipes, kids jostling and pushing for the best positions, grabbing at the sticks, sliding the goal, engulfing St. Anne and fighting over who got to pet her, picking up loose lacrosse balls and throwing them off the wall, and, finally, Neil let loose a primal Chippewa war whoop that triggered St. Anne to howl along and then the fifth grade boys joined in the chorus and soon Neil had managed to corral the entire throng into a not so terrible harmony and the jostling stopped and the kids wound down the wolf chorus and their attention was focused again on the solo baying of the man who had started the whole mess in the first place.

St. Anne tore after her tail, chasing herself in tight radiuses as if she'd been prompted by some unholy force or single inescapable image, cutting circles on the gym floor like a discus thrower who can't unwind and the kids were beside themselves, pointing at her and laughing and then chanting, *St. Anne Four, St. Anne Four*, and she kept spinning for as long as the kids made rain and finally she stopped but could not keep her balance. She staggered over to Neil and the girls found this all way too cute to even absorb into their eyes and they covered their mouths and they drawled over and over about how cute she was and finally Pascal Lefebvre said, *Can anybody do this?* and grabbed his right ankle and placed it above his head, still as a statue in his y-scale and of course the kids all had to try this and of course none of them could even come close and bodies collapsed in heaps, banging on the hardwood floor like so many laughing bowling pins and we were on the cusp of another free-for-all when Jan stepped in.

"Enough!" she bellowed. She glowered at Neil and me, disappointed by our ineptness. "I want fifth grade boys only," she said sternly. "Everybody else back to your seats."

Even as we waited for Archie's "Oh, I see," Parry Four Bears was planning his own assembly as if Archie had already said it. He had beautiful strong features, Parry Four Bears, and close-cropped gray hair like a diplomat, terra cotta skin, large brown ears and a straight spine. He was in his seventies. He was a former lax All-American at Finger Lakes, the first ever Native All-American in any modern sport. He thought nothing of driving a thousand miles. He lived on the Onondaga-Iroquois reservation near Syracuse and journeyed frequently all the way out here to meet with me when the full team was in town. His grandson was Orin Beauchesne, one of my first-line middies, though you can bet the house that he wasn't treated any differently because of it. I put Parry in front of the team every chance I get, which happened for the first time the weekend before Jan's assembly at the Periwinkle Middle School gymnasium. He was a sachem to them, a Jim Thorpe, an elder whose credential was that he played the game himself once, with great honor. People decried his choice of me, a Great Lakes Chippewa, for the Indigene Nation coaching job, but I was not in charge. Whatever power I wielded flowed to me from Parry Four Bears Beauchesne.

I had asked Parry to address the team. We needed to get ourselves thinking right about training for this competition, for those were no superficial changes. Neil came too. I figured, better to get the news from the sachem and the stickmaker than from the coach who would have to manage the fallout. I wanted them to see this was a line we all had to toe. Neil led off. He could speak with such a clear head sometimes.

"I heard you guys are calling it PMS, that's good. Periwinkle Middle School, your home away from home when you come up to the U.P. They give you the run of the gym and showers, the fields, the cafeteria, a computer lab. Not a bad grab, and all thanks to the best gym teacher PMS has ever had, your coach Birchwalker Charlevoix. Hey, now, listen. If all goes according to plan, Drey Foss and Team USA, Russell Pape and Team England, Team Denmark and Team Canada, Team Japan and Team Germany, they will all be shelving their precious titanium and graphite sticks to play with *these* bastards, you see, hickory sticks in the Iroquois style. They're as heavy as a war club. They don't feel right in your grip, out of balance like." One at a time, Neil picked a stick and approached each man with it, thrusting it with both hands into theirs with a grunt, hanging on until they felt compelled to grab it away from him and really take possession of it. "You will not like these sticks for a good long while. They don't cradle well because the pocket isn't as deep, the head is maybe larger or smaller than you're used to, they're heavier so there's less whip—goddammit, they're just plain clunky, but we're turning back the clock here, aren't we, so before you even start complaining, get the hell over it. Practice all the time, from both sides, overhead and underhand. Throw, scoop, catch, break it in the best you can. Eat with it, sleep with it, brush your teeth with it, caress it, love it. It's your weapon in a historic battle, your war club in the skirmish known as 'war's little brother,' baggattaway. Don't blow this! We're stacking the deck for you. Those other bastards have never held a weapon like this before, and let's just say I won't be in a big hurry to fill their orders when they do come in. And don't think you've got it made once you get practiced up on the sticks, because there's plenty more to do…"

Neil was on a tear. He was unstoppable, haranguing them on every aspect of the 2010 proposed rules. He barreled through, even stole, most of Parry's presentation. Permitting not so much as a question or a maple taffy or a bathroom break, Neil's monologue continued in this vein: "You better start walking around barefoot, too, because the teams will not be wearing any footwear. No sneakers or turf cleats. No socks. No helmets. No pads. Nothing. Shorts or your grandpas' breechclouts, shirts if you want them. And that's going to take some getting used to, gentlemen. You're going to have sunburns and blisters and corns and calluses, and the sooner you get your shoes off and train outside the better off you'll be. Same with checking. No pads or helmets means you think more about contact and pick your battles as to when to throw your body at someone. You all know the stories from your tribes. In the old days, the whole village including old people and kids would go over the playing field the night before the game and clear it of any debris, sticks, stones, everything, until it was considered playable by real men, barefoot men. Your bare feet will be running on a one kilometer by one-half kilometer track with no nice, white sidelines but natural sidelines like a lake or a forest or a river or a hillside. That's one kilometer, now, ten times more than a hundred ten yards! The teams will all have twenty-five players, no substitutes; Jerome will have to break in a second goalie to man the twelve-foot goal; there won't be face-offs, so Russell, you'll have to learn Ball Up. Maybe you should put your sleeping bag under the hoop and dream of rebounds. I think I'll leave it there," he finished,

having left nothing for Parry to say. "By the way, have you all seen
The Other White House?"

True. Parry Four Bears' chieftain car was cool, so cool that
like Tipi it ought to have had sunglasses. Instead of a pep talk for the
stallions, Parry gave them a tour of his vehicle. It was the official
vehicle of Iroquois Nation, their Air Force One. Did the chief of the
Six Nations not speak for the American Indian at the United Nations?
At college commencements? At peace and environmental
conferences? Of course he did, and he required transportation
commensurate with his status and the weight of his mission. Thus, the
Grand Council saw fit to furnish him with a trademark. Metallic white
with purple trim, it was a custom conversion van, a prowling thing
called the Ohian, that featured dark wraparound windows, fridge and
wet bar which Parry stocks with ice tea only, two moon roofs, GPS
navigator, flatscreen TV and DVD player, laptop, voice-activated cell
phone and perforated leather seating for seven including the driver.
And if you somehow missed that this vehicle carried the chief of the
Onondaga and the Elder Brother on the Grand Council of the Iroquois
Nation, well then, the purple and white flag of the confederacy
emblazoned prominently on the driver's door, the passenger's door
and the roof would surely remedy this ignorance. It was dubbed The
Other White House. The stallions ogled it inside and out and wanted
to make it the official car of Indigene Nation lacrosse. Parry was
headed west, out to Oklahoma and South Dakota.

"Far from it," he had said when I suggested that the trip might be a grueling one for him. "I can't wait to go. I'll take Lila and Naila, the two sisters who work in the tribe's history department. They'll share the driving with me."

"Roundtrip three thousand miles," he'd said, "no sweat in The Other White House. Kid stuff," said between the two stops and including the tribes in Michigan and Ontario he could reach half a million Natives. We had talked about it late into the night, reviewed the numbers I'd given Drey Foss at Hull, in detail, and it came out like this: 106 thousand Chippewa, 88 thousand Choctaw, 49 thousand Iroquois, 16 thousand Potawatomi, 9 thousand Delaware. Then we added the Creek, the Seminole, the Cherokee, Sioux Nation, the Alabama, the Arapaho, the Kiowa, the Osage, the Cheyenne, the Crow, the Mississauga, Nipissing, the Michpicoten, Iroquois Nation, the Chickasaw, Kansa and Wichita, the Arapaho, Mandan. We talked about media, news coverage, publicity. We would need plenty of that. He wanted news helicopters buzzing The Other White House, showing the Iroquois flag on national TV. He wanted *SENE* in on the promotion early, refusing to countenance the possibility that they wouldn't pick it up.

We talked about ceremonial wampum for his meetings and developed the idea that he'd carry one of Neil's sticks for each of the major tribal sachems. "Have him craft me a beauty,' said Parry, "three of them, in fact, ask him to carve symbols of our story into the handle—a moon, a bridge, a vermilion-stained baggattaway ball, a burial mound. Indian diplomacy, Birch! A war plan is agreed, wampum is exchanged, a pipe is smoked, forearms clenched in a just cause."

I said he'd have to explain about the venues for the games, the forts, Green Bay and Michilimackinac, that their people would sleep on the playing fields. I told Parry I thought this enterprise needed a name, and within five minutes we came up with *The All-Americans Tour*.

"I can see it painted on the Red Dog buses," said Parry. He explained to me that we would have to charter hundreds of them. We would have the corporate sponsors put together a package to include roundtrip bus fare, admissions tickets for the games, food vouchers. He had caught the fever. And he was not about to idle The Other White House much longer waiting for word from Archie.

Neil had all the Sault Elementary kids reciting a poem at a fevered pitch, 'Hiawatha.' Each kid in the three sections of the bleachers held a copy of one of the stanzas. He stood there in front of them like he had for the rainmaking, almost pulling the verses out of them, a conductor with wisps of hair fallen out of his braid, and of course they were in fullest throat. Louder than a pep rally. I glanced at the stallions and they were singing it too. How could they not?

"Fifth graders!"

> *By the shores of Gitchee Gumee,*
> *By the shining Big-Sea-Water,*
> *Stood the wigwam of Nokomis,*
> *Daughter of the Moon, Nokomis.*

"Fourth graders!"

Dark behind it rose the forest,

Rose the black and gloomy pine-trees,

Rose the firs with cones upon them;

Bright before it beat the water,

"First, second, and third graders!"

Beat the clear and sunny water,

Beat the shining Big-Sea-Water.

Neil walked a stick over to me and said, "This time, my friend, you play Bad Sky and I play Makoons." He loped over to the double doors where the teachers were all standing and theatrically shooed them away. He opened the right side door and flipped down the stop with his moccasin. He proclaimed to the kids that these doors represented the land gate at Fort Michilimackinac and that they were to watch carefully. "Have you ever been to the moon?" he asked into the mic. About thirty kids raised their hands. St. Anne barked.

"Me, neither," said Neil without looking for the show of hands, "but I bet you've heard of the man in the moon, haven't you?" They went wild, like the man in the moon personally tucked them in each night. "Well, listen to me, children, I know him!" They went wild again, breaking into chants. "But I do," he told them. "His name is Bwon-diac, and he is tied to the moon, and every year on the second day of June, just before the end of school, he floats down on his moon buggy very close to our bridge Big Mac and to the field where we play at Fort Michilimackinac, and he watches my friend Birchwalker and me perform this little ritual of ours."

There was no sound except Neil's voice.

"And it has everything to do with the greatest game of all, baggattaway, and its most famous moment. It occurred in 1763. That's two hundred forty-six years ago, children, not all that distant. Bad Englishmen took over the fort, and the Indians who lived in Michigan back then before it was Michigan wanted to take it back. They call in Makoons," he said raising his stick up over his head, "because he has the bravest stick and the truest, strongest shot of all. But he needs to make the shot into the open land gate from quite a distance and his friend Bad Sky decides to hold his stick out flat…"

He motioned me over to the middle of the floor, and I stood in front of him with my back to the half open gymnasium door.

"…so he can run up to it and hit his stick against Bad Sky's so that the ball will fly as far as it can into the gate." We demonstrated the sequence of Makoons and Bad Sky's famous collaboration in slow motion for the kids. After retrieving the ball from the corridor, Neil addressed them again. "There are no videos of what happened, and for that you should consider yourselves lucky. Maybe they should make the story into a video game, because it was as violent as any war game you've played on your game boxes. Those Indians tricked the bad men by throwing the ball into the fort and then they took tomahawks and scalping knives from their women's blankets and killed all the English soldiers, but they got their fort back for only a short while before losing it again. Oh, children, what a sweet victory that was!" His voice trailed off, and he was suddenly far away, as he often was out on the Straits in his canoe. "Violence is a big part of life, children, but if it knocks you in the face you have the memory of it to think about, and that pain never goes away. The Chippewa no longer gather pike from the Great Waters. Steel mills dump sludge into the St. Mary's. Our perfect game was kidnapped…"

He could not have wanted the assembly to end on this low note, risking Jan's wrath with his inappropriate sadness in the process, and yet he had sunk into an Indian despair so deep I thought he would break down and cry. So I jumped in. I slung my arm around him.

"But Makoons," I said, spreading my free hand out over a vast, imagined landscape, "we have our man in the moon. We have the soaring eagle and the baying gray wolf. We have our June Two celebration, and we have our sport as well. It has simply been *borrowed* by the white man, my friend. One day he will give it back."

On the day of her invasion, Marla somehow saw that I should teach, and for a second I felt it here, in this crummy elementary school in the middle of nowhere, the recycled, true passion of a new school year. I remembered little Obie Crick, Jerome French, the little big man he was in seventh grade. I did. I run the open fields with snotty-nosed kids, show them how to chase down lacrosse balls with sticks made by my friend Neil Longbow LaSalle, teach the fine arts of scooping, cradling, running and passing, how to stand in the net of life and defend it against all those shots that people take on it. We play it in the snows and in the heat, in the rain and in the wind. We drill it in the gym. When I'm finished with them, they know everything about our game. They've written tests and essays on it, and they have played it for hours, too. They know the word *baggattaway*, its history, the rituals, the grueling borderlessness of it, the smackdown thrill of it, the prayer of it, the fairy tale of it. I have stood with them at Lake Superior and made them look northward over the great water into Canada, watching and listening for geese and barges. I take them on field trips to the fort, explain to them for Louis's sake what qualities beets and vermilion baggattaway balls have in common, and for Neil's sake how each of them is an ephemeral drip that has condensed onto Anishinaabewaki holding a lacrosse stick. I recite *The Cry of Bwon-diac* and bid them to take it into their hearts, to honor our chieftain who is lashed to the changing faces of the moon in the Afterlife, his anger held in a vise grip until the forts are reclaimed and the English thieves are deposed.

Anyway, my rescue afforded a happier ending, a signal to the assembly that the worst had passed. They could breathe out finally. They'd had their lesson. For that day at least, the Chippewa had the fort, and their beloved stickmaker and rainmaker and storyteller Neil Longbow LaSalle would wake up to try again tomorrow.

New Beginning

Archie finally broke his silence, on Columbus Day! Irrepressible, unimpeachable, wrong-hearted Columbus Day. Its peak foliage the harbinger of festivity and year's end, we overlook the holiday's gory subtext—the incidental slaughter of Carib innocents on their own pristine beaches at the mighty hand of desperate careless empires. Nonetheless, the time of year shocks the Upper Peninsula into life, shakes it out of its summer doldrums. Forests suddenly beam their vital waves of color into the clear cool air. Lush reds, righteous yellows, luminous oranges and arrogant purples crown black treehides and sparkling white birch bark. We just don't want Columbus to get all the credit for a climactic transformation that would occur with or without his vaunted blessing.

The three month wait had worn on me, exhausting me with imaginary scenarios, what ifs, ups and downs and backs and forths until I had capitulated and darkly settled back into the tedious rhythms of a life, slighted. I had convinced myself there would be no baggattaway adventure. Who had I been kidding? What was I thinking? Drey Foss and Russell Pape by now would have lobbied Archie's ears off in favor of the precious status quo, and none among us had ever met the mysterious President of the WLC, and so could not begin to guess at his leanings in the matter of our proposal. Marking periods, ghosts and goblins came and went. Thanksgiving was already in the air. Neil should not ever have begun his stickmaker's marathon, I thought, Parry Four Bears should not ever have set out halfway across the country on behalf of our stillborn idea. But they had more courage than I did, I guess, more faith. Not that Neil had suddenly turned into an optimist, though. In fact, he was frustrated, stalled out, laboring over the design of Parry's three wampum sticks. They had to be just right. They had to be perfect. "Have you ever tried to carve a tiny little suspension bridge into a hickory lacrosse shaft? And then paint it with an eentsy little brush no bigger than an eyebrow? You want art, Birchwalker, and I am only a technician."

And then Archie called and, for Neil and the rest of us, all hell broke loose.

Like that very first luminous orange leaf in a glade of greens, he popped up out of nowhere, called me from the Hotel New Beginning. Like he lived here, called every day, no big deal. Drey Foss, Andrew Sophie, Russell Pape and I were to host a press conference with him. He gave no details. *Just meet me for dinner*, he said. Marla whooped and hugged me excitedly.

"You're in, Birch! Why would he come all the way up here and stage this big elaborate press conference if the answer was no? Watch. One or two of the wire services will pick it up and then it's Times Square. The world will know. He flew Russell and Drey all the way in for it, didn't he? I think it's incredible that Archie is making the announcement here. It'll happen, Birch," she assured me. "June

Two will be the next national holiday! Now we have to find you some decent clothes for the big show."

"*Wear?*" I said, "What am I going to *say?*"

The New Beginning was the only decent Lockside hotel, its front yard the trail of tears, its patio garden the locks on the St. Mary's River. You could watch the locks grinding through the restaurant windows. Tilt your head a degree or two and look across the river to Canada. Somehow the border setting was appropriate.

"Gentlemen," Archie opened up with the International Bridge sitting on his head like a matador headpiece through the big plate glass window. "I'll spare you the blow-by-blow description of all the horse trading that went on before we hammered out the final...formula. Suffice it to say, I authorized a vote, as you all know, a vote from which I abstained, an up-or-down vote on the Indigene Nation proposal—namely, that, without going into specifics, the championships of 2010 be constructed in such a way as to honor the American Indian traditions of the sport and to incorporate as much of the original game as possible into the tournament."

"Tell me we're not doing it," said Drey Foss.

"Hold your tongue till you hear how the vote went," shushed Russell Pape like a nanny.

"Sound idea," said Archie. "Because it's interesting, to say the least. There were nine yes votes—Germany, Wales, Czech Republic, Ireland, Indigene Nation, Japan, Korea, Scotland and Denmark. Four countries voted no—U.S., England, Australia, New Zealand. Three nations abstained—Canada, China and Sweden."

"You didn't vote, Andrew?" shrieked Drey Foss. "That's it? We're doing it?"

"Majority vote. We're doing it."

"Does this pig shit come gift-wrapped with dates and venues?"

That's when I knew. When I watched Drey Foss's face contort. It was going to happen. I floated to heaven.

Archie stared him down before answering. "London and Shanghai in mid-May, Green Bay and Michilimackinac in late May into the first days of June. Look, Drey, I'm not asking you to love it. I'm telling you you have to play along. We're doing history now. You three have a bye into the round robin. By the way, try a cup of their gumbo," he said nodding at the menu. "You'll love it."

"Come on with the rest of it, Archie. I can see there's more. Out with it."

"It's gonna be a great show. But the WLC left me no wiggle room. It has to work. If it doesn't..." He drew a steak knife across his throat.

"It can only succeed," I said. "We've never *promoted* the championships like this. All we have to do is suit up and play our game. The paying public will be there."

"So, I guess you're not leaving us any wiggle room, either, right, Archie?" surmised Drey Foss with an eye on us other coaches.

"Bingo. We sink or swim together. No screwing around here, no politics. We all go down or we all survive. We are a team. Only a team can make a gamble like this pay off."

"Did he get *every*thing?" asked Russell Pape heavily.

"Nearly. We toned down parts of it, like the dimensions of the playing field. We'll require one kilometer long by one-half kilometer wide. That's roughly ten times the size of the current playing fields. We'll keep an area behind the goal in play, twenty-five yards; that's ten more than today's rules allow. Instead of the current ten, each team will field twenty-five players—eight defensemen, nine middies and six attackmen, in addition to the two goalies. The spruce sapling goals will be set at twelve, not eighteen, feet. No substitutions. Individual coaches will have a lot of latitude in how they configure their offense and defense. Two zebras patrolling the field. No offsides. We will do Ball Up instead of face off."

"Team USA is appealing this."

"Be my guest."

"Did we get *any*thing?" Russell was keeping score.

"Well, we're using standard white rubber lacrosse balls. That count?"

"Archie, please promise me we are not using those goddamn Indian sticks, those fucking …war clubs."

"Can't do that, Drey."

Drey laughed into his gumbo, a disgusted throaty laugh.

"And then, gentlemen, there's the pièce de résistance," he said with a wry smile pointed right at me. Archie was the only one eating at that point, jawing a juicy bite of prime rib.

"What, then?" demanded Russell.

Archie had them baited, strung them out.

"Oh, Jesus." Drey Foss looked away.

"Barefoot, we're playing barefoot."

"Bloody hell we are!"

Drey Foss leaned back in his chair and blew a cynical snort through his nose and showed his teeth. "This is starting to sound like a payoff, gentlemen. You into him, Birch? How much is it? Barefoot. Uh-huh, barefoot in the park. Isn't there a gay little musical by that name? I'll tell you what, Archie. This sucks."

"Can it, Drey."

"Yeah, but you don't even know the first thing about lacrosse, do you? This is a masterpiece of bullshit and a house of cards and it's all going to come tumbling down on us. I predict that not only will Birch not deliver the crowds he's promised but also that you will be forced into true retirement over this, Archie."

"You go ahead and predict, Drey. You are the coach of Team USA and I can't even hear anything past that. I just don't seem to hear you. Look, if you don't think I know that my job is on the line, you've underestimated me. I'm a born risk-taker. True enough, I know little about the sport, but this is an enterprise that has a balance sheet to manage, web sites and newsletters to maintain, worldwide development programs, doping tests to administer, revenues and business partners to look after, member programs, but most importantly, Drey, it can flourish only in the hands of the right people. I don't hold your inexperience on the business side and your lack of people skills against you. I *have* immersed myself in the game's history and I *have* spent the last few weeks of my life in contact with all kinds of people and all kinds of agencies to get this thing sold and organized. There is a whole lot more to this venture than knowledge. No one will undermine us now."

"You got to have balls," I smiled, "big brass ones."

"Well, that's probably true, Birch," said Drey Foss sanctimoniously, not even bothering to look at me, "but you won't have to worry about that since yours have already been cut off."

"Can it, Drey! That's enough," said Archie. "I will also announce the venues for the final rounds, and I will announce that Birch will be making a promotional trip before the tournament to help fund raise and build awareness and interest overseas."

"Oh, this is beautiful. He goes on a fucking world tour too. Where to?"

"Probably London, Prague, Shanghai. We'll sort it out later, but something like that."

"And what were those venues again for the U.S. round?"

"Green Bay, Michilimackinac."

"Sounds like a very U.P. event," Drey said caustically. "I take it these are colonial forts where the Indians got it handed to them?"

"Hey, look. If you don't put a cork in it right now, I will recall you as the U.S. coach. Is that clear?" Archie's neck and face flushed with exertion. Drey threw his white napkin on the floor, slammed the menu shut and stood up facing Archie.

"Okay. Just don't ask me to sit through this crap then. Don't try to wheedle me into it. Tell me what I have to do and stand back and watch us kick everybody's ass, Archie." He stormed out of the dining room.

"Andrew, you've been pretty quiet."

"Seething is more like it, Archie. I just manage it better than Drey." He hesitated, eyeing me intently as he continued. "There's evidence that the Indigene Nation squad may be doing a little end run off the field as well as on it."

"What do you mean? Out with it."

"I think Birch might be poaching. He's got one of my players, Pascal Lefebvre."

"True, Birch?" before I could even respond.

"True that I've got him. Doubtful that he's Andrew's player."

"Go on. Explain it."

"He's Chippewa, or at least he has Chippewa blood in him. He was referred to me and I learned he lived in Ontario. I can make a case to keep him because he's Indian."

"Did you ever think of picking up the damn phone? Jesus, don't undermine your own agenda, Birch! Do we need a blood test on this Pascal guy? Are there any other cases like this? Can you two make this go away?"

We looked right at one another and both nodded our heads yes.

The three of us cooled off after Drey left. It had been far more head banging than compromise for the other coaches, but me? I was beatified, haloed, anointed. I streamed pure radiance into the heavens just like the trees of the Hiawatha. For that one moment at least, the grimy reality of how to actually win baggattaway games was wholly rubbed out by thick beams of color.

Though it was pretty late by the time I passed PMS on the way home, I stopped in to check for emails from The Other White House, and I found this:

"Birch,

So far Parry has wampumed (is that even a word?) with the sachems of eight tribes including the Cherokee, the Seneca and Cayuga who were removed out here in the nineteenth century, the Delaware, the Seminole, the Creek. It's been quite a history lesson for us historians. The response has been great and completely supportive. They are coming, Birch! The only questions are logistics, like money and time off from work and traveling plans. So, we will be finishing up here and leaving for South Dakota the day after tomorrow and are really looking forward to it.....Please tell Neil the wampum sticks are a big hit. The Choctaw had some of their teenage boys perform a baggattaway dance using the two sticks as their ancestors did, it was a moment. We have been wined and dined and the chief has smoked many pipes. Our arrival was announced in the tribal newsletters all over the state and thousands of people came out to greet us. Parry said that he never doubted this outcome, that it was right as rain from the beginning and pure as the driven snow. Everyone wants to sign up right away. We even made the local television news here in Oklahoma City...The chief is nervous, though. Any word yet?

Lila and Naila for Chief Parry Four Bears"

I flipped a light on and started to type.

"Boozhoo, Lila and Naila. Neil will appreciate that his wampum sticks are scoring points with the chiefs of our brother tribes. News from here just as good: Archie Mellon is holding a press conference Monday in the Soo. I'm going to mention Parry's trip and would expect media attention if I were you. Can you call me tonight? I'll have all the details about the press conference.

Baa Maa Pii, Birch."

Caught between good news and recent loss, I didn't sleep a wink Sunday night, waking up every half hour to the nightmare of a funeral casino, some kind of gaming parlor at the edge of the Path of Souls where my father was caught, wandering. I had to play my way through it to get to him. The wrinkle was that the slimy grinning hosts were Drey Foss, Russell Pape and Bone Digger. They walked me around the funeral casino, schmoozed me like I was some innocent mark, past roulette wheels and blackjack tables, baccarat and poker tables, bingo and keno lounges. We threaded our way through a maze of pop-culture, chiming one-armed bandit pits, clouds of cigarette smoke. There was a Rocky, a Beverly Hillbillies, a Fort Knox and Uno. The Price Is Right man wanted you to come on down. High Stakes, Monopoly. It was endless, and I yelled out in this dream to my father that it was impossible, I could not help him pass from this Purgatory to the Land of Souls where he belonged. Old ladies hunched, vacantly pulling at the slots, entirely unmoved by the splashing metal sound of a few coins in the silver tray. Listen: What do we name the grievous desperation that drives my people to build casinos where a father's soul is trapped forever?

High noon under a blinding sun on Columbus Day. Archie took to the podium. The press conference was organized by the hotel in a spot just down the street in Brady Park where a treeless manicured lawn sloped down to the bending river and its north bank, Big Soo behind it all. Archie had them mount two life-size canvas-backed action photos of rearing, firing lacrosse players on some aluminum frames as a visual aid for anyone who didn't know what the sport looks like. For all the sunshine it was brisk, around fifty-eight degrees, and we were wrapped in foliage, of course. The air was crowded with noises of the river. You could hear foghorns bellowing, gulls cackling, tourists waving and cheering as they lit out on a boat tour of the St. Mary's, a baby wailing. Drey and Russell and Andrew and I sat behind Archie. Andrew waved to his Team Canada who had come across for the event. It was easy to pick out my mother's bobbing head and her crutch Minerva, smiling and waving away at me. Marla and Sheila and Sandrine were there, our Lockside merchant buddies, too—Tony, Mickey Blake, Tommy McKeon. The King and his permanent sneer. I had called a practice for the weekend, so all of the stallions were there, most wearing the same dress clothes they wore at my father's wake. I'd say that sixty or seventy curious souls showed up, maybe a hundred. I saw some young faces from PMS. They were bunched with their parents and pointing me out, the crazy gym teacher who teaches them about baggattaway. Neil was missing, up to his eyeballs in hickory. The press was lined up directly in front of the podium, holding out microphones and jotting down notes and bustling around until Archie cleared his throat and said, "Good morning, ladies and gentlemen," in unmistakable Australian, and I suddenly realized sitting cross-legged in my new beige dress slacks and blue tweed sports coat that I was a complete moron: I had told Archie nothing about Parry Four Bears and his whereabouts.

"On this beautiful fall day I am proud to be with you in Sault Ste. Marie to make a series of announcements concerning the World Lacrosse Council. As you can plainly hear, I'm not from around these parts, and that alone may signify to you how international this sport of lacrosse has become. It is played all over the world today, including much of Europe, some in Asia, and, of course, in Australia, Canada and the United States. My name is Archie Mellon, and I am the Executive Vice-President of the Council. This seemed the right place for me to deliver such an important piece of news about our sport, not alone for the fact that Canada, the birthplace of modern lacrosse and hockey, is just behind me—who but the Canadians would have devised the concept of box lacrosse, all those ice hockey rinks sitting idle in the spring? But also because those Canadian boxes would become the last, shrunken vestige of a playing field for Native athletes.

"You would hardly mistake the game played by Natives hundreds of years ago for what we call lacrosse today. The sport was taken up by the white man, refined, given an order of play not found in the Native versions, and, some would say, weakened by the addition of helmets and pads and sidelines. Still, the relationship is undeniable. Baggattaway is the sire of lacrosse, and this lineage merits honor and celebration. From the first, humble world championships in 1978 when just four teams participated, we have done our unswerving best to build participation amongst all the world's countries. In May of next year, 2010, we will field sixteen teams— Germany, Denmark, Czech Republic, England, Wales, Scotland, Sweden, Italy, Japan, Korea, China, Australia, New Zealand, Canada, the United States, and last but certainly not least the team representing the indigenous peoples of America, the Indigene Nation team. But we will program the tournament in an unusual way.

"Indeed. There is no grander way to honor than to reenact, and that, ladies and gentlemen, is precisely what we will do. We will break with one tradition to honor another."

He pointed to the picture displays.

"It won't look like this, mate. We will toss out our rulebooks, dig up the sidelines, widen the goals and use stripped spruce saplings as posts. We will shelve our graphite and titanium sticks and play with hickory shafts from these very forests bent to the specifications of Native players long before there was a United States by your own Mr. Neil Longbow LaSalle of the Pope County Indian Reservation. We will break out of the stadium mold of thinking and spill out into the countryside where hills and rivers and lakes mark the out of bounds. Our players will wear no shoes or pads or helmets. Not that we want them to get hurt, mind you, but we believe they will slash and check more…thoughtfully. They will run barefoot, yes, barefoot, over fields of play more than a half mile long."

The crowd rounded its mouth, oohed and ahed at this revelation.

"And, perhaps best of all, we have selected nearby historical venues for the final rounds —Green Bay and your own Michilimackinac. Three of the four charter teams of the World Lacrosse Council, whose coaches are flanking me on this rostrum, will be given a bye in the first round of the tournament, a bow to their countries' roles in shaping the modern game. They will be honorary hosts of this traveling tournament. But the rest of Europe and even Asia will contribute teams too. A total of five international teams will emerge from regional play-in games and come to the upper Midwest of the United States. And yes, even the Asian and European players will compete according to the old ways, and that should be very interesting to see. Those eight teams will contest the 2010 World Lacrosse Championships, with the round robin to be played at Green Bay and the semi-finals and championship game at Fort Michilimackinac. That is a special choice, made in honor of the surprise attack by the Saulk and Chippewa tribes against the English in 1763, where baggattaway itself was used as a ruse to retake the fort.

"Before I yield to the coaches, let me say that such a bold reshaping of our tournament requires us to be prepared to instruct and promote in order to achieve a fair competition and to convey the full measure of enjoyment to all people in the celebration of the Native American origins of the sport. To that end, I am announcing that Mr. Birch Charlevoix, coach of the Indigene Nation team, former WLC charter player for that same team and proud member of Chippewa

Nation, will embark on an overseas campaign to assist member teams abroad in fund-raising, in the ways and equipment of the Native game and in building public awareness and interest. In many of these countries, lacrosse is still in its infancy, but I can assure you that it is played with no less fire, and we hope that a number of international fans will follow their teams here to this place."

Archie closed his speech with an extended apology to the mayor of London, Ontario, where the 2010 tournament had first been scheduled. He conceded he'd had to be a bit heavy-handed in yanking the championships from the fair city but said he was certain the mayor had understood why. He'd agreed to remunerate any expenses incurred by the city and gave his word that as recompense both the 2014 and 2018 games would return to Ontario.

We coaches all said the same things coaches always say, explaining our attitudes toward the changes, urging people to come out to the games, assuring them of unpredictable and hotly contested matches. Drey led off, in snide tones, and asserted that his American team would come ready for battle, even barefoot, and win it all. Andrew referenced bare feet, too, and felt that the rules change might level the playing field somewhat for the newer teams from Europe and Asia. Russell Pape didn't say much of anything, his messages garbled by a sneering manner and vain attempts at humor. He did offer to show me around London, England, though, when I go and then signed off with just a *Cheerio*. I got a wild reception from the crowd. I talked about my stallions mostly, their tribes, their dedication in getting all the way out to the U.P. for practices every two weeks, how they are every bit the young and modern American team, used to playing lacrosse with helmets, cleats, pads, and on a hundred-ten yard field. I told them we had nothing to lose and that we would play our hearts out for all American Indians. At the end, I slipped in the headline about Parry Four Bears and Lila and Naila out in Oklahoma and South Dakota, fanning the flames of Indian support with wampum sticks made by Neil.

Then Archie hustled back up to take the mic and told the press, "Fire away!"

The Detroit *Free Press* had a question for Archie. "This is quite a gamble for you, isn't it, Mr. Mellon? You've been with the organization only a short time and never actually played the game yourself. How do you feel so confident that such big changes will be good for the game, for the growth of its spectator base, for its fans?"

"We believe that the turnout from Native tribes will be extraordinary, that promotion from our corporate sponsors will create interest among a fan base curious about the genesis of sport, that the players reenacting that beginning will learn to appreciate their chosen sport all the more."

The *Soo News* asked if the fort in Green Bay was still standing and how he got approval to play at the sites.

"Unlike Fort Michilimackinac, Fort Edward Augustus is but a memory. We'll play instead on a beautiful piece of nearby real estate, the Thunderbird Country Club, specifically on holes eight, nine, seventeen and eighteen. I met with the mayor of Green Bay and the chief of the Oneida reservation there, as well as the appropriate state and local agencies in Michigan and Wisconsin, so I've had a little practice at my pitch," he said with a wide grin.

"A question for the coaches!" yelled the *AP* reporter. "Kilometer-long fields, Indian sticks, no helmets, no pads, no *shoes*! Gentlemen! Can your teams do this? How do you prepare them?"

We looked at one another. I finally stood up and answered that it'll take some doing. Hard practice and learning new skills in a game we already knew. We would need calluses on top of calluses and stronger arms and shoulders to work those sticks, and better wind. It would not be easy, I promised everyone.

Archie then pointed, unwittingly, to my cousin Henry Charlevoix, who worked for the *Sault Tribe News*. He wanted to know where the overseas travel would take me. He also asked about the incoming Indigene spectators, how they would be housed, how they would pay, how many there might be.

I gulped and said it right out loud, a hundred thousand. *A hundred thousand!* "Our plan is to bus them out to Wisconsin and Michigan. We plan to call it 'The All-Americans Tour.' We're hoping to get chartered buses to shuttle them back and forth from Oklahoma and South Dakota to the forts." I tipped off the news organizations that a big white Ohian conversion van with a purple Iroquois Nation flag should be easy to spot from a news helicopter. I told my cousin I'd have stops somewhere in Europe and Asia, and he wondered if he could go with me.

The Sault *Star* reporter asked Archie a couple of straight-up questions. "Would an Indian from Canada play for the Indigene

Nation team? Or Team Canada? Any idea who might pick up title sponsorship and broadcast rights for the tournament? And do you have a web site?"

"Baggattaway.com!" Archie enthused as, again, I jumped in to help him on that first question. I said if we played by Indian rules, then, technically, historically and in all other ways, the question was moot because Canada and the United States don't exist yet. *Do you know what I mean*, I asked the reporter. But he looked confused. Archie didn't have much to give him on sponsorship, only his expectation that quality television and radio networks as well as numerous corporate sponsors would queue up to bring this spectacle of Native American sport and culture into living rooms around the world.

My fellow coaches left quickly without so much as a finger wave.

The response was as Marla predicted—we were everywhere. Front page news in big city newspapers and magazines, full cable and network news coverage, suddenly and unsettlingly, everywhere. I felt like a faceless charity that had suddenly grown a face and a clear narrative that put us in the discussion around dinner tables across the nation. Maybe instead of blindly accepting that each precious American timepiece first ticked to life on July 4, 1776, Americans would be reminded that in actuality they just took somebody else's clock and reset it. And going even further back, they might get the picture that when Mr. C. Columbus stumbled lost onto the beaches of

San Salvador in 1492, ours was a civilization at its peak, taking its recreation by playing divinely-inspired baggattaway in all times and places. But Archie Mellon was no C. Columbus, slaughterer of Tainos. Quite the opposite in fact, he was the jaunty white man who rode into Anishinaabewaki and handed out *favors* to the red man, including the handwritten purchase order from the WLC to a Mr. Neil Longbow LaSalle for '...four hundred twenty baggattaway sticks, white ash or hickory, to measure 44 inches long and be constructed with 8 inch clockcord-rawhide pockets...' which he stuffed in the breast pocket of my new blue tweed.

Archie was making it happen, I tell you. Skeptical at first, the country's biggest sports magazine, *American Athlete*, derided him as '...that vain Aussie huckster and former pacemaker exec who is trying for a global rollout of a uniquely American sport as if it were a worldwide medical product launch...a sport given ample opportunity to make a splash on the world stage when it was accorded exhibition status in two early twentieth century Olympics, and it didn't pass muster then...the WLC can't even fill the bleachers for its own quadrennial championship games. They'll never break even...' Contrarians. There's always contrarians. But, no matter the light in which it was presented, baggattaway was the belle of the media ball. Any publicity, even bad, was good. They all led with baggattaway buzz, excavating stats on players, teams, records, and serving up preliminary picks for 2010 to the online legions whose scanning pupils now took in our light. Major publications sent reporters to scour the playing fields of Europe and Asia to independently plumb lacrosse's alleged global appeal. They would find it uneven, certainly, but not lacking and clearly on the upswing. They would interview international head coaches like Russell and Lars and Graeme. Polls on *SENE On*line asked readers where they stood on the rules change, whether any team could best the United States, how many games Team Indigene Nation would win, and whether they planned to go to the games.

Archie had even turned my pig-headed insistence on the symbolic date of June Two for the championship game into a bonus opportunity for live TV coverage. He had found a gap in early June sports programming, a perfect slot for Pontiac-Looking-Down Day. It fell just before the NBA Finals and well before the baseball pennant races and arena football would heat up. The Masters would be over and nobody cared about the European red clay tennis season, so we had our slot. They would just slide us right in.

The Canadian government was first to the table, asking to bid on the exclusive broadcast and radio rights in their home market. Then the Pontiac Division called Archie and unsubtly offered his company as title sponsor of our event, gushing over how their snappy cars were the only thinkable match for a televised baggattaway tournament on Pontiac-Looking-Down Day. Then, *SENE* called. With over ten billion in revenues and seven channels dedicated exclusively to sports and entertainment and a vast international operation dangling on the line, Archie did not hesitate to uncradle the phone. On the other end were the executive vice-president of *SENE* International and *SENE*'s senior vice-president of programming. They told Archie they'd like to meet, discuss all the options, examine the whole WLC enterprise as a clean slate upon which to write a new chapter in sports television history, that they could deliver any number of well-heeled corporate sponsors with well-known international brands and that, still, they would work with whatever cadre of existing sponsors we had in our stable. They said only half jokingly that they probably already owned them anyway. They said that the 'The All-Americans Tour' was a sure-fire winner that would have no trouble whatsoever attracting sponsors and that the tournament format at first blush seemed a noble venture that extended into the very realm of righteousness, for which they had a department.

I had to ask myself: Was baggattaway a looking glass on the human spirit?

And: Who would pay the price of this celebration, in human terms? Because it became clear pretty quickly that a fortune was waiting to be made in this casino and that a spring lamb might need to be sacrificed as payment in kind. Businessmen did not love our game, they loved business. Alchemists who created riches out of nothing. They would conjure wealth from the smoke and mirrors of a global media campaign, a jingo, a hologram logo, a human face, all mixed in a beaker over a Bunsen burner until that precious something dripped into the mind of the public, and who, then, should their human face be if not the coach of Team Indigene Nation? But in their payday lay our redemption, that pinnacle where the wide eye of humanity would scour our sport for saintliness and, if it were to be found worthy, enshrine it. Would this be such a moment? Did the ancient Indian sport of baggattaway contain all of this? That was the bet I would make. Who else but me should lay his tender neck on the chopping block? Had another man come of age in two separate worlds, played the game on both sides of the fence, passed on wisdoms to the next generation of players, received divine orders to return his game to its people? I would stand accused of grandstanding for forgotten history. But nothing more nefarious than that. Our goal would be to win games, not to reverse fortunes. We would dig down through the hides of sand and stone, soft-brush the edges of the original fossil deposit, raise it up and say, yes, look, that was the forerunner, those are the genes, a beautiful thing happened here—in its dying act, one civilization bequeathed to another its game and let it be what it would, I understand the beginnings of sport. Place our amber-encased proteins on the altar at the top of the mountain and let the world say if baggattaway was a piece of humanity's bedrock. It came down to that one daring wish.

I talked with Lila that night of the press conference and met with Parry when they came motoring through the Soo on their return from South Dakota. Parry was like a victorious diplomat returning from abroad, aglow and basking in the unanimous support he'd drummed up for 'The All-Americans Tour' from Sioux Nation. TV and radio had covered his meetings in a huge teepee in the Badlands. News choppers had shadowed The Other White House in a state-to-state relay from Rapid City to the Soo. Yet a problem was weighing him down, a single concern so big that it alone could unmake everything—public safety. A simple question from the Oglala chief had keyed it. "Parry," he'd asked coolly, "what precautions will be taken for the protection of our people? I mean, a couple thousand chartered Red Dogs going up a thousand miles on the interstates. Every kook in town will be able to watch on TV, get the route and do something we could all regret for a long time."

While that dialogue added a new dimension to already frantic levels of planning and organization, Archie and I worked out the trip. I was to go in mid-December and return just in time for New Year's. There would be stops in London; Prague, which boasted the most energetic lacrosse program in continental Europe; and Shanghai. Archie had taken charge of the agenda, set up meetings, baggattaway exhibitions, fund-raisers, TV appearances, visits to schools, you name it. I was scheduled to meet an English earl, evidently at the earl's request, conveyed through Russell Pape. Prince Frederick was his name, the Earl of Essex, seventh in the line of succession to the British throne and a rebel royal who had actually played lacrosse. He wanted to get his hands on one of Neil's Native sticks, too, and had thoughtfully offered the hilly terrain of his Midlands golf course as the English play-in venue for the European regionals. Then, right at Christmas time, Prague. I would huddle with my colleague Karel Kovac, from Hull, the smoker with the odd sense of timing and the condescending smirk. And the final leg of the trip, the eleven-hour flight to Shanghai. I had no business going to Asia, I thought, but what if our sport caught on in a country with over a billion people?

Neil showed up, morose, for Thanksgiving morning, pushing a wheelbarrow full of sticks-in-the-making, reeking of fireplace ash and sap and moving hangdog. He looked tired. He didn't say two words to us over Marla's turkey dinner. He just told us that Thanksgiving was for fasting, not for feasting. And he did. He fasted in Zen-like peace, resisting our pleas to eat, sipping at a black coffee and quietly stroking the fur of his fourth beagle.

"Will you at least listen to the *Ameritalk* program on the radio tomorrow?" I asked him.
"Two p.m. They're talking about baggattaway, nation-wide, call-in, heavy hitters. Four Bears is on." But not even that could stir him.

"You mind if I borrow Marla to help me lace again?" was all he asked me.

And that was the last thing I saw before crashing into bed in the middle of my long Thanksgiving weekend, Neil and Marla setting up to do some serious stick lacing. Maybe he was overworked. The man had, at last count, two hundred eighteen more sticks to make in order to get them out to all the other teams by Christmas. Oh, and while he was at it I would throw in one more for Prince Frederick. It was piling on like they do to a running back in football, I knew, enough already, a poor Indian at the bottom of the heap struggling for air. He paid no mind to the cold, nor to the extra fingers of Jack Daniels he was downing as he worked his mysterious sons into being. He would come over to see if I wanted to go into the Soo and do the trail of tears:

"Stickmaking is breaking my head. Look, c'mon, we'll have a pizza and a vanilla coke with Tony."

"But you don't have any Bigwig maple goods to sell him. Plus, with snow coming you just know he'll be ramming snowmobiles down your throat."

"Okay, so we ditch Tony and steal a Montecristo from Mickey Blake for making a cigar-store Indian out of me, maybe stop into Tommy's for a quick beer and a fight with the Frenchies and maybe we'll see you on *SENE*, Mr. Big Shot, then we cap it all off with a haircut at Thaddeus Sokolowski and a little barber pole watch. Who can beat that, Birchwalker?"

He would look at me with doleful eyes borrowed from his beagle.

I know. I should have gone. I wanted to go. I wanted more than anything to do the trail of tears with my best friend. I wanted to have a meal with my wife, too. I wanted to get a full night's sleep so I could be right with the kids I teach everyday. I hadn't even seen my mother and Minerva since Columbus Day. Between leading team practices two weekends a month and having to beg travel subsidies for the distant stallions just to get them out here, and doing phone interviews from every kind of local, regional and, now, national news-gathering outfit and preparing myself for this trip to Europe and China, well, I was often too busy to even eat. I had not seen a clear sky since October. I had lost touch with the moon and the Afterlife, and that included my aanimendam father who wandered in Afterlife casinos, as well as my chieftain Bwon-diac in his moon buggy.

Even Marla was awash in her own truant officer busywork and now had her own issue to deal with, and the issue's name was Pascal LeFebvre. In Marla's mind, he was stalking her. Cozying up to her as she ran on the rez, coming out of nowhere and just scaring the hell out of her. Asked her questions about my trip and when I'd be gone. Then just as suddenly he'd peel off and leave. She wanted me to react, to be a husband, get in his face and threaten him to within an inch of his life, or be a coach and bench his ass or even flat-out expel him from the Indigene Nation team. But it was easier not to come down too hard on your best player unless the alleged stalking escalated or turned weird.

The biggest weight of all, though, however little we may speak of him, was Louis. His passing had cast the longest shadow. Sheila was as morose as her Uncle Longbow; Louise would ramble on, still clucking away at him; Minerva had lost her tongue, and Marla, Naanganikwe, was still his daughter-in-law. Louis's life swirled around us still, talked to us on highways and bridges, we were its milk trucks, carting his former existence around like Neil pushing his sons in a wheelbarrow, the exquisite burden of love.

When I came to the morning after Thanksgiving, I looked out the window and saw that it had snowed five inches overnight. "Shit," I said pulling on a T-shirt and almost tripping down the creaky half flight of stairs thinking of where we could practice, then remembering Pascal telling me we could use the new arena in the Big Soo if we would agree to work around the home schedule of the hockey farm team. As I got to the foot of the stairs, I remembered the stick making party, and there was Marla, the back of her head wedged into the seam of the couch, fast asleep. She was wan, her scar washed of its color. Her fingertips glowed red and her arm rested limp on a stack of fully-laced sons of Anishinaabewaki. I was held momentarily by the profile of my moonless woman at rest when I heard St. Anne panting and remembered Neil. I turned around...Listen: I don't think I was ever more startled in all my life. Behind me, in our rattiest chair, a wobbly old thing with no arms, sitting in an intense silence, was Neil, looking right at me with such a face. The look was not anger, not exhaustion. That look was something else, ghastly in its way. The look my friend wore that morning of the season's first snow was the look of forlornness, forlornness. He finally spoke.

"Birchwalker, four hundred twenty sticks is as much as I've made in some decades. What do you think I should charge the white man for my sons?"

"Welcome to Ameritalk," sounded the program's host Danielle McCann. Introducing her subject on the day after Thanksgiving 2009, she called baggattaway '...the little sport that has raised up a big debate over colonialism, athletics and Native culture in America.' Neil and Marla and I sat staring at the radio around the kitchen table, Neil still fasting and sipping black coffee while she and I nibbled on what my friend had not eaten the day before. St. Anne was running with some kids outside. Danielle introduced her distinguished panelists, Chief Parry Four Bears Beauchesne; Reed Seiss, a professor of colonial history; Michael Pierce, S.J., a Roman

Catholic priest who had written a book about the early New World settlements of the French Jesuits, and Will Jansen, a noted sports psychologist. Neil's eyes were heavy as the program began.

Within two minutes I hated the professor. He wanted to know '…why we should reminisce about a divisive story so bloody and violent as if it were some grand old time we all had? The greater good was served in the outcome, and we move on.' That pissed Parry off, because he shot right back that '…relocation and assimilation were not that grand a time for Native Americans.' They discussed the merits of playing the tournament at Green Bay and Fort Michilimackinac, and it was about to degenerate into a shouting match when the Father interjected. Neil's eyes popped wide open and Marla reached for her scar as he started to talk about *The Cry of Bwon-diac*! Our poem. And he knew all thirty-six stanzas by heart. He spoke parts out loud, in perfect meter and inflection, wielded each syllable like a history lesson, not only to support his won positions, but to say to Danielle's listeners, as he did, 'Hey look. Here is a chronicle of annexation that catches the feelings of what it truly is to be a vanquished people. Tied to the moon, you know, like the sunk feeling you have in a dentist's chair with a drill an inch from your numbed nerves? The dentist owns you.'

Neil doubted that the good priest knew it by heart. He looked at me and said, "Don't be a fool, Birchwalker. He's probably got it on the desk in front of him."

Danielle asked the sports psychologist what he thought and he said, 'I mean, if America is a giant oak, its roots are soaked in the blood of Native peoples, and that is hardly cause for celebration. You just can't separate all this stuff, the war from the sport from the civilization. You can't just pull up the root that's labeled baggattaway, dust it off and do a dance around it. You also get the roots marked colonialism, racism, Christianity, you see, and it becomes a woeful mess of exhumed guts that was just supposed to be a ballgame. You have to understand here. Baggattaway is the tip of an iceberg.'

To him Neil said, "Sometimes a cigar is just a cigar, Mr. Noted Sports Psychologist."

Next a kid called in, a high school lacrosse player and I'm pretty sure the only reason they let him on the air is that he came from La Crosse, Wisconsin. Too good. He said he would crawl to the games if he had to.

"So, you'll go to Green Bay?" asked Danielle.

"Oh, absolutely," said the kid.

And then it was Marla's turn for outrage. A senator from Kansas had called in, made my moonless woman go for her scar when he said, 'As much as I champion the playing of sports for the betterment of ourselves and our society, this particular proposal is nothing but the enshrinement of a terrorist act, dressed up as sport. Look, I smell payback and revenge afoot here. What's important is the integration of our population, not a demonstration of our apartness. We don't want distance between Native people and their adoptive culture. This idea is misguided. It must not be allowed to stand, and I frankly don't think any red-blooded American could see it any differently.'

"Terrorist act?" she shouted. "Smug-ass bloviator!"

We listened to a girl from Alabama who claimed a part-Choctaw bloodline. Katelyn said that not only did she love the title of 'The All-Americans Tour' but also hoped the tournament would be a monster success and spawn many more just like it.

On that most positive note, Neil came to his feet, shuffled over to the radio and turned it off. "Heard enough of that crap?" he asked, rather beside the point. "Anyway, the sponsors, whoever they are, will be happy."

Indian Diplomacy

Good to the last drop, good all the way to the very last damn irreducible quark. That's what I was thinking as the plane tilted up off the tarmac and pinned my spine and shoulders into the back seat cushion. We upright fossils were as good as fuels eventually, compressed, exhumed and sweetened by the weight of modern white culture, then exhausted by their jets as vapor at forty thousand feet, white plumes from which we drifted away, finally and utterly spent. It was pitch black and bitter cold in Detroit. Below me and falling fast I saw all the other upright fossils, the mighty trees and people of the Three Fires. The upward push into the atmosphere was irresistible, yet it was nearly balanced by the pullback of the immovable great waters and the rooted trees and tribes. The separation tore me in two, cleaving the part of me that could not leave Marla and Neil and my mother and sister and the team—especially the stallions, our last practice ever present in my mind—and peeling the rest of me forcibly toward a dream we all needed to become real.

"Coach, you're serious?" That was Trev Fenton as he spun the head of his stick in front of me like it was part of his body. He was hopping from one foot to the other. "Can we at least keep our socks on, coach?"

At ten in the morning, Saturday, December 1, 2009, I was standing barefoot on a piece of the PMS athletic fields blown clear of snow, pawing my whistle and watching my exhaled breath tail away on the stiff breeze, yelling mantras at the stallions and pretending it was the most natural thing in the world for the soles of feet to freeze to dead grass. I could just see the headlines: *Toes litter field at baggattaway practice. Frostbite leads to serial amputations, death. Team Indigene Nation withdraws.* I supposed I did overdo the barefootedness a bit in that early cold weather, but accommodation to the new rules had to begin. Pascal and Obie and Russell Phaneuf ran barefoot all the time anyway. I did manage to enforce other WLC commandments in the last practice before my junket, like the long field, the new sticks from Neil, the twelve-foot goals with twinned goalies. That all turned out to be more than ambitious enough anyway. Afterwards, I had scheduled y-scale practice and a mini Hiawatha marathon.

I gave them an early New Year's resolution. I said, "You need to start thinking of yourselves as players of baggattaway. Representatives of your people. Don't complain about sticks and rules. This was your game once. It was called baggattaway. Think like favorites, think like top seeds." They laughed at me.

Of course it would have helped if I'd had a full roster. But it stood at seventeen, so I was short eight players on attack and defense, and it was not immediately clear from which genie's lamp these eight would materialize. But that was a coach's worry and I distracted them from the thought with over-the-top workouts. I ran them like horses over fields without boundaries. I pounded *Stop* signs twelve feet apart into the almost frozen ground, target practice for the likes of Trev Fenton and his twin Robbie and fellow attackman Danny Brown to fling their lightning strikes at. *Make it sing from thirty-five yards*, I told them. Jerome French and Elias Lane stood in front and tried to block the shots. Even without a full roster, I would need to dream up a middie configuration. Under normal lacrosse rules, the coach rotated three lines of three in and out of the game, but in next year's tournament they would all be in the game at the same time. The coaches would be stumped at how to distribute play among the middie lines. This was the chaos that Drey Foss had predicted and which I would make come true. With my one asset, speed. Pascal, Orin Beauchesne and Herschel Seavey would be my first line, backed up by Aaron Bell, Jesse Olsen and Ronnie Philibotte for the time being. Delbert DesMarais and Evan Crosse would be in the mix, too. I would envision them as units, gliding over the field in tandem, three rabbit-quick little Indian trinities I could sic on Drey Foss.

I worked the fast break. I worked their stick skills and returned them to scoopers and jukers and passers. I put middies in their trios and had them practice stick and poke checks on one another, run quarter-mile wind sprints, build vital interdependence. The sticks were war clubs, tough to handle when you were used to sleek, whippy titanium. *Listen*, I said: *That ball's going to pop out of your pocket. Learn how to control it. Let it bounce off your chest. Control it, then scoop it up and run for the hills. Practice your barefoot turns and dodges. Practice double-teaming, flipoffs and cutting. Practice everything!*

My defensemen stuck to your ribs, or so I liked to believe. Tall, tall Russell Phaneuf, fast Obie Crick and Elias Lane. Strong quiet types, intense and competitive. First step was getting them to believe that defending was even possible without their accustomed six-foot defenseman sticks. There was going to be twenty-five yards behind the goal to defend, and offenses would stack up there, looking for a seam in the defense. They practiced breaking that stack maneuver. *Deny your man his lane*, I cried. *When your man starts his drive, you get that stick up to high-port, in his face. Strip the ball! They can't cradle it anyway so it'll be loose*! They would work hard. And if an opposition attackman somehow succeeded in penetrating my defense, he would find himself face-to-face with Jerome French. Not to be underestimated, he was pudgy, looked anything but the athlete. He had a baby face, and I wasn't even sure if he shaved yet. This was my advice: *Do not engage him in any contest having hand-eye coordination as its main skill, for you will lose. Whether your poison is video games or ping pong or baggattaway, he will smoke you. He can take up his goalie stick, stretch it out at an advancing attack-man or middie with a mind to shoot on him, and turn it in response to the shot on any plane in the blink of an eye. His reaction time is zero*. I couldn't remember ever seeing him blink. He stayed so cool under fire, he should have had sunglasses like Tipi and The Other White House. Attackmen were devious in this game. They lived to outfox goalies. They would stand in front of a goalie just to block his view of an incoming shot. They would put ridiculous head and body fakes on them, they changed direction on a dime, they took quick-stick shots high on the weak side or bounced it in front of the goal line when the goalie was up high with his stick. They juked like fleas.

Goaltending in our sport was the single most valuable skill, the final stand of the defense. Though Jerome had remained wordless about any of the changes, he was clearly thinking about them. He knew the pressure would be on him. The twelve foot crease doubled the width of the modern goal, and he was going to have to share a piece of his turf.

We would go for two and a half hours like this. It was at our last huddle, when out of the corner of my eye I saw Bone Digger coming around the corner of the school. In a navy blue pea-coat and matching tuque, no less, hands stuffed in his pockets. Come to pick over our bones. Tommy McKeon was with him. The King was working his chewing gum through his sneer. He wanted to know about Pascal, how he was doing. I sang Pascal's praises to him, but an ulterior motive began to seep from his unctuous features. I realized he'd heard about my roster shortfall. Then he asked about Neil, reported that he'd been coming to Tommy's all hangdog. The two of them left as quickly as they'd come, no obvious reason for their call. Then it was as if his mere presence had poisoned the stallions. We carried on with our scrimmage, up and down the snowy meadows behind the school. They dropped balls on long downfield runs, they missed passes and shots on goal, their arms hung like rubber, they cursed Neil and the sticks and bounced them off the ground until, born of frustration, came the breakthrough. Pascal Lefebvre, maybe the only one actually encouraged by Roy's visit, saw that an extra ingredient was needed, patience. The same patience we used to have with mere manual control of a television before the remote came along—you had to *get up* out of the easy chair, *walk* to the set and *turn* the knob. Likewise with baggattaway, you couldn't scoop on the fly, catch on the fly, or pass on the fly with Neil's blunt instruments. You first had to get your feet planted and then catch, first cover and then scoop, first lay the stick back and then cradle. The burden was on you and your hands and feet, not on the technology. Then, Danny Fenton figured out that shooting underhand would give more control because the ball would pinch between the frame and the lacing. And Russell realized he could let his arms do the work of the longstick he missed so much on stick checks, letting that natural advantage of big reach work for him. "Coach, this is like mowing a lawn with scissors," Jerome complained only half joking. He had the hardest job of them all, defending the goal with a stick whose diameter was half of what he was used to. He too would figure this out, learn to rely on his God-given talents and not on the fat goalie stick and the titanium. His hand-eye coordination produced the same kinds of exhilarating saves I always credited my father with in my imagination, in the crease on those windy days on the Ontario box rinks, digging balls off the ground, snatching them out of mid-air and then running like mad for the late steamer back home.

"Hey! Charlevoix! Right here, right now. I got a bone to pick with you." That was Andrew Sophie in the parking lot, practically on my hip as I opened the driver's door.

"Pascal," I said.

"You're damn right Pascal," through clenched teeth.

"He's Canadian, right?"

"Right."

"He should be playing for you, right?"

"Right."

"Not the way I see it. He's Anishinaabe."

"What the fuck does that mean?"

"Ah-*nee*-shee-*nah*-bay. You can say it, Andrew. It means Indian, that before there was a Canada or a United States of fucking America, there was the Council of the Three Fires, and if you haven't checked, we're playing the 2010 tournament by Indian rules. Canada doesn't exist yet, Andrew. There's no damn Maple Leaf."

"He's got a Canadian passport, Birch. I could sue your ass."

"Legally, Andrew, he is what the WLC says he is and what *he* says he is, and so far the Chippewa in him is doing the talking."

He was ready to take a swing at me. "There's a rumor that your team is going to practice at the Memorial Gardens Arena for the winter. That true? Just tell me yes, because I want a nice big package of infractions to take to Archie."

"Yeah, maybe. It depends."

"And I'll bet Pascal's setting it all up for you, right? You know we're practicing there too, and you know that I will do everything to prevent this, Birch. That's no shit."

"No shit? You're making me want to do it even more now! Remember the Hotel New Beginning, Andrew? Remember Archie told us to sort out our own messes? Well, let's do that, Andrew. There's two ways that I can see—the way you've chosen, which I would call...ambush, or the way I would choose which is by gentlemen's agreement."

He couldn't answer.

"Remember how Archie handled the mayor of London? There's nothing hard about this. We could meet at the Gardens, have a cup of coffee, sit down and talk. What do you say, because I've got to run, literally."

I told him to follow me to Pope County and to Neil's.

"You're the stickmaker?" he asked in a kind of enchantment, like he'd stumbled onto a house made of candy in the woods. "You're making all the sticks for the tournament?"

"Would you happen to have the sticks for Team Canada ready, Neil?"

Neil played along with me, bowing and scraping as he gathered Team Canada's sticks from the double wide and loaded them into a defanged Andrew's trunk. "Free of charge...and no tipping, please," said Neil.

Forty-five minutes later, the stallions were gathered at the trailhead. "I'll go easy on you, coach," Obie said, breaking up the trail.

"Y-scales at Tahquamenon," I yelled out. I noticed Pascal had the ribbed blue tuque on and was still barefoot. The two of us ran together a few strides and I asked him point blank, "Why are you running with my wife?"

"No reason, coach," he said coolly. "I just run a lot."

"Yeah, but you live across the river. What the hell are you doing down here at Pope County?"

"I come down to run in the Hiawatha, you know, sacred grounds?"

"That's bullshit, Pascal. Try again."

"Coming back on Six Mile Road, coach."

"That's one hell of a lot of extra running, co-captain. You're scaring her, you know."

"I know I startled her a couple of times. I didn't mean to."

I grabbed him by his sweatshirt, rougher than I should have. "Listen, a lot of the promise of our team rests on your shoulders. You get that, don't you? You teach these guys that y-scale at the falls, and stay off my rez!"

"You got it, coach," he said, and we both put it in gear again, pacing ourselves to catch the others. We ran faster and faster, bumping shoulders if we had to, and then accelerating into a full-bore sprint through the twisting paths of the Hiawatha. We were steeple-chase runners, picking our way over its cradles and graves, hurdling its fallen timber, splashing through its iced-over streams. Finally, with the others again in sight, he relented and fell back a few yards, as if he wanted the others to see nothing but deference on his part toward me. Only I got the same eerie feeling Marla must have had when I sniffed in this show of his not a hint of deference, but boundless contempt.

My ears were buzzing as the plane put down at Heathrow Airport. It was seven-thirty in the morning. The ankle was real sore. I was picked up by a guy named Mike Campbell, one of Russell's middies, and I wondered why the hell Russell couldn't have picked me up himself. I left a wake-up call for noon and went straight to bed, hoping Neil's sticks had arrived and that the Earl of Wessex, His Royal Highness Prince Frederick, had received his already. At one-fifty that first afternoon, I was waiting in the front lobby for Russell, but for the second time that day Russell Pape didn't show. He had sent another one of his players, and by the time I arrived at the ELA office—that's for English Lacrosse Association—I was more than slightly pissed off at the English coach.

"Birch," he said, beaming at me, as if we were old friends.

"Russell. You people play lacrosse in this weather? Did Prince Frederick get his stick? Did you get the sticks?"

"Absolutely, Birch." He had personally delivered one to Freddie the day they arrived. He, the Earl, wanted to have dinner with me that first night. "I've told him all about you," Russell grinned.

Before I left the ELA office, Russell filled me in on the agenda for my stay. There were to be school assemblies in London, baggattaway exhibitions on golf courses with players from the few league lacrosse clubs in the country, none with his players. He was only mildly on board with the idea of celebrating baggattaway, I thought, and he got prickly about putting me together with his sponsors, his team, anything at all meaningful.

"Russell," I said to him, "aren't you going to have me play around with your lads, at least watch them in action with the new sticks and new rules…meet with your sponsors?"

"You mean the old sticks and the old rules, Birch?" he answered. "I gave that some thought and decided I'd prefer to be quite on my own with getting the team adjusted. Like I say, we want to have you do some photo ops and Q&A with the team. Other than that, no need to take down our pants for you, is there? Divulge trade secrets to the enemy? I rather doubt it," he said with hard English T's. It was pretty clear Russell and I wouldn't be chumming around London together, taking in shows on the West End and dining out. I was pleased to have any company for dinner that night, much less royal company.

"Prince Frederick? It's an honor," I said as we shook hands.

"Listen, Birch, may I call you Birch? Call me Freddie, and please don't bloody scrape or bow or treat me any differently from your pals at home. Besides, we have a lot in common—no pun intended, I assure you—and it starts with lacrosse." He leaned back in his chair and played with a see-through cocktail, eyeing me curiously. He didn't look like a complicated man to me— mid- to late thirties, unmarried, trim, fit and very energetic, disarmingly open for an Earl of Wessex.

"Oh, I despise cricket and football," he said as dinner was served. He talked non-stop, once in a while asking me a rhetorical question I didn't have time to answer before he continued on. He had short, wiry blond hair close cropped on the sides and a little lock of which fell onto his forehead and dangled there like a loaded spring. You could call him eligibly handsome, but given the pile of money he was sitting on, his looks probably didn't matter all that much. There was a dimple in his chin, and even his slightest movements were crisp and athletic. "I much prefer the faster moving games, like lacrosse and, from what I've learned since receiving your stick a day or two ago, baggattaway, too. May I call them your people? You are American Indian."

"Yes, Chippewa, from the Great Lakes," I told him.

"I see, Chippewa. But not full-blooded, I take it."

"No, less than half."

"Fabulous, and you've come to promote this wonderful idea that Russell Pape has explained to me, this celebration of baggattaway, right?"

He listened attentively as I detailed the differences between modern field lacrosse—which, it turned out, he had played on the club level in his college days in eighties' Boston—and our Native game. He was fascinated.

"Russell tells me that your team don't stand a chance regardless of the rules you play by. True?"

"On paper, that's true," I said.

"You're confident," he said with a twinkle in his eyes.

He asked all about the rules changes, about this friend of mine who was responsible for the marvelous Native sticks, about the forts, everything. And when I told him about Bwon-diac and Pontiac's Lament, that got him talking about history.

"You can imagine, Birch, being related, however distantly, to the royalty of colonial England, one finds it relatively easy to know certain things. Though we don't exactly discuss them over dinner, we are well informed about the base calamities wreaked upon the Native populations of the present United States and Canada by our forerunners; we know of the smallpox blankets, the fur trade disruptions, the plundering of scared grounds and waters, the seizing of your women."

I pressed him about the boy king, King George III, the nemesis of Bwon-diac.

He roared with laughter. "Indeed I am, Birch. Well, he was, of course, in the house of Hanover and I am in the house of Windsor, but it is correct to say that if you trace our lines back far enough they will converge. Dear old Queen Victoria was the last Hanoverian monarch, and your George III was in that line above her. Then, during WWI, being a Hun just wouldn't do, so George V renamed the family after the location of its first royal residence, Windsor. Imagine, Birch. Victoria and Albert even summoned one of your American adventurer-artists to Windsor Castle for a private performance of his traveling Indian gallery. The Chippewa performed for them in our house, in the Waterloo Room. George III was a right dick, that one. Lost the thirteen colonies. Lost the whole bloody continent of North America, didn't he?" Our waiter delivered another drink to him. "He went mad at the end, quite mad," he continued. "The doctors gave him tartar emetics and bled him on a regular basis. He's buried at Windsor. It's really a barrel of laughs," he assured me. "Would you like to see his vault, Birch?"

Freddie's hunter green, custom Land Rover glided into place under the canopy of my hotel entrance, and one of the back doors opened to me on its own. Windsor Castle was massive, a cathedral, parts of it constructed as far back as 1070 A.D., and that included a room called the lower ward of St. George's Chapel where the remains of my chieftain's nemesis have lain since 1820. After leading me through long passages lined by ancient stone walls, past countless rooms, each with its own fireplace, past untold servants and butlers, Freddy suddenly turned to me and said, "Fancy a game of snooker before dinner?"

So, there we were, the Indigene and the Earl of Wessex, standing at his private snooker table in his family's thousand-year-old castle, hunkered over the angles of shots that would travel the green felt and disappear into small leather pockets. He poured cognac and lit himself a cigar. He waxed philosophical about snooker as a metaphor for baggattaway, the meadow of green felt; the leather pockets with their handsome scent as goals; the wooden cues that tapered like the heads of our sticks; the colored snooker balls racked and clustered like players on the field, the two contestants like coaches pacing the sidelines.

"Let's go see the vault," he said.

"Which one is his?" I asked as soon as we got there.

"He really pisses you off, doesn't he? You must tell me why."

I told him about Michilimackinac, the game on George's twenty-fifth birthday. About the sight of those redcoats and the twisted martial music of their fifes and drums, the bayonets fixed on their muskets.

"This I really enjoy."

"You may not enjoy the slaughter part of the story," I warned.

"Try me."

"The Indians tossed the ball into the land gate of the fort as a ruse. Their women and children were hiding weapons…"

"What kind of weapons?"

"War clubs, tomahawks, scalping knives."

"Lovely stuff."

"They cut out the hearts of the soldiers and drank their blood."

"There are times I'd have done it as well."

"This doesn't bother you?"

"I don't care about the gory bits, the details of war back then, or today for that matter. War is a blunt device, always brutal and inhuman, the least creative invention of man. All offensive war is travesty, I find. Don't tell anyone. That's not the kind of thing you admit to around here. Not many pacifists lying here under the High Altar, you know. There are something like thirty royals buried in the Royal Vault here, from infants to teenagers to cohorts to crumbling old men, every one of them an ancestor to me. Yet my heart is not with them. It is with the losers of history. The reason winners win is that they possess overwhelming force, and, in my book, the mere possession of force is no vindication for war; they're the ones who must learn restraint, a bit of the dexterity of a good laugh, I tell you, a ribald laugh in the face of provocation."

I had to challenge him. "England was always on offense, and they almost always won."

"That's why I'm in Italy so often! I would have been cheering Bwon-diac. He was tomahawked it says in the poem."

"Freddie, I came here to spit on your boy king's grave."

"When a foreign power kills your king, you must always hate them. Power speaks and you are voiceless."

"In the poem we are called upright fossils."

"There are those who have called *us* that for quite some time now…"

"England or the monarchy?"

"Touché, Birch. Both, to be precise. The toothless monarchy, a parody of itself, a laughingstock. The punchless Brits. The very royals that encased you in amber, Birch, are them-selves likewise encased. One might dare say entombed, as we're standing in this horrid chamber of fallen monarchs. I quite like the notion of the upright fossil. I had forgotten it. It's funny even while it is terribly sad. We are in the same boat, Birch, the boat of upright fossils. Let's toast to it!" His eyes sparkled. "Your story will live on."

"We are the names of places," I told him under my breath. "Chicago and Ocala, Chattanooga and Sheboygan; we are the names of rivers, like Mississippi and Monongahela and Ohio; we are the names of states, like Michigan and Oklahoma and Dakota! This is the fate of the upright fossil, labeled and gathering dust…"

He was with me. "Whether in a museum or a crypt. Birch! Windsor, our place name! Don't you see? We are upright fossils as well. Our identity buried in such places as these, we are place names like you."

"It is a state between life and death, a perpetual dying, like Bwon-diac on the moon."

There came over us one of those exquisite silences. We are brothers, I thought, the Earl and I every bit as related as Neil and I, as Marla and I. One of the richest men in the world is my brother. We gazed over the dust and ashes of dead kings and talked about history, and it hurt, it hurt, it hurt, to be in the brotherhood of upright fossils.

"So, Birch, it's the revenge of the fossils, isn't it? He exclaimed. "I get it now. You have changed the rules of the game that was stolen from you to reflect its perfect state, before its contamination by the white man.

Just then, he sounded like Drey Foss in Hull, and I didn't know if I could disagree anymore.

"Birch, you must hold on to your hate," he said. "Only keep it hidden below the surface. You must hold it in and use it to win the baggattaway championships. There can be no second place, do you hear? You must defeat Russell and his lads, and I, for one, will not only cheering you on in spirit…I will be there in person."

I couldn't see a thing out my airplane window, no stars or clouds, no moon, just my own vague reflection in the pitch-black. Five days before Christmas and I was going the wrong way, the long way home. As it happened, though, Christmas in Prague would be an entirely memorable experience. In the hollow metal tubes of the airport with seasonal hymns swaying above me and Christmas firs wishing *Velike Vanoce*, Karel Kovac approached me wearing a long, olive-green loden coat. His breath, of course, smelled of cigarettes. His odd sense of timing was reinforced in our first words.

"Birch."

"Karel."

"England, you saw the countryside. The English shires are the most pristine on earth, and, I assure you, so are the Czech hillsides...pastoral." We left the terminal. He smiled and stepped to the side to show the open door of his big black Mercedes. He drove it white-knuckle fast, through the boulevards of Prague and into the old city where the streets turn to cobblestone and just like that, openly coveting the wampum stick, he was wishing me *Velike Vanoce*, saying he'd pick me up at nine the next morning.

I limped into the room and flung my suitcase and bag and wampum stick and then my own tired body on the bed. I counted down baggattaway sticks like sheep, backwards from seventy-four, and drifted off to visions of Marla and Neil, toiling away at home. But I awoke encased in self-doubt the next morning. Who was I kidding? I asked the mirror. Why did the heady estimate of a hundred thousand spectators roll off my tongue so easily, so recklessly? Was I being cavalier, misleading, aanimendam? What right did I have to assume that Birch Charlevoix's wispy dream should materialize in the blood of modern Indigenes, awakening them all to my cause? Four Bears' tour notwithstanding, what would make my removed, assimilated, integrated, segregated people get up off their asses in a kind of reverse trail of tears and come to watch, in my mother's phrase, 'a bunch of sweaty guys play ball?' What kind of pre-American, pre-Columbian, pre-literate, pre-Enlightenment, retroactive pipe dream had Neil and I invented? Maybe we'd taken the long view of history. The European white man claimed this land, America, whatever you wanted to call it, dirt and sky, the land, rooted to the intelligence of the earth like a sensory tunnel, an ear, an eye, a mouth. Vanquished First People survived in the eternal mind of this land, and always would, recorded in its continuous dream, filed under *U* for *Upright Fossils*. One day the white man too would be swallowed by the land and archived, under *C* for *Colonizers*, and the ones after him, and the ones after them, each and every squatter catalogued in his turn. *The land owns us. The land owns us.* My little mantra for the day carried me through my morning shower and shaved me and dressed me and put me in the elevator and was still singing to me right behind my eyes as I shook hands with Karel in the lobby.

"I thought we might take a little drive today, out in the countryside. Does it suit you?"

I fought back the urge to tell him about the mantra, knowing it would spawn a debate I wasn't ready for. He lit a cigarette and inhaled sharply. One of the critical conversational tactics with Karel, I would come to understand, was the abrupt change of topic that was really a clever continuation of it. For some reason I dared to pit my limited skill against his.

"Coach Kovac, I present you with the wampum stick." He was taken aback, studying the carved icons intently. I explained the custom of wampum, reminded him of the fort and the lacrosse deception.

"I'd love to think about it," he said. "Can we take it with us today? "He turned his chin sideways, his eyes never coming unglued from the stick. "Birch, why don't you check out?"

I pretended that I understood what he meant.

"I invite you to stay with us, with my family," he explained.

"Did you receive your sticks, Karel?" I asked.

"Of course. Then you accept my offer."

Minutes later, we were zipping across the pleasant Czech countryside. Vienna was eighty miles to the south. We came into the Moravian lowlands, a landscape turned of lush hills and farmlands, hushed in December's frozen mists, brimming with rye and sugar beets in season. There was almost never snow early in the winter, and the grass stayed green. English weather, fog and cold rain.

"The sun will burn this off by noon," he said. We crossed a bridge over the Morava River; the fog began to yield sunlight like a sieve. "This is the field." I had never seen anything like it. An enormous alpine meadow. No dwellings in sight. A beautiful, gentle slope to the land, away from the river on either bank, out a half mile to the surrounding hills. The Morava was a broad river, three or four football fields across with a healthy current running north. It sliced right through the middle of a long wide pasture. It was the most perfect baggattaway field I had ever seen. "There you have it, Birch," he said, pointing to distant human figures coming toward us, "Team Czech Republic."

He cuts a smart figure, I thought, out there in the foggy meadow in a white shirt, a blue cashmere sport coat, expensive loafers and gray slacks, even the cigarette dangling from his mouth served the look.

"What's the matter, Birch? Don't you like surprises?" The entire team surrounded us, buoyant, youthful, athletic, tall. Piles of their clothes were strewn at the riverbank. "Ahoj!" he yelled to the team.

"Ahoj!" they yelled back. Then they all looked at me.

He draped his arm on my shoulder and said loudly, "This is Mr. Birch Charlevoix. He is the man who makes you use the new stick, play on a big field; it is he who makes you run barefoot!" At this, they all raised up their sticks and jeered me, feigning revolt. I could see they used their hands well, the way they managed the sticks, twirling them around absently; they could cradle and scoop and check with anybody. After the captain, Adámek, introduced himself, I shook hands with them all, tried to pronounce the strange names and promptly forgot them all except Šimon, Karel's son.

With his raised eyebrow doing the talking, he waded into the bodies, showing the green, black, red and yellow icons of the wampum stick. He motioned his team to sit on the wet ground.

"Because the American Indian is a primitive people," he began provocatively, "their ideas are simple, yet very strong. Myths and legends surround their game of baggattaway. Take note, please," he said to his rapt team, holding the stick above his head. "This wampum stick is what we play for, the green hill, the black bridge, the red ball, the yellow moon."

After the riverside rendezvous with his team, he took me to his home on the north side of Prague, and I was moved into the manor. Any description by me would not do justice to his place, but listen: it was a red-brick wonder, husky and elegant and if the trees would have just magically disappeared, we could have played the baggattaway tournament right there on his hilltop. The car. The house. The adoring team. The family, too. The wife named Irena and her high Slavic cheekbones that floated when she smiled, strangely, a bloodshot eye. I learned over champagne and goose and walnuts that Šimon was twenty-two and in the middle of his senior year at a college in Virginia. Another son, Stanek, explained how his father had come from soccer into lacrosse, how, thanks to Šimon playing the game, Karel had fallen in love with it and taken on the Czech bureaucracy single-handedly to establish a national team, winning instant celebrity as its first coach and access to ministries and officials in the process. Šimon told his father he thought the Czech team would make it out of the European play-in and get to Green Bay.

"The Scots, the Italians on a good day, the Danes, they could all trip us up," he cautioned. "I too want to win Europe. I do not want to be just one-of-two to make the final round; I want to go as European champion. We make it to Green Bay, Šimon, but we must play over our heads and the only way to do it is to practice and play exhibition games in the style of Birch's ancestors until your confidence is so high that no one can shake it loose. No one."

The next day Karel disappeared in the black Benz while I was running his hilltop through horizontal stripes of fog. Irena, Šimon,

Stanek, no one knew where he'd gone, but their reaction told me that this was not at all out of character. It was three days till Christmas. My ankle had swollen up badly from that jaunt with Pascal in the Hiawatha and just would not go down. Irena packed ice around it. Saturday evening came, a rainy Sunday dawned and set, Christmas Eve was upon us. Finally, at mid-afternoon the black Benz and its quirky owner skidded to a stop in the cobblestone drive of the manor. I thought he'd come to explain, to look in on his guest. He did not come to speak to me. I was getting fed up with his queer charm.

Before dawn on Christmas morning he woke me, and the lines of a rationale for his absence would quickly emerge. Karel did have charm by the boatload; he had wit; he was certainly arrogant and aloof; he was by turns flattering and insulting; he had power and was clueless; he was sensitive and hard as nails. The list was confused, I know, it was also endless, the combination punches he could land on you if you let him in. The man also had some serious pull, pull that could roust high-ranking officials out of bed on a foggy Christmas morn, pull that could produce a command exhibition of nine other (Germany, Italy, Sweden, Denmark, Holland, England, Scotland, Wales and Ireland) European lacrosse teams on that same Christmas morn for a six-hour mini-tournament he called the *Velike Vanoce* Games, pull that got his *Velike Vanoce* Games splashed in all the papers and advertised on radio and television.

First, I was hurried in the black Benz to Prague's Old Town Hall where I met with the mayor and three Czech ministers—Education, Youth and Sports; Health and

Culture—plucked from their families on Christmas morning. I had my picture taken a thousand times if it was once, an amazing photo opportunity in the face of many cheering thousands in the main square of the city, strolling Czechs who might have been returning home from Christmas Mass and who had followed the crowds into the square where they were then exhorted to board the buses arranged for by you-know-who that would ferry them out to Otrokovice where they could spend the fine day amusing themselves at a celebration of baggattaway. Karel himself took the microphone many times and spoke in Czech. He brandished the wampum stick at one point to a thunderous round of applause. He had charisma. Plenty of that. Opportunistic as well. Who would have said no? The buses were idling just off the square; there was the promise of barbecue pits smoking carp and chicken and beef at the fields, and where such local delicacies abounded, could dill soup and Pilseners be absent?

Lars Asferg was the first to find me in the absolute throng of spectators said to number in the early tens of thousands, all jammed like Woodstockers onto the Otrokovice playing fields where two games were always in progress thanks to that gorgeous twin meadow. He was very warm to me and congratulated me on what he called the rebirth of baggattaway. The weather at Otrokovice was perfect in the afternoon. The fog had burned off, the temperature was in the low forties again, and a topless sky showered deep blue upon the battle formations drawn around the rustling Morava. Not one of the teams had mastered Neil's sticks, though they were definitely catching on. Watching this scene, strolling through it on Christmas morning, I had to pinch myself. Lars was right. Karel had produced the kind of opportunity no coach could turn down—an exhibition that would surely kindle a loyal following, the chance to gauge the competitiveness of future opponents in a friendly competition, a test for the players who would run barefoot on a kilometer-long field of baggattaway. You simply could not afford to miss it. Swells of players from both sides pursued free balls, sometimes moving so far downfield the spectators lost sight of them completely and waited for news of the attack to filter back to them. Had a goal been scored? Yes! Sprained ankles, bruises, cuts, they all happened about as expected. *Ball-up* was a hit with the players and the basketball-loving Czech crowds. It was a sight for sore eyes to see Neil's sons stretched into the sky to rip down the hanging ball. I walked down the river to the far goal and studied the tandem-goalie system in practice. It was awkward if the guys weren't talking to one another and they ended up crashing into one another like two fielders going for a fly ball. I made a mental note to put Jerome in charge of calling every single shot on the Indigene Nation goal.

There were some excellent games. With ten teams and only four or five hours of daylight, the games had been shortened to forty-minutes or the first team to five goals, whichever came first. Karel's team and Denmark, Lars's team, played one another to a draw and settled it like a soccer match, by penalty shots. Karel's team eked out the victory. It surprised me how quickly their players were adapting to the sticks and the rules, as if they had not had a lot to unlearn about modern lacrosse. In the final game of *Velike Vanoce*, Harald

MacManus's Scots outlasted Karel Kovac, taking the title, 5-3. A joyous noise was the exodus from the fields back to the cars and buses. Vendors and politicians and fans and coaches and kids and of course the athletes them-selves took away the concept of our game. And when photographers and chroniclers from the papers had finally photographed and chronicled the last images and words of the *Velike Vanoce* Games until only the gurgling Morava remained, I gave thanks for the first baggattaway matches held in over two hundred years.

But there would be more to Karel's Christmas surprise, its exclamation point, the gala dinner at Prague Castle. Some ninety minutes after the Games had ended the same throng of players and coaches, together with Karel and his family and sundry local dignitaries, filed into Hradcany Castle. "The president may make it for dessert," boasted Karel with that smirk as we walked into the Vladislav Hall. Still basking in the runner-up finish in the *Velike Vanoce* Games. We entered via the horses' staircase, a set of long, low, brick steps over which knights once rode their jousting steeds into the hall. Karel called it a state dinner and soiree rolled into one. Imagine a lavish banquet hall, its long dining tables set regally for three hundred guests. There must have been fifty Christmas trees. Candles flickered on the tables. You could hear the echoes of footsteps on the cold stone floors. A string quartet which had escaped my notice suddenly burst into a series of chamber pieces from the eighteenth century. Champagne bubbled in fountains. The medieval walls all but swallowed the conversation of the three hundred, and then the lights went up. From that same horses' staircase came the unmistakable clatter of iron shoes on cobblestone. Ten riders on ten white stallions rode in single file, stealing the attention of every guest. Someone pointed out that each horse wore as its saddle blanket the colors of one of the ten countries that had played in the *Velike Vanoce*. It was true. There was the black-red-yellow of Germany, the green-white-red of Italy, the red-blue-white of the Czech Republic. Each rider held a baggattaway stick solemnly above his head as the white horses cantered around the guests and the chamber music swelled. The humble Native American game of baggattaway was set in a whole new regard, ennobled. Karel had managed to raise its profile in far away Europe, gave it a Moravian baptism. I stole a glimpse of him. He was clapping and whistling and there were tears in his eyes. The horses pranced and snorted around the perimeter of the hall many times before gathering themselves in a tight shoulder-to-shoulder formation away from the tables, and a hush came over the crowd. Karel rose and spoke eloquently about Christmas and baggattaway. He called me forward and draped his elbow over my shoulder. How the cameras clicked and whirred. How they applauded us.

It was almost a circle, the Snow Moon that escorted me like an owl's eye from Amsterdam to Shanghai. It flew alongside me, a silent hitchhiker on the wing of my plane, an angel on my shoulder. It was so perfect that it took my breath away. The moon was closer that high up, set theatrically against the void of space. I did not see him, but I heard him, Bwon-diac, those gorgeous war whoops belted out into the vacuum of space.

"Hi yi yi ya yo! Hi ah ho ay yo! Heya, heya, ha i ya ho ay oh!"

Father, why have you forsaken me? he said.

"Hi yi yi ya ya! He yi yi ya yao!"

Retake my forts! he said.

So I replied to him.

Around the world, Bwon-diac, I am circumnavigating the earth just like you. Many people say it was from Asia that distant ancestors began the trek across the land bridge to the tundra above Hudson Bay. Many people say this is the reason that the red man and the yellow man are both the brown man, their broad, round, flat and hairless faces a mirror of one another. Many people say that our two cultures understand the moon, its primacy in the affairs of men, that we keep our time to it. It is the clock of life and death, a pipe of peace shared between the Chinese and the American Indigene. Do you not think, Bwon-diac?

By now, I hoped, Neil and Marla would have baptized their last stick, and I was thinking, sucked in by lunar light, that my friend had probably gone on a major bender to celebrate. His sons would soon be scattered out into the world, missionaries sent abroad to spread the gospel of baggattaway. He must be happy, I thought. Hats off to you, Neil Longbow LaSalle, I thought. You have accomplished the task of a lifetime. Four hundred twenty baggattaway sticks, each one shaped by your own hand, alive with your own spirit. It is a beautiful thing. I bet you went Lockside right to the trail of tears, bellied up to Tommy's bar, ignored the taunts of our good friend Roy LeRoi and ordered yourself up a few frosty mugs inside those frosty windows where the Frenchies and the Irish huddle around the single, inescapable image of sixteen football games. You did, didn't you? I wish I could have been there with you, preceded you into the bar, rolled out a red carpet and announced you to the patrons. I wish I could have watched St. Anne Four, who was probably happier than yourself that the long night of stickmaking was over, as she chased her tail, fully beset by all that televisual chaos. I would have hoisted several myself in your honor. I would have looked for an opening to ask you to make twenty-five more wampum sticks for the winning team at our tournament. I would have bought you a Montecristo at Mickey Blake's, a pizza and vanilla coke at Tony's. I would have given my eye teeth to be there with you. I would have placed my coat around your overworked shoulders as we stood guard at the barber pole at Soo Locks. Is it cold at home, my friend? Has the snow piled up on Ashmun Street? Have the Great Waters frozen over this year already?

My God, that moon was something to see. I had the illusion that I was at its height, that it was just over there, off the port wing. It glided through space like a birch bark canoe through water. I studied its face for hours, looking for my chieftain. There were fissures and fractures, pocks and craters, on its surface, but its edge was round as an eye. The pull on the poets and the oceans and the women below must be profound tonight, I thought. The urgings on the hearts of man must be irresistible. The rivers and lakes of Anishinaabewaki must overrun their banks.

I saw Marla's face, my moonless woman. Have you forgotten me in all this fury of travel and baggattaway? Or is my fury your boredom? You have given of yourself. Like a midwife, you have helped my friend give birth to his sons, lacing them all at the moment of their becoming as if you were wrapping them in swaddling. I send to you a thank you for the invasion of thirty-one years ago. You walked out to the rez in your pink Converse and took this Indian shirt off the rack. If we are severed by this noble baggattaway mission, then it is this moon that rejoins us tonight. The little yellow moon on the wampum stick, the moon in the sky over you, the moon on my wing. It's going well, Marla! Baggattaway is a hit! A hit in England and with the Czechs, with the players and with the spectators. I have seen things. I have met people. I have learned things. Neil's sons have been raised overhead on horseback in a thousand year-old castle. I have been claimed as a Christmas present by a wealthy Czech with rhetorical pauses. Have you put up a tree? Has Neil given his annual Christmas prayer, the one where he says that Indians are like fir trees in the wild, cut down and taken into the white man's den for fifteen days at Christmas, the one where he says that a fir tree sawed from its roots and locked onto a tree stand by a warm hearth no longer has the spirit of a tree, that it is doomed? I am thinking of you. I am going to repay you for the kindness of your invasion. I am going to take your breath away with the engagement ring I have saved for ever since you started working at PMS.

I did not, could not sleep. My soul stayed up to drink in the light of that Snow Moon. I would happily have perished in its hold. I watched images and faces and memories and dreams popping up from its surface as my stewardess taught me about Chinese teas. I asked her how the weather was for our landing in Shanghai.

"Under the clouds is rain," she replied. "Much rain."

Inside the international terminal of Hongqiao International Airport an ocean of humanity roiled below me. Cresting atop the waves was a tall young woman, moving her right hand back and forth like a windshield wiper at me. A huge clock behind her tolled precisely 11 A.M., 27th December, 2009.

"How did you recognize me?" I asked her over the din.

"I am very happy you carry the lacrosse stick," she smiled.

As we puttered along into the city, she pointed out the vital signs of Shanghai life: Jiaotong University, where she majored in English; the clangy boat traffic on the Yangtze River and the central rail station; the Oriental Pearl T.V. Tower; Yuyuan Garden, where the old people do their t'ai chi at dawn; People's Square. She parked her tiny blue Xiali and walked toward the European-style promenade they call the Bund, turned to me.

"Would you like a cup of tea, Mr. Birch?"

In the cool rains of December, the warm smells hung low. Steam shrouded the Mandarin signs. Ramen and Mexican, laundries and fruit stands, Tandooris and the acupuncturists' bitter moxa merged and wafted in every direction. I was overwhelmed by the idea that the Chinese are an indigene society. And that no one ever came to kill them off. Thirteen million Shanghaiese alone, just doing life, leaving footprints we never could.

Li Mei is twenty-eight, and she harbors the dream of going to America one day. Since graduation she has worked at the People's Daily Online. Li Mei showed me to a table where Li Rui, her father, hovered over a teacup. Rain poured relentlessly, and I was beginning to wonder if our lacrosse exhibitions might get washed out completely.

"Mr. Birch," offered Li Rui in almost unintelligible English, "you like tea?"

"Father would like you to try his favorite with him," said Li Mei, "a spicy black tea. Very tasty." Her father drew her to him and whispered in Mandarin, urged her to tell me something.

"Mr. Birch, my father asks you to pour his tea."

Then, for show, Li Rui held out his right fist to me palm down and extended his index and middle fingers as if he was dipping them in holy water. He then folded them back to the second knuckle and gave four or five light raps on the table. It brought a smile to his face that Li Mei explained.

"It's the thanks knock," she said, a little perturbed with her father. "In the Ching Dynasty long ago, the emperor liked to dress as a commoner and visit his kingdom. Servants were told to stay incognito to keep secret their master's identity. One day in a restaurant, the emperor poured himself a cup of tea, then filled the servant's cup as well. To the servant, it was a huge grace having the emperor pour him a cup of tea. He wanted to kneel down and thank his master. But he was stopped because that would give away the emperor's identity. So instead of kneeling on his knees, the servant kneeled with his fingers." She showed me the folding fingers again in case I missed them "kneeling." With a certain ceremony, Li Rui stood and lifted the teapot and poured one for me, returning the favor. I inhaled the sharp spices and performed the thanks knock as a little white Shih Tzu dog I hadn't even noticed before yapped like a soprano St. Anne.

The torrents of rain finally washed out all hopes of baggattaway and left us with plenty of time on our hands. Through the swinging wipers of Li Mei's windshield, I did get to see the Dze Chiang Country Club where the teams from China, Japan, New Zealand and Australia were to have played. There was no point, though, in waiting out the rains and I decided to leave early. When I told Li Mei, she became very anxious and begged me for help.

"Please, Mr. Birch," she began, "say nothing to my father. I want to cover the games? You please to come with me, tell my boss to send me to America?"

That final night of my trip I dreamt a disturbing duo of dreams. In one dream Marla's vermilion turtle, which she gave me to wear for the trip, suddenly lit up like a message light on a telephone. It was Marla. I knew it; she was trying to contact me. In my dream, I saw it flashing on a woman's neck, in the little swale of skin between the collarbones, ringing, and then I saw that the swale belonged to my moonless woman, and she was jogging through the alleys of the Pope County Indian Reservation. Her face writhed in the pain of being pursued. Pascal ran beside her, cool as a cucumber, laughing and joking as she tried in vain to get away from him. He ran her into the Hiawatha and I woke up in a sweat, panting. The second dream was the bloodletting dream. Neil was in it. Neil, of all people, whispering urgently to me in the dream that the white man is like a phlebotomist, a blood-letter, standing over the outstretched arm of the prone Indigene, stabbing our veins and slyly drawing up precious Native blood until we are dry. It ended with Neil shaking his head and saying darkly, "This is how the dust has settled."

Something was going on at home. I tried to call from Hongqiao Airport, but there was no answer. The phone just kept on ringing. All I could do was get on the plane.

It seemed whole weeks had passed until finally I was on the final leg, nervously bouncing both knees up and down as I sat staring out the Red Dog bus window, sipping bad coffee from a plastic cup. In the other hand I had a hold on Marla's vermilion turtle as if it were a rosary, something more than the colonial heirloom that had brought me full circle and back home. The signs for farm towns and county roads in Michigan floated by my tired eyes like pieces of driftwood on the black sea of the new year 2010, exits for Flint, Saginaw, Bay City, Sterling, St. Helen, Grayling, Frederic, Gaylord. Michigan was too long. Finally there was Wolverine and Mackinac City. We were more than half way. Next stop Big Mac and then another fifty miles on I-75. At long last, I hailed a cab to cart me the final miles out to Periwinkle and the reservation. I could smell the Hiawatha, the cold fir. It was New Year's Eve, and Michigan was covered in snow. The moon was not to be seen—had it snowed down all its light on Pope County and faded away forever? There had to be thirty inches on the ground, and the temperature was cold enough that it was sure to stick around for a while.

St. Anne Delivers

"What are you doing here, girl?" I ask St. Anne Four, the one being I did not expect to see after the longest day of my life. "You better get yourself a new stylist," I tell her. Her fur is clipped short in many places, uneven, like she was attacked by a mad dog barber. Can I even begin to describe how good it feels to be home again?

"We all alone?" I ask the dog. "Where's Marla and Neil?"

So, if this is New Year's Eve, where's my bride and my best friend, and why is St. Anne here by herself? I toss my bag and the wampum stick in a dark corner. Why is the house so dark? She must have gone out when it was still light and not come back as soon as she thought she would. God, has she left me? Has she finally left this poor Indian dog, I wonder, finally had enough of the rez and the alley ways she runs four days a week and the damn tenement holes she drags her truant PMS kids out of? Has she finally gone back to the Soo, recrossed the river to her own people's encampment? Was she just waiting for me to be gone so she could make her move without having to explain? A memory assails me, a single inescapable image, Roy pointing his chin at Pascal as he's being led out of Jimmy Blackbird's banquet room at my father's wake. That nod of the head. It was loaded. And what of my team? Did they practice in the arena in Big Soo? Any problem with Andrew Sophie? Are they fasting and growing calluses and blisters on their soles? Is Archie signing corporate and broadcast partners? Has Parry Four Bears rounded up a hundred thousand Native Americans to come to three baggattaway fields in the upper Midwest and eight new Choctaw to play for me?

"What's this, girl?" I ask her, picking up a cylinder of paper that's caught my eye. It's lying on our kitchen table, a couple pieces of paper I could just as easily have mistaken for coupons or something and thrown away. They're rolled up so tight, it looks like they've been stored in a cigar tube. Something about them is saying Neil to me. I pick them up. Maybe the hint of his unmistakable lettering that bleeds through from the front. The papers are resistant to any attempt at straightening, and it's so darn dark even with the light on that I decide to light a candle. St. Anne starts barking and won't stop and then I see she's.....talking to me. This dog wants me to sit down and read this letter. I hold it open with a hand at either end, and, right away, it's Neil.

"If you're reading this, then St. Anne
O'er Great Waters has swum bravely
And across Big Mac has sprinted
Did she pay the toll, I wonder?"

"Sounds like Neil's sense of humor, doesn't it, girl. Now, what the hell is he talking about? Pay the toll?"

"In this moment I have stacked up
Twelve lacrosse sticks in a pyre;
On the Straits of Mackinac light
Polka-dots of snow are flying."

I can feel my face falling. A pyre? The Straits? And I remember the little framed picture at the peace van, where the baggattaway players have stacked up their sticks for a blessing by the shaman.

"St. Anne Four has learned the way home
She has mastered swimming shoreward;
Soon I'll toss her in the Waters,
But her legs I will not bind up."

I look quickly to St. Anne who, in turn, is regarding me unblinkingly. "Oh, no!" I yell out. "What has happened here?" And I realize she knows everything and that she always has. For some reason I begin to read Neil's poem out loud. I do not want to hear what I am hearing in my head over the echoes of shrieking jet engines and that is the sound of Neil's distant voice chanting these very words with me from the Path of Souls.

"Swim, St. Anne! Swim for your life now!
Aazhawaadagaan, my beagle!
Make your way back to Birchwalker;
Ram his leg until he sees you."

"Oh, Jesus." My breath is catching even as I laugh through the welling tears that my friend would talk of his dog ramming me. "Dear God," I cry out to the dog, "did he throw you off his canoe on the Straits? Did you swim to shore and run all the way home?"

"She has run the Mackinac Trail;
She has run through two cold twilights;

Up the U.P. she's ascended;
Please look after her, my dear friend."

How long does it take a beagle to run fifty miles in the dead of winter? Is it possible? I look again at St. Anne. She is still staring *me* down, urging me to read on. "Yes," her eyes say, "I ran the Trail." Am I seeing Neil in her? "Are you the same one that went to the moon with me?" Am I having some kind of nervous breakdown? Am I finally going aanimendam?

"Try to understand, I beg you,
Though I know it is not easy—
I am ashes now Birchwalker,
I am ether in the Sky-world."

"Neil!" I howl in anguish, but St. Anne doesn't budge. I am completely lost. There is a pounding in my head, right between my eyes, that is strong and getting stronger, a demon leaning on a chord in a very minor key, a dark chord, a dirge, and I am broken for all time by my friend's passing. I give up on this day. I am beyond touching now. I am immune to it all.

"Did I tell you not five full moons?
Does the full Snow Moon not draw me?
Bwon-diac himself is wailing,
And I dare not keep him waiting."

That night with Archie. Stickmaking and stinking Tennessee sour mash. He said it, didn't he? Told me outright that he would be gone in five moons. But right away I hurt again, I am no longer immune. My mind, nimbler than I would have believed, has made certain calculations as I prepare to mourn. It reports the memory of that night flight from Amsterdam to Shanghai where the full Snow Moon rode on the wings, that I gazed out at it for hours and believed that the pull on dreamers and lovers must be irresistible. Was it at that very hour that my best friend, my brother, dragged his boat out onto the lower Straits and set it on fire? This is an utter impossibility and I will collapse altogether if I do not stop reading these words.

"I must tell you, I must tell you,
'Ere I set my boat afire
How this ending did befall me
How I came to this departure."

"Do you Ashmun Street remember
And the barber pole of Soo Locks,
How I guarded it with St. Annes
Like my life depended on it?"

Again I look at the dog and it is true that she knows everything. The pupils in her eyes are as black and shiny as the dark side of a new moon and there is a corona on their rims suggesting a light on the back side where Bwon-diac and Louis and now Neil are all aboard. She is also St. Anne One, Two and Three, and she is also Neil Longbow LaSalle. She has made baggattaway sticks and guarded barber poles. She has consumed sour mash whisky and sung poems at the birth of her sons. She has told the story of Wakayabide on Pontiac-Looking-Down Day. She is the grandfather of man. Now I am

seeing in the way I saw on the moon with Bwon-diac. Neil's words
are button candy, a ticker tape behind his beagle's pupils.

"You remember too Soo Theater
Kitty-corner from the Soo Locks
That they always played two features
That at night I'd spy unseen there."

"And if lovers came a-strolling
From the movies out to Ashmun,
From my quiet little station
I could eye them unattended."

    "No, dear God."

"I remember still the titles,
The big films of Seven-seven—
Annie Hall (I thought I loved her),
Close Encounters of the Third Kind."

    I speak to St. Anne, laughing through fresh tears. "Yes, I
remember. You loved Annie Hall. You said she was the only white
woman you could ever love, that she had gotten life just about as right
as white could get it."

"After all had left the movies
And I stood my watch for Frenchies
Came a young man and his woman
And they stopped and there was tension."

"'I am late, Roy! I am late, Roy!'
I can hear her voice today still
Echo off the dark, wet pavement

How she pled with him for pity."

In my head, alongside the shriek and the dirge, an alarm begins to sound, and all three of them circle around inside my skull. Close encounters are at hand here. It was Roy. It was Roy.

"But he looked not kindly on her,
Merely coiled his big right hand back,
Lashed her cheekbone harshly with it,
Left her sprawled out on the street there."

"Marla."

"Should I help her, Should I help her?
Wondered I with much confusion,
Or my Injun nose not stick in
To the matters of the white man?"

"Help her! Don't just stand there like a fucking cigar-store Indian, for God sake!"

"She was bleeding, she was crying;
In my head there came a great ache,
For she struggled to her feet then;
On the gash she held her hand down."

The move that signals my love for her comes to my eyes, the fingers raised just to the point of touching the smiling red scar, and withdrawn at the last second. I am doing it now myself.

"In her face I saw a sorrow
A dilemma of existence:
When the Soo has sent you packing
You have nowhere else to call Home."

I close my eyes. I know I am watched by St. Anne. I see young Marla crossing over to the rez, baby Sheila bouncing on her back. Rejected from the Soo is the bottom of any barrel.

"Barely twelve moons had transpired
And that scene had left me no peace;
I was looking out my window
In the alleys of our rez here."

"You recognized her," I say to St. Anne.

"It was Naanganikwe walking,
A papoose upon her shoulders;
She was striding in those pink Cons,
Making for the house of Louis."

"Naanganikwe. What you called her the night of our wedding, the night of the full moon like a baggattaway ball through the trees and the vermilion turtle and the pink Cons."

"You will ask me how I knew it—
When I married you that evening
And her smiling scar I did see,
I put two and two together."

There are manidos jumping into my skin from everywhere, swarming me, my crazy father's forearm frogs, the evil spirits he used to taunt Minerva and me with. The news from my dead friend's voice regarding the secrets of my life makes me shiver like life is passing from me. A bare wire is draining me.

"You will ask me, 'Why not tell me
Of these stories? They're my answers!
Whence the smiling scar and baby
Of my moonless woman Marla?'"

"'And so now you deign to tell me
Of all people Roy this asshole
Is the answer to both questions:
Fathered Sheila, pasted Marla?'"

"'And you've known it, and you've known it,
Thirty years or more you've known it.
Yet you could not tell me of it;
Please explain yourself, my brother!'"

"Yes!" I scream at him. "Please explain yourself, my brother! After thirty-one years, please explain yourself! Please explain how you kept Roy and his scar a secret for thirty-one years!"

"It's that scar that gives me goose bumps;
At the wedding black I made it;
For Roy's voice was speaking through it,
So I sealed it up with war paint."

I remember that. I remember how you reached out to her face and smudged the charcoal and bear fat over the scar. Neil: Did you really see his lips?

"Please envision now Roy's red ring
Barely fits upon his finger
I am sure that was the weapon
Ruby red begat the bleeding."

He still wears that fucking ring. Right under my face. Every time we go to Tommy's, every time we fight, at practice the other day. Coward has tried to light up my chin with it, too. Bastard can't get the evidence off his goddamn finger.

"And for all of this, Birchwalker,
Do you think you can forgive me?
That I chose not to reveal this
Haunts me even at my burning."

"Neil, how is it I should hate you? You have set yourself on fire. Ancient secrets you have carried. Painted lips will not be silenced. Did you never see it glimmer, that red scar that Roy did give her? Oh, my friend, what have you done here? What insanity befell you?"

"I could hold it in no longer;
Yet I could not let it out, so
From the seam twixt sky and water
I can let my secret go free."

"Please do not a coward judge me;
I could not bear that dishonor;
Rather Noble Savage call me
Call me Unencumbered Spirit."

Oh, oh. Your toast at my father's wake. Your fellow aanimendam. You said this during your toast to Louis: *Isn't that what life is, denying the soul its range, its running room?* You told the assembly that your sons would forever run around the edge of the earth under the gaze of the gods playing the eternal game of baggattaway with my crazy father's beet balls. And through my grief and anger and confusion I ask myself if Neil hasn't broken free himself, his thousand sons sown like seeds around the world by Birchwalker. Is this the beginning of understanding of what he's done? Who will call me Birchwalker now?

"These disclosures make me nervous;
He will stick you with that big shiv
For he comes to claim his daughter
And he wants his Annie Hall back."

I am crying again, crying at the thought that my friend, as a young man, watched our Annie Hall have a Close Encounter of the Third Kind, that he bore his guilt so alone for so long. I do not know if I can read any further. I want tea.

"Of his guile you must be leery
Turn your back not lightly on him;
There's an agent, too, the middie,
That he planted on your roster."

"In the alleys of our rez here
Pascal jogs with Naanganikwe
Arabesque move notwithstanding,
Can you trust him, can you trust him?"

      "Pascal."

"But the Soo has ground me down now;
Barber pole must twirl without me;
You and St. Anne Four can guard it;
Now the trail of tears is ended."

      "Tony, Mickey, Tommy, Thad: He's gone."

"Of your woman do not think ill
That she such a past has shrouded
All this time you have been guarded
In the knothole of the ash tree."

"But the dingo dam herself is
Now the object, now the quarry
You must place her in the knothole;
And stand guard against the serpents."

"Was it Louis led me out here,
Dying face-down in his red beets?
Dirt to dirt and ash to ashes,
Now poor Sheila tends his garden."

"May the Natives come in droves to
Cheer your team against the English;
I'll look down upon them playing
Pray you, put a whuppin' on them!!"

"We are brothers, we are brothers
In Baggattaway we live on;
With our June Twos do continue
I will meet you in the Meadow."

With visions of the field at Michilimackinac before me, I am out the door and running like an amped-up middie through the alleys to my mother's house. They will have news, mother and Minerva. They will know what has happened. But at midnight on New Year's Eve, neither of them is home. Backtracking to Neil's, I pass my own house, and I hear their voices before I see their faces. My wife, my mother, my sister and another woman whose voice I cannot make out approach me in the dark first minutes of 2010.

"That you, Birch?" my mother calls out.

At our humble front stoop I step out to greet them. A hug from Minerva, a bobbing hug and kiss from Louise.

"You're home early!" says Marla, wrapping me in a hug that was a little quick. "Look how skinny you are, Birch!" And she hugs me again, better this time. "Thank you for coming home early. I'm sorry."

Thank you? I'm sorry? "Why didn't you tell me?" I scream at her over the jet engines.

They all look very tired, but their faces reveal none of the trauma to which I have been exposed in the last few minutes. It turns into a standoff, none of them knowing who should speak or where to start.

"Come on!" I yell at them. "I know he's dead. I just read his poem." Suddenly I realize that St. Anne Four is standing right by me, that she must have followed me out the door and run alongside me the whole way. "Anyone care to tell me about it?"

We stay up the whole night talking and crying, the wounds still bleeding, the insult of suicide still raw. I learn that the other woman is Neil's cousin Samantha, his only known relative come to our rez to help with the packing up of his estate. I never even knew he had a relative. She is a Plains Chippewa from Oklahoma. She saw Parry Four Bears on T.V. last fall. I learn that my friend tossed his beagle overboard and set himself on fire under Big Mac at moonrise on the day after Christmas, on the very night of that full Snow Moon that rode with me to China. It turns out that the only clues as to his motive are contained in the poem. Among the scant physical evidence: charred fragments of the canoe blown onto the shore at the fort by the strong north winds, frozen strands of catgut and clockcord hooked on the edges of ice floes and on the southern buoy a deposit of his silver and turquoise armband, a pair of kingfisher feathers from his headdress, the kerosene jar he'd used. Everything else was burned to smithereens. That would include, besides Neil, the wooden frames of the twelve sons who comprised the pyre, his beloved birch bark canoe, and who knows what else? Poof! Up in smoke. It was Marla who reported him missing to the village police in Periwinkle and they who had pieced her report together with a police report from Mackinac City where residents had phoned in an early evening fire on the Straits. I cannot imagine her pain at seeing St. Anne limp up to our front stoop in such terrible condition, hypothermic and dehydrated, frost-bitten, on the verge of not only collapse but probably death. Neil had trained her to run across Big Mac and onto the Mackinac Trail which would take her right into Periwinkle. On the basis of the reports and the poem and the time St. Anne appeared at her door, Marla figured it had taken her eighteen to twenty hours. To make her visible to night traffic, Neil had painted her up in reflective orange war paint. Marla had scrubbed and scrubbed at it and finally had to take a pair of scissors and clip it out of her pelt. As if this weren't shocking enough, there was still no indication to her that anything had happened to Neil. Marla gave the dog some water and cupped her face in her hands to study her. It was then she noticed a silver tube tucked into her collar, a Montecristo cigar tube sealed with cork on both ends. After a frustrating ten-minute struggle to remove the corks during which she tried an ice pick, scissors, a bottle opener, a corkscrew and a blue streak of profanities to pry them out of the tube, she finally dislodged them with a pair of pliers and then needed still more frantic seconds to get the scrolled papers out and finally she had the poem and those little tribal prints from his living room wall before her wild eyes. She thought it was a practical joke at first, a gruesome playful Neil joke, but a further look at his beagle who had just completed a double marathon in the middle of December was all the persuasion she needed to believe that the lump in her throat and the knot in her stomach were inklings of the unthinkable. She said he must have thrown her overboard at the buoy which is fairly close to the shore and the bridge, otherwise how could the poor thing have swum in that freezing water more than a few dozen yards. Marla reasoned that Neil would have put her in a life preserver if only she didn't have the long run ahead of her after the swim. He *expected* her to come through, she said, he *expected* her to understand what was at stake. How she then had the presence to run the entire width of the U.P. after…She had to have seen the fire. It had to catch the corner of her eye, as she chugged over the bridge. She had to know exactly what was going on there, that Neil was in flames, that she had a mission—to get over that bridge, to find her way to the Trail, '…pace yourself, find Birchwalker and ram him until he notices you…' How did Neil even get himself down to Cap Gros where he hides his boat? He doesn't drive, never has, so Marla figured that he probably hired a taxi and she tracked down the driver who helped him drag the boat into the chilly twilight water and load onto it his twelve lacrosse sticks and kerosene and St. Anne Four and whatever else he took with him. Marla took the taxi driver to the police station herself and made him tell his story.

I imagine the moments of fire. I see whitecaps and gusting winds that were his tools to perform a final Indian pirouette—can you hear him chanting with his oar dipped to pivot, singing thanks to the wind and the water? Yet that same wind rocked the canoe and made it difficult to construct the pyre. I agree that my friend probably moored at the southern buoy sixty or seventy yards from the shore of the fort. I believe he was calm. I believe St. Anne was as well, despite the cold and wind. They had prepared for this moment. Like the little print from his living room wall, he would have bound the twelve sticks together, wedging their butt ends between the bottom and the gunnels until they balanced their heads against one another like the frame of a wigwam. He would have tied off the top of the pyre with several of those long splinters of white ash or hickory he used to check the wood for suppleness. I am certain that when this was set up he turned his face up to the full Snow Moon and greeted Bwon-diac, knowing that the only thing that separated them now was the bridge itself. *My friend wanted to climb the bridge to get to Bwon-diac.* There is not the slightest doubt in my mind. Do you remember how he said that there is a seam between water and air where we humans appear only briefly and that we are reborn to the sky at that seam? My friend put himself in the seam. He was past guilt. He had known for months that this would be his end, so that, when he tossed St. Anne ceremonially over the side of the boat and doused his sons in kerosene, he was a happy man with a place to go. Neil didn't think of this as a separation from me; why should he if he is on the moon with my spirit guide and if, in the fullness of cosmic spacing, I will be right there with him in no time.

The women and I never get around to speaking of my trip. We never get around to the disclosure of the scar's origin in Neil's poem, to whether Marla has shared the news with Minerva and my mother, to the shock she must have felt when she realized Neil had known her secret all along, to whether Sheila is to be told of her paternity, to what nuclear dust would settle on Marla and me. At dawn they fall asleep in our family room. As I too am finally drifting off, I see Neil sitting in that awful cane chair of ours. I am way too tired to be surprised even by a ghost, but he's right there staring at me like he was that Friday morning after Thanksgiving when he and Marla laced sticks the whole night. He is wearing the same face, the one past oblivion and past exhaustion and at the gate of forlornness. I am about to ask him if he knows he's dead when he says to me, "Birchwalker, what do you think I should charge the white man for my sins?"

Did you get that? Not sons, sins.

PART TWO

L O N G B O W

MAN ON THE MOON

After all is said and done, what
Can a person say he is then?
Is he only splendid Feeling
Risen off a fetid body?

Does he carry with him into
Afterlife his aches and troubles
Or are such mundane sensations
Left behind like molten
snakeskin?

Did a specter gently lift off
From this former Upright Fossil
Leaving body parts to harden
And ascending to Forever?

To these questions I've no
answer
In this new state of existence
Either way you cut the cookie
I remain a sentient being.

Into verse have I been taken
It goes with a higher vision
My expression's been upgraded
Prose is just so damn prosaic.

I no longer speak in circles
Words come flying out like
bullets
Trochees spurt from me in
tempo
Any other form is muted.

When I set myself afire
And ascended through that
tunnel
Afterlife constrained my

speaking
Forced my thoughts into a Funnel.

Like my chieftain was before me
I am stranded on this Oval
To this cratered hell I'm strapped
down
Of wrongdoings stand convicted.

Here you are who you have hated
What you've loathed and
persecuted
All your envy, spite and bile
Concentrated in a tumor.

So on every Injun hater
I look down and spit my oaths out
On the white man's day in general
And on Roy LeRoi in person.

I'm no better than my worst
thoughts
And they course around inside me
Marinating my existence
Irrespective of repentance.

Blisters, pocks and welts of lepers
Curdled up inside my entrails
Till I feel a nauseation
Like a kitten with a hairball.

Like a bubble in a level
Tumor rises, falls and wriggles
And my only job it seems now
To evacuate it, purge it.

Did you dress me? Someone
dressed me.
I could not have done it better
For my eyes are circled white and
Black and red paint do adorn me.

Polished quail bone through my
nose and
Buckskin quiver at my mid-
thigh
Braided ponytail bisected
By the feather of green heron.

I can see my native country
Cruising past on this moon
buggy
Oh, Anishinaabewaki
Oh, the Land of Upright Fossils.

Please forgive me the
irreverence
Of Bwon-diaclike rotation
But it seems that Indigenes of
Every clan and stripe are fated

To this ceaseless Purgatory
Tethered to the spinning Luna
Half the time is recollection
And the other half is Vultures.

The wen-di-goes, the red-gee-
bis
And the dread Mit-chi-mani-tou
Name your demon, name your
goblin
See the Vultures of the Cosmos.

When I gaze upon my home
lands
And remember how I lived
there
It's my sins called up before me
I see all the sins before me.

And when turned to face the
Out Side
I am easy, easy quarry
Sitting duck for all those

Vultures
Wreak their cosmic justice on me.

I am bound at hand and ankle
Leather cord grips at my gullet
I am free to move my torso
But to claws and beaks it's open.

For deceit and friend-betrayal
For the secrets I did harbor
From this timid heart I call mine
Let the Vultures have their
Nibbles.

I will gladly pay this Penance
Deed the Demons all my organs
For a chance to do it over
For a chance to save Birchwalker.

MEA CULPA

From upon the lofty perch here
I can see my grievous error
That I should have told
Birchwalker
Where his Marla got the red
scar.

But I cannot go back down
through
The mitéwin's sacred tunnel
Cannot douse the pyred son-
sticks
Cannot recondense, be reborn.

St. Anne Four cannot be
untossed
From the waters of the Straits
nor
Can I take the poem delivered
In the tube of Montecristo.

Thirty-one years, thirty-one
years
I will pay that debt forever
Yet my sentence carries over
To the Present, to the Present.

I have watched him, I have
watched him
I have watched Birchwalker
struggle
The predicament I left him
All the consequences of it.

He has faced his challenge
squarely
He has fought the way he
knows to
But the cards were stacked

against him
And to that I must plead Guilty.

Naanganikwe and Birchwalker
My disclosures made them part
ways
To my peace van he retreated
Time to strategize his future.

Naanganikwe was exposed now
Her red scar had a beginning
Very mark of their communion
Now the reason for disunion.

"Please don't leave me now," said
Marla
"Don't you dare lay this upon me!
Don't you dare take St. Anne
either,
Don't you go to that damn peace
van!"

"On the day your father passed on
I helped carry him inside from
Beets he thought were red
lacrosse balls—
And your sister and your
mother?"

"Don't you think that I too suffer?
That we need each other more
now?
Look, I know this is confusing
But he was our common best
friend!"

"I laced rackets till my hands
broke
Bucked him up through all his
down times.
It's the place where we were
married

Can't you love me just the
same, Birch?"

Sheila too had a beginning
Finally knowing who her father
Can you feel her indignation
Worthless bitch-child of a
drunkard?

Maybe this quote you'll indulge
me
Sheila at my funeral said it
Uttered poem in my honor
Tender things that made my
eyes flood:

"Aanimendam Uncle Longbow,
Four St. Annes dance all around
you
And a thousand sons are
orphaned
And a Sheila from the rez too.

"You're too beautiful for this
world
What you saw that night did kill
you
When you burned I fasted for
you
Your black ashes are my
manna."

Marla bore the brunt of all this
Can you blame her? Can you
blame her?
Guarding secrets with her bared
teeth
Like the dingo dam protector.

Still the separation lingered
Birch did ponder situations
Team and fam'ly tribulations

Six long weeks he sat without her.

There was never any question
That they'd soon be back together
From upon the Moon I cheered it
Sprinkled moon dust on
Birchwalker.

But Birchwalker had forgotten
The engagement ring he'd bought
her
Long ago at Hull's big meeting
On installments he had put it.

And that diamond it did glitter
In a little velvet blue box
On my erstwhile nighttime table
Near the famous turtle necklace.

A GAME NEEDS
SPECTATORS

As to tourney organizing
Men in business suits came
calling
Paying last respects and selling
Their ideas for promotion.

Did it not make sense right
after,
From my passing to make profit
Timely telling of my story
Folksy Native ashwood Bender?

Gather footage rare as can be
Splice and edit, glorify me
Animating ancient custom
Put it out on SENE.

But so many pressures rained
down
On the shoulders of
Birchwalker
And originated by me
I could see the ending coming.

From the Team Pascal was fired
For infraction oft repeated
Son of Roy and Sheila's brother
He'd stalked Marla and was
banished.

And the Team it was in chaos
Those eight players were still
missing
Practices were hardly useful
Downward spiraling their coach
was.

I have struggled since in vain to

Get my hand down to my side
here
Tomahawk pipe in my quiver
Toss it to Him Who will need it.

Four Bear's van I watched from
orbit
As it crossed the Mississippi
Archie, Birch, Minerva, Parry
Lila, Naila and Prince Frederick

And my cousin Sam was there too
She had come east for my funeral
They would drive her back to OK
Meet the chieftains, firm the plan
up.

Sheepishly did Birch concede that
To my double-wide he'd move
out
And the party said, "You're
crazy!
Leave your Wife exposed to
danger?"

For who knows what can transpire
If Pascal again should stalk her
Or his Injun hater father
Tries to reclaim his possession?

Archie Mellon bore down on him
Details of the tourney telling
Things had surfaced while Birch
traveled
Which he must be made aware of.

Radio and television
SENE had it covered
They had lined up corporate
sponsors
Toiletries and pills and autos

And he told him of the format
For *Baggattaway Moon* tourney
End of May, June 1st and 2nd
Winner crowned on Pontiac's
Day.

Play-in rounds in England,
Shanghai
Who would move on, who
would move on?
Five teams only could advance
on,
Aussies? Czechs? The South
Koreans?

Bye teams waited for the
winners
U.S., Canada and Birch did
In Green Bay's round robin
matches
Those eight teams would play
for glory.

Jamboree that's what it was, for
In two days they'd play twelve
games full
From the Red Pool, from the
Blue Pool
Two from each into the next
round.

Four teams went to Mackinaw
then
To the fort the Ruse was played
out
Seventeen and Three and Sixty
Very day so much time later.

Winning team would need just
five wins
But if that should prove too
many

Only three would earn the semis
Three wins got you to the Big
Dance.

Archie pressured him about it
For, to keep the cameras rolling
And to keep the turnstiles
swinging
Birch would have to win those
three games.

Winning three would move the
masses
From Green Bay across the State
Line
Into Michigan they'd migrate
To Anishinaabewaki.

Nineteen hundred Red Dog buses
Chugging through the copper
landscape
From round robin in Wisconsin
To the climax on Great Waters.

And beside himself with fervor
Archie told him of the Red Dogs
Of the tour to cart the Natives
To Baggattaway's Rekindling.

They would be a hundred
thousand
Coming on those Red Dog buses
Oklahoma, South Dakota
From a hundred different Nations

From the Kansa and the Choctaw
The Oglala, Alabama
Seminole, Kiowa, Cheyenne
Creek, Apache, and Osage

Cheering section for Birchwalker
And his Indigene lacrosse boys

They would be there for their
Heroes
Tribal difference unimportant

They would root against all
comers
'Gainst the English most
intensely
In Baggattaway's Return as
The Creator's favored Pastime.

With no record to rely on,
No particular advantage
They could only hope that
History
Would propel their Team to
Victory.

Breathlessly did Archie tell him
Of the proceeds they expected,
Eighty-four plus million dollars
Indigene, meet Resurrection.

But when Archie heard of
Pascal
That Birchwalker sent him
packing
He could see the head coach
hardly
Shared his outsized
expectations.

In addition they were still short
Eight men on their final roster
Archie, fuming, squared up to
him
Looked him right into the
eyeballs

"You must make it to the semis
Nothing less will be accepted
By your People by your family

By Bwon-diac or by Archie…"

"But I had to let Pascal go
And the Choctaw are not here yet
And the stickmaker has walked on
And my marriage is a shambles.

"With my team I have not
practiced
Since before my trip to Europe.
If they're practicing in bare feet
If they're catching on to Neil's
sticks

"If they practiced in the Big Soo
I can't even say I know it.
All I know is that they're anxious
Over Pascal disappearing.

"It's a little disconcerting
For he is our best lacrosse man
But he also frightened Marla
And his father's Roy LeRoi and

"He and I have had our issues.
So the King has infiltrated
Indigene Team operations
And it threatens to unmake us."

THE EVENT TAKES SHAPE

When they got to OK City
There was bedlam in the
meeting
Someone asked "Will they be
safe when
On their way in Red Dog buses?

"Every nut who owns a gun and
Has the route from television
Finds a perch upon a knoll and
Licks his thumb and flips the
safety

"Or let's say another nut says
We should blow them all to
ashes!
Look beyond Baggattaway now,
Can we get them up there
safely?"

Parry guaranteed they would
and
Then the chiefs gave them their
blessing
Off to Green Bay in Wisconsin
And Michilimackinac too.

SENE had decided
The event's name was promoted
Dubbed it *All Americans Tour*
And from here I gave a war
whoop.

SENE wants a scrimmage
Exhibition games on TV
Whet the appetites of viewers
Let them see the game's new
style.

So the bye teams take the meadow
Fort Michilimackinac's field
Indigenes, Canucks and U.S.
The three bye teams'
demonstration.

For Baggattaway was different
Long long fields along Great
Waters
And the players all run barefoot
Wield my cumbersome creations.

They would tease a TV fan base
Fatten up the viewer ratings
Make Baggattaway commercial
Fatten up the sponsors' wallets.

And the sponsors then relented
Under pressure from Chief Four
Bears
To pay all incurred expenses
For each Indigene spectator.

Housing, transportation, food and
Best of all the entry tickets
Every single Sioux or Kansa
Ancient Game's Rebirth would
witness.

At $300. valued
Indigenes would all be covered
They would sleep out on the fields
and
Ride their Red Dogs all for no
charge.

Ever closer came June Second
And in fits and starts it happened
That the Choctaw Eight did show
up
At the peace van of Neil Longbow

With Birchwalker did they stay
and
They did get to know the
stallions
They did learn to handle one
stick
For with two their People
played it.

A DATE TO REMEMBER (1)

Then one day Birchwalker
realized
Without Marla he could not live
Moonless woman who had
claimed him
Who out 6 Mile Road did walk
out.

Who had worn the turtle
necklace
On the evening they were
married
That he still had at my peace
van
That had glowed and blinked in
Shanghai.

And for Marla too the diamond,
Sat right next to turtle necklace
He resolved that she should
have them
Even though they weren't
together.

And he did become excited
Knew he couldn't bear to leave
her
Irrespective of her Soo past
Marla was his moonless
woman.

He was staring at the runner
On the hutch I kept my knives
in
And the clockcord for stick
lacing
When he hit on an idea.

He would fete her, he would

fete her
This most precious of all people
He would plan a celebration
On a pedestal he'd place her.

At the Hotel New Beginning
(And how perfect was that place
name?)
He would organize a dinner
For his moonless woman Marla.

He would make a reservation
For June Third or shortly after
When Baggattaway had ended
When the tournament was over.

No expense would he forgo on
This occasion of reunion
Sumptuously they would dine and
Champagne bubbles would
delight her.

Then pièce de résistance comes
Maitre d' will have it brought out
Laid before her shining eyes that
Feast upon her husband's true
love

Jú-ah-kís-gaw! Jú-ah-kís-gaw!
How did Birchwalker conceive it?
Naming ceremony dinner
For his squaw of 31 years.

Chippewa word Jú-ah-kís-gaw
Meaning 'Woman with Child on
Back'
Papoose cradle board he'd make
her
They would bring it out with
coffee.

Irresistible idea

She'd embrace it without
question
Like a baby she would tear up
And he wasn't even finished.

With the pleasant meal behind
them
He'd get down on bended knee
and
Open up the diamond ring box
Slip it on her left ring finger.

He would ask her hand in
marriage
New beginning, new beginning
She would cry and say, 'O, yes,
Birch,
Thought you'd never think to
ask me.'

And just when she thought it
over
He was only getting warmed up
He had one more oath to swear
her
It would rob her of her
breathing.

CELEBRITY

Phys ed. teachers don't get
famous
The kinetic arts they teach us
Skills like shooting and
defending
Fitness, teamwork, being good
sports.

SENE found its man though
Former player, coach and
Native
In the person of Birchwalker
Their campaign's own TV idol.

Out on stages they did push him
Shining face of their new
Project
TV, radio, AM talk
Sell the Program to the Nation.

In the media he featured
Sports talk, magazines, GMA
On the Internet in chat rooms
How Birchwalker was the rage
now.

For the tournament was coming
Waxing was *Baggattaway
Moon*
June the Second was upon us
Birch alone could represent it

He would fly to New York City
For a live spot in the morning
Tape an interview for FM
Lecture college kids by evening.

He was frazzled, deer in
headlights

He was eating very poorly
He was missing lots of school
days
And his team still had no rudder.

He had taken on the mantle
Spokesman for his Sport and
People
Face of Indigene Revival
See the costs of Fifteen Minutes.

But, he thought, Our Cause is
worthy
And who better than myself to
Shine a spotlight on this Moment
Sport and History, Collision.

Quite unnerving was the chatter
For Birchwalker on the
airwaves—
Did the Injun have the Spine for
Brutal contests of desire?

When the Game was on the line
did
Injun Will rise up defiant
Overcome his deficits in
Strength and prowess and
nutrition?

For the white man had co-opted
What was once the Indigene
Game
Stuffed it into nice white lines and
Added helmets, gloves and quick
sticks.

Taken balls of red drilled tree
knots
And replaced them all with rubber
Moved the goal posts ever closer
Faced-off now instead of Ball Up.

Birch's players in this sense
were
Just as white as any white kids
They had learned Lacrosse like
others
And Baggattaway forgotten.

So the coach's challenge
doubled
He must make them all
remember
That which courses in their
veins and
Naps in brainstems, sleeping
giant.

He would run his young men
barefoot
He would run them mile and
mile
He would teach them their own
game new
He would fire up their Instincts.

He would make them angry to
have
Ever ceded such a Symbol
Indian-style recreation
Healing prayer, Creator's
Pastime.

"Take your Game back! Take
your Game back!"
Lectured to them like my
grandpa
After running through the
Forest
To the falls of Tahquamenon.

Where they talked and did their
y-scales
To the roar of water falling

And their coach's words imported
And they started to believe them.

They had half as much a chance
as
Did their weakest rival out there
And they knew so much was
riding
On the outcome, on the outcome.

Legacy of Fallen People
Breathe life into Upright Fossils
If Baggattaway they named it
Indigenes would have to win it.

With or without Captain Pascal
With a coach beset by problems
Playing teams that ought to crush
them
They should somehow find the
Spine to

Upset every pundit's wisdom
That they didn't stand a chance to
Make the semi-final matches?
They could maybe beat the Danes
though.

FIGHT AT TOMMY'S

But before the Dream could
happen
Birch would have to go on
Offense
And I don't mean in the sports
sense
Rather give a foe a licking.

And perhaps he even heard me
For I yelled it from the Moon
here
'Take St. Anne and kick the
King's ass!'
And he headed for the sports
bar.

He went after Roy LeRoi then
Injun hater, Pascal's sire
For he knew the King could
shatter
Any Dream Birch could
imagine.

(Had he not killed Birch's
father?
Yanked poor Louis through the
beet bed
Every single Indigene too?
Who knew what this man was
thinking?)

On a bitter snow-filled week
night
Quiet time at Tommy's Sports
Bar
Birch resolved to forestall
mishaps
Take the King out of the
picture.

For his hands had blood upon
them
Maybe mine too if you ponder—
If he didn't set the fire
He took matches to the kindling.

I would like to review for you
Some details of this back story
How it redefined Neil Longbow
Both in This World and the Prior.

From the corner of his eyeball
In a fraction of a second
Lurking underneath the street
lamp
Maybe saw me, maybe didn't

Had to know that I was present
At the moment of his Great Shame
When he battered Naanganikwe
Prior to her Birch invasion.

And upon assaulting Marla
Lashing her across the cheekbone
Leaving her to bleed on Ashmun
Certain things were set in motion.

I'm a coward! I did nothing!
Watched him swagger from poor
Marla
Ruby red ring readjusting
Knuckles rubbing in departure.

Other red men might have stepped
out
From the shadows to confront him
And to help defenseless Marla
Whose mistake was being
pregnant.

Should have called the police on
him

But what beat cop would believe me?
Senseless Injun guarding Pole's poles
Fighting all the time at Tommy's.

I saw 31 years later
That same scar stroll onto our rez
Out my window did I see it
Recognized her, Naanganikwe.

Wearing halter top and short shorts
Baby Sheila in her backpack
Sheila's father had no honor
Disregarded her existence.

Less than 90 minutes later
She and Birchwalker came to me
And I married them that evening
In Anishinaabek fashion.

I could not look at that red scar
Smiling smugly from her cheekbone
It was Roy whose smile came through it!
Yes, the King was taunting through it!

I was frightened to my marrow
Such a thing could even happen
So I covered it in bear fat
And I smothered it in charcoal.

'Cause it seemed his lips were saying
Like a priest asks in a church vow

'He who knows of any reason
Why this wedding is not valid

'Here and now please speak your reason
Or your peace hold for forever.'
I just had to shut him up so
I kept smearing charcoal on it

And I knew it in my bones that
This eternally would haunt me.
I confess this private Failing
Which in Afterlife I pay for

I'm the priest who knew the Secret
That the newlyweds could sunder!
Not just that! I set in motion
Chain of lethal consequences.

Birch went out that night on Offense
Thinking Four Bears the next target
Famous, visible and Indian
Couldn't Roy assassinate him?

As he got to Tommy's sports bar
Saw his breath rise over snow banks
And Roy's famous red Toyota
Parked askew like he's the mayor.

Generators in the truck bed
Diesel gas cans half a dozen
Fertilizer in abundance
Bags ripped open, some still sealed up.

Saw machines for blowing snow off
Shovels thrown in, heaped together

But Birchwalker only saw red
As he crossed the street to
Tommy's.

He could not see in the
windows
None inside could see him
coming
They were frosted up so thickly
It was minus ten that evening

He and St. Anne unexpected
Burst in to the quiet gin joint
Were stopped cold by 16
Birches
On the TV screens above them.

Of St. Anne this made a dervish
Circling round on her own
backside
Spinning like a top she rounded
Too much eyeball stimulation.

SENE'd interviewed Birch
And they ran it at that moment
It was Birch himself times 16
And his image froze him solid.

Frenchies watched them with
amusement
Spinning Top and Mouth Hung
Open
And they mocked him, Pascal
with them,
'Ain't ya never seen a nigger?'

It was Roy LeRoi who said this
Snapping Birch and dog from
daydream
St. Anne growled in her chest
and
Made a mad run for the

Frenchies.

St. Anne rammed him like a
fullback
Hit him full force with her
shoulder
Like she always brushed
Birchwalker
Only harder than the normal.

When the thug bent down to swat
her
She attacked him with a
vengeance
Piercing both his flannel shirt and
The Bone Digger's rawhide
forearm.

How he yowled, how he yowled,
From upon the Moon I heard it
And saw St. Anne hanging from
him
Gripping jaws he could not
unhinge.

With her teeth inside his
bloodstream
He foreswore all further yowling
He paraded her around then
Showing guts to all his cronies.

St. Anne then reached up and
swiped him
Dug his face out with her four
claws
Left four bleeding tracks upon it
Just like once Roy'd done to
Marla.

In the meantime Birch was
charging
And the dog relented finally

Ran to supervise the Frenchies
While Birchwalker and Roy
squared off.

In the middle of his rushing
Tommy threw Birchwalker
something
A straight razor, for he'd need
one
Tommy'd stolen it from Thad's
shop.

For Birchwalker Time was
slowed down.
And he couldn't really hear it
But he thought that Tommy told
him
'*Kill* the fucker, do you hear
me?'

Birch continued now his lunge
at
Roy who turned around to face
him
And they circled one another
Around chairs and tables
slowly.

Sized each other up and
shuffled
The Bone Digger's arm was
spurting
And Birchwalker only hoped
that
He could knock this bastard's
head in.

'So you cuffed your pregnant
girlfriend
Left her bleeding in the dark
street,
Didn't have the decency to

Even help her back to standing.

'And you've known it all along
that
She is living on the rez now
With a loser Injun teacher
Knew your secret would be safe,
right?'

The Bone Digger took a wild
swipe
Did not catch Birch, came up,
sniffled
Birch kept taunting as he circled
Looking for a chance to end this.

'Now that I am someone famous
And the limelight is upon me
And our Injun game is featured
In the mind of every white man

'And your woman makes lacrosse
sticks
And your daughter knows the
truth now
It's a little much to handle
For an asshole like yourself, huh?'

Roy LeRoi just laughed the taunts
off
Said he'd heard that Marla moved
out
Now Birchwalker did reside in
My dilapidated trailer.

Said the tournament would
happen
Only over his dead body
Said they'd never win a game if
Son Pascal was not among them.

Then Birchwalker said, 'You

killed Neil,'
With the straight blade did
lunge at him
Falling forward sliced his left
thigh
Ripping deeply in the tissue

But Roy paid him back in kind
then
Cut him over top the shoulder
Made a gash behind his left arm
They both fell down in a
writhing

Tommy's shirt, a tourniquet
now
Wrapped around the coach's
armpit;
Pascal to his father tended
Birch could hear his cries of
anguish

Knew he'd really stuck it to him
Knew he'd maybe rescued Four
Bears.
Knew he'd made a declaration
Knew he'd stood up for Roy's
victims.

NO REST FOR THE WEARY

That's the last thing he
remembered
That and faithful St. Anne
Four's breath
Raining heavily down on him
As he sank into unconscious.

When he woke up in the clinic
After shoulder reparation
Feathered out on Percoset now
Dennis Charpentier was
bedside.

Maybe you do not remember:
He's the beat cop for St. Mary's
Took their statements in the
ward beds
Charged Birchwalker with
assaulting

First-degree with deadly
weapon
And intending to inflict harm
Class A felony he told him
And that Roy was charged in
like ways.

Even Tommy was complicit
Said this pudgy Soo policeman
Jeopardized his liquor license
If it ever again happens.

Also St. Anne was remanded
To the dog pound where she'd
be held
Till such time as Jimmy
Blackbird
Could come down and
recognize her.

A grand jury would convene then
Three weeks later, three weeks
later
Birch was ROR'd till that time
Asked of Tommy 'How is Roy
now?'

Tommy told him all about it
As he from the bed did listen
How he'd had to have them sewn
up
Major vessels thigh and forearm

Both St. Anne and he had
punctured
One with teeth and one with razor
Good, said Birch, I hope he bleeds
out.
Hope he never walks like normal.

He could even lose his leg if
Circulation was not bettered
And he'll have a limp forever
From St. Anne's patellar ramming

And from Tommy also learned
this:
St. Anne wrecked his face forever.
Even surgery would not hide
Those four tracks along his
cheekbone.

Tommy left him with this
warning:
That the King would look for
Vengeance
That he'd strive for nothing less
than
Laughing last upon his victims.

But Birchwalker wouldn't listen
Said 'Just how's he gonna do that

If he's lame and scarred and
beat up
How's he gonna get his
Vengeance?'

But McKeon then insisted
'Mark my words,' he said, 'and
watch out
Take the bastard at his word
Birch
Settled score is what he's
thinking.'

Under cloud of an arrest now
Scarred of shoulder and not
working
Birch did contemplate the
notion
That on June Two he'd be
locked up.

This of course just could not
happen
Archie Mellon hired a lawyer
Miss J. Pino was her name and
With Birchwalker did she
huddle.

Marla picked him up at
discharge
They had been apart for weeks
now
Was uncomfortable between
them
She still reaches for that red
scar.

She came by and cooked him
hot meals
Cleaned my house for him a
few times.
Would embargoed feelings

surface?
Would positions harden badly?

Archie Mellon called and told him
Red Dog buses were confirmed
now
Over hundred thousand Natives
From points south and west to
Green Bay

They would board in Rapid City
A long caravan departing
Also Oklahoma City
Chugging northeast to Wisconsin.

Archie also showed his ire
For the error at the sports bar
Had he taken leave of senses?
Going after such a low life?

Drawing negative attention?
Giant pay days must be nurtured,
Not discarded in a bar fight
Petty local bullshit bar fight.

And he wouldn't sit and listen
To Birchwalker's cogent reasons
That this jerk could bring the Tent
down
He'd protected the investment.

Archie told him he'd decided
Now to station cops at practice
Of his team Birch had not thought
much
Would they ever let him lead
them?

Telephone calls with Ms. Pino
Homebound rehabilitation
Interviews of every sports kind
Visits from the team and Marla.

From Jerome and Obie,
captains,
Learns Birch of Pascal's
resumption
Seized control in Birch's
absence
Countermanding direct orders.

Learns that players have
responded
Very well to Pascal's coaching
He refined the goddamn y-scale
Ran the drills and blew the
whistles.

Ran the team above all barefoot
They've the calluses to prove it
For Pascal they will do y-scales
But the captains want their
coach back.

As co-captains they felt strongly
That with Birch they had to face
up
Sundry problems that the team
faced
Irrespective his condition.

Captains wanted custom jerseys
Like the other teams were
rumored
Russell Pape and Drey Foss
dreamed up
Chauvinistic fashion statements.

Union Jack and Maple Leaf and
Then Old Glory, snare drums,
fifes too
They just wanted purple and
white
On their uniforms imprinted.

And then finally they fessed up
That Pascal had disappeared since
Fateful knife fight in the sports
bar
Pascal's father v. lacrosse coach.

Also what about the Choctaw
Just how would we integrate them
On and on like this they plagued
him
Though he only thought of Pascal.

Let's concede the ugly truth that
Birch had knifed his player's
father
He was put in a dilemma
Should I play or should I boycott?

But he felt Pascal would show up
As *Baggattaway Moon* drew near
He would not resist the call to
Captain Indigene lacrosse team.

They were worried over Red
Dogs;
Would Birch reinstate Pascal too
Even though he had released him
In the light of revelations?

Things had tied themselves in
knots here
And Birchwalker had to ponder
On his team, Pascal and Marla
Legal matters, Archie, school too.

And his problems just got bigger
When his principal relieved him
Placed him on indefinite leave
Due to recent misbehavior.

Dropped him from the faculty list
Like a snow day from the school

year
Alan Ficek did dismiss him
Lest on kids he have an impact.

Benefits, a while he'd keep
them
Half his take-home pay was left
him
'Here is hoping that by next
year
All your messy dust has
settled.'

This said Mr. Alan Ficek
Showed his teacher-coach the
way out
Two-plus decades of his service
For PMS not sufficient.

That same week he learned a
new term
Very legalistic sounding
Ms. J. Pino did explain it
'Charlevoix, you have been
true-billed.

'That means this thing goes to
trial
Or you to the charges plead out
Take your chances on the
sentence
I will do the best I can here.

'Mr. Mellon wants no trial
But if you decide to challenge
I can have the date continued
Past the tournament finale.'

Ms. J. Pino had advised him
Either way he would do some
time
Best case was six months

suspended
Worst case one year-plus behind
bars.

Archie Mellon's thought was
simple:
Keep this snafu from the papers
Make the charges disappear and
Worry later over jail time.

Harsh, perhaps, he had his reasons
Major press conference was
scheduled
He and Parry April Fool's Day
On security arrangements.

For those Red Dog riding Natives,
Poor souls, targets on the
highways
As they caravanned en masse to
Their beloved game's Rekindling.

For the *All Americans Tour*
To get safely to Wisconsin
There could be some prickly
hand-offs
As from state to state they
plodded.

Politicians worked together
To forestall a Devastation
Deathly frightened were officials
Of catastrophe on their watch.

Who would want to answer for it?
Eight Midwestern governors not
So with Washington they pleaded
'Homeland office, please assist
us!'

A DATE TO REMEMBER (2)

It was right about this time that
Birch decided for Reunion
That his moonless woman
Marla
More than ever before needed.

He would look past any
Misdeed
Whether past or present time
frame
He would have to swallow hard
but
He could see she'd never
wavered.

Sure a secret had been jimmied
And she'd not been fully honest
But besides his bruised-up ego
And some tension with his
captain

And some hate that crystallized
for
Lifelong Injun hater LeRoi
Who turns out to be the father
Of his captain and
stepdaughter…

The Coincidence was painful
And then I too was a factor
In Birchwalker's frantic
thinking
Two friends kept him in the
Darkness.

A conspiracy it was not
As to that let me assure you
Marla, I had separate reasons.
From each *other* kept our

secrets.

Was Baggattaway of all things
Brought the actors into conflict
Pascal, Marla, Me, Birchwalker
Roy LeRoi and all St. Annes too.

Cradle carrier he fashioned
In a fit of new-found Purpose
No, they'd not had any children
Yet was Hope itself their
offspring.

Talking loudly to himself now
Ricocheting off my cheap walls
Did he flash back to 6-Mile Road
And her long hike in those pink
Cons.

She had come direct to claim him
Her predicament announced by
Baby Sheila in the back pack
And the smiling red scar shining.

Suddenly his blood awakened
And he rummaged round my
trailer
Stripped the runner off that old
hutch
Pulled the top drawer for the
cradle

Found my drawknives, clockcord,
catgut
Stoked the fire in the chimney
Took a piece of hickory wood
Bent a handle for the top end.

Tied it to the drawer with
clockcord
Bent a strip of ash for border
Flashy sidewall for adornment

He would paint the symbols on
it

That I painted on the
wampum—
Yellow moon, green grassy
mound and
Black lines diving for Great
Waters
And the red lacrosse ball flying.

He was bursting at the seams
now
Like a man possessed by
demons
It consumed him every hour
How he'd make the
presentation.

But distractions there were
many—
Speculating writers seeded
Eight most likely teams to
tussle:
U.S. first, Indigene last seed.

Anyone else didn't matter
Play-in rounds had not yet
started
But the time was pressing
forward
England, Shanghai would
decide it.

Five teams from those foreign
play-ins
Would advance to play round
robin
In two pools they'd be divided
Red and Blue pools would each
yield two.

Final Four would face off next
with
Semi-finals June the First then
All the marbles on June Second
At Michilimackinac's fort.

But regardless his excitement
Close to vest he'd play his hand
out
He would ask her out to dinner
For June Third when all was over.

He would make like it's no big
deal
Just two friends out having dinner
But surprises he had planned out
Just would knock her off her
keister.

Until then he'd play it coolly
Just a few more weeks to while
There was no need to foresignal
Anything but calm, collected.

Can you beat it, just for timing?
Pontiac-is-Looking Down Day?
Maybe stallions in the semis?
Maybe skunk the English
squadron?

And June Second is the day when
31 years back I married
Chippewa man to a red scar
Surely that's a match eternal.

So June Second was his D-Day
Planetary realignment
That's the day of celebration
That's the day old sparks rekindle.

At the Hotel New Beginning
He would wine her, he would dine

her
After dinner have a cordial
Then he'd get down to his
business.

The blue velvet box he'd pull
out
Genuflect upon one knee then
He would say, 'I am your truant
Will you kindly take me back
home?'

Moonless woman would be
wordless
Tears would well up in both
eyes and
She would reach for Birch's
hand and
Search his eyes for all his
meaning.

Then comes Naming Ceremony
He would reference
Naanganikwe
But bestow on her his own
choice
How she'd cry at Jú-ah-kís-gaw.

She would feel that she is part
of
Chippewa tribe she'd adopted
When she came to claim her
Injun
Off the dime store's rack of
misfits.

She would redden at belonging
It would mean the world to
Marla
An Anishinaabek arm clasp
She would cry and cry and
laugh some.

She would love the honorific
Nature of the appellation
It would sate her more than dinner
Her eternal just desserts be.

Cradle board would then be
brought out
Maitre'd would gently lay it
In her lap after she pulled back
To receive her final course and

In the moment that she figured
What this work it represented
Tears would well up in her once
more
And she'd put it all together.

She would hardly find her focus
Through a steady tearful misting
She would see the wampum
symbols
Like her scar she'd reach but not
touch.

She'd say green mound indicates
Death
That a black bridge signals
Portage
That the red ball signs Good
Fortune
That a white moon means Bwon-
diac

In his mercy has reclaimed her
That she is no longer moonless
Like the Indian existence
Hope for Dignity must live forth.

So emotional would this be
He could see it all before him
She would reach up for her scar
then

She would take her Truant back
home.

And just when she thought it
over
He'd have one more Favor for
her
Deadly serious he'd face her
He'd remake himself before her.

Fundamentally a Native
On Pope County rez conceived
and
Raised in Chippewa tradition
Proud as ever was he of it.

But he'd entered a new Outlook
In his thoughts of reuniting
It was time to pay his Wife back
For the Life she'd given to him.

So he'd tell her he's retiring
Crossing back over the River
That she'd come across herself
when
She had left the World of white
men.

From Baggattaway he'd step
back
And Pope County he'd
relinquish
This Illusion of a Boundary
He would cross it to repay her.

For a long time they had
labored
In the service of his People
Marla as a truant seeker
Birch the ageless phys ed.
teacher.

Marla was no Upright Fossil
And no longer must Birchwalker.
He'd insist that they together
Back 6 Mile Road to the Soo
walk.

It was necessary for them
Such reversing of direction
From the Rez back to the City
Hand in hand and looking
forward.

It was such a big decision
Birch could hardly keep it secret
Wanted so much just to tell her
Often they'd see Sandrine, Sheila

She'd have memories of Louis
And they'd both be laughing-
crying
And they'd take them to their new
life
And their tears would cleanse the
anguish.

Birch was thinking, he was
thinking
Were they too old for a baby?
It would not, it seemed, surprise
him
That's how Special, New
Beginnings

PRESS CONFERENCE

In the meantime came the
Choctaw
Eight to tighten up his roster
And they stayed a while at my
place
Nearly drove Birchwalker
crazy.

Kendall Peet and Arthur
Branson
Ryan Embry, Two Dogs
Henshaw
Bobby Cooper, Kyle Clovis
Ricky Prendergast and Pat
Winch.

In the double wide reigned
Chaos
Eight guys cradling with my
weapons
Checking, juking, poking,
shooting
As they wended through the
trailer.

The big press conference was
airing
Birch was watching through the
maelstrom
Twenty-five officials so grave
Parry Four Bears, Archie with
them.

Seeing such a thing on TV
Made Birchwalker sit, take
notice
How much bigger did this Trek
seem
Now that all the Nation knew

it?

Now that shows were interrupted
Now that governors had gathered
Now that politicians fretted
Now that Terror hovered on it.

There they stood and took turns
warning
Of potential dangers lurking
For the hundred thousand Natives
In a caravan of Red Dogs.

Homeland people from each state
and
Homeland people out of D.C.
Colonels of highway patrols stood
Facing grimly toward the
cameras.

Breaking news is how they billed
it
Gravitas is what's projected
Great concern about the Welfare
Dire outlines of prevention.

The Director of the Homeland
Tries to reassure the public.
For contingencies he has planned
Shows a resolute demeanor.

They are meeting in Chicago
At the Hotel Interregnum
April 1 is April Fools' Day
Snowflakes fold into the river.

Microphones of every ilk are
Catching every hushed
pronouncement
Foreign, sports and cable, network
Every citizen must know this.

He announced defensive
measures
Military terms he uses
Ground and air support he
mentioned
Deft deployments of the Guard
troops.

Helicopters from the Navy
Interstates would reconnoiter
Power-Point displayed the two
routes
Both the northern one and
southern.

Out from Oklahoma City
Trail of Tears descendants
riding
Chugging north along the River
Headed for the games in Green
Bay.

And from Rapid City eastward
Carting members of Sioux
Nation
Out across the blooming
cornfields
And on up to Packer country.

It was opened up to questions
What about those Natives
drinking?
What about the less secure spots
Like the Mississippi levees?

Or the Dells in mid-Wisconsin?
What about the corporate
sponsors?
Will they pull out overanxious
And despoil this humble
Venture?

Nerves were at the point of
fraying
Was a Bloodbath in the waiting?
Who would sweat out all the Ifs of
Hundred thousand plus in transit.

'There will be no great disaster!'
He reiterated boldly
Though he could not guarantee it
Who would make such foolish
promise?

The Director did insist that
Police presence would be massive
Armed with pistols, rifles
shouldered
Zero tolerance for misfits.

Checks for booze and steel
detectors
Pregnable would neither Site be
Homeland office, state and
federal,
Seemed to have its act together.

May 13 was billed as Day One
When the operation started
Interlocking safety programs
Midwest Region and the Nation.

Then another writer asked him
'Who is paying for this service?
Who is underwriting this most
Costly, daring undertaking?'

'It's a combination public-
Private plan of high financing.
Federal monies have been granted
States have unforeseen expenses.

'Helicopters overflying
Extra staff hours in the thousands

Friskers, screeners doing
searches
Of a hundred thousand people.

'Hand-held sweepers under
buses
Undercarriage is inviting
A good place to hide a car bomb
Such inspections do cost
money.

'Federal marshals on the Red
Dogs
One per bus that's 1900
Then there's marksmen on the
routes and
More surprises we are certain.

'Are they open to attack at
Cloverleafs and dells and
levees?'
He was asked about specifics
But Director had no comment.

He was asked about the Chatter
Was there any foreign intel
SATCOM terrorist discussions
Re the *All Americans Tour*?

'Will you have to raise the
level?'
And for that he had an answer:
'For the three weeks from May
13
To June Second for the Finals

'Status red will be enacted
In the Midwest Region only.'
Kyle Clovis looked at Birch
then
'Wouldn't that mean
Oklahoma?'

And the cameras then zoomed in
on
All those chiseled stoic faces
All those promising officials
They had sounded the alarm bell.

SENE then came on air
With a brief appeal for reason:
'In good conscience we must plan
but
Chance is nothing bad will
happen.

'Confident are corporate sponsors.
Come support *Baggattaway
Moon*.
Do not let this news deter you
Come and witness sporting
History.'

THE NOTES

Ultimatum, ultimatum
In the bottom of a bucket
Out my kitchen window saw it
Birch bark bucket in the side
yard.

It was hanging from the dye
plate
Chipped and peeling maple sap
pail
Birch went out to look into it
Fished a Marla note out from it.

Wrote that twelve weeks was
sufficient;
And in spite of all his tensions
Asked him once more for
forgiveness
Wrote him that she still did love
him.

Wrote she would not wait
forever
Gave him only till the end of
The Event to make his mind up
Wrote that if he didn't want her

She would quit as truant person
To Sandrine and Sheila move
back
And against her every fiber
Quit her life there at Pope
County.

Marla signed her good-bye
letter
With an 'M' inside a sad heart
A frustration built inside Birch
She had ruined his surprises!

'She has beat me to the punch
here
Read my mind and stolen
thunder!'
He just turned the paper over
Penned his answer in the kitchen.

He did not want to reveal it
The big plan he had for dinner
At the Hotel New Beginning
Gifts of cradle board and
diamond.

So he wrote of recent dreaming
Wrote of crazy dreams and
visions
Madjikiwis, Wak'abide
To the man dog is grandfather.

Wrote that waking in a full sweat
Panting heavily from dreaming
Troubled by its symbolism
Face-to-face he'd come with St.
Anne.

How she stared right at him,
through him
Seemed to know just what he's
thinking
Maybe even tried to warn him
Would he ever know what she
knows?

Wrote he'd never felt so wounded
Wrote he leaked love like a sieve
now
Wrote he'd lost too much to deal
with
Wrote he wished she wouldn't
leave yet.

Birch agreed to Marla's deadline

Wrote he'd call her, they'd do
dinner
After tournament had ended
For till then he was too busy.

BAGGATTAWAY MOON (1)

Thus began a month of
weekends
When our Sport held center
stage, oh,
Ancient Sport of our forefathers
Moonlong tournament would
honor.

Birch and Jimmy drove the milk
truck
May 13 down to the fort for
SENE's exhibition
How the sun bounced off the
Waters.

St. Anne yelped and barked at
something
Nearly broke all of their ear
drums
Till Birchwalker did discover
She was having canine
flashback.

As they passed my old marina
She had recognized the
concourse
That she ran while I was
blazing.
Fifty miles in the Winter.

Birch and Jimmy of the games
talked
Whether his team could
compete and
Whether Pascal would show up
and
How the Games had gone
commercial.

SENE cultivated
Hunger for the coming tourney
Offered clips of bursting
fireworks
Out upon the Strait's dark waters

Pageantry galore was broadcast
As the Natives and the others
Made their way into the fort for
Tribal music celebration

Powwow, dancing, color guard
and
Wampum stick held elevated
By a horseback Native player
My four icons were the logo

Even had it animated
And etched into all their ads for
Razor blades and pills, casinos
Banks and cars named for Bwon-
diac.

Flute and tom toms spiced the
venue
Natives mulling through the gates
and
Taking in the great fort's history
Till the one o'clock *Ball up!* call.

At 12:55 precisely
Cannon shots rang out and
bounced off
Our Big Mac and its steel girders
Louis helped to build its caissons.

Reminiscent of a track meet
Jamboree and reenactment
Pig roast and a big Greek wedding
Festive sporty and historic

Elementary school's fifth graders

Swarming all around the players
Hanging out and running wild
On the meadow with no
boundaries.

In Baggattaway they found joy
Barefoot players did astound
them
And the cool new sticks that I
made
And the sight of Indigene men.

It could not be lost on Birch
though
As he walked that Meadow pre-
game
That our own June Two
enactment
He'd be doing on his own now.

Echoes of Makoons and Bad
Sky
In his head did surely rise up
Catapult shot in the front gate
Momentary Justice Reset.

Had to break up fisticuffs down
At the far goal out of sight from
All the viewers one excepting
Man with camera on a hillock.

'Fucking Choctaw, fucking
Choctaw!'
Cursed his erstwhile Captain
Pascal
His own players locked in
combat
At the far goal in the netting.

Yes Pascal he had reentered
Competition could not sit out
Knife fight to Lacrosse took

back seat
Though he'd surely not forgiven

What his coach from Roy had
taken—
Face all scarred up, gait impaired
so
Pascal meted out his anger
On the Choctaw Bobby Cooper

'Coach, they will not do the y-
scale!
That's a sign of team belonging
Its what sets apart us Injuns
From the rest of all this bullshit.'

Obie Crick was quick to chime in
That the Choctaw hard were
trying
But just couldn't seem to master
Single sticks and y-scale balance.

Pascal's face was terrifying
How he sneered at Bobby Cooper
For his insubordination—
At his team's face did Birch
shudder.

Pascal self-defended bravely
In the face of Birch accusing
That he'd yeoman's service
rendered,
In Birchwalker's absence held
things

He insisted to Birchwalker
He had come today for winning
Caged-up lion he resembled
Set to play and then devour.

Save your venom for Opponents,
Everyone was wont to tell him

You did not want to offend him
Crazy look inside his eyeballs

Then he and Birchwalker faced
off
And Birch asked him straight
out calmly
If to Roy he was related
Would he claim him as his
father.

'Bet your ass, he is my father,
But today's the Exhibition,'
And they saw each in the other
Unavoidable dependence.

Tried to warn Birch in my last
note:
Careful of your Captain Pascal
For he's filled with something
bitter
And he'll be the last one
standing

Tommy also tried to warn him
Of his father's vengeance
penchant
Tommy meant just what he'd
said then:
Roy would find a way to strike
back

But what choice had our
Birchwalker,
He relied on hostile parties
Had to tolerate the danger
Tribe and Woman, Sport and
History.

Relegated to assistant
Sitting out the Exhibition
Keeping stats for Coach

Birchwalker
Pascal prowled up the sidelines

I could not myself have told you
At that team-negating moment
Whether for *Baggattaway Moon*
Captain Pascal would be present.

The Americans were awesome
Played as if it were a real match
Left both Canada and Injuns
Junior varsity appearing

Birch was pleased with what his
team did
Choctaw seemed to come alive as
Competition made them wake up
To the skills that they required

And without a doubt the crowd
played
A big role in the event too
Sliding up and down the sidelines
As the play flowed hither and yon

There was freedom in this format
Though the players cursed my
weapons
Running wild afield like centaurs
In some mythical unwinding

If May weather stayed inviting
And the crowds could be coaxed
out then
All ingredients were at hand
For a very special season

So the Exhibition made clear
A sensation's in the making
Both with media and public
SENE'd set the table

For a sports extravaganza
Only two weeks in the future,
Even for the foreign play-ins
Oxford, England; Shanghai,
China.

BAGGATTAWAY MOON (2)

What a semi-final upset!
Czech Republic beat the
Scottish
In a European match up
On an Oxfordshire golf course.

In the other semi-final
Russell Pape had home
advantage
Asferg's Danes though thrashed
the English
Staged another stunning upset

6-0, 6-0.
So it's Danes v. Czechs in Final
And the winner has momentum
For the next round in the U.S.

On my lousy set Birch watched
them
Three a.m. on May the Twenty
Barefoot Aussies and Koreans
Czechs and Danish wielding
war clubs

Reading magazines with one
eye
Settled in to watch the finals
Of the Euro, Asian play-ins,
8 Seed had to do some scouting

On that lovely rolling golf
course
Over four holes on the back
nine
Did those barefoot players
tussle
Raising cumbersome lacrosse
sticks.

Over hill and dale competed,
Through the mist and sun
perspired,
Thousands cheered them from the
side lines
Pulled along by sprinting middies.

Kovac's Czechs that day did
vanquish
Asferg's Danes, but it was so
close
4-3 that was the final
Czechs were getting used to
winning.

In the meantime poor Birchwalker
Watching all of this on TV
SENE till the wee hours
Knew his team needs motivating.

In the ill state of affairs that
Hovered on his rag tag ball team
Had a challenge set before him
To compete against those Euros.

All the pundits called for Aussies
Asian play-in to win hands down,
(Like the English, Welsh and
Scottish
Commonwealth teams always
favored).

It was thought to be a cake walk
But another major upset
There in Shanghai on a golf
course
With a half a million present.

South Koreans v. the Aussies
In a yawner of a final
Only Aussies didn't win it
South Koreans 10-7.

Birch had watched this play-in
final
SENE had it covered
Back-to-back he watched the
play-ins
With St. Anne Four right beside
him.

Exhibition and the play-ins
Now behind them and decided
The *Baggattaway Moon* tourney
Stood already halfway finished.

He'd received no note from
Marla
Whether yes or whether no-go
For the date he'd asked her out
on
On June Third or shortly after

A full month had thus transpired
No word from his Moonless
Woman,
Left him fitful and despondent
Had no time though for self pity

With policemen standing duty
And the Choctaw still outsiders
And the coach's woes
impinging
Stallion practices were
downbeat.

Indigenes' team lacking Spirit
Fractured, torn by all the
troubles
Seeded eighth, derided for it
People gave them next to no
chance.

So Birchwalker spoke directly
Did not mince or parse his

phrasing
Gave an undiluted message
Brutal honesty was called for.

'Once you wanted to compete in
This *Baggattaway Moon* tourney
Felt you had the upper hand and
Rules change tilted in your favor.

'Now you seem to me deflated
Expectations and the limelight
Put a weight upon your shoulders
Well it's time to pull together.

'And I don't care how you do it
Through intensity or fasting
I don't care about the y-scale
Nor distaste for Neil's lacrosse
sticks.

'I don't care what you may think
of
Pascal fighting Bobby Cooper
Nor of my own recent problems
Everybody's got opinions.

'Look, I know you've been
neglected
Starting with my trip to Europe
Left you stranded in the winter
And Pascal stepped in the
vacuum.

'Wish that never would have
happened
But he held the team together
At a point I couldn't help you
Enough problems for a lifetime

'As you know my best friend
walked on
Took his birch canoe and St. Anne

Made a funeral pyre from it
Threw his dog into the water.

'New Year's Eve I finally
landed
I was happy just to be home
To Anishinaabewaki
To my wife, my job, my best
friend.

'In the minute of homecoming
All that joy was dissipated
By my finding a cigar tube
Awful letter scribed within it.

'It contained a private history
Which I do not care to tell you
It suffices though to say that
I was forced to reconsider

'How and where I lived my life
out
I was simply no more able
To absorb the blows and
punches
Had to move out to the peace
van.

'I admit to judgment errors
Should have never picked that
knife fight
Got myself carved up and
charged with
An assault on Pascal's father.

'Lost my job and lost myself in
Marketing *Baggattaway Moon*
A celebrity on TV
Hot shot coach on every cover.

'Radio and big newspapers
Till you prob'ly couldn't stand

it
Pearly whites belied my true state
Private life in great turmoil.

'It has taken toll upon you
Witless orphans of my Calling—
To the cause of this Renewal
I have given every effort.

'All that said I need to tell you
Time is now to dust our hearts off
Reunite ourselves in Purpose
Set aside all those distractions.

'Each man really lives but one
time
And he must be open to it
Sense the Moment of Potential
Flesh and Blood in tandem raging.

'And so clearly is this our time
Eighth Seed, First Seed, what's it
matter?
They have given us our Game
back
And to that gift we must rally.

'We are used to giving in to
All the forces armed against us
But this time there'll be no towel
Thrown to signal our surrender.

'Grow a Seventh Sense I tell you
We will name it Big-Game-
Instinct
We have owned this gene forever
We just seem to have forgotten.

'No great thing can hatch in self-
doubt
You believe it, you believe it!
Even talk yourself into it

Irrespective of naysayers.'

Then he tossed them all a copy
Green Bay's ordering of play
times
Indigenes played in the Blue
Pool
England, Aussies and Koreans.

In the Red Pool Czech Republic
U.S., Canada and Denmark.
Twelve games stuffed inside of
two days
Come this Saturday and
Sunday.

'We have nothing left to lose, so
You must play with wild
abandon
We must find our way to three
wins
I will not allow a wallow.

'They expect us to get
slaughtered
Laughingstock before our
People
Dormant fossilized sports Has-
beens
Don't you give up! Prove them
wrong now!

'Teams can go on winning
streaks, and
You've just seen it in the play-
ins
Czech team's peaking at the
right time
Could've anyone predicted?

'Do you think it really matters,'
He provoked them with this

notion
'To the world Out There that
Choctaw
Fathers on the Trail of Tears
walked?

'That our present Choctaw
brethren
Here among us have returned to
Use a single stick and cradle?'
And the team all stared at
Choctaw.

Thinking, *Jesus, we are lucky*
That they even came to help us
All the way from Oklahoma
And Birchwalker, seeing, moved
on.

'Do you think Out There they
realize
'Just how fucking good Jerome
is?
Standing tall inside the crease and
Flicking shots away like cow
flies?

Then the team burst out in
laughter
And perhaps they reconsidered
That the guys who were their
leaders
Just might pull the others up too

Then into applause they burst out
As they knew Jerome was worthy
'Do you think they really know
how
Goddamn fast our Obie Crick is?

"How Elias Lane can juke you
Leave you standing with no jock

strap?
Do you think Out There they
realize
What a Sauk is, what a Fox is?

'Do you think that others know
of
Names like Grubby Spratt,
LaFramboise?
Can they know what it is like to
Be embalmed with white man's
fluids?

'Do they know that Russell
Phaneuf
Tall, tall Russell got his height
from
Not his father's side, the Creek
side
But his mother's Choctaw
bloodline?

Then a silence overtook them
As he rounded on their senses
Stood behind the eight new
Choctaw
Asked of Russell to say
something

Then you could have heard a
pin drop
Russell deep in cogitation
'Oklahoma red-clay country
Has delivered us these eight
bums

'Once they played like girls
with two sticks
But we're teaching them just
one now
I will play with them as
Brothers

From today we are all Choctaw.'

Stallions roared and stallions
whistled
Banged on tables, raised a Spirit
Was it so hard to believe that
Indigenes would win three ball
games?

'We have got a hearty meal plan,'
Said Birchwalker now to calm
them
'England Saturday nine-thirty
And at three p.m. the Aussies.

'Are you up for that?' he shouted.
'Yes!' in unison they roared back.
'Can you go out oh-and-two,
then?'
'Yes, we can!' to him they yelled
back.

'We take one game at a time so
Put your blinders on, no blinking
Concentrate on what's before you
Over future matches fret not.'

'Do you think Pascal will play,
coach?'
Asked a timid Kendall Pete then
And the coach addressed it head
on
This most central of all issues.

'If he is or if he isn't
Does it change how you approach
it?
Single men don't make a ball
team
It's a game of skilled team
players.

'I would like you to think rather
Of the hundred thousand
Natives
Who are coming up to cheer
you,
In your playing resurrected.

'Don't you fret about their
safety
They'll be fine with all the
escorts
You're what stokes Imagination
In their Upright Fossil heads
now!'

He explained about the game
clock
Halves are five and thirty
minutes
Skulling halftimes twenty
minutes
First to four goals wins the
contest.

They were mildly concerned by
Reputation of the English
Their first foe, what was the
game plan?
Birch's eyes came up like fire.

'Bloody bastards do not want it!
Hearts have never been around
it
Hate the barefoot, hate Neil's
rackets
Lost to Danes; they are all
finished!

'Do not waver but believe me
We will beat the English easy
Then we'll smoke the goddamn
Aussies

Half the Commonwealth for
breakfast!

'Then the next day we will stifle
With impenetrable defense
Vaunted offense of Korea
And leave Green Bay undefeated!

'But be careful of Korea
They have just dethroned the
Aussies
Just like us nothing to lose and
They are playing like they mean
it.'

Just one more time did they probe
him
On his personal dilemmas
'Loss is life, Jerome, I tell you
Each one has to learn to bear it

'But then come along those
Moments
When a loss cannot be shouldered
And you simply dig your heels in
Perish in the war if need be.'

Then Jerome let out a war whoop
Leapt up to his size 13 feet
'That's the leader we've been
waiting
That's the order we've been
craving!'

Walked around the room with
chutzpah
'*You're* the reason we all came
here
And we want to know you're
alright
You're the one we learned
Lacrosse from

'Taught us cradling at PMS
Taught us running and
defending
Fought for rules change in this
tourney
Never made fun of my freckles.

'Promise to you, just you watch
me
Swat opponents' shots on goalie
Watch us all just find a way,
coach
Watch us get you to the next
round!'

Then Jerome obliged them all to
Put their money where their
mouths were
Take a voice vote, In or Out be
And he danced around the table

Taking high fives like an usher
Taking up a new collection
Putting Spirit in the basket
And the team responded to him.

At that moment I was gleeful
As, I know, my friend
Birchwalker
For disaster'd been averted
For Pascal there was Jerome
now.

BAGGATTAWAY MOON (3)

It was May the 26th and
Birch was on his way to Green
Bay
O'er the U.P. highways
speeding
All exhausted yet excited.

He was contemplating history
There in M. Virkanen's milk
truck
How he paralleled the route of
Nicolet in 1600s.

Out past Hiawatha Forest
Vision quest sites, waterfalls too
On failed marathons he did
muse
Ancient, personal and fateful.

Due west out along the U.P.
Through the time zone to
Wisconsin
Down the bay into Brown
County
Had a meeting with the mayor.

Nothing but a photo-op but
Still he had to make the effort
LiMei, Freddy, Archie, Parry
And himself would all shake
hands there.

Even as they there assembled
Former lands of Winnebago
All Americans Tour started
Nineteen hundred Red Dogs
rumbled

From the south and from the
west too
Made their plodding way to Green
Bay
For round robin games they'd be
there
Barring any terrorism.

Police escorts, cameras whirring
Pilgrimage was underway now
Jubilation in the air as
Homeland people watched and
fretted.

You could watch live the
Procession
Snake along across the Midwest
State police would say 'Good
riddance'
As they passed them to the next
state.

On board somewhere was an Earl
who
Underdogs was moved to favor
He'd decided to ride with them
Fellow Upright Fossil royal.

Birch had flown again to New
York
Final network morning news
show
Final SENE taping
Scarcely made it back and then
left.

Hours now until arrival
He was listening for a newscast
But with Matti's ancient tuner
And the poor reception out there

He could only guess their status
Escorts, handoffs at state borders

Joyous Natives sliced through
wheat fields
Joyless politicians scowled.

Are there Injun haters hiding
Behind levees, mounds and
hillocks?
Who could know it, who could
know it?
Yet the passengers were happy.

Who could rule out any bedlam
In Birchwalker's mystic
Venture?
Like Bwon-diac did before him
Gambled with his People's
welfare.

Thus Birchwalker did get cold
feet
Second-guessed the whole
damn Venture
Could he ever live it down if
They fell prey to some damn
racist?

Just as I do on this Luna
He would bear the blame
forever
Working off his earthly sinning
With the Vultures pecking at
him.

What if hundreds were to die in
An explosion or a bombing
What if dozens taken hostage
In some hate group's bid for air
time?

The entire world was watching
That I think you can imagine
Everybody concentrated

On the daring undertaking.

Spectacle of all those Natives
And an English earl among them
On their way to see a ball game
Invitation for Disaster.

It was almost voyeurism
Something bad just had to happen
At a rest stop or refueling
Which nut had them in his
crosshairs?

And the ever-present cameras
Never interrupted coverage
They pre-empted normal
programs
Just to bring you this in real time

With the routes surveilled
completely
Split screens showed the two in
tandem
Out front cop car cherries flashing
Running interference for them

Eight patrol cars rode behind them
Overhead buzzed helicopters
Red Dogs all in triple file
Highways closed for their safe
passage

Had the feeling of a funeral
Head of state whose corpse was
borne to
Sacred resting grounds or
homeland
Drawing maximum attention

Birch from anxiousness delivered
Sudden patch of good reception

And he learned that in that
moment
All went well along the
highways.

South Dakota Red Dogs
halfway
OK City Dogs at Springfield
'Woohoo! Yeehaw,' yelled
Birchwalker
St. Anne's head hung out the
window…

Then they roared into the depot
Nineteen hundred Red Dog
buses
Horns and fireworks a-blasting
Winnebago greeting party

Hanging out the small bus
windows
Waving, chanting for the
cameras
All the world could safely
exhale
Caravans had got there safely

All the Sioux tribes and the
Kansa
Cherokee, Cheyenne and others
Bounded off the belching buses
In their midst an earl named
Freddy.

In this biblical congestion
Swirling tribal congregations
Self-congratulating wand'rers
Like already their team had
won…

From my perch I watched them
walking

St. Anne Four and old
Birchwalker
On the grounds of Green Bay's
golf course
Where the eight teams would do
battle.

It was twilight on the back nine
I could almost reach and touch
them
Quiet introspective moment
Moon threw shadow on the
bunkers

Long par fours had been selected
In contiguous relation
To two short par fives alongside
Field of dreams Baggattaway
style.

Thus kilometers were wrung from
Rolling knolls of short-cut
fairways
Any sand traps would be live-ball
Had to keep off every green
though.

Grassy contours in the starlight
Constellations clear and hanging
Flower Moon on the horizon
I was peeking round the petals

The Big Dipper a lacrosse stick
Stars bouqueted in floral clusters
Lit up bundles out in deep space
And a dead man doing Penance.

And surveilling from these
heavens
Old best friend and erstwhile
canine
One I tossed out in the Straits and

Threw the other in hot water.

But for now Birchwalker
dreamy
Thinking on the coming
contests
And if in that sporting drama
For his People take the forts
back.

TV towers cast their shadings
Banner ads proclaimed the
sponsors
Flags of all competing nations
Flew above the golf course pro
shop.

Soon the horseman would come
riding
Wampum stick up high would
brandish
Featured on the jumbo screens
for
Hundred thousand mouths held
open

Late that night the women,
children
Came out on the course and
swept it
As in ancient times the custom
Working goals up to the
midfield

Fanning out in single file
Picking stones and splintered
tees up
They pushed slowly toward the
middle
The white circle of the *Ball Up*!

Bottle tops and cigarette butts

Dung chips, shards of glass, ball
covers
Sensed them with their eyes and
bare feet
So the players would not have to.

Migrant workers, oh so happy
To perform a role in these Games
If it gets to dark to see then
Red Dog high beams light the
field up

Now a huge throng all had
gathered
Looking up toward Number Eight
green
Fairway bunker cut the side hill
Much anticipated Op'ning

Under canopy so starry
Giant bonfire thirty feet high
Flames shot up into the night sky
And the dry wood crackled
loudly.

From the crowd a huge ovation
Prologue raising high the spirits
They could not make out the
gauntlet
Forming up above in darkness.

Onondaga horseman rode out
Full regalia and splendid
Clear suggestion of pre-Contact
Of an Ind'an world in balance.

Of a world that was untainted
Well before the smallpox blankets
And the Trail of Tears processions
To an earthly Purgatory.

Of a People's recreation

Also pure and bound to Nature
Lay along the rivers, hillsides
And Baggattaway we called it.

Played it for the watchful gods
that
They might show upon us
mercy
Like a prayer they would
receive it
Heal our wounds and bless our
Walked-On.

Red, black, yellow shot the
horseman
Through the gauntlet formed by
Natives
Gasps of awe shot from the
public
As he raised my wampum
racket

Silhouetted arm kept pumping
Carried with it the spectators
Their acclaiming grew much
louder
Whipped up higher, ever higher

First came out the South
Koreans
Stoic jogging in flag jerseys
Then came Asferg and the
Danish
Then came Kovac and his
Czech team

Kovac stared out messianic
In the pitchblende Green Bay
darkness
Looking like a conqu'ring hero
We would see if that would
hold true

And the pitch of the ovation
With each passing introduction
Found an ever higher level
Till you thought you would be
deafened

Aussie squad and Russell's
English
Andrew Sophie's proud Canucks
then
Commonwealth teams all together
Union Jacklike flags upon them

Then out strode the USA team
Drey Foss' grimly twitching game
face
Wampum sticks refused to carry
For their partisans showed Bad
Ass

Drey was macho and defiant
Gave no player introductions
They just stood there like Marines
would
Crowd was prompted into
Anthem

Swollen wave of human sound
fell
Out in ripples o'er the huge crowd
Even gathered up resistors
And *O, say can you see* rang out

After that there fell a Silence
Lasted just about two minutes
As they slowly came to notice
Only one team left to intro

Then before they even came out
Indigenes did start to rally
And the whole place took the
chant up

To the fire came Native women

There were just about a hundred
Fifty faced out to the people
Fifty others faced their sisters
And they then performed the
ball dance

Line dance spread into the
watchers
Then the tribal celebrations
Danced in columns to the sand
trap
Red Dog drivers blew their big
horns

Red Dog drivers flicked their
headlights
Sweetest bedlam had erupted
There was no hope to contain it
Could have gone on till the
morning

With a tear in every eyeball
Indigene team made its way out
Stood between the big bonfire
And the *All Americans Tour*

There was no chance to
continue
War whoops sounded in the
night air
An incessant approbation
For his underdog lacrosse team

Then in front of that huge fire
In the sand trap it was burning
Our Pascal assumed the y-scale
Improvising on a grand scale

I am sure Birch didn't say to
But it was a thing of Beauty

He just held his ankle up and
Struck a perfect gymnast's posing

Well this made the people wild
Acrobatics in the mix too?
The long shadow of his y-scale
Thrown out over all the public

What a gesture, what a statement
That LeRoi's son had displayed
there
And the cheering surged up for
him
With his foot did he salute them

When he finally put his toes down
Noise did of a sudden lessen
And into that waning sound bank
Did Birchwalker then step
forward

But again they raised a roar up
Deafening beyond all measure
Drew Orion's rapt attention
Great Bwon-diac pricked an ear
up.

(Mortal noise, could that bestir
them?
From eternal duties wake them?
A Great Wrong was being righted
Fallen People being raised up)

And it lasted ninety seconds
Till he raised his hands above
them
Microphone he then was handed
Introduced them to his players

Jerseys purple-white in color
Wampum logo print upon them

Tom-toms, ball dances resumed
and
Sticks were blessed with river
water

Stacked into a pyre formation.
Damping blanket billowed
down then
From the mind of great Bwon-
diac
Hushed crowd came up to its
tiptoes

All Americans were greeted
By Birchwalker and invited
'Root for anyone you want to,'
And the Upright Fossils cheered
him

Then he thanked me Neil his
best friend
That I made so many rackets
And he thanked his Moonless
Woman
That she helped me with the
lacing

Then he thanked his father
Louis
For vermilion beet lacrosse
balls
Introduced then his team mascot
St. Anne Four who was not
nervous

Birch's heart was overladen
And the crowd could see it well
so
Someone yelled out in the quiet
'Win 'em all, Birch, take the
trophy!'

This Event electrified him
It rewired him completely
Then he saw that he'd already
Come away with something
special

Didn't matter much the outcome
Of the games, he'd try his hardest
For upon this Midwest golf course
Long Oblivion he'd bested...

So it came down to the contests
And excitement there was plenty
After Day One some surprises
Also some games per predictions

In the Red Pool USA team
Took out Denmark and the Czech
team
But the Czechs then beat up
Sophie
And then Sophie beat the Danes
up

So it was a bit surprising
That the Danes could notch no
vict'ry
Czechs and Sophie's team were
one-one
And the US had a clear lead

In the Blue Pool Birch beat
England
One-to-nothing with his defense
And Australia beat Korea
As did Russell's English squadron

But the Aussies beat Birchwalker
4-1 it was a yawner
So Koreans hadn't won yet
Aussies had the lead in Blue Pool

Birch was pleased with how his
team played
He could see they were a Tough
Out
That their defense would sustain
them
And if offense they could
muster

All the coaches learned it
quickly—
Their effect upon the players
By field distances diminished
And the crowd noise in addition

Made instructions to combatants
And encouraging coach barking
Near impossible to be heard
And the Midwest winds did not
help.

And the crowd was ever-
moving
Up and down the field was
swaying
Out of sight and then upon you
Always cheering for their
players

For although you could observe
it
From upon the jumbo screens
there
Watching bare-eyed was much
better
Tens of thousands ran alongside

They would run o'er empty
fairways
When the play was at a goal
stand
Just to see it from that angle

Was five hundred yards across
field

And they craned their necks and
ran fast
When Attack had penetrated
Midfield line and longstick
defense
When the crease under duress was

When two goalies hunched
intently
And their four eyes wide and
anxious
How they dug their bare feet in
and
Overlapped their sticks defiant

In commotion round the goalies
Heaving bodies sought advantage
That is what spectators wanted
Confrontation at the goal line

Like twin matadors they stood tall
Like two daggers drawn, their
rackets
And the big black bull came
charging
Who would win these tests of
mettle?

For how does one score a goal
here
When within the twelve-foot
spacing
Eight or nine guys have
maneuvered
To deflect or block away shots?

Crafty scooping, faking, juking
And the little guys could sneak
through

Going low among the big trees
From their bellies they could
score one.

And the players did complain of
Injuries unto their bare feet
People stomped and chopped
with rackets
And no refs to call the fouls

Much more physical was this
game
Than that rugby Aussie rules,
say,
Or that bloody Irish football
Padless, bare of foot, my
weapons

It was all up to the players
How they field-coordinated
Everybody had realized it
Coaches rendered mute
cheerleaders.

Young Pascal did not play Day
One
Kept the stats, advised
Birchwalker
Brain trust on the Injun sideline
Pascal, Freddy and Birchwalker

For the earl was playing
favorites
He was not too proud to say it
That for Indigenes he rooted
Underdogs and Fellow Fossils

But Drey Foss discovered
something
Sending plays out with his
fingers
And you had to give him credit

The obnoxious man could coach
well

Figure-eight weave he had started
Middies five across the fields'
width
Back and forth and bare
advancing
Hypnotizing, hard to break up

In the forefield did they stall it
Till the defense finally came out
To frustrate the endless passing
Leaving hidden scorers lurking

Of a sudden came to life then
Pushed the ball into the red zone
Snapped the ball to an attack man
Cutting right across the middle

By the time the coaches saw him
And the fans had yelled their
warnings
They could not avert the outcome
Split the upright sapling goal
posts

Day Two's games did pit
Birchwalker
With the winless South Koreans
And the Czechs would play the
Danish
In a rematch of their play-in

Czech Republic had their way
with
Listless Danes, score four-to-
nothing
And Koreans left with no wins
Losing four-one to Birchwalker

So with sleeping bags all rolled up

And the Red Dog buses
groaning
Here's the tally of round robin
As to Michigan they journeyed

South Koreans and the Danish
With no wins Green Bay
departed
A surprising outcome that one
As they both had won their
play-ins

And advancing from the Red
Pool
Czech Republic and the U.S.
Blue Pool sending on
Birchwalker,
English team by razor's margin

There had been a three-way tie
in
Final standings of the Blue Pool
Aussies, Indigenes and English
With a 2-1 record finished

So net total points were counted
Spinning out the hapless
Aussies
Leaving Indigenes and English
To advance into the semis

Birch had not gone three-and-oh
as
Everyone had said he'd have to
But he squeaked through to the
next round
Final Four Baggattaway now

In a ruckus on those Red Dogs
Injuns pounding on the side
boards
All Americans Tour plodded

Up the bayline for the U.P.

Freddy put himself on board of
One of those mad frantic buses
Company kept with his People
In the aftermath of glory

On an afternoon so sunny
On Memorial Day weekend
Did the caravan re-form and
Chug back east through copper
country

Not an untoward thing had
happened
Not a breakdown, not a sniper
Just a bunch of good lacrosse
games
And en route those hordes of
Natives

And somewhere aboard is Li Mei
For the Chinese fans reporting
Birch had promised her a sit-down
When the Red Dogs parked and
rested

He was thinking in the milk truck
All the good things that'd
transpired
Had to pinch himself about it
Stallions made it to the semis

He was guessing that the Final
Would between U.S. and Czechs
be
He would root for Karel Kovac
Any day against a Drey team

Indigenes would face the Yankees
Chances clearly were against
them

They would likely be routined
by
The American attackmen

Then his happy mind kept
drifting
To the sav'ry things awaiting
Tasty dinner and a hot date
With his moonless woman
Marla

Steered the milk truck cross the
river
Cross Menominee he drifted
From the Central time zone
back home
To the Eastern Daylight Savings

It was in this time-warped
bubble
In this little remote pocket
With his mind on all the good
things
That his dream began to sputter

In his rearview did he look back
Smiled on the sight of Red
Dogs
Chugging up and down the hills
and
Cruised along on Route 2
eastbound

Out of nowhere, out of nowhere
Westward speeding Mich. state
troopers
Really speeding, doing ninety
Cherries flashing but no sirens

*They're supposed to meet the
Red Dogs*
Thinks Birchwalker in a second

Like for all the other hand-offs
Escorts met them at the borders

Then he sees a red Toyota
Overtaking those state troopers!
Must be doing near a hundred
Sees a face inside the cabin

And askance the face looks at him
Lifts his chin and then he realized
Was the same look he
remembered
From his father's wake when
Jimmy

Showed the King the door for
brawling
Tilted back his head at Pascal
Pointed at him with his chin up
Motioned at the tomahawk pipe

*So that's where the pipe had got
to!*
Figured Birch in that split second
King's smug face was speeding
by and
Pascal had the tomahawk pipe.

Three containers made of plastic
Fifty, sixty gallon drums and
Fertilizer bags all emptied
Pinned along the red truck's bed
sides

He was speeding by the cop cars
Taken by surprise were they too
In the rearview watched
Birchwalker
As the scene unfurled behind him

Up the hill came Red Dog buses

Vanguard Red Dogs now in full
view
Happy Injuns celebrating
Still the vict'ries of Birchwalker

Slammed his foot onto the
brakes and
Jacked emergency brake up and
Wheeled his truck around to
watch it
Through St. Anne's eyes also I
watched

Now the troopers tried to catch
him
But the King had gotten by
them
Birch and St. Anne hunkered
down then
Through the windshield they
would witness

*Was he really going to ram
them?*
Gasped Birchwalker as he
realized
Crazy Injun-hating LeRoi
Had crossed over in the bus'
lane

Swerving wildly, gunned it
harder
Taking dead aim at the lead bus
Two explosions, two explosions
Birch did jerk back in his seat
then

Fireballs shot in the air and
Plumes of smoke rose up and
spread out
White-black cloud formed all
around them

Crashing metal sounds around
them

As the wind dispersed the crash
clouds
And Birchwalker saw the damage
Saw that lead bus torn asunder
Front from back half separated

Human bodies catapulted
Twenty, thirty feet and land dead
Birch stopped breathing altogether
Vultures pecking at his innards

Anguished crying screaming
yelling
Floored the milk truck to the
carnage
Looked around for Roy LeRoi and
Any sign of his Toyota

Scanned the scene for signs of
living
Overlooked those ones that were
not
Twenty, thirty, more were dead
there
From the front half of the Red
Dog

Then of all the horrors one should
Never ever have to shoulder
Birch saw Freddy's royal body
Face down in a pile of Kansa

Found the driver of the lead bus
Innocent man, Red Dog driver,
SENE's lead reporter,
Marshal's corpse was ripped and
broken

Caravan behind had pulled up

Screeching halts and Natives
running
To the awful scene before them
Friends and loved ones to
recover

Where's the cop cars when you
need them
'9-1-1 call!' cried Birchwalker
And the sirens started wailing
He heard screaming from the
back half

Ran back into hellish chaos
Caught the people as they
jumped out
From the inside that was
burning
Poor Birchwalker cried and
caught them

Victims of his dream half
finished
But its ending was a Nightmare
Bleeding badly, some survivors,
And as many or more would not

Laid the corpses by the roadside
Lined up columns there on
Route 2
Breathing black smoke
unawares and
Going back to pick up others

Rows for living, rows for dead
and
More would die before the help
came
SENE helicopter
Ferried bodies, Mission: mercy.

THE QUICK AND THE DEAD

How can anyone so stupid
Have that kind of dumb luck
with him
Do you think that he had
planned it
That the troopers were delayed
there?

That a dumb miscalculation
Between central, eastern time
zones
Led to showing up a bit late
Speeding up to meet the buses?

Let your guard down for a
second
Even in these thin backwaters
And the snake will have your
puppy
From within the knothole snatch
it

Planned or not, that's how it
happened
You ad nauseum can watch it
On the TV in the morning
On the TV all day running

Every sick and twisted angle
In slow motion if you want it
In disgust you turn away but
Cannot take your eyeballs from
it

Forty-seven people perished
In the King's attack on Natives
ANFO bomb configuration
Fertilizer bomb he'd built it

Diesel fuel was mixed together
With ammonium of nitrate
Add a booster TNT stick
And he meet the Red Dog head on

Fully sealed off was the U.P.
To Superior from Big Mac
Total lockdown in the Soo where
Seven Rosebud Sioux to life clung

Blast had set the whole world
reeling
Everywhere reverberations
From security alerts to
My *Baggattaway Moon* tourney

From the grizzly work of rescue
To the nearing date with Marla
From apologies to England
To the ID of the victims

Setting broken bones in plaster
Notifying friends and family
In this setting comes a survey
Of the accidental tourists

By the press it was determined
Polling all remaining Natives
Since they're stuck for the
duration
They might better play the games
out

Felt their safety now not
threatened
That the whole damn U.P.'s
sealed off
What can happen now? they
grimaced
Lightning strikes not twice the
same spot

354

Marla went down to the peace
van
With Birchwalker made a visit
Had to check in on his progress
See what traumas he still
suffered

Broke down crying then herself
and
Blamed herself for the Disaster
'If out 6 Mile Road I'd not
come
None of this could ever happen

'Had I just stayed with that
Loser
Roy LeRoi and made my life
there
Misery would surely own me
But those fifty'd still be
breathing.'

Did the King intend for this
too?
Was he really such a Thinker,
That in dying he did deal Birch
Yet another fateful setback?

Did he in his prescience scheme
to
Importune poor Marla further?
Not just guiltiness inspire but
Seal her off to Birch reunion?

Must we credit him in death
with
Brilliant strategy, a grand plan
On Birchwalker's bliss
foreclosing
Blocking Jú-ah-kís-gaw from
him?

Did he know of New Beginning
Gleefully rub hands together
When he realized that his ex-girl
Would herself blame for his
actions?

That into a funk she'd be thrown
That she'd close off all her
feelings
Stopping any planned rekindling
With her erstwhile Injun husband?

Oh, to be outsmarted by one
As dumb-luck as Roy LeRoi was
Left Birchwalker in a funk too
Ruing all the stupid outcomes.

But he would not cede him vict'ry
Saw instead a coward's motives:
• Roy had lost his will to go on
• Sheila, Marla both despised him

• With that gash that made him
gimp and
Scarred-up face that made us
wince and
Sundry other lasting ailments
Said 'I've not a thing to lose
now.'

• Knew that in Superior Court
He would surely be convicted
Spend more time inside a jail cell,
Barred from Tommy's bar for life
too

Birch refused to give his plan up
For June Second was tomorrow
And besides big plans with Marla
There were games yet to compete
in

Looking at her face he saw it
She was shell-shocked, self-
accusing
"But so many've died,' she said
then.
'You and I are still alive
though,'

Said Birchwalker soft to Marla
Face to face there in the peace
van
And her face began to brighten
So their date he did confirm it

In her mind it's just a dinner
Though a nice one to be certain
Prob'ly thinks it's meant to
soothe her
Ruffled feelings from his
absence

Irrespective of conditions
Morrow brings Bwon-diac's
name-day
When he hoped he'd still be
playing
And renewing with his woman

So in spite of the Disaster
Things had turned out almost
normal
He was playing in the semis
And would dine at New
Beginning

It was all so very clear now
He had tended all the details
It would start off with the best
seats
Overlooking broad St. Mary's

And the locks would be uplifting
And he'd ask her to consider
If she'd marry such an Injun
As at that time sat before her

And he'd say, 'Not in the shadows
Of two ash trees in the moonlight
But a genuine church wedding
By a priest who won't be
drinking.'

(I did not take any umbrage
At Birchwalker's reference to me
Even now I am not sorry
How I married those two kids up)

Marla Langevin would sit back
She would cover up her mouth
and
She would reach up to her red scar
But she'd never ever touch it

They would dine on juicy red
meat
And perhaps a beet greens salad
Savor only vintage red wines
Money was to be no object

They would chat and banter
lightly
How their wedding would be
styled
Birch would signal maitre'd to
Bring his best desserts and coffee

And of course the cradleboard too
Would be set upon her table
She would probably stop
breathing
Reach out to it but not touch it

Maybe then she would take
comfort
That her walk out 6 Mile Road
had
Brought her with her man
Birchwalker
Happiness just like she'd
wanted

Simple, hidden kind of life style
Raised her Sheila out of harm's
way
From the deadly world
protected
Dingo dam had found her
knothole

As she eyed the cradleboard
though
And thought on her walk in
pink Cons
She would scarce believe she'd
done it
All those many years ago now

She would ask him if he'd made
it
Turn it to the light, inspect it
Fine embroidery and quills of
Porcupine and 'What's it mean,
Birch?'

Then he'd stand and walk
around and
Take the ring box from his
pocket
Genuflect down on one knee
then
Velvet blue box lid slow open

Diamond ring so long in coming
She would simply not believe it

Throw her shoulders back and
reach for
The red scar that started all this

He would fit it on his wife's hand
Slip it on her shaking finger
Looking at her he'd fall silent
Make her wonder what he's doing

"Jú-ah-kís-gaw,' he would utter
And she'd wonder what that word
was
'Jú-ah-kís-gaw,' he'd repeat and
Then he'd tell her what that
phrase meant

She would likely cry and faint
when
Phrase in Chippewa was tendered
'Pretty-Lady-with-Child-on-Back'
Words would feather down upon
her

And his meaning would be crystal
Striking clearly in her new mind
She would know she'd been
accepted
By her Chippewa adopted

She would look around herself
and
Reckon which gift was the dearest
Cradleboard or diamond ring or
The proposal or the Naming

He would laugh, 'I've finally
stumped you!
I have rendered you here
speechless!
And I haven't even finished
Like another cup of coffee?'

He would take her hands inside
his
So she couldn't reach her red
scar
And he'd look into her eyes and
Inside out for her his soul turn

'What's important now is us
Two
That's the only thing that
matters
Not Pope County, not my
family
Not my Chippewa ancestry

'No more Roy LeRoi will there
be
No more trail of tears with
Longbow
There'll be Sandrine, there'll be
Sheila
We will make our way together

'No more truants no more gym
rats
Periwinkle, Schmeriwinkle
No more stallions no more Old
Ways
Even no Baggattaway too.'

By this time she'd be in
shocked state
Look at Birch with arching
eyebrows
After 30 years of rez life
She would scarcely find an
answer

'It is time to face the world
now,
It is time for Purifying

Bury hearts and head and start
new
Set aside all lame excuses.

'I will turn my sorry ass in
I will serve my jail time coming
We will march like smart
survivors
From the Forest to the City

'It is your world, it is your world,
Can you show me how to live it?
Will you with me to the Soo go?
I'll wear pink Cons, just you
watch me

'Want to walk back out 6 Mile
Road
Pink Con steps of yours retracing
Holding hands depart Pope
County
Turn the page upon Extinction

'In reverse, though, in reverse so
I can abnegate your hard times
Walking ceremony act out
Jú-ah-kís-gaw and
Birchwalker...'

So the next day they would play it
On June Second Pontiac's day
Irrespective of Disaster
For the marbles they would play it

The attack of Roy LeRoi had
Changed the mood from
celebration
To a kind of resignation
That the tourney should be played
out

The spectators were morose now

Filing in and out of diners
Filling churches with their
praying
Sipping pensively at coffees

Teams were staying out of sight
and
Some had whereabouts
unknown so
Cheerful banners that were
hung out
Seemed incongruous at best
then

Perfect May skies too seemed
ill-timed
It should be more overcast here
And for all four teams in semis
Spirit must be truly lacking

Little call for fiery speeches
Coach could only hope that
somehow
Stallions find that stingy
defense
And become again The Tough
Out

But Birchwalker had a notion
He believed that in the Forest
Indigenes would find Renewal
Rediscover motivation

So he called a Hiawatha
Marathon, it was an option
He would not force any stallion
But for him it had a meaning

Halfway point and resting stop
was
Tahquamenon Falls, the
cascade,

And the falls would be refreshing
He expected no big turnout…

At this point inside my story
Thick clouds settled twixt my
Luna
And Birchwalker down below me
So no longer could I see him

Then the Vultures were upon me
Did not want me to forgo this
Final outcome of my misdeeds
Never-ending penance, torment!

For I am the one blameworthy
Of the fate that my friend tasted
And the buzzards made me watch
it
On their bloodshot eyeball
cameras

I could watch in all their four eyes
Culmination of Birchwalker
While two others at my innards
Customary organ feeding

Divine justice one may call it
That at Birch's final moment
By these Hell Hens I was gnawed
at
In their replay never blinking

They had pinned me down and
forced me
Fate of Birchwalker to witness
They had captured every moment
My attention was assured now…

He and St. Anne Four were
stretching
At the trailhead so familiar

When co-captains three did pull
up
And Pascal was even barefoot

Obie yelled in Birch's face loud
'Have you anything to lose
now?'
And Birchwalker fired back
thus
'No, I've not a thing to lose
now!'

Then they mounted up the trail
and
In the Hiawatha sprinted
Under canopy so green and
Shafts of light around them
strobing

Over roots, half-fallen firs and
Scaring squirrels on pine cones
nibbling
Over ferns and through the May
flies
Even those pests could not slow
them

St. Anne Four had pulled away
now
All the runners' chests were
heaving
Second wind would soon relax
them
Set their pacing for six miles

Effortlessly ran Pascal in
Spite of bare feet he was
graceful
He was running with the
captains
And Birchwalker lagged behind
them

He could see there was jaw-
boning
Pascal scolding at the captains
They were looking at him funny
They were looking back at Birch
too

He remembered here his failed
quests
He remembered here my grandpa
How we built my birch canoe and
How we laid him in the forest

He remembered his own father
Louis Charlevoix' black walnut
Overlooking Tahquamenon
Till he saw the gods in battle

He remembered how the moon
shone
How St. Anne and he'd
transported
Of a sudden on the moon stood
Gazing at his roped up Chieftain

In his reveries he'd lost them
Can't see St. Anne or his players
He imagined them already
Doing y-scales at the water

Rays of sunlight piercing low now
Patch of pink sky on the river
In that clearing, wondrous light
show
Wrapped inside the roaring rapids

Birch pulled up and caught his
breath then
Looked around him for the others
Watched clear droplets in the
spray arc
Prism'd sunset water bubbles

Then a cold weight on his neck
came
Starts mad ringing in his
eardrums
Metal edge had made a dull
thud
Like a melon being parted

Planted just below his right ear
Wedge of metal split it open
Thrust him forward, sent him
stumbling
Toward the riverbank, arms
flailing

Tomahawk, that's what it was,
sure!
Missing tomahawk pipe of mine
Pascal had it all along from
Wake of Louis until this time

Who had struck this mortal
blow here?
Who'd assailed the Indigene
coach?
Face-down twelve feet from the
river
Saw his blood sieve through the
pebbles

Numbness starts to overtake
him
Little prisms still danced for
him
Light green leaves of Hiawatha
Mottled in the shafts of sunlight

Heard a footfall from behind
him
Sun was warm upon his Being
Could not move his head to
look at

Could not thus a self-defense
make

Lay still bleeding at the waters
Heard the crunching of the
pebbles
Underfoot this slow sure
crunching
Someone'd come to oversee him

Tanned and callused feet turned to
him
Saw the feet just at his shoulder
No face needed he to see, just
Bare feet of Pascal LeFebvre

Turned Birch over to face sunlight
And Birchwalker saw the trees
now
Thousands of them and
considered
Upright fossils would protect him

Every one an eyeball witness
To the awful crime transpired here
Millions mourn him in the
shadows
Though they're powerless to stop
it

He was losing now his vision
Pascal just a fuzzy shaping
Gloating over Birch's body
Saying absolutely nothing…

Then the buzzards had their fill
and
Cursed clouds between us broke
up
Eyeball replay was suspended
I again directly saw him…

Then St. Anne Four came a-
running
Eye-to-eye now with
Birchwalker
My poor friend would never
know it
Thought himself hallucinating

For 'twas I who spoke then
through her
I was St. Anne Four in person
Spoke through her to my
Birchwalker
Into Afterlife then talked him

At this point he seemed to savor
What this moment did afford
him
Healing Balm spoke through a
beagle
Of his best friend's voice
possessed now

Hearing war whoops in the
Forest
Thinking on Jerome and Obie
Chanting chorus in the Forest
Upright fossils' gath'ring voices

Blood still trickled on the
pebbles
As he listened to me talking
We could see his vision failing
Cursing out at Roy and Pascal

Forest floor was getting darker
And the sky had changed to
cobalt
And the full moon that I rode on
Was the bare bulb in his
darkness

I was present at his Going
In the eyes of St. Anne Four and
In the guise of our old Chieftain
Dropping down upon moon
buggy.

He did not have any notion
That Bwon-diac's not on board
here
But that Longbow'd come for
vigil
Hear him cry out to the Chieftain:

'Help me climb the tree, Bwon-
diac!
To the Luna with you pull me
I beseech you flood the earth now
Swell Great Waters till they rise
up

'And destroy Civilization!
Cause the ocean to inundate
All the cities in its pathway
And remake this land we cherish

'Send it crashing down upon us
Soak your lands in milk and
honey
Till Anishinaabewaki
Be reclaimed and reconfigured!

'Shine your beacon light down on
me
Float me up into the treetops
Plant me firm in that black walnut
Where my father saw his vision.'

But by now hallucinated
Also Birch inside his hearing
Were those flutes and tom-toms
playing

Or man's grandfather who
counseled?

"My Birchwalker,' so I
whispered
Then I started with our poem
Yes, the one we learned as
children
Called *The Crying of Bwon-diac*

And I watched it slake his last
thirst
Give him comfort from his
death throes
Soothing Trochees in a four
beat
Like embalming fluid for him

So I sang it, so I sang it
Through my beagle's mouth I
sang it
Lullaby for poor Birchwalker
Two-way street of purifying

*Though a French priest be
unworthy,*
Of a heathen to sing praises,
Nonetheless I must regale you,
With the story of a War-Chief.

Brave and true Anishinaabe,
Once he plotted a rebellion
*'Gainst the hated English
redcoats,*
But it ended in his own fall.

*Must they hunt him? Must they
kill him,*
Noble savage who defied them?
Must they vanquish every vestige
Of the unencumbered spirit?

At this point he seemed to fathom
Tried to lift his head up toward
me
Said he'd meet me in the Meadow
Said to get the red balls ready

Then I watched Pascal his arms
take
And then drag him toward the
water
Through the beagle's eyes I
followed
Then for Marla did he cry out

'Who will tell you that I love you?
Who present your cradleboard
gift?
Who will go to New Beginning
To explain the feting to them?

'Who will give her then the
diamond
She has waited all her life for?
Who will watch my moonless
woman
'Case she cries and needs a
shoulder?

'Most of all though do I beg you
Who will tell her of her Naming?
That her Chippewa have claimed
her
Who will call her *Jú-ah-kís-gaw*?

'Who will tell her I've
surrendered?
No more upright fossil living
6 Mile walking ceremony,
O, Pascal, can you assist me?'

'Do you think that you could
stand in?

I will not be there to do it
You're the only one who knows
now
All the ways I want to love her.'

Man in moon's beyond emotion
But with tears I filled the
Heavens
That I'd caused such human
grieving
Martyred in his desperation

So I had no other choices
With the poem did continue
Through the beagle's face I
sang it
Put him through his dying paces

So they got him in the forest,
Laid his noble skull wide open.
Where they laid him, where they
laid him
Not a man can say for certain.

His revolving eyes do well up,

At his Nation's humors draining,
Mighty forest of the Great Lakes,
Oh, the lost Anishinaabek!

Pascal dragged him to the water
Walked him out into the rapids
I and St. Anne on the shoreline
Watched his head go under water

Blood did mingle with the white
crests
Made the churning waters brown
then
Sunset spread its gorgeous blanket
Little prisms turning silver

Whirlpool funnels on the surface
In the spray a hole has opened
A mitèwin hole is forming
And Birchwalker is ascending

I will greet him like a hero
For his singular achievement
We have taken back the forts and
I will meet him in the Meadow.

Printed in the United States
216238BV00001B/2/P